EXTRAORDINARY ACCLAIM FOR TREVANIAN

"Trevanian is one hell of a pleasure to read."
—*The Washington Post*

"Trevanian has both wit and intelligence . . . Something for everyone."
—*The New York Times*

"Trevanian is primarily interested in giving the reader a good time and he resoundingly succeeds."
—*The New York Times Book Review*

"When you pick up a novel by Trevanian, you know you've witnessed a pro at work."
—*Pittsburgh Post-Gazette*

INCIDENT AT TWENTY-MILE

"[Trevanian's] hero is a finely crafted jewel of contradictions . . . A treat that belongs on the same shelf as *True Grit*, *Shane*, and Richard Condon's slapstick send-up, *A Talent for Loving*."
—*New York Daily News*

"A riveting piece of storytelling by a genuinely original author."
—*The Chicago Tribune*

More . . .

INCIDENT AT TWENTY-MILE

TREVANIAN

St. Martin's Paperbacks

INCIDENT AT TWENTY-MILE

Copyright © 1998 by Trevanian.
Revised edition copyright © 1999 by Trevanian.

Library of Congress Catalog Card Number: 98-19401

ISBN: 0-312-97023-4

Printed in the United States of America

St. Martin's Press hardcover edition/October 1998
St. Martin's Paperbacks edition/July 1999

10 9 8 7 6 5 4 3 2

Dedicated to Owen Wister and Frederic Remington; the first for creating the mythotypic characters and the distinctive motivational values that power the narrative engines of the Western genre, and the second for establishing its visual vocabulary. Between them, they provided the idioms and the inspiration, not only for all subsequent writers of the genre, but also for the Western film, from John Ford to Sergio Leone.

February, 1998
St. Etienne de Baïgorry

THE COMING OF AUTUMN to Vermont never fails to stir an irresistible wanderlust in me. Something minor-key and seductive in the fading melancholy of the season, something in the tart-within-sweet taste of old-fashioned pippins, in the smell of bonfires, in the rustle of ankle-deep leaves, makes me yearn to hit the road; and for me the direction of "going" is west, just as "coming back" means returning to New England. Perhaps this homing instinct is a tidal tug in my eleven generations of Puritan blood, but I suspect it has even more to do with the unnumbered generations of my Iroquois ancestors.

The Fall of 1962 sent me drifting westward. I was an hour or so beyond Laramie, driving into the setting sun, when I recalled an intriguing place-name on an old map: a town called Destiny somewhere up on the northern flank of the Medicine Bow Range. It would be foolhardy, or at least barren-spirited, for a drifter to fail to keep an appointment with Destiny.

There was no sign indicating the turn-off for Destiny because it was no longer an incorporated town, so it was nearly dark when, after two fruitless runs down long dirt tracks, plumes of red dust rising behind my car into the low-angle light of sunset, I found what was left of Destiny: two houses (one empty and for sale) and a gas station-cum-general store. None of them had felt a paintbrush for a very long time.

The old man who ran the general store told me that back at the turn of the century Destiny had been a thriving little city serving a silver mine up in the mountains as well as the surrounding country. But when the Surprise Lode went bust, the spur line that connected Destiny to the Union Pacific Railroad was left to rust, and the community quickly dwindled to a handful of old folks with nothing to do but wait to learn the answer to the Final Question. Now most of the houses were gone; some had burned down, some had been pulled down, some had just fallen down during storms. "Hey, you could pick one up pretty cheap, if you're in the market!"

I laughed this off and asked if he'd sell me some gas and put me up for the night, and he said, "Sure...if you're willing to sleep in your car. You can have breakfast same time as me. Crack of dawn. As for the gas, it's been five–six years since the tank was filled. I don't sell but sixty-seventy gallons a year, mostly to people hunting for souvenirs up around the old mine."

The gas pump was a lever-operated affair that brought gas up into a glass cylinder with gallon measurements down the side. "What about some supper?" I asked. "Sure. But it'll cost you a buck."

An hour later we were sitting at his oilcloth-covered table eating fried eggs and beans while we word-whipped the goddamned government, this rock-'n'-roll crap that passed for music, and indeed, "progress" in all of its confusing or threatening forms. He brought out a bottle of rye.

Mr. Pedersen was a seventy-four-year-old loner who sometimes hankered for a chance to talk about what interested him most: the old days in Destiny and in the ghost town of Twenty-Mile halfway up the mountain. He had been a child in Destiny, but his family left when everything went bust. They moved to Cheyenne, where he grew up, found work, and married. He never had any children. ("Don't know why. God knows we tried hard enough, Meg and me!")

Such was the lure of Destiny that he returned after

Meg's death and took over the gas station-cum-general store, but when Interstate 80 came along and siphoned off the traffic, Destiny was condemned to economic strangulation. Mr. Pedersen soon became the town's only inhabitant, and his few customers were either folks who'd gotten themselves lost, or the occasional trophy-hunter who came to climb the old narrow-gauge railway up the mountain, looking for historical mementoes with which to decorate his den. One such history scavenger returned from the hard climb up to Twenty-Mile proudly exhibiting several "quaint" wooden burial markers he had pillaged from the burying ground. After he left, Mr. Pedersen decided he had better take a look around up there while there was still something left to see. He made the climb (a demanding task for a man then in his late sixties) to Twenty-Mile, and he camped out for two days in the old marshal's office, where he sketched a map of the town, naming the buildings and their functions. He also recorded all that was legible on the grave markers. I cite several of these epitaphs in this novel.

It was fortunate for me that he made the map because a couple of years later a party of curio-hunters started a fire in the pot-bellied stove of Twenty-Mile's Mercantile Emporium. The rust-clogged stove pipe caught fire; it spread to the roof, whence the wind snatched the flames from one weather-dried old building to another until, in the end, only three were left standing, the three that stand there to this day ... if something hasn't happened to them since last I was there, more than fifteen years ago now.

Mr. Pedersen asked me what I did in life; I told him I was a writer; and he said that figured: a man with a real job isn't free to wander around the country. But for all that writing wasn't "real work," he admitted that for a long time he thought about writing a book himself, a book about what had happened up in Twenty-Mile, and what became of Destiny. He said he had poured one hell of a lot of rye into old-timers to get them to tell him what they remembered, and he'd written it all down. But what with the rheumatism in his knuckles and his eyes going dim on him, it didn't seem likely that he'd ever get around to writing that book now.

I told him I'd love to read it.

He eyed me from beneath shaggy eyebrows. "So's you can steal it?"

"That's right."

He scowled fiercely . . . then wheezed a laugh. "Maybe I'll show it to you tomorrow. I ain't promising, though. We'll see."

It was evident that he hadn't had his fill of talking and he intended to keep my willing ear around for a while.

The next morning after breakfast, I sat on the front steps of the general store and read Mr. Pedersen's randomly organized swatches and tales and notes, written in a round, painstaking Palmer hand, and revealing an uninhibitedly creative approach to spelling. I am thankful that he reproduced the old-timers' tales verbatim, capturing those sound-licking idioms and image-drenched similes that gave Western speech its unique piquancy, before it fell victim to television's anemic homogenizing of our culture. I have tinted this novel's dialogue with that evocative idiom, even stealing a few of those earthy Western similes: to be busier than a one-legged man in an ass-kicking contest, for instance.

Several times while reading Mr. Pedersen's manuscript my eyes defocused through the page as I envisioned the novel I could confect around these rough recollections, a novel firmly embedded in the conventions of the Western genre, but dealing with wider and more contemporary issues: with the end of a century, the end of an era, the end of a defining, and for American males a limiting, dream. . . . A last Western.

State Prison, Laramie

ALTHOUGH WYOMING HAD BEEN a state for eight years, the older guards still called it the Territorial Prison. Guard Private John Tillman (nicknamed "BB" by guards who ragged him about the "Baby Butt" smoothness of his cheeks) had been on regular shifts for only a month when he drew the duty of guarding the "moonberries" in the upper-deck security wing. He didn't know why the criminally insane were called moonberries; he had never asked, fearing it might be just another of the tiresome gags with which old hands tormented and humiliated new guards.

Tillman started his first tour of the special cells, stopping at each door to open the spy-hole and check on the inmate. The first moonberry was sitting on the edge of his cot, rocking himself and humming. The smile of perfect contentment on his bland visage gave no hint of his deeply held conviction that it was his duty to throw acid in the faces of children. "If I don't do it..., " he had explained to the judge "... who will?"

"The Politician" in the next cell was engaged in an ill-tempered debate with the space in front of him.

The third moonberry recoiled into a corner when he heard the spy-hole being opened. He cowered there, hiding behind his hands and babbling, "Please don't hurt me! I didn't mean to do it! Honest to God, I didn't mean it!" "The Spook," as the guards called him, was afraid of everything. During the morning mucking-out rounds, a guard had to go in and get his shit-bucket because he was too frightened to bring it to the door, as the other prisoners did. Tillman humanely closed the spy-hole as soon as he had verified the Spook's presence. The old

man repeated, "I didn't mean to do it!" then he slumped
in relief and his eyes narrowed with cunning. He had
fooled them again. He really *had* meant to do it. And
he'd do it again if he got the chance! Those kinds of
women had it coming to them!

Tillman passed by the large two-bunk cell that was
currently unoccupied and went to the last door on the
corridor. A wave of horripulation ran up his spine as he
reached out for the spy-hole because this moonberry, a
man named Lieder, was the most dangerous man in the
prison. The guards always spoke of Lieder with a certain
pride. He was the baddest of the bad, and they were the
ones chosen to keep society safe from him. "Which must
mean we're pretty tough ourselves, right? After all, we
managed to keep 187 inside." Number 187 had been
their most famous inmate, Robert LeRoy Parker, a horse-
thief who did eighteen months in the Territorial Penitentiary under the alias George "Butch" Cassidy.

"But 187 was a Sunday school teacher compared to
this Lieder. Don't be fooled by that fella's smooth manner, kid. He's slick as greased shit. Keep on your toes
all the time. He's busted outta two places, and chances
are he'll try it again, sooner or later. You just make sure
he doesn't do it on *your* shift, or the warden'll reach
down your throat and snatch your lungs out!"

"Yeah, kid, and do you know what Lieder does all
day long, lying up there in his cell? He does what your
mama told you would ruin your eyesight. He *reads!* His
cell is chock full of books and magazines and newspapers! Read? He's at it from first light to last. Mostly
history and politics. But he's got one favorite book that
he reads over and over."

"What book is that?"

"Oh, you'll hear about it. You'll hear *all* about it."

It was the guards who provided Lieder with books and
magazines, in part because it was the easiest way to keep
him calm, and in part because they were afraid of him.

He had once informed a watch sergeant, with calm sincerity, that if he didn't get a newspaper every week, he would punish him and his family when he broke out. The sergeant had dismissed the threat with a sniff, saying there was no way no moonberry would ever get out of the security wing. None never had, and none never would. But the next day he came with a newspaper under his arm. Well, hell's bells, what's the point in taking chances? Look at his record, for the love of God.

When he was only fourteen years old, Lieder had inflicted a weekend of hell on his hometown just south of Laramie, shooting out windows, setting fire to the school, and holding three children hostage in a livery stable he threatened to burn down if anyone approached. He was eventually cornered and sent away to a privately run home for wayward boys dedicated to "reforming" tough kids through a combination of spirit-crushing punishments and long sessions of prayer on their knees with their arms stretched out until their shoulders knotted with pain. At eighteen, he broke out after seriously injuring his spiritual mentor while they were praying together for his salvation. A three-month rampage characterized by gratuitous and inventive cruelty had the whole southeast corner of Wyoming peering into shadows and flinching from sounds before Lieder was recaptured and committed to the Territorial Prison because no other institution had the facilities to deal with the boy who had punished a tenaciously evangelistic preacher by shooting him four times, once through each palm and once through each foot, to provide him with the stigmata of this Christ.

Lieder was rescued from a lynch mob and sentenced to perpetual confinement as a menace to society. Once inside, he became a model of good behavior, never causing trouble, always polite, often helpful. But he escaped while working in the prison broom factory (as foreman), and was on the loose for nearly four years. After joining up with the northern, "Union Pacific" stream of Coxey's army, that uniquely American blend of lofty intent, quixotic diversity, righteous wrath, and carnival hokum, Lieder became disillusioned and returned to cleave a trail of pain and violence across southern Wyoming and northern Colorado. At some point, he experienced a kind of political revelation; victims reported that even while he was torturing them to discover where they had hidden their money, he ranted on about how he had joined William Jennings Bryan's crusade to save the farmer and workingman from being crucified "on a Cross of Gold," and to protect them from the hordes of foreigners swarming across the ocean to steal Americans' jobs and contaminate their pure blood by seducing their women. His frenzies of violence culminated in an assault on a farmer who had expressed his intention to vote for McKinley over Bryan. Beginning with the farmer, Lieder had methodically punished the whole family with an axe handle, and done it so thoroughly that none of them were able to testify later. The farmer's memory never fully returned; the two children were left brain-damaged and with an abiding horror of strangers; and the wife's catatonic withdrawal from reality was so total that she ended her years in care. Despite Lieder's claim to have been "sorely provoked" and to have acted for the good of his beloved United States of America, the judge condemned him to life internment in maximum security.

"That Lieder's crazy, all right," the guard Tillman relieved explained, "but he's not stupid. He's done folks all kinds of hurt, but he never *kills* anybody, 'cause he knows he'd hang for it. No, he's no fool. What he is is evil. Pure distilled two-hundred-proof evil. And crafty? He can talk the birds down from the trees. So you be careful, kid. And I mean *careful.*" All this made Tillman wish he hadn't promised his wife that he would speak to Lieder. But . . . a promise is a promise.

He opened the spy-hole to find Lieder pacing angrily across his field of vision, a book open in his hand. "Yes!

And this 'time of tribulation' must mean the war in Cuba! What else could it mean?'' He disappeared from sight for an instant as he reached the near corner of the cell, then he turned and strode the five paces back to the opposite corner. '' 'The tribulation will pass,' '' he quoted from the page before his face, '' 'and the nation will rejoice! But in its rejoicing, it will little note the insidious rot eating out its core! This rot will spread, until a leader rises from among the People to smite the invaders!' '' Lieder softly closed the book and looked out through his barred window to the horizon. ''...to smite the invaders...'' he repeated in a tone of wonder. Then he threw himself onto his bunk. ''*Smite them!*'' In a suddenly calm tone he spoke to the ceiling, ''You'd be the new guard. What do you call yourself?''

''Ah...Tillman.''

''Tillman,'' he repeated. ''I like to know a man's name. I think it's important to know a man's name. Well, Mr. Tillman, welcome to the land of the moonberries. You got something for me?''

Tillman cleared his throat. ''I got this week's paper.'' There was an embarrassed silence. ''How...ah...how do I...?''

''You're wondering how you can give it to me without opening the door.''

''Well...ah...'' Tillman certainly didn't intend to take any chances.

Lieder stood up. ''They roll the pages up and push 'em through the hole. And you know, I honestly believe that's the best way to do it. A man would be a downright fool to risk coming in here.''

Tillman ineptly rolled up the first sheet of the four-page paper and slowly introduced it into the spy-hole. It suddenly flew through his fingers as Lieder snatched it in.

''Good news,'' Tillman said as he started rolling up the second sheet. ''Looks like the fighting in Cuba's all over. They've signed a . . . a something . . . with Spain.''

Lieder stared fiercely at the paper. "A protocol . . . whatever the hell that is. Those pig-ignorant bastards in Washington have been tricked! Fine young American boys fight and die to teach foreigners who's who and what's what, and the politicians sign a protocol! Spain palms off Puerto Rico and the Philippines on us! And that stupid McKinley thinks he did good! Those sly Spaniards have slipped us the poison spoon, Mr. Tillman. Slipped us the poison spoon! They've palmed off a couple of million illiterate greasers on us, and first thing you know they'll come streaming over here to steal jobs from Americans! Give me that!'' He snatched the second sheet in through the spy-hole and scanned it rapidly. "Stupid bastards!''

Tillman had been looking for the right moment to speak to Lieder about what his wife had suggested, but this sure wasn't it.

"I'm interested in your opinion about something, Mr. Tillman,'' Lieder said. "Who do *you* think blew up the *Maine*?''

"Ah . . . the Spanish, of course.''

"*The Spanish?*'' Lieder laughed. "It was those anarchists! One of those immigrant bastards put a time bomb on board when she was still in harbor in America!''

"But . . . why would they do that?''

"To lure us into war! To draw our soldiers out of this country and leave them free to take it over!''

"That's crazy! There ain't—''

Lieder spun and glared in rage at the spy-hole . . . then he smoothly masked his fury behind an eye-smile. "Well now, maybe you're right, Mr. Tillman.'' He showed his teeth in a broad grin. "Crazy men do sometimes say crazy things. That's how we know they're crazy, isn't it? Mr. Tillman, would you tell me something?''

"What's that?'' Tillman's tone was stiff. No slick moonberry was going to talk *him* down from the trees.

"Are you a reader? Me, I believe a man ought to read. Keeps his mind sharp and his horizons broad."

"I don't read but the Bible. A man don't need nothing else, 'cause all the truth in this world is right there. Me and my wife read from the Good Book every morning and evening."

"Your wife? Oh ... yes. Yes, a guard told me that the new man had just got married. It is a crying shame, ain't it, how some men feel they've got to say smutty things about newly married folks? Joking about what they get up to, and how many times they do it, and how sore the wife is afterward! Men think they're being funny, but all they're being is filthy-minded. So you don't read anything but the Bible, eh? You know what I was reading when you came calling at my door? I was reading the most important book ever written—other, of course, than your Bible. I was reading *The Revelation of the Forbidden Truth*, which was written by a man who signs himself simply The Warrior. You ever hear tell of *The Revelation of the Forbidden Truth*, Mr. Tillman?"

"Can't say I have," Tillman said, his curt tone showing he was no soft touch.

"I'm sorry to hear that. But then, I suppose it isn't given to everyone to receive and understand the Forbidden Truth. Only to those who have been chosen to smite the politicians in Washington who are despoiling this beautiful land of ours. And the immigrants! And the papists! And the stockbrokers! And the—" He smiled suddenly. "But just listen to me, will you? Babbling away like a crazy man. Sane people, they don't care if the foreigners and the Catholics and the Jews blow up American battleships and get off scot-free! No! And they don't care if America's turning into a garbage pit for Europe to dump their ignorant scum into." He dropped onto his bunk and threw his arm over his face.

"Ah ..." Tillman began uncertainly. "Talking about reading and all, do you ... ah ... have a Bible in there?"

Lieder did not respond.

"I'm asking because my wife..." Tillman shrugged.

"Because your wife what, Mr. Tillman?" Lieder asked from beneath his arm.

"Well, I told her about you, and she said I should... I mean, she thought maybe you'd like to..."

"Maybe I'd like to do what, Mr. Tillman?"

The guard cleared his throat. "Have you accepted the Lord Jesus Christ as your personal savior?"

Lieder smiled into his arm. But his voice was gentle and receptive when he answered, "Well now, I can't honestly say as I have, Mr. Tillman."

"You haven't been washed in the Blood of the Lamb?"

"N-no. But I confess that something in those words attracts me mightily." He lowered his arm and looked toward the spy-hole, his eyes vulnerable and sincere. "Your wife, she wouldn't have something I could read, would she? Something to guide my feet along the right path?"

"I'll bring you some tracts tomorrow."

"Will you, Mr. Tillman? I'd be so thankful."

"You can count on it." Tillman closed the spy-hole and drew a deep breath. Mary will be pleased as punch when I tell her. Pleased as punch!

Alone, Lieder's lips compressed into an astringent smile. "*Well*, now! I guess there's something to what Paul said in Friesians: 7, 13. Praise the word of the Lord, for it is Truth, and the truth *will set you free.*"

DUTCHMAN'S FINGER, YANKEE PROMISE, Sally's Drawers, Why Bother?, Easy Squaw, Eureka Ditty...the Wyoming silver rush left so many short-lived and whimsically named towns in its wake that "Twenty-Mile" seems mundane by comparison, until you discover that the town wasn't twenty miles from anything. It sprang up overnight beside a narrow-gauge railway that connected the boomtown of Destiny to a high mountain silver mine called the Surprise Lode. The distance between these terminals was only seventeen miles as the crow flies, but if that crow had been obliged to take the train, it would have had to endure a tortuous forty-three mile crawl up the vertiginous switchbacks of the Medicine Bow Range, with solid rock walls almost brushing one side of the train and, on the other side, a series of stomach-fluttering drops into deep ravines.

Some claim that Twenty-Mile got its name when the railroad surveyors, having chosen a point at random from which to measure distances, discovered a two-acre shelf of flatland about twenty miles up the line that would serve as a way station for supplies while they were blasting out the roadbed and laying track. The little cluster of unpainted, false-fronted buildings that sprouted up overnight came to be known as Twenty-Mile. Admittedly, it is not very gratifying to learn that Twenty-Mile was so called because it was twenty miles from a spot twenty miles away, but we are unlikely ever to get a better explanation because Twenty-Mile now exists only in small print on the survey quads, where its symbol indicates *uninhabited agglomeration*, map-maker language for a ghost town.

This ghost town attracts occasional memento-hunters who, after working their way up the now-derelict and dangerous railroad cut in search of souvenirs from America's Vanished Past, report feeling a disquieting "chill" upon reaching Twenty-Mile's little scattering of abandoned, sun-bleached buildings. Old-timers say that the town's "bad totem" comes from what happened there in 1898 when, already slipping toward decay after its brief flurry of growth, it was inhabited by only a handful of hangers-on. But every Saturday evening a rattling five-car train used to carry the week's output of silver from the Surprise Lode down to Destiny to be smelted and shipped back East. The snorting narrow-gauge engine made a brief stop at Twenty-Mile to drop off sixty-or-so miners for their weekly bender. It would pick them up again on its return Sunday morning, as it brought coal, equipment, and supplies up to the Lode and to the residents of Twenty-Mile. This arrangement had been worked out by the mine managers to prevent their work force of misfits and drifters from getting down to Destiny, where they might find work that was less backbreaking, dangerous, and poorly paid, or even desert to the new gold fields up in the Klondike. But the Surprise Lode miners were a feckless, burnt-out bunch, content to stay where they were so long as they had all Saturday night to raise hell and squander their wages; and it was this hell-raising and wage-squandering that constituted Twenty-Mile's only excuse for existing, after its role as the mine's principal supply station had been superseded by Destiny, and the flood of independent prospectors that used to comb these mountains had dwindled to a trickle of half-crazed diehards.

Even before the train came to a full stop, the fun-hungry miners would scramble down from the boxcars, whooping and shooting their slack-hammered old dog-leg pistols into the air as they descended upon Bjorkvist's Boardinghouse, where they would devour huge quantities of pretty bad food. Then most of them would go to Kane's Mercantile Emporium to buy overalls or work gloves or muscle liniment or flannel shirts or chewing tobacco or patent medicines, and sometimes frilly little gifts for someone's birthday back home. Mr. Kane would keep their purchases for them until just before they scrambled back onto the train Sunday morning.

From Kane's Mercantile, some went to Professor Murphy's Tonsorial Palace, where a coal-stoked boiler wheezed dangerously as it struggled to heat water for the four wooden tubs. You could get a bath for 35¢, and a

15¢ shave came with enough bay rum slapped onto your cheeks to make your pals hoot and whistle when they smelled you coming into the Traveller's Welcome Hotel (which was not really a hotel, just a whorehouse with a bar). The reason some men got all bathed and shaved and bay-rum'd was because they believed they might get special treatment from the hotel's whores if they looked their best. No one ever specified what this "special treatment" might consist of, but the words were usually accompanied by winks and nudges and knowing snickers.

Three "girls" worked the Traveller's Welcome: Frenchy, a tall, lean, yellow-eyed black woman from New Orleans; Chinky, a shy Chinese girl who spoke little English and never looked a man in the eyes; and Queeny, a loud, laughing, sloshy-breasted old Irishwoman who was said to be able to drink anything that didn't eat the bottom out of the glass before she got to it. The older miners preferred Queeny, saying she was a "barrel of laughs" and a "good ol' gal at heart"; the younger boys went for Chinky because more experienced girls might poke fun at them; and those who passed for connoisseurs went for Frenchy because everyone knew that black gals were just naturally better at it, and if she was also French . . . ! Well, hey there! Stand aside!

The miners greatly outnumbered Twenty-Mile's permanent population, which had shrunk from more than two hundred at the high tide of the town's fortunes to just fifteen souls, so few that they occupied only a handful of the unpainted wooden buildings that had been slapped up during the heady years of boom and hope, when the town's motto had been: Watch Us Grow! Now those empty buildings creaked and groaned softly as they surrendered themselves to the patient and deadly embrace of gravity.

Twenty-Mile's fifteen residents included Mr. Kane, owner of the Mercantile Emporium ("Everything a Person Really Needs"). Mr. Kane's independent-minded seventeen-year-old daughter, Ruth Lillian, was accounted the town's beauty. Professor Murphy, as we have seen, sold hot baths, shaves, and generous splashes of bay rum at his Tonsorial Palace. Mrs. Bjorkvist ran the boarding-house, which was really just a big dining room that served "steaks" (the quotation marks are meant to suggest the same level of dubiousness as those around "girls" when describing the hotel's whores). These steaks came with cabbage, baking-powder biscuits, and canned peaches at every meal. There was a long room at the back with wooden bunks and skimpy straw mattresses on which miners stumbling back from the Traveller's Welcome could sleep. Bed, supper, and breakfast cost an all-in price of one dollar—robbery, the miners always grumbled, but they paid up. Although Mrs. Bjorkvist spoke with an accent that could blunt a hacksaw, she managed to make it known that she never wanted to see any of the Traveller's Welcome's "girls" around her establishment. There was a Mr. Bjorkvist skulking in the background, a hefty, scowling man with whose assistance she had borne two children. (One wag said he must have struck pay dirt each time he put in his spade.) Kersti Bjorkvist was a heavy-shouldered, thick-featured girl of twenty-two who worked in the kitchen and waited on tables, and her brother, Oskar, was a slow-witted boy a year older than Ruth Lillian Kane, whom he ogled in a moist, slack-jawed way that made Mr. Kane frown irritably. The Traveller's Welcome and its three girls were run by Mr. Delanny, who coughed a lot, wore sparkling white shirts with frills down the front, and was thin as a rail. Mr. Delanny was understood to have been a "big-time gambler" in his day, a reputation burnished by Jeff Calder, the one-legged Civil War veteran who served behind the hotel's bar and often complained that although he'd done more than his share in the defense of the Union, this no-account government refused to treat its wounded heroes like it ought to.

As for the remaining three citizens of Twenty-Mile: B. J. Stone dealt with the donkeys they used up in the mine shafts. He was accounted "odd" because he read a lot and had a way of looking at you as though he knew something he wasn't telling. B. J. Stone's helper-of-all-work was called Coots, a gruff old mixed-blood, part Black, part Cherokee, who kept to himself and was rumored to be a dangerous man to fool with because he had been a gunfighter. Finally there was "Reverend" (see "steak" and "girls") Leroy Hibbard, who received a stipend from the mining company for accompanying the men back up to the Lode every Sunday morning and laying a soul-scourging sermon on the entire work force, which the Puritan Boston mine owners obliged to assemble and receive this bludgeoning enlightenment. Hibbard always stayed overnight at the mine after his exhausting witness and returned Monday afternoon, walking the fifteen miles back down the railroad track. The Reverend was locked in constant battle against the Depravity and Evil that lurk within all descendants of Adam, but every couple of weeks his moral fiber would begin to fray, and he would sneak in at the back door of the Traveller's Welcome late at night to drink with Jeff Calder, then he'd go sin with Frenchy, after which submersion in the sloughs of iniquity, he would stagger down the street in that blackest hour just before dawn, sobbing and crying out that he was a disgusting creature! a loathsome sinner! a fornicator! an unworthy vessel undeserving of God's forgiveness! Mrs. Bjorkvist made no secret of the fact that this was pretty much her own evaluation of the Reverend, who eagerly lapped up her loathing as a deliciously appropriate punishment for his wickedness. B. J. Stone (the Livery man who reads a lot?) found the Reverend ludicrous and openly laughed at him. And for this reason the man of God detested Stone with that marrow-deep hatred that the righteous claim to reserve for the sin but always visit upon the sinner.

Every Sunday morning, after the train dropped off supplies and picked up the miners to carry them and their furry-mouthed hangovers back up to the Surprise Lode, Twenty-Mile was left feeling stiff and leaden, as though it were suffering its own kind of hangover, dazed by all the shouting and laughter, soured by drink, drained by loveless sexual excess. Most people slept late on Sundays, but Kersti Bjorkvist could usually be found sitting at her kitchen table, slump-shouldered and staring, and over at the hotel Jeff Calder would be stumping one-leggedly around the barroom behind his push broom, while upstairs the public girls sprawled in tangled, sweat-damp sheets.

The spring bell over the door of Kane's Mercantile jangled as Mr. Delanny came in to pick up the bottles of Mother Grey's Patented Suppressant he used to keep his cough in check. Departing, he met Mrs. Bjorkvist at the door, and he lifted his hat in a sarcastically theatrical gesture that made her sniff and turn her head away. She wanted no truck with the man who owned The Traveller's Welcome, with its . . . its . . . its Whores of Babylon! Mrs. Bjorkvist's moral abhorrence of the hotel did not, however, extend to denying herself the profit she made by supplying that iniquitous den's residents with their daily dinners and suppers. Unable to lower herself to having such people in her establishment, she sent her daughter over with covered pots containing the meals, but she watched the clock to be sure the girl was gone no longer than was necessary to put the food under the warming hood of the hotel's kitchen stove, because . . . well, because you never know, do you?

Knowing that Mrs. Bjorkvist never bought anything, Mr. Kane continued his Sunday morning routine of listing the supplies the train had brought up from Destiny, while his customer pecked along the counters, fingering the new stock and muttering over its price and quality. "Have you decided to celebrate our victory in Cuba with a little shopping spree, Mrs. Bjorkvist?'' She compressed her lips and sniffed. "Caught a little cold, have we?" Mr. Kane asked in the flat, dental accent that would have revealed his ethnic roots to anyone less accent-deaf than Mrs. Bjorkvist. "Maybe you should try some of Mr. Delanny's Suppressant." Mrs. Bjorkvist's neck stiffened at the thought of taking anything into the tabernacle of her body that was used by that...panderer, that...that...! Something outside the store window snagged her attention. "Vat's *dis* den?" she demanded to know. Mr. Kane lifted his head to see Mr. Delanny standing in the middle of the road, talking to a young man who was carrying a heavy pack and had an ancient, oversized shotgun on an improvised rope sling over his shoulder. Except for the occasional prospector, the arrival of a stranger was a rare enough event in Twenty-Mile to justify Mrs. Bjorkvist's irritated "Vat's dis den?" And this young man's wide-brimmed farmer's hat and wide-toed farmer's boots said he was no prospector.

"Vere d'ee tink *he* come from, den?" Mrs. Bjorkvist asked, her eyes riveted on the stranger, as though to nail him in place until she had made up her mind about him.

"I have no idea, Mrs. Bjorkvist," Mr. Kane said in an indifferent tone he knew would irritate her.

They watched Mr. Delanny smile and shake his head in response to a question from the stranger, then turn away to his hotel with a flip of his long, thin fingers that clearly said, "Good luck to you, boy." This was followed by a shake of his head that added, "You'll need it."

The young man shifted the weight of his pack, tipped his hat back on his head with his thumb, and walked off. Mrs. Bjorkvist pressed her cheek against the window to peer diagonally down the street after him. It wasn't that she was nosy, but if she didn't have a perfect right to know what this stranger was up to, then who did? When he turned in at B. J. Stone's Livery, she nodded to herself. She might have guessed! What with the way that old man was always reading books and looking at people like they were funny, or stupid, or... *something!* Imagine him daring to call other people funny! Him, who's nothing but a foul, vile—But she wouldn't contaminate her mind by even *thinking* that word.

In a tone that said "Wouldn't you know it?" she informed Mr. Kane that the stranger had gone to the Livery.

"Gone to the Livery, has he?" the shop-owner responded dryly. "Vat's dis vorld coming to, den?"

Ruth Lillian Kane came down the stairs from the living quarters above, having washed the breakfast dishes while her father was opening the store. She greeted Mrs. Bjorkvist brightly (a little too brightly, because she didn't like her) and asked politely after her daughter. But the proprietress of the boarding house limited her response to a disapproving glance at the new gingham dress Ruth Lillian was wearing. Frills and vanity! He spoils her, that man. Trying to make up for the way her mother... well, enough said. Enough said. No good ever came from spoiling children. She ought to give him a piece of her mind, but she didn't have time to stand around talking nonsense. That stranger would be wanting to sleep and eat at her boarding house. Well, maybe she'd let him, and maybe not. It would depend on what sort he was. She'd just wait and see.

Without further socializing, she left the store and crossed to her establishment.

"Good-bye, Mrs. Bjorkvist," Mr. Kane called after her in a sing-song. "Always a pleasure to serve you."

B. J. STONE TIPPED HIS chair back against the slab wall of the shoeing shed, carefully folded the two-day-old Cheyenne newspaper he had been reading, and

scrubbed his grey-stubbled cheek with his knuckles.
"From Nebraska, eh? And walked all the way! Well,
there's cold water in the barrel. Help yourself. Dipper's
right there. I'm sorry to have to tell you this, son, but if
you're looking for work, you've come to just about the
worst place in the Republic. There's absolutely nothing
happening in Twenty-Mile. And that's on busy days. This
is a town without history. Its past is only eleven years
long, and it has no future at all. I'd offer you a little tide-
over work, but what I make handling donkeys for the
Lode is barely enough to keep my soul from leaking out
of my body. I wouldn't even be able to afford old Coots
here, if he wasn't willing to work for just bed, vittles,
and my eternal gratitude. Isn't that right, Coots?"

The wiry old Black-Cherokee didn't look up from
scraping rot out of the hoof of the donkey whose foreleg
was folded up onto the leather apron on his lap. "And
piss-poor vittles they are," he muttered.

"Sorry I can't help you, son. But you're welcome to
a cup of coffee."

"A cup of coffee'd do me nothing but good, sir." The
boy grunted as he slipped off the straps that had dug into
his shoulders during his all-night walk up the railroad
track from Destiny.

"Fetch our guest a cup of joe, Coots," B. J. Stone
said grandly.

"You want to take over scraping out this hoof?"
Coots asked.

"No, no, you're doing just fine."

"Then *you* fetch the goddamned coffee. You ain't
done nothing all morning but sit there with your nose in
that paper, grumbling about *imperialism* and *jingoism*
and Christ only knows whatotherism! While me, I been
busier'n a one-legged man in a ass-kicking contest!"

B. J. Stone leaned toward Matthew and whispered,
"I'm afraid poor old Coots is a miserable excuse for a
host. And as for his coffee . . . !"

"If you don't like it, don't drink it!" Coots snapped.

"Touchy old bastard, too," B. J. confided behind his hand.

The young man smiled uncertainly; he'd never heard a black man sass a white man like that before. B. J. Stone stood up with a martyred sigh and disappeared into the kitchen, where a pot of coffee simmered on an iron stove, growing thicker and blacker since its grounds had been sunk with egg shells first thing that morning.

The young man set his shotgun beside his pack and gently pressed his sore shoulder with his fingertips as he watched Coots's skilful, pale-palmed hands work at the donkey's hoof. He was intrigued by Coots's face: the blend of Negro features and Cherokee eyes.

"Where'd you get that gun?" Coots asked without looking up from his task.

"My pa's."

"Hm! And he must've got it from his great-grandpa, who must've bought it off Methuselah! Where do you find ammunition for an old monster like that?"

"Pa used to make it himself." He untied the thongs of his backpack and rummaged in it for a canvas bag containing the shells he had taken with him when he hit the road. "Here's one. Ain't she a dandy? Pa, he'd cut open two ordinary double-ought shells and leave the primer and powder in place in one, then he'd make a longer jacket with stiff paper and add the powder from the other shell and the shot from both, then he'd tamp everything down tight—that was always the spooky part, the tamping—then he'd crimp the paper and dip it into wax to make it stiff and waterproof. They came out real good. But I'll admit the gun has a pretty fair kick."

Coots turned the waxy, double-size shell between his fingers and shook his head. "I'll bet! A man'd get tuckered out, having to pick himself up and walk back to the firing line each time he shot it!" Coots tossed the shell back. "Seems a waste of time, making shells for a gun that's no good for hunting. You hit an animal with that cannon and there'd be nothing left but a tuft of fur and a startled expression.''

The boy laughed. ''Pa only shot it once in a blue moon. He'd blow old barrels apart, making the staves fly ever which-a-way. Showing off. He liked having a bigger gun than anybody else.'' He returned the shell to his bag. ''To tell the truth, Pa didn't have all that much he could brag on.''

''But that antique's dangerous, boy! And with hand-made ammunition...whoa there! And you lugged that old monster all the way from Nebraska?''

''Yes, sir. I don't rightly know why I brung it along. I just didn't want to leave it behind. But *heavy?* A hundred times I thought about dropping it off along the trail.''

''But you didn't.''

''No, sir, I didn't.''

''Why not?''

''I don't rightly know.''

''You must like it a lot.''

''No, sir, I don't like it. Fact is...I hate it.''

''I don't blame you. Sooner or later that old thing's going to blow somebody all to hell.''

''Yes, well...that's just what happened. It was this old gun that done for my pa.''

Coots's knife stopped moving in the donkey's hoof. ''I'm sorry, boy. I never...I mean, I was just blathering. Sorry about your pa.''

The boy lifted his shoulders and said dully, ''Things like that happen. They just...'' He lowered his eyes and shook his head. ''...happen.'' He idly picked up an old leather-bound book from the bench. It smelled like his mother's Bible, but he couldn't figure out the words.

''That's Latin, son,'' B. J. Stone said, returning with a tin cup in one hand and the coffeepot in the other, its hot handle swathed in a clump of rags. ''It's a collection

of Roman satire from Lucilius to Juvenal. I don't suppose
you read Latin.'' He gave Matthew his cup.

''No, sir,'' the boy said, putting the book back gingerly, then holding out his cup to be filled.

''Satire deals with our vices and our—whoops!'' B. J.
Stone absent-mindedly over-filled Matthew's cup.
''...deals with our vices and our absurdities—in short
with the bulk of human activity.'' He turned to Coots.
''Well, do you want some of this miserable sludge, or
are you just going to keep on fussing with that hoof?''

''*Somebody's* got to do the work around here,'' Coots
retorted, holding out his cup to be refilled.

''You wouldn't be interested in the Romans by any
chance, would you, boy?'' B. J. Stone filled his own cup.

''No, sir, I can't say I am. I know that one of them
just washed his hands and let them kill Jesus, and . . . well,
that's all I know about the Romans. To tell the truth, I
don't read all that much.''

''That's too bad. A book's a good place to hide out
in, when things get too bad. Or too dull.'' This last
seemed to be directed at Coots, who ignored it.

The tin cup was so hot that Matthew had to suck in a
lot of air to keep from burning his lips, but the coffee
felt good going down into his empty stomach. ''What I
said about not reading all that much? Fact is, we moved
around a lot, and I was snatched from school to school
so much that I can barely recognize my name.''

''And what *is* your name?''

''Well, sir . . . they call me the Ringo Kid.''

Coots and B. J. Stone exchanged glances.

''*Do* they, now?'' B. J. Stone said. ''The Ringo Kid,
eh? So when your ma wants you for chores, she shouts
out, 'Hey, Ringo Kid! Come here, and chop me some
kindling!' Is that it?''

''No, sir, she doesn't say that.'' He paused a moment
before adding quietly, ''My ma is dead.''

"And his pa's dead, too!" Coots hissed in a tone that accused his partner of lacking tact.

"Oh." The teasing tone leached out of B. J.'s voice. "Have you been on your own for long?"

"About two weeks. After my folks died, I decided to pack up and go west and..." He shrugged.

"I see. Hm-m." B. J. Stone took a long sip of coffee to conceal his discomfort.

After a silence, the boy volunteered, "My ma named me Matthew. She wanted to have four boys. Matthew, Mark, Luke, and John."

"And what became of the other three evangelists?"

"The fever took Luke when he was just a baby. And Mark, he ran off about two years ago."

"And John?"

"There never was a John. My ma stopped having kids after Luke died. I guess it didn't seem worth the trouble, if the fever was just going to come along and take them off." The boy drew a long breath and stared out toward the cliff that ended Twenty-Mile. Then his focus softened into a gentle eye-smile. "Truth is, I ain't *really* called the Ringo Kid. I just said that because...well, I don't rightly know why. It just seemed like a good name to start my new life with. I got it out of the books by Mr. Anthony Bradford Chumms. You know the ones? *The Ringo Kid Meets His Match*? Or *The Ringo Kid Teaches a Lesson*? Or *The Ringo Kid Takes His Time*? I've read every one of them over and over until the pages started falling out. On the back cover of *The Ringo Kid Evens the Score*, it says that Mr. Anthony Bradford Chumms is 'an English gentleman who lends a cultured richness of expression to exciting tales of the American West.'"

"Well, now!" B. J. Stone said with mock respect. "Lends a cultured richness of expression, does he? My, my!"

"Yes, sir. For my money, Mr. Anthony Bradford Chumms is the best writer in the whole wide world!"

"Me, I'll stick with old Lucilius. But I thought you said you could barely read your name?"

Matthew lowered his eyes and was silent for fully three seconds. Then: "Yes, sir, I did say that. But it was a lie. I said I couldn't read because the Ringo Kid can't read, but everyone respects him anyway, because he's honest and fair. And I've always wanted to be like him."

"Hm-m. You do a lot of lying, do you, Matthew?"

"I'm afraid I do, sir. I know it's a sin, but..." He shrugged. Then he grinned. "But it sure saves a lot of trouble."

"I see. Well, look here, Matthew—You don't mind me calling you Matthew, do you?"

"No, sir. You can call me anything, so long as you don't call me late for dinner!" He forced a chuckle at his pa's tired old joke.

B. J. Stone scrubbed his cheek stubble with his knuckles. "Uh-huh. Well, look, Matthew. If you're hungry— and boys usually are—you can get something to eat down at the Bjorkvists' place. I'm not saying their food's good, you understand. Matter of fact, the best that can be said for it is that a strong man can keep most of it down."

"Oh, I'm all right. I'm not hungry." In fact, he hadn't eaten for a day and a half.

"Suit yourself. But it would be a good idea to get something inside you before you push on up to the mine."

"The mine?"

"Aren't you on your way up to the Surprise Lode to look for work?"

"Well, no, I...To tell the truth, this is the first I heard about there being any mine in these hills."

"Didn't the people down in Destiny tell you about the Lode?"

"I didn't ask. Everyone was running around, hooting and shouting about our glorious victory in Cuba."

"Victory!" B. J. Stone snapped. "A strong young nation bashes a tired old one that has nothing but worn-out ships commanded by inbred aristocrats, and you call that glorious? Under the cover of spreading democracy, we snatch off the Philippines and Puerto Rico. And while we're at it, we just pocket the Hawaiian Islands too! Thomas Jefferson would be spinning in his grave if he knew we'd become imperialists!"

Coots closed his eyes and shook his head. "You just *had* to bring Cuba up, didn't you?" he said to Matthew.

"But, I—"

"Victory?" Stone pursued. "Victory? William Randolph (I'm-so-rich-I-can-do-anything-I-goddamn-well-want) Hearst decides to boost the sales of his newspapers by whipping up a pack of mindless ruffians until their mouths foam with patriotic fury! And that publicity-hungry Roosevelt hires a bunch of polo players and a few out-of-work cowboys to charge up San Juan Hill—with plenty of reporters on hand, of course! But he quickly brings his Rough Riders back to Long Island to avoid the only real dangers in the whole war, malaria and yellow fever! Victory? You know how we won Guam Island, boy?"

"Ah . . . well, no, sir. But I—"

"I'll tell you how we won it. One of our ships pulled up and fired at the harbor, and the Spanish commander—who didn't even know there was a war on, for Christ's sake!—sent a messenger apologizing *for not returning our salute*, but he couldn't because there was no ammunition on the island. So we sent a rowboat ashore and claimed a valiant victory! *Victory!*"

The force of this tirade made Matthew glance nervously at Coots, who shrugged and asked his partner, "You just about all through?"

B. J. Stone growled and sniffed. Then he nodded. "Yes, I'm through. But . . . goddamn it, the idea of spilling young blood just so a few old men can—! Oh, don't get me started again.'' He drew a deep breath, then said, ''So, Matthew. You say you didn't even know about the Surprise Lode? You just decided to walk all the way up the railroad cut on the outside chance that you might find work at the end of the line?''

''Well . . . I figured there must be *something* at the end of the line. Else why would they have built it? And it seemed like it might be nice up here, tucked away from everything.''

''You took one hell of a chance,'' Coots told him. ''That track's mighty narrow, and the train could of flatten you like a turd under a wagon wheel. Hey, *wait* a minute . . . !''

''That's right! That train come near as nothing to killing me! I was walking up the track, fat and sassy, then all of a sudden I felt the rails shaking, and the next thing you know I heard the train coming up behind me. You better believe I started looking around for someplace to be, but it was all rock on one side, and nothing but air on the other! So I scrambled up-track as fast as I could, lugging my pack and gun, and just as the engine come round the bend, I found this crack in the wall and I squeezed into it with my face jammed up against the rock! And that train came roaring and sucking past my backside so close that every car knocked against the butt of my gun, click, click, click! I was sure something was going to catch on the strap and snatch me out to be killed. I was just certain that damn old gun was going to do for me, like it done for my pa.''

''Lord! That *was* a close shave!''

''*Close?* After it passed, I set down right there on the tracks, limp as a rag, my heart pounding away. To tell you the truth, if I would of known—''

''Let me give you some advice, boy,'' Mr. Stone said. ''You should break that habit of saying 'to tell the truth' all the time, because people usually say that as a stall while they cook up a lie. And if you're hell-bent on being a liar, you might as well be a good one.''

The boy nodded thoughtfully. ''Thank you, sir. I'll remember that.''

''So I suppose you'll be pushing on up to the mine?'' Coots said.

Matthew looked down and studied the ground. Then: ''No, sir, I don't believe I will. I think I'll just stay around here for a while.''

''But I just told you there's no work in Twenty-Mile,'' Stone said with some exasperation.

''Yes, sir, you did. But there's something about this place that suits me.''

''There *is?*''

''Don't you worry, sir. I'll find work. Say, can I ask a favor?''

''Anything that doesn't cost me worry, work, money, or time.''

''Can I leave my bindle and gun with you while I look around town?''

''Suit yourself. But it's no use.''

The young man nodded and grinned. ''You're probably right, sir.'' He stood up. ''Well, I sure do thank you for the coffee. It truly hit the spot.''

As they watched the boy walk back down the rutted street, B. J. Stone sipped his coffee pensively. ''What do you make of him, Coots?''

''Beats my two pair.''

''Why would a bright kid like that want to stay here, at the end of the world?''

''Could be he's hiding.''

''From what?''

''Beats my two pair.''

''Well, one thing's sure. He's not going to find work in this played-out town.''

''I wouldn't bet on it.''

State Prison, Laramie

WHEN HE ARRIVED TO take the midwatch, Guard Private John "B B" Tillman was sorely troubled.

He had been surprised, but pleased, by the way Lieder had received the tracts his wife selected for his guidance. He had half-expected him to scoff and jeer, the way his fellow guards scoffed and called him a "Bible bug" when he sought to share with them the precious gift of faith. But Lieder didn't jeer. He drew the rolled-up pages of the tracts in through his spy-hole respectfully, almost tenderly. And when they quietly discussed these messages of hope through the door, Lieder's whispering voice always carried tones of sincere yearning...a man seeking his way. And several times Tillman had opened the spy-hole to find Lieder on his knees by his bunk, his face buried in his arms, praying fervently.

Lieder's blasphemous habit of making up scripture and ascribing it to "Paul to the Mohegans," or "Paul to the Floridians," had caused Tillman heartache. But Lieder assured him that he didn't mean any disrespect, and he promised to pray for the strength to break all his bad habits. From that day on, his acceptance of Jesus as his personal savior seemed to lift a mighty burden from him. Tillman often heard him singing to himself in his cell, usually old-time revival songs, and he once declared that he willingly accepted the imprisonment of his body for the rest of his natural life, knowing that he could now hope for the liberation of his soul through all eternity!

At first, Lieder's rapid progress was uplifting to witness and a tribute to the benevolence and power of the Lord. But lately . . .

"I purely don't know what to do," Tillman had confessed to his wife. "He seems to have fallen into darkness. Sometimes he just breaks down and sobs like to make your heart break. He says his sins are so black and piled so high that he doesn't deserve the Lord's forgiveness. And sometimes he just lies there on his bunk, staring at the ceiling. The fact of it is, Mary, that man's soul is burdened down with sin."

"But he *mustn't* despair, John. Despair is the greatest sin of all."

"Don't I know it? But what am I to do?"

"You must never, never relent in your efforts to save him, John. You must tell him that he's got to persist through this Slough of Despond, for the Lord's mercy is as vast as it is eternal."

Tillman promised he wouldn't give up on Lieder. He would pray with him that very night. His wife agreed that prayer was the sovereign remedy for all Man's illness and woe, but she reminded him to be careful in dealing with this... what's that you call them?

"Moonberries."

"Well now, don't you take any chances."

"You think I'm crazy, darlin'-heart? You think I want John Junior to grow up without a dad?"

She blushed and pushed his chest with her fingertips, as she always did when he mentioned her "condition," a condition that they had celebrated with an exchange of presents. He gave her ribbons to braid into her hair, and she gave him a braided leather lanyard with a slide that he could wear in place of a tie. They laughed over the coincidence of both presents having to do with "braid," and she said it was a lucky omen.

The first thing Tillman did when he came on watch was to check on Lieder, whom he found lying on his bunk, staring up at the ceiling, lost in misery and self-loathing. He greeted him in an encouraging tone, but Lieder muttered bitterly that there was nothing left for him in this life, and probably nothing in the next. So what's the use? What's the use?

Tillman reminded him that despair is the greatest sin of all. Despair is a trick of the Devil, making us doubt the Lord's promise of salvation for even the least and lowest of us, but Lieder only shook his head miserably and turned his face to the wall.

Tillman sighed and returned to the watch-desk.

It was almost dark when Tillman made his last round of the moonberries. Through the spy-hole he found the acid-thrower sitting on the edge of his cot, rocking himself and humming, as always. "The Politician" was disagreeing violently with a space in the corner that he addressed as "you ignorant little pinch of duck-shit!" At the sound of the spy-hole opening, "the Spook" cowered in the corner. "Don't hurt me! I didn't mean to do it! Honest to God, I didn't mean it!"

The next cell had long been empty, but now it contained two men who had been transferred to the moonberry wing to protect new young prisoners, whom they routinely dragged into dark corners and... "broke in" was the prison term for it. As he approached the door, Tillman heard sounds of grunting and panting as though a fight was going on. He opened the spy-hole and found a neckless, bullet-headed giant bent over the end of his cot, and behind him was a little gnome with a twisted face. They were both panting and grunting. The gnome leered toward the open spy-hole, and only then did Tillman realize that they were... *Lord Jesus in Heaven!* He snapped the spy-hole shut and turned away.

He took several deep breaths to settle his stomach before going on to Lieder's door. He had been rehearsing the words of comfort he would share with the despairing sinner who—

But Lieder wasn't on his bunk. Through the twilight gloom, Tillman could see him over by his barred window, half-standing and half-kneeling, as though—*Lord*

Jesus! He had torn a strip off his blanket! One end was tied to a bar and the other around his neck! *Don't let this be happening, I ask it in His name!* He yanked down the locking lever, threw back the thick iron bolt, rushed in, and lifted Lieder to take the weight off the blanket strip around his throat. He held the sagging body in his arms, then sighed with relief when Lieder's eyes fluttered open. Tillman breathed a prayer of thanks that he hadn't been too late, but something had snagged on the leather lanyard his wife had given him, and it was tightening around his throat so that...*Argh!* The two men were pressed face-to-face, the lanyard threaded through Lieder's strong fingers. He made a fist and twisted, and Tillman's eyes bulged.

Lieder gently lowered the boneless weight in his arms to the floor.

Now! Now, he was free to follow The Warrior's instructions as set forth in *The Revelation of the Forbidden Truth.* He had thought about releasing the moonberries to form the nucleus of his American Freedom Militia, but he rejected the men at the end of the corridor as too old and crazy to be useful. He would take only the new pair in the double cell, the gnome and the bullet-headed one.

He felt sorry for young Tillman. But...a man's got to play the cards he's dealt. And anyway, going a little early to collect your reward ain't all that bad, is it? Not for a true believer.

RUTH LILLIAN KANE WAS alone in the Mercantile, her father having gone up to the living quarters to make their noon meal. He had done all the cooking, even when her mother was with them, because Mrs. Kane had had no intention of ruining her looks with domestic work. Ruth Lillian inherited her mother's looks and love of pretty things, but her father's no-nonsense brand of crisp, practical intelligence. She had arranged the new stock on the shelves attractively—she had her mother's eye for that sort of thing—and she was standing behind the counter, paging through a pattern book from the Singer Sewing Machine Company, approving styles that would suit her with a little nasal sound of appreciation, and dismissing unsuitable ones with a slight frown and a curt shake of her head, when the spring bell over the door jangled. It was so bright out in the street that she had to shield her eyes to see the customer silhouetted in the doorway. "Can I help you?"

"I truly hope so, ma'am." He approached the counter, taking off his wide-brimmed hat.

For a second, she stood with her hand still shielding her eyes. A stranger in Twenty-Mile? And a young one. "What can I do for you? Like our sign says, we got everything a person really needs." She smiled. "You'll notice it doesn't say everything a person might want, just what he really needs."

"I'm glad to hear that, because what I really need is a job." He smiled. "My name's Matthew."

"Pleased to make your acquaintance, Matthew. I'm Ruth Lillian Kane. This is my pa's store."

"I don't believe it."

"Well, it is. Why would I lie?"

"No, I mean I don't believe your name is *Ruth Lillian.*"

"What's wrong with my name?"

"Nothing! It's just that . . ." He shook his head. "Well, I'll be!"

"What'll you be?" Ruth Lillian asked.

"Well, to tell the tru—Ruth Lillian was my *ma*'s name, believe it or not!"

"There's lots of people named Ruth. It's a Bible name."

"If you were both called Ruth, *that'd* be a coincidence. But to have the same middle name too! Now, that's something more than coincidence.''

''Like what?''

''I don't know what to call it. But it's *something*, that's for sure.'' Matthew became aware that Mr. Kane was standing at the back of the store, having come down to tell Ruth Lillian that dinner was ready. ''Good afternoon, sir. I was just telling your daughter here that her name and my ma's—''

''I heard you,'' Mr. Kane said dryly.

''He came looking for a job, Pa,'' Ruth Lillian explained, and she flushed with resentment at being made to feel she was in the wrong in some way.

''There's no job here, young man. Nor anywhere else in Twenty-Mile, to my knowledge.''

''Yes, sir. Mr. Stone up to the livery stable told me the same thing. But it's an awful long walk back down to Destiny. And I'm pretty near tuckered out. To tell the truth—What I mean is, I'm not exactly sure what I should do.'' He looked at Mr. Kane with an open expression that invited him to make a suggestion.

''Have you got any money?''

''Yes, sir, a little.''

''Well, the Bjorkvists would probably put you up tonight. You could start back down in the morning.''

''Yes, sir, that's a possibility. I'll give it some thought. Thank you.''

''I don't suppose Matthew has eaten in a spell, Pa,'' Ruth Lillian said, ignoring her father's frown.

''I didn't make a meal,'' Mr. Kane said. ''Just leftovers.''

''That'd suit me just fine, sir,'' Matthew said cheerily. ''Left-overs is my favorite dish. My ma used to say that when it comes to vittles, I'd eat anything I could outrun!''

Ruth Lillian forced a little laugh at this, then looked at her father with calmly arched eyebrows until he shrugged, turned on his heel and started up the stairs, saying, "Well, we might as well eat before it gets any colder."

During the meal, which Matthew praised frequently and lavishly, he mentioned that he hadn't eaten this well for weeks, because he'd been on the road since the day his ma and pa had died within a couple of hours of each other.

"The fever, was it?" Ruth Lillian asked.

Matthew settled his eyes on her. "Well, you know how it is, Ruth Lillian. Sometimes the fever comes swooping down and takes a whole town. Other times it takes some folks and leaves others to get on as best they can in this world."

"You were left all alone?" Mr. Kane asked. "No brothers or sisters?"

"No, sir. I was their only child."

Ruth Lillian nodded slowly. She was an only child too. "How old are you, Matthew?"

"Eighteen going on nineteen. But I suppose everybody that's eighteen is going on nineteen. If they don't die first!" He grinned at his joke.

"Where are you from?" Mr. Kane asked dryly.

"Well, sir, the truth is, we moved around a lot, my folks and me. We ended up in a little town back on the Nebraska border. But my pa never had much luck getting jobs and even less keeping them, so we were fixing to move on when the fever come and..." He lifted his palms and made a little sucking sound with his teeth.

"What did you say your name was?"

"Chumms," Matthew said quickly. "Matthew Bradford Chumms. Ma named me after the writer. The Ringo Kid books? I guess that's why most people call me Ringo. Except for Mr. Stone up to the livery stable. Him and Coots, they call me Matthew."

"Oh, you know B. J. Stone, do you?"

"Well, I wouldn't want to say we're *close* or anything. But we sat around talking about Cuba and books and Romans and such like. Mr. Stone particularly admires Mr. Anthony Bradford Chumms, so naturally we hit it off. I told Mr. Stone how I didn't think our victory in Cuba was all that glorious, what with how we snatched islands off of the Spaniards just to sell newspapers, and them not even having any ammunition while Teddy Roosevelt was running away from the yellow fever, and all. I think he pretty much agreed with me. Sir? Excuse me, but there's something I've really got to fess up about.''

''Oh? What's that?''

''A while back you asked if I had money, and I said I had a little. Well, actually, sir, that was...'' He swallowed. ''That was a lie. Fact is, I ain't got a thin dime. I spent my last cent getting something to eat down to Destiny yesterday afternoon.'' He looked down into his plate. ''I know a person shouldn't lie, sir. My ma was at me often enough about lying, but... Well, my folks and me, we've always been poor. And I've always been ashamed of it. When I was little, I used to pretend to have things I didn't have. Spending money. Toys. I even used to pretend I had brothers named after the other three evangelists. I don't know why. Maybe I thought that made me seem interesting.'' He looked into Ruth Lillian's eyes with the simple sincerity of a person wanting very much to be understood. ''I guess what I've always wanted more than anything is for people to respect me. Like they respect the Ringo Kid. But people don't respect you if you're dirt poor.'' He turned his eyes to Mr. Kane. ''And that's why I lied to you about having money, sir. But it's not right to lie to people who've been good enough to invite you into their home and set you down to their table.''

Mr. Kane cleared his throat and grunted. ''Well, lots of good men have been poor. That's nothing to be ashamed of. A man can hold his head up, so long as he's willing to work for what he gets, and play fair with—''

"Oh, I'm willing to work, sir! Don't you worry about that. You just point me at what needs being done, and I'll do 'er!''

"I told you there's no work here."

"Yes but, I'm not talking about a permanent job. Just odd chores like chopping wood, or touching up a little paint, or fixing things that's busted, or toting stuff from here to there. Little stuff like that."

"There's lots of things we never get around to doing, Pa," Ruth Lillian put in, braving her father's dour glance. "You *know* you could use help with the heavy work."

Matthew had noticed that Mr. Kane had been slow in mounting the stairs and that he had stood at the top, drawing shallow breaths and pressing the flat of his hand against his chest.

But Mr. Kane was not going to be forced into a decision against his better judgment. "I don't need help. Not even temporary. I'm sorry, son, but that's how it is."

"I understand what you're saying, sir," Matthew agreed reasonably. "Look, I'll tell you what. Why don't I just go off and look around town while you two talk things over?" He pushed his chair back from the table and rose. "I don't know how to thank you for that fine meal, sir. It was what the Ringo Kid would call 'fair to middlin'.' That means it was *real* good. Mr. Anthony Bradford Chumms always has the Ringo Kid express himself that way—saying things are less than they are. Like calling a wild shoot-out 'a bit of a dustup,' or like saying he's not feeling all that jaunty when he's been shot in the shoulder and lost buckets of blood. So when I say that dinner was fair to middlin', I really mean that it was—gosh, I don't know why I'm blabbering on like this! I guess I'm nervous because your decision means so much to me. So I'll just leave you to talk things over in private. I'll come back in a few hours, and you can tell me what you've decided about the job." He turned to his hostess and made a gesture like tipping the brim of the hat he'd left downstairs on the counter. "Much obliged, Ruth Lillian."

"I'll walk you down and unlock the door for you."

"That's mighty civil of you." He stood aside to let Ruth Lillian precede him down the stairs. Before following her, he put his head back into the dining room, where Mr. Kane was resting, his elbow on the table, his head in his hand, his eyes closed. "Thank you again, sir."

Without opening his eyes, Mr. Kane waved him away.

———————

"THE THING IS THIS, sir," Matthew explained as he handed Professor Murphy the long-handled brush he used to scrub out his bath barrels after the miners went back up to the Lode. "Mr. Kane just doesn't have enough chores and odd jobs to keep me busy full time. Lord knows he *wants* to help me out, what with my ma and Ruth Lillian being so close and all."

The barber lifted his splendidly curled head out of the barrel and cocked a dubious eye at the young man. "You're related to the Kanes?"

"Oh, I wouldn't say we was *related*. But Ruth Lillian has the same name as my ma. You know how it is, sir. There's small towns back East where just about everybody's related to everybody else. My pa used to say that the dogs was even related to the cats!"

Professor Murphy contributed no more than a snort to the boy's self-appreciative laughter as he grunted his belly over the edge of the bath barrel and continued to scrub it with strong-smelling Fels-Naphtha soap. "Well, I'm afraid I ain't got any work for you," his voice echoed woodenly.

"Yes, sir, I understand that. The only reason I asked was because Ruth Lillian's pa and old B. J. Stone both thought maybe you could use some help with the dirty work. Like scrubbing out those barrels and such. But if you can't afford it, I'll just tell them so. I'm sure they'll understand.''

Professor Murphy emerged from the barrel again, his splendid head of salt-and-pepper curls slightly askew. ''It ain't a matter of being able to afford it!'' He straightened his hair with a deft jerk. ''It's a matter of needing help or not needing help!''

''You're absolutely right, sir. And I can see I'm wasting your time, and like my pa used to say: time is money. Matter of fact, I figure that scrubbing out those four barrels real good, then sweeping up your place, and washing the windows and stuff like that, would take me about... oh, about two hours. And I wouldn't be able to work for less than two bits an hour, so the whole job would cost you half a dollar, and the good Lord knows that half a dollar ain't chicken feed. Not in these hard times.''

Twenty-Mile's only licensed purveyor of Chief Wapah's Patented Tonsorial Rejuvenator snorted. ''If you think you could do all that work in two hours, boy, you been chewing on crazy-weed.''

Matthew looked at the barrels with a measuring eye. ''Hm-m-m, well, I'm pretty sure I *can* do it in two hours ...three at the most. Tell you what. I'll do the job for six bits, and if it takes me all day, well then that's just skin off my own nose. I honestly don't believe a man could say fairer than that, do you, sir?''

''Six bits? Four barrels, scrubbed as clean as I want 'em? *And* my shop swept out? *And* my windows washed? *And* the trash dumped over the cliff, down across the tracks? *And* the sink scrubbed? You're saying you'd do all that for six bits?''

''Yes, sir, that's my price for the first two weeks. And after that, if you don't think that's fair—or if I don't— well then, we can work out some sort of agreement.''

''Hm-m. Yeah but, even at six bits, the fact is I don't need no help.''

''...plus advice.''

"What?"

"My price would be six bits *plus* some advice."

"Advice? What sort of advice?"

"Well, sir..." Matthew smiled slackly and looked around in embarrassment. "It's my hair, sir. I'm afraid I'm starting to lose it."

"You?" The Professor regarded the boy's oak-brown, sun-glistered mop with a mixture of envy and irritation. "It's your *mind* you're losing, boy, not your hair. You'll have that hair till hell freezes over."

"I wish I could believe that, sir. But my pa, he was only forty-two years old when he died, and he was already getting a little thin on top. He used to say that early balding was a sure sign that a man was strong with the women! My ma'd get mad when he said that because he had a reputation for... well, you know. So along with six bits for doing your chores, I'll be wanting advice about what to do, if I want to have a head of hair like yours when I'm your age."

"You want hair like mine, do you? Well then, *here!*" He snatched off his wig and thrust it toward the boy, who jumped back startled. In fact, he actually *was* a little startled to see that the Professor was a good two inches shorter without his thick salt-and-pepper curls.

The Professor sputtered with laughter, and Matthew stood blinking. "Well sir, you fooled me, and that's for sure! I never in the world would of guessed!"

As he replaced his hair, still chuckling at the effect of his wit, Professor Murphy agreed to give their arrangement a try. "In fact, you can start right now." He tossed him the long-handled brush. "What'd you say your name was?"

"Folks call me the Ringo Kid. Sir, would it be all right if I started first thing tomorrow morning? You see, I'm supposed to talk to the man who owns the hotel. What's his name again?"

"Delanny. And it ain't a hotel! He gives himself airs,

calling that three-stall whorehouse a *hotel*.''

"Ain't that the truth? Some people do just love to give themselves airs. But I got to get me a little work from Mr. Delanny, too. Old B. J. Stone confided in me that there wasn't a real job to be had in Twenty-Mile, so I guess I've got to build me one out of bits and scraps. I'll be back bright'n early tomorrow, and seventy-five cents later, those tubs'll be cleaner than a . . . a . . . Gosh, I can't think of what you say things are cleaner'n a.''

"Whistle."

"Whistle? I thought things were *slicker* than a whistle.''

"I always heard *cleaner!*''

"You know, sir, I believe you're right. I believe smart folks say cleaner'n a whistle, and only us country folks say slicker'n a whistle. Well then, I'll be seeing you tomorrow morning.''

MR. DELANNY HAD BEEN sitting at his table, laying out his usual game of solitaire, when he was interrupted by the young man's apologetic request to have a few words with him. The gambler looked slowly up from beneath the brim of the carefully brushed black hat he wore level on his head, and surveyed the boy with heavy-lidded, cynical eyes. But he listened, wryly amused, as the boy "played out his trumps," describing how everybody in town was doing their best to scrape up some chores for him to do. Behind the deserted bar, Jeff Calder stumped around on his peg leg, shifting bottles and glasses that didn't need shifting, his every gesture radiating irritation at the presence of this outsider begging for work. Just barely audible from somewhere above, a woman was humming in a husky contralto: a Negro spiritual. Matthew interrupted his pitch to tell Mr. Delanny that the song reminded him of the time his mother brought him to a traveling revivalist's tent, a "Cathedral of Canvas," where a man dressed all in yellow silk preached and sobbed and begged God to come down to heal those who believed, and punish those who didn't, while three Negro women stood behind him in white gowns, swaying and humming that very song. His ma had given a two-dollar bill (a lucky one, with the corner torn off) into the collection plate, and his pa had been so mad when he learned about it that he had slapped her around some. That was only last year, and now both his ma and pa were...gone.

"That was pretty slick," Mr. Delanny said in his soft, phlegm-burred voice.

"Sir?"

"You know what you are, young man? You're a natural-born con. That was pretty slick, the way you picked up on one of my girls singing upstairs and parlayed it into telling me that your ma was religious, that your folks were dead, and that you were all alone in this cruel, cruel world."

"Gee, sir, I don't understand what you're saying. I mean...My folks *are* dead!"

Mr. Delanny chuckled—and this brought on a bout of coughing that ended with his spitting into a large white handkerchief, then looking into it with clinical curiosity before folding it to conceal the blood. "Oh, I don't doubt that your folks are dead. Nor that your ma was religious. It's the way you use those facts that reveals you to be a natural con." Mr. Delanny's speech was slow and his diction precise. Everything about him, his gestures, his dress, his speech, had a precious theatricality. "The successful con doesn't risk lying, except as a last resort. He uses the truth—selected bits of it—cleverly. It's a sleight of mind that can't be learned. You've got to be born with it. This world's divided into two kinds of people: the marks and the cons. And every human relationship—politics, business, romance—can be described in terms of who are the marks and who are the cons. And you, boy? You're one of Nature's own cons.''

"Well, ah...thank you, sir....I guess.''

"But there's one thing you better remember.''

"Sir?''

"Never try to con a con.''

"I don't understand, sir.''

"Oh, I think you do. Now, I don't mind your coming in here and trying out your line of patter. Matter of fact, it's amusing to see how you lay out your cards. But I wouldn't want you to think you were scoring on me. Professional pride, you know.''

"Yes, sir. I know all about pride. That's why I can't let people take care of me, and I've got to find ways to support myself.''

Mr. Delanny laughed again—and coughed. When he got his breath back, he said, "You are some piece of work. You know perfectly well I've got you pegged, but you're still trying to score on me. Trying to con a job out of me.''

Matthew grinned. "Well, sir, I really do need it.''

For a long moment, Mr. Delanny looked at him from beneath the rim of his black hat, a glint of wry amusement in the feverish eyes deep in their sunken sockets. He nodded. "All right. I'll try you out. What's your name?''

"My name is...'' Matthew covered his hesitation with a clearing of his throat. "...Dubchek, sir. Matthew Dubchek.''

"That's your *real* name?''

"Yes, sir.''

Mr. Delanny's eyes narrowed in evaluation. Then: "You know, I think Dubchek just might be your real name. It isn't one that a natural-born con would make up. Too foreign. Well then, Matthew Dubchek, why don't you start tomorrow morning? You can give Calder there a hand.''

"I don't need no hand!"

Mr. Delanny ignored this and told Matthew he could help Jeff Calder make breakfast for the girls and...

"But I don't *need* no help."

...then he could do whatever other chores Calder set for him. Might be washing the dishes, or making the girls' beds, or doing the laundry up at the spring, or throwing garbage over the cliff. Whatever Calder said needed being done.

Matthew rose from the table and went to the bar. "Well then, Mr. Calder, I guess you're to be my boss."

"Yeah, but I don't need—"

"I gotta be honest with you, Mr. Calder. I ain't any great shakes at cooking. But I'm a quick learner!" Matthew smiled, and the peg-legged veteran grunted and muttered that he'd damn well *better* be a quick learner, because he didn't have time to tell somebody how to do something more'n once!

"I understand that, sir. And I'll see you tomorrow morning, bright and early."

"Not *too* bright and early," Jeff Calder said, making it clear right from the beginning who was boss.

Matthew nodded and put on the hat he had been holding by its rim. His broad smile concealed the nausea that the barroom medley of stale cigar smoke and whiskey brought to the back of his throat. Particularly the whiskey. He hated that smell! He had turned to leave when Mr. Delanny's beckoning flick of a forefinger brought him back to the card table, where he took off his hat and sat.

"Tell me, young Dubchek, how did you happen to come—"

"Excuse me, sir. I'm sorry to interrupt you, but I'd just as soon you didn't call me Dubchek because ... well, you see, somehow Mr. Kane got the idea that my name was Matthew Bradford Chumms—same as the book-writer?—and I didn't bother to set him straight because, well, because I didn't know I was going to stay in Twenty-Mile long enough for it to matter one way or the other. But now if I tell him that Chumms *isn't* my name, he'll think I was lying to him, and—'' Matthew stopped short and looked into Mr. Delanny's amused eyes. He lowered his own eyes to his lap. ''All I been saying is a lie, sir. Fact is, I *told* Mr. Kane my name was Chumms.''

Mr. Delanny chuckled through his nose without smiling. ''That's a well-worn, but nevertheless effective, ploy: confessing that you've been lying when you realize the other fellow's got you cold to rights, in the hope that you'll end up seeming honest because you've admitted to being a liar.''

Matthew didn't look up. ''I don't lie, Mr. Delanny. Not really what you'd call *lie*. I just . . . I tell people what I think will please them, or interest them, or make them respect me.''

''Is that what you want from people? Respect?''

''More'n anything, sir. But it's hard to get respect if your name's Dubchek, and everybody knows who your pa is. And *what* he is.''

''I see. So you're not to be called Dubchek.''

''No, sir. Just plain Matthew will do. Well, you could call me Ringo, if you want. That's what Professor Murphy calls me.''

Mr. Delanny didn't laugh because he couldn't afford to trigger another cough, but his eyes glittered. ''It would be a pity for you to waste such a natural gift for duplicity on Twenty-Mile. There's nothing for you here, boy. Not even any respect worth having. The people in this town, they're just driftwood carried here on the crest of the silver boom, then left beached when that flood subsided, and they hadn't the strength or the courage to get back into the current.''

Matthew smiled crookedly. ''Even you, sir?''

''Even me.''

''Why do you stay here, if it's all that bad?''

Delanny's mouth creased in an ironic smile that did not illuminate his eyes. "I'm here for the mountain air. It's good for my lungs. Keeps me alive—if moving cards around on a table and watching the days sift away can be called living. All right then! You can start tomorrow morning. The girls eat and sleep here in the hotel because Mrs. Bjorkvist wouldn't have them at the boarding house. She'll take money from the miners who use them, but she won't have the girls. A typical God-fearing Bible-pounder who believes that money in the bank is a sign of God's approval."

"She's certainly that, all right!" Matthew agreed with a knowing chuckle.

"Oh? You know Mrs. Bjorkvist, do you?"

"Well, no, not exactly. But if you say she's God-fearing, your word is good enough for me, sir."

Mr. Delanny sniffed and shook his head. "You're a real chameleon, boy."

Matthew rose. "Well, I promised I'd get back to Mr. Kane's so we could figure out what sort of chores I'll be doing for him." He raised his voice. "Good-bye, Mr. Calder. I'll be back in the morning—but not too bright and early, like you said."

Mr. Delanny, who had returned to his solitaire layout, glanced up when Matthew asked, "Sir? Excuse me, but just what exactly is a kameel—keemel—what you said?"

"A chameleon is a lizard that protects itself by changing its coloring to match its surroundings."

"I see." The boy nodded slowly. "Well, then!" He waved and went out into the glaring sunlight.

MATTHEW HAD NO LUCK with the Bjorkvists, even though he found a way to mention right off that his ma, who had passed over into Glory only the week before, used to read every night from the Bible, which he, for

one, reckoned was the finest book in the world, even
better than those Ringo Kid books written by Mr. Anthony Bradford Chumms, after whom he was named—
except for his first name, which was Matthew . . . like the
Matthew who helped write the Bible?

He stood in the doorway to the big dining room, further penetration into the boarding house being blocked
by Mrs. Bjorkvist, whose arms were folded over her
chest. Her husband sat at one of the back tables, sullen
and silent in a long-sleeved red undershirt that was sweat-
bleached under the arms. Curiosity had drawn the thick-
featured Kersti Bjorkvist to the doorway of the steamy
kitchen, where she stood dabbing at her glistening neck
with a cool dish cloth, while her slack-eyed brother, Oskar, stood against the wall, sizing Matthew up, wondering
who'd win in a fight.

No, Mrs. Bjorkvist did *not* have any work she needed
done—particularly by somebody who'd come to her directly from Delanny's den of vice, after spending time
up at the Livery with that B. J. Stone and that *Coots* of
his! Didn't he know that this *Coots* used to be a gunman
in wicked river towns, protecting gamblers and Jezebels
from being strung up by righteous citizens, like they de-
served? No, she didn't need any help, but if Matthew
wanted to stay at her boarding house, it'd be a dollar a
day for two meals and a bed. Matthew said that he was
sure that was a fair price, but to tell the tru—he wasn't
even sure he'd be *making* a dollar each and every day,
but maybe he could work off his bed and board by doing
odd jobs around the—Didn't he hear her say that she
didn't need no odd jobs done!? She had her own men to
do odd jobs. And it was a dollar a day, take it or leave
it.

"Well, ma'am, I guess I'll have to think about it.
Nothing would please me more than to be a regular guest
with a family that lives by the Good Book, but at a dollar
a day . . . Well, ma'am, I want to thank you for your help

and advice, and I...well, I guess I'll just be on my way.''

————————————

"DON'T SAY I DIDN'T warn you,'' B. J. Stone said, looking up from the month-old Laramie newspaper he had been picking clean, down to the social announcements and "for sale" notices. He had devoured the paper that came up with the train, and now he was reduced to rummaging through his stack of back issues for something he hadn't read to the bone. "I told you there wasn't any work in town.''

''Yes, sir, you did. But, you know, it's amazing how helpful people can be. Everyone found some little job that I could do. Everyone except for Mrs. Bjorkvist.''

''That doesn't surprise me none,'' Coots said as he continued sharpening a knife on a whetting wheel that was no longer round and had to be "chased" to keep the blade in contact. ''That woman wouldn't give you the time of day. She might *sell* you the time of day at so much the minute, but give it? Not hardly.''

''She said you used to be a gunman in river towns.''

''Did she, now?''

''Yes, and she said you used to shoot people and break up lynching parties and all.''

''Well now, how about that? Sounds like I was a real heller.''

''Why don't you get our young guest here a cup of coffee, Mr. Heller?'' B. J. said.

''Your legs broke?'' Coots wondered, continuing his work.

B. J. sighed deeply, pushed himself up from his chair with a grunt, and went off to the kitchen.

Coots tested the edge of the knife with his thumb and, satisfied that it was sharp, stopped the wheel and turned off its water drip. ''Yes, you'd play hell getting any work from that tight-fisted Bjorkvist woman. She squeezes every nickel so hard the buffalo shits itself.''

''Mr. Coots?''

''Hm?''

''How'd you come to be a gunfighter?''

''How does any fool start doing stupid things? After the war I was like lots of men: nowhere to go, nothing to do, didn't know anything but fighting. I was young, and I had a lot of anger in me.''

''You fought in the Civil War?''

''That's right. I signed up with an Arkansas regiment.''

''You fought for the *South*?''

''Most of the Five Tribes were with the Confederacy. After all, most of us owned slaves, too. The South promised us tribal rights and better land after the war was over. And you know how Indians are about white promises. They just keep swallowing the bait and swallowing the bait and *swallowing* the bait.''

''I didn't know Indians had slaves.''

''Could be there's lots of things you don't know.''

''And were you one of them? A slave, I mean?''

''No. I was never a slave. Indians don't make good slaves. Either they rise up and kill their master, or they just pine away and die.''

''But you're...''

''Black? Yes. There were two kinds of Negroes with the Cherokee. There were field slaves that the Indians bought and used just like white people did. Then there were blacks who'd run away to live with the Indians... mostly because they'd done something to a white man, and they knew what'd happen if they got caught. Now, my father—Hey, why the hell am I talking about all this when there's work wants being done!''

''Oh, go on, Mr. Coots. Your father was a runaway, was he?''

''That's right. Most Indians will accept you if you're

willing to live their way. They don't think about race the
same way as whites do. Or blacks either, for that matter.
My mother was a breed. So I'm three-quarters Black . . .
and at the same time all Cherokee.''

''What is war really like, Mr. Coots? Must of been a
real adventure.''

''War? Mostly war's boring. You're always cold and
wet. And you're tired. And itchy with bugs. Then all of
a sudden everyone's shooting and shouting and running
around, and you're so goddamned scared you can't swallow. Then it's all over, and some of you are dead or
wounded, and the rest are back to scratching and being
bored. That's war.''

''And after all that, your side lost.''

''N-not exactly. By the end I was fighting for the
North. After the way Choctaw and Chickasaw troops got
blooded at Pea Ridge and Wilson's Creek, Chief John
Ross decided we were goddamned fools to fight for the
Carolinians and Georgians who had driven us off our
land, so he led the Upper Creeks and a bunch of us Cherokee mixed-bloods to join the North, and next thing I
knew, I was wearing the blue of the 2nd Cherokee Rifles.''

''You fought on *both* sides? And to think I didn't
know that Indians had fought in the war at all!''

''The Five Tribes suffered greater losses in the war
than any American state, North *or* South.''

''Gee, they never told us about that in school.''

''There's lots of stuff they don't tell you in school
about Indians, boy. And about whites, too.''

''I guess so.'' Matthew digested all this. Then: ''Can
I ask you something else?''

''No, you can't!''

''All right.''

''My mouth's worn out with talking!''

''I understand. . . . but if I *could* ask something else,
Mr. Coots, I'd ask how come you and Mr. Stone haven't

given me any work. I mean, I understand why Mrs. Bjorkvist hasn't. She's bone stingy, but *you* two... But I guess it's not up to you to decide. You'd have to ask Mr. Stone before giving out work, and he'd probably—''

"I wouldn't *ask* B. J. nothing. I'd just tell him."

"Tell me what?" B. J. asked, returning with the coffee pot and Matthew's cup from earlier that morning. He flipped it empty.

"We're going to give the boy some jobs of work to do."

"We are?"

"Yes. A few hours here and there. And we're going to pay him fifteen cents an hour. He's not afraid of hard work. Unlike *some* people I could mention."

B. J. Stone passed Matthew his cup. "Well, I guess you're part of my staff. Though God knows why a healthy, bright young man would want to stay in this godforsaken excuse for a town."

"Thank you, sir." Matthew accepted the scalding coffee and drew in a long, air-filled sip. It was even stronger than before, but he didn't make a face. "I don't know why you bad-mouth Twenty-Mile so much, Mr. Stone. It seems to me a nice town full of helpful people."

"You're mistaken, boy! Twenty-Mile is moribund! And its citizens are the lees and dregs of this world: the lost, the lonely, the losers, the lazy, the luckless, the low-minded. And that's only the *L*'s for Christ's sake!"

Matthew's mouth had slowly opened in awe at this flow of words. He looked over at Coots, who shrugged and said, "He used to be a schoolteacher. Some trades leave their marks on a man, like those little burn-scars on the arms of a blacksmith, or the black spit of a coal miner. School-teaching leaves a man with incurable mouth-flap."

"I'd give anything to be able to talk as smooth and

slick as that, Mr. Stone. You use words almost as good as Mr. Anthony Bradford Chumms.''

''Who? Oh, that British hack you're so fond of. The one who—how did it go? '...lends a cultured richness of expression to exciting tales of the American West'?''

Stung by this mocking of the man who created the Ringo Kid, Matthew said, ''No matter what you say, Mr. Stone, I don't agree that everybody in Twenty-Mile is losers and lonely and low-minded, and all that. Take Mr. Kane, for instance. Him and his daughter seem to be good people.''

''It isn't a question of good or bad. It's a question of being whole or crippled. Once Twenty-Mile started dying, only the lame and the confused stayed behind. Everyone got out who still had a modicum of health, or hope, or heart—''

''And that's just the *H*'s,'' Coots said with annoyance. He was used to B. J.'s misanthropic outpourings, but he didn't think he should parade his unattractive bile before a stranger.

''But you're right about the Kanes, Matthew,'' B. J. Stone continued, the bit well between his teeth. ''Kane's not a bad man, just weak. He's let bitterness and self-pity gnaw at him until it's eaten half way through his heart. And his daughter...? Well, I feel sorry for her, growing up in Twenty-Mile. But she's got spunk and she'll find a way to get out one of these days, I'm sure of it. As for the rest of us...'' He flipped his hand, as though to clear the air of such rubbish. ''You've met the Bjorkvists. Now *there's* a fine upstanding family for you! A grasping woman who wrings money out of the miners. And her hulking bully of a husband! Oh and don't forget that simple-minded son with a slop-bucket for a mind. And Kersti, a poor pack animal cruelly short-changed by both Nature, who made her ugly, and Fate, who dumped her in this lost chunk of Nowhere. One might feel sorry for Kersti, if it weren't that she's sure to produce a litter of her own, a litter bearing her parents' lethal blend of cupidity and stupidity.''

''And that's just the 'iditiy's,' '' Coots muttered, looking out to the northwest, where the low angle of the setting sun was picking out textures on the hillsides.

''The Bjorkvists left Sweden with a sect that found the *Loo-tern* church too forgiving and sinner-coddling for their taste, so they set up a religious colony back in some Iowa or another. But they threw the Bjorkvists out. Imagine being rejected from a fundamentalist sect! How low on the intellectual ladder can you get?''

''What did they get thrown out for?''

''Who knows? The mind boggles! The imagination staggers! The stomach turns! The skin crawls! And as for *Professor* Murphy, our tonsorial entrepreneur! He arrived in town trailing rumors behind him like the stench of his potent bay rum.''

''What sort of rumors?''

''The vilest you can imagine, boy. The only reason he stays here is because there are people in the lowlands who would shoot him and leave him to rot in the gutter if they ever came across him.''

''Lordy!''

''And as for the denizens of the Traveller's Welcome? Well, you've met Jeff Calder, the only obvious cripple among us. And Delanny, our theatrical whoremaster? Coughing up his lungs bit by bit, but still playing the role of the mysterious, tragic figure to the hilt. Any man with real dignity would put a quick end to a life that's no longer worth living. But he clings to every second, hoping the dry mountain air will prolong his life. But it doesn't! It only prolongs his dying! I'll give him this much, though: he isn't a pimp. He contents himself with the profit from the liquor, and he makes his girls salt away most of their wages of sin in the bank down in Destiny. And speaking of the girls, have you seen them?''

"No, sir, not yet. But I suppose I'll meet them tomorrow morning, when I help make breakfast."

"Well, you've got a treat in store. There's a toothsome trio of hetairai for you! Frenchy, the black one, has a bumpy scar running from the corner of her eye to the corner of her mouth. It was done by a broken bottle, and it's a real heart-stopper, partly because black skin scars worse than white, and partly because of the surprise you get when she turns her head. From one side, she looks just fine, but then she turns her head and—look out! Grab ahold of something! Then there's Chinky, the little Chinese. Delanny bought her from a couple of Chinese prospectors who'd been sharing her but needed a grubstake. Delanny offered to let her go, but she's backward and timid and can't speak more than a dozen words of English, so where could she go? How could she keep herself? And Queeny? Well, poor old Queeny'll never see the sunny side of fifty again. Maybe not of sixty. Half of her sags and the rest jiggles. The red dye she pours into her hair never quite hides the white roots. And the whiskey she pours into her gut never quite hides the fact that she looks like someone's grandmother who got into the elderberry wine and went wild with her makeup box. So the girls stay on in Twenty-Mile because there's nowhere else they could find work. You have to feel sorry for them. And they're not the worst of our citizens! Not by a long chalk! The sorriest sack of garbage in this town is 'Reverend' Leroy Hibbard! Now *there's* a reason to wish Noah's boat had gone down with all hands! He's the most contemptible—"

"Well, then!" Coots said, standing up and dusting his palms against the seat of his trousers. "I guess that'll do us for today! You must be feeling better, now that you got all that shit out of your system." He turned to Matthew. "These fits of cussedness come over him ever now and again. Christ only knows why I put up with him, and He ain't telling."

Matthew sensed that the best way to play it was to imitate Coots's joshing tone. "So everyone in Twenty-Mile is low and vile and contemptible, is that it, Mr. Stone?" He grinned and glanced at Coots for approval.

"That is exactly it."

"What about you and Mr. Coots? Are you low and contemptible too?"

"Most people in town think we're the lowest of the low and the vilest of the vile. And in Coots's case, there's some foundation for that opinion. You've tasted his coffee? There's nothing lower and viler than that, and you can *experto crede*, as Virgil said."

"And you, Mr. Stone?" Matthew said, grinning ever more broadly. "Are you low and vile too?"

"Certainly not! I'm telling the tales, and the gossip always comes off cleaner and nobler than his victims. Well, I can't sit around all evening flaying my fellow creatures for your amusement. It's supper time, and I better get something burning in a pan or Coots'll get nasty and evil and vile and low and all the rest of it." He started toward the kitchen, then stopped. "You hungry, boy?"

"I'm just about always hungry, sir. But I'll be eating with the Kanes. . . . At least, I think I will."

"Suit yourself." And he left.

Coots had sat down again and was watching the far horizon, his mind seemingly adrift. "Sorry about that," he said, half to himself. "Ever now and again he gets these fits of cussedness, and he starts bad-mouthing everybody and his uncle."

"Oh, I know the people in Twenty-Mile aren't as bad as he made them out to be. He was just funnin' and exaggerating."

Coots blinked away whatever it was he had been turning over in his mind and settled his eyes on Matthew with a slightly irritated frown. "No, he wasn't funnin'."

He pushed himself up. "And he wasn't exaggerating neither."

THE SUN HAD SETTLED onto the westward hills, red and molten on the bottom; and evening was spreading in from the northeast, where long slabs of cloud turned pink, then briefly mauve, before dulling into gray.

Within the Mercantile, Mr. Kane looked up from his account ledger, set his pen down, and reached his two forefingers in under his glasses to rub the red dents on the sides of his nose. "Is he still there?" he asked in a weary voice.

Ruth Lillian leaned back from the counter to look out the window, though she knew perfectly well he was still there, for she had glanced sideways from the pages of the Singer pattern book half a dozen times and seen, tangled in her eyelashes, the profile of Matthew sitting on the wooden steps, his pack beside him and the heavy old shotgun across his knees. He was looking out past the rim of Twenty-Mile's bowl toward the last sunset glow behind the foothills. In fact, he wasn't so much looking at the dimming foothills as letting his eyes rest on them while his mind wandered elsewhere. Sensing at the nape of his neck that someone was watching him, he smiled up at Ruth Lillian, then he settled back against his pack, patient and immovable.

Ruth Lillian turned back into the darkening store. "He's still there, Pa. Just sitting and waiting. Why don't you light your lamp?"

He grunted negatively.

"You're going to hurt your eyes, doing those accounts in the dark."

"I don't need to be told when I can see and when I can't!" But it wasn't her solicitude that irritated him. "That boy's been sitting out there for an hour!"

"Nearer to two."

"Well, he is not going to push me into anything, not if he sits there all night long."

"I don't think he's trying to push you into anything, Pa. He said he was going to give us time to talk things over, and that's just what he's doing. Waiting for your decision."

"My decision is we don't need him. I'm not going to waste half the day thinking up make-work chores for some drifter, then waste the rest of it keeping an eye on him to make sure he does things right—things that don't really need doing in the first place!"

"Then call him in and tell him. It's not right, just letting him sit out there in the dark."

"Oh, so now it's my fault he hung around all day, instead of making his way back down to Destiny? I suppose you think I should feed him. And maybe put him up for the night as well?"

"Nobody said anything about feeding him or putting him up. But you might have the common decency not to leave him sitting there, hoping against hope that he might get some work from us."

"Why doesn't he go over to the Bjorkvists'?"

"Because he doesn't have any money, Pa! And you *know* Mrs. Bjorkvist ain't going to put him up for free."

"And all this is my fault, too, I suppose?"

"No one said it's your fault."

"You're trying to make it *sound* like it's my fault."

"I ain't trying to make it sound...! All right then! *I'll* tell him we don't need him." She crossed to the door and snatched it open, setting the spring bell to jangling wildly. "Matthew? Will you come in here for a minute?"

Leaving his pack and gun behind, the boy entered the store, his bearing at once humble and eager. "Evening, Ruth Lillian," he greeted, taking off his hat. "Evening, Mr. Kane. I been watching the sun set. Lordy, it sure is beautiful up here! And to think you have this show every evening.''

''Oh, we get more'n our share of rain and storms, don't worry,'' Ruth Lillian said. ''Sometimes the first snow comes as soon-as October. And when blizzards choke up the railroad track, we're cut off for a couple of weeks at a time. And sometimes we get a rip-snorter. That's *really* something.''

''A rip-snorter?''

''That's what people around here call the storms that come raging down almost every fall and do their best to scrape us off this mountain.''

''Nobody calls them rip-snorters but you,'' Mr. Kane said grumpily.

''They're something, those rip-snorters,'' she told Matthew. ''First the air starts humming with electricity, then in she comes! With wind ripping from every direction at once, and rain slashing down, and thunder crashing and shaking the mountain, and lightning cracking and smelling like the air was frying! I love it!''

''I know I'll love it too. I really like this place, what with the sunsets and the nice people. Except for the Bjorkvists, everybody's pitched in to help me out.''

Ruth Lillian cast a glance at her father, who cleared his throat and said, ''Look here, boy. I've thought it over, but I'm afraid I can't use any help.''

''None at all, sir?''

''No, none at all.''

''...I see...''

Matthew allowed the silence to lie there until Mr. Kane felt impelled to say, ''As I was telling Ruth Lillian, all right, maybe there *are* a few things that need fixing and sorting out. But I simply don't have the time to work out what needs doing, and when, and how. So that's that.'' As though to punctuate his decision, he scratched a lucifer to light his lamp, but the match head broke off and flew hissing onto the pile of receipts he was copying into his account book. He jumped up and slapped it out with his hand, giving himself a painful little blister. "I can't *afford* any help! That's all there is to it!"

"I understand, sir." Matthew nodded gravely, his brow knit, as though hefting Mr. Kane's problem in his mind. Then: "What would you say to me looking things over and deciding for myself what jobs need being done? That way you wouldn't have to waste time working up a list or anything, and you could just come look at the work when it's finished and tell me if it's good enough. And as for pay...? Well, I'll just do the job, and you pay me whatever you think it's worth. And if you don't have the money to hand, well, you can pay me when you do. Now, I honestly can't think how I can offer any fairer than that, sir, but if you've got some other way we could work things out, it'd be just fine with me." He waited respectfully to hear what this other way might be.

Ruth Lillian donned her most concerned expression and waited too, watching her father with a glint of amusement in her eyes.

Mr. Kane touched his blistered finger with the tip of his tongue and blew the wet spot cool. Then he drew a long sigh.

He later realized, with some irritation, he never *did* hire Matthew. Not in so many words, anyway. He just growled and returned to his accounts. Ruth Lillian scratched a lucifer and lit his lamp for him, and Matthew asked her if they had any drippings up in the kitchen, because there was nothing better for a burn than drippings.

Although, of course, butter would do, too.

In a pinch.

———————————

AFTER SHARING THE KANES' supper, Matthew insisted on helping Ruth Lillian wash the dishes. He turned from the draining board to explain to Mr. Kane that he always used to do the dishes for his ma when she was tired or when she'd been ... well, she wasn't feeling well.

Later, as they sat around the table, coffee mugs between their hands and the kerosene lamp in the middle, flat-lighting their faces and throwing their shadows against the walls behind them, Matthew asked Mr. Kane intelligent, insightful questions about the running of a general store. The thoughtful tone of his questions and the rapt expression with which he absorbed the responses drew the best out of Mr. Kane who, before bitterness had soured him, used to like nothing better than talking late into the night with cronies. Occasionally, Matthew glanced across at Ruth Lillian, who was only half listening to her father's rambling, excessively detailed explanations. Her eyelashes were lowered, and she was adrift in some daydream. The lamplight burnished her high-piled cupric hair, and Matthew knew there was no more beautiful girl in the world. This was the sort of girl the Ringo Kid helped when she was in trouble, and he never asked anything in return, because he was only doing what any real man would do in the circumstances.

That night, Matthew slept on the counter down in the shop, beneath a four-tail Hudson Bay blanket Ruth Lillian had taken out of stock. He woke twice during the night, intensely aware of the girl sleeping above him.

LONG BEFORE MR. KANE started making breakfast for himself and his daughter, Matthew had folded up his Hudson Bay blanket and returned it to the shelf, then slipped out to explore the abandoned buildings of the sleeping town before going to the Traveller's Welcome, where he found Jeff Calder stumping around the kitchen. He had started early to make breakfast for the girls and Mr. Delanny to show that he didn't *need* no help! Mat-

thew was careful not to get under his taskmaster's feet,
while at the same time being cheerfully helpful. Rustling
up breakfast shouldn't have been a complicated matter,
for it consisted simply of coffee, bacon, and canned
beans; but the first boiled over, the second burnt, and the
third had to be served tepid because in all the years Jeff
Calder had been battling the smoky Dayton Imperial
stove, he had never got the hang of the goddamned-
useless-sonofabitchin' thing! Matthew knew how to stop
the stove from smoking by adjusting the air intake, because he had often had to cook when his ma wasn't up
to it, but he also knew that it would be a mistake to show
Jeff Calder up, so he just watched the old soldier fuss
and fidget and cuss. Every once in a while Matthew
would mutter things like "So *that's* where you keep the
mugs," or "Yes, sir, I think I got the idea," or "I'll
remember that, so's I'll be able to get everything tomorrow morning."

Following Jeff Calder's curt instructions, Matthew set
up three places for the girls out in the barroom, and one
place at a distant table for Mr. Delanny, who was strict
about maintaining his distance and dignity. He experienced again the clogging thickness that the stench of
whiskey always brought to the back of his throat, but this
was soon supplanted by the smell of charred bacon,
which drew the girls down early, and Matthew hurried
to carry their breakfasts in, saying a bright good-morning
to each in turn as he set down her plate of beans and
bacon. They hadn't bothered to do more than put on
wraps and flick a little water into their puffy, wear-
stained eyes.

"Well, look what the cat drug in," Queeny snorted
with a husky laugh that caught in her throat and made
her cough wetly over her first cigar of the day.

"I'm the new help," Matthew said, snatching his eyes
from Queeny's half-revealed breasts so quickly that he
inadvertently settled them on Frenchy's—oops—then

away quickly to her face, but he didn't want her to think he was staring at the rumpled scar that tugged her right eye toward the corner of her mouth, so he lowered his eyes to her breasts again—oops—then glanced quickly over at Chinky, whose breasts (thank God) were small and didn't bulge out of her loose wrap. Having followed this maladroit display with her slippery yellow eyes, Frenchy sniffed and shook her head dismissively.

"Well?" Queeny demanded. "You going to bring us our coffee, or are you just going to stare at our udders?"

Matthew swallowed but maintained his aplomb. "Coffee coming right up, ma'am." He stopped at the door and turned back with a boyish grin. "But such fine udders are a terrible distraction to a poor country boy."

Queeny hooted with laughter, Frenchy smiled, and Chinky wondered what they were talking about.

Having come down to the barroom during this exchange, Mr. Delanny shook his head and smiled thinly. A natural con, that boy.

After he finished washing the dishes and sweeping the kitchen, Matthew found Jeff Calder fiddling around behind the bar and Mr. Delanny setting out a hand of solitaire. "Well, I guess that's about all, Mr. Calder. Thanks for showing me the ropes. I think I'll be able to manage breakfast by myself tomorrow."

"I ain't sure I want you managing any—"

"Oh, excuse me, sir, there's something I want to ask before I forget. Tomorrow, should I set your place with Mr. Delanny, or at a table of your own?"

"What? Ah, well...ah...well, I suppose a table of my own will do good enough." He hadn't anticipated being served breakfast from now on. Well, now!

"Good luck in your game, Mr. Delanny," Matthew said brightly as he left.

The gambler nodded without looking up from his layout. "You too, boy."

BY THE TIME HE had scrubbed the bath barrels until
the wood was furry, it was past noon, and Matthew was
damp with soapy water and sweat. After washing up and
putting his shirt back on, he went into the barbershop to
tell Professor Murphy, who was dozing in a shaft of sunlight, that he'd be back to sweep out later that afternoon.
''Meantime, sir, would you mind taking a gander at the
tubs—when you find the time, that is? Tell me if they're
done to your liking.''

When he came down to reopen the Mercantile after
dinner, Mr. Kane found Matthew sitting on the porch.

''Afternoon, sir.''

Mr. Kane produced a hybrid between a hum and a
grunt.

''Tell me, sir. Does Mr. Delanny have a slate with
you?''

''He does. He settles up monthly.''

''That's good, 'cause I want to put some flour on his
account. And some baking powder. Oh, and do you keep
honey?''

''No.''

''How about molasses?''

''I have corn syrup.''

''And butter?''

''No one uses butter up here in the summer. Everything comes up from Destiny, and butter would melt on
the way.''

''Oh, I see. Well then, I'll just have the flour and the
baking powder and the corn syrup.''

Mr. Kane was up a ladder fetching down a quart tin
of corn syrup when Ruth Lillian came down from their
kitchen. ''I thought I heard voices and—Pa, you know
you shouldn't climb ladders! How things going, Matthew?''

"Just fine, thank you, Ruth Lillian."

"You sleep good last night?"

"Never better. But you know something funny? I think you and Mr. Kane showed up in my dreams."

"You *think?* You ain't sure?"

"Not rightly. When I first woke up, the dream was clear as clear, but as soon as I tried to think about it, it started to crumble away, and the harder I tried to remember, the faster it crumbled. Do dreams ever do you that way? But I remember that in my dream Mr. Kane was kind and friendly, telling me interesting things about how to run a store and all. And you were sweet and smiling, and you had your hair up, like it is now." He chuckled. "Funny how the good dreams slip away before you can get a grip on them, while bad dreams . . . hoo-birds! Once they sink their fangs into you, they *never* let go. Oh, Mr. Kane? Speaking about dreams and sleeping and all, you know those deserted buildings between here and the railroad? Do they belong to somebody? Or could a body just move into one of them?"

"I don't see why not," Ruth Lillian said. "That's what Reverend Hibbard did when he came to town. He took over the abandoned railroad depot."

"Reverend? I haven't met anyone that looked like a— Oh yes! I remember B. J. Stone saying something about a Reverend Somebody-or-other."

"No, you wouldn't have met him. Sundays he sleeps over up at the Lode. He won't get back until this evening."

Mr. Kane put the tin of corn syrup, the sack of flour, and the box of Calumet baking powder on the counter. "The only place fit to live in is the old marshal's office. The roof is still good, and the miners haven't shot out the windows."

"Which one's the marshal's office?"

"This side of the street, down from the big burned-down building across from the hotel."

"Well, I'll be darned! That's the very one I sort of picked out for myself when I was out early this morning. It's got an old stove that looks like it might still work. And I saw some sticks of furniture left in some of the other places. Do they belong to anybody?"

"I guess they belong to you, if you want them," Ruth Lillian said.

"It's going to be fun, making a little nest for myself."

That thought had occurred to Ruth Lillian at the same instant. Like playing house.

"You know what I'm going to do? Soon as I get my place fixed up, I'm going to ask you two over to dinner to repay your kindness."

"We'd be honored to come," the girl said with a firmness that dared her father to say otherwise. "People in Twenty-Mile never do anything social like having people over to their houses. They're all so ... *small*. I think it's a good thing to invite people to dinner."

"No, I couldn't, Ruth Lillian. Thanks, but I really couldn't. The only way I could take my meals with you folks would be if you let me pay board money. 'Course, I suppose you could take my meals out of what you pay me for the jobs I do around the place. That way you'd be saving money, and I'd be having the pleasure of your company. But it'd only be two meals a day. Noon and evening. 'Cause I'll be having breakfasts over to the hotel, after I feed those folks."

Mr. Kane had been blinking, trying to catch up. Now he cleared his throat sharply. "We're not in the boardinghouse business."

"Of course you're not, sir. What was I thinking about? There's nothing in the world more natural than a father and daughter wanting to be alone at mealtimes, so's they can talk and such."

"Shoot!" Ruth Lillian said. "We eat a whole meal without saying more than 'pass the salt.' "

"But last night we talked and *talked* and talked."

"You mean Pa talked and talked and talked."

"All I know is that it was real interesting and I learned a lot. Well look, I really got to get to getting." Matthew collected his purchases and went to the door. "I'll ask Mr. Murphy to pay me for my day's work so's I can drop by this evening and buy vittles for my supper."

———————

"THAT WAS FINE, SIR. *Mighty* fine." Matthew pushed his chair back from the table and pressed his hand to his stomach with mock tenderness, as if too much pressure would make it burst. "You could of knocked me over with a feather when you said you'd decided to take me on as a boarder. Even if it is for just a few days. To see how things work out."

"It was more Ruth Lillian's doing than mine," Mr. Kane said pointedly.

"Well then, let me thank you, too, Ruth Lillian. How come you're so good a cook, Mr. Kane?"

Mr. Kane waved the compliment away. "I'm not a good cook. I only know how to make four or five things, and we have them one after the other. Nothing fancy."

"Well, it's fancy enough for this ol' boy, believe you me! Don't you ever give a hand with the cooking, Ruth Lillian?"

"Only when Pa's sick. And he always tries to get well quick, so he won't have to eat my cooking any longer than he has to."

"I don't believe one word of that," Matthew said.

"Ah, but it's true," Mr. Kane affirmed. "My daughter has never shown any interest in the domestic virtues, other than making herself dresses from pictures in catalogues. She doesn't like to clean up either. But she'd rather clean up than cook, so I do the cooking, and she does the cleaning up."

This might have been the time to ask about Mrs. Kane,

but something warned Matthew to avoid that subject. Instead, he said that it must take *buckets* of know-how to make a dress from a picture in a catalogue, and Ruth Lillian said it wasn't all that hard, once you got the hang of it, and Matthew said shoot, *nothing* was hard once you got the hang of it, the hard part was getting the hang of it; then he turned to Mr. Kane and asked how he got started in business, but Mr. Kane shook his head, saying it wasn't all that interesting, but Matthew just sat, smiling, his expression open and eager, until Mr. Kane shrugged and said reluctantly that he had been born in Germany—in the old ghetto section of a city—but the only memories he had of it were smells of rich cooking—oh, and a curiously carved wooden clock that looked like a bird with a multicolored tail that swung back and forth to the rhythm of its ticking. He was five years old the very day their ship arrived at New York Harbor, and he grew up playing on the floor of the two-room basement apartment where his father and mother toiled from early morning until late into the night, doing ''out work'' on garments they delivered to the great, barn-like sweatshops of the Lower East Side. His father's most treasured possession was the pair of fine tailor's scissors he had brought from Westphalia—none of this cheap-jack American stuff. You want to do good work? Use good tools. The only time his father ever hit him was when he caught him cutting paper with the precious scissors, and that was only a cuff on the side of his head. His mother never completely got over feeling homesick. She often wondered if they had done the right thing in leaving the safety and comfort of Germany for a chance at success in the New World. She sometimes sighed and envied those who had stayed behind. But, after years of hard work and careful scrimping, they managed to save enough to launch themselves into the business of supplying buttons, thread, and imitation lace to garment-making enterprises owned by immigrants who had arrived a few years before the Kanes.

"That's the way it was. When you arrived, you were exploited by those who had come before you. Then, if you were clever and hard-working—and lucky! Don't forget lucky—you could become exploiters in your turn. That was the Great American Promise!" Mr. Kane poured himself another mug of coffee.

. . . *the Great American Promise*, Matthew repeated to himself, savoring the words.

"I remember the day my father put the sign in our window. Fancy lettering in red, white, and blue. *The American High-Class Finishing Materials Company (Reliable Service at Competitive Prices)*. He was very proud of that sign, my father. Well, after all, he had paid two dollars for it. In cash!" He chuckled to himself and for a time looked into the lamp flame in silence. "But then . . ." he continued in the soft voice of a man fingering old memories, ". . . then, just when my parents could see a little daylight at the end of the tunnel, cholera swept through our neighborhood and my father . . ." He shrugged. "He died early one sunny morning—it's not right, somehow, to die on a sunny morning. People ought to die at night. Like my mother did, the very next night. And the morning after she died, while neighbors were dealing with the bodies, I . . ." He looked into his mug, and his jaw muscles worked with the effort of reliving painful things. ". . . I went out and delivered their last order. Four boxes of buttons—imitation shell, four-hole, recessed. Funny that I remember those details after all these years. The order had been promised for that morning, you see, and my father prided himself on being reliable. 'Reliable service at competitive prices.' That was us."

Ruth Lillian, who had been staring into the lamp, looked up and searched her father's face, trying to see past the dark spot that the lamp flame had printed on her vision. He had never before mentioned delivering the four boxes of buttons while his parents were lying at home, dead.

"Well!" Mr. Kane said gruffly, passing over the painful memories. "When that autumn came, I was traveling with an old Yankee drummer who made the rounds of farms, selling needles, thimbles, pots and pans, ribbons, rush brooms, almanacs, pain remedies—whatever. He sold goods out of the back of his wagon. But mostly he sold himself: his gossip, his cheerfulness, his stories. These stories came in two flavors. Sweet for the women, salty for the men. People would buy things they didn't really need, just to have his company. 'There's thousands of drummers out there,' he told me. 'And they're all trying to figure out how to sell more. But it isn't *how* you sell, it's *what* you sell. If you try to sell a woman thread, you only make your sale if she happens to need thread at that moment. But if you sell her the dream of a fine new dress... ah! Or better yet, the image of her daughter wearing that dress at her wedding... a-ah! She'll buy your thread because it's all tangled in dreams of new dresses and weddings.' He told me how he started off by running a sausage stall at county fairs back in Vermont, but he didn't do very well until he learned that you don't sell the sausage, you sell the sizzle! 'You got to be a dream merchant,' he told me."

A dream merchant. Matthew liked that. *The Ringo Kid: Dream Merchant.*

"The old peddler died of pneumonia after a downpour caught us on the road. And me? Well, I was about your age, young man. So naturally I went west to make my fortune. My fortune! Look around you."

"Well, you have the treasure of Ruth Lillian."

"True, true. Such a docile, obedient child! And what a cook!"

Ruth Lillian made a face across the table to Matthew, who smiled.

"Yes, I decided to go west and make my fortune in the gold rushes and silver bonanzas, but not by prospecting. The old Yankee peddler had once described how oceans of men were flowing towards the West, picks and shovels over their shoulders, and dreams of gold and silver in their heads. 'Out west! There's where a man can make his packet, boy,' he told me. 'Prospecting for gold?' I asked. 'Hell, no! Selling picks and shovels!' And he went on to explain that for every prospector who struck it rich, a hundred thousand ended up with nothing but blisters, chilblains, and a handful of stories to bore their grandchildren with. But every single one of them needed a pick and a shovel, and trousers, and beans, and tobacco. 'Yes,' he said, 'if I were younger, I'd be heading west myself.' 'With your wagon loaded up with picks and shovels,' I said. He was silent for a time, then he said, 'No. No, I'd probably be prospecting for gold along with all the others. Like everyone else, I'd be fool enough to imagine that I'd be that one in a hundred thousand to strike it rich. No, I'm afraid I'd be out there chasing the dream, because it really ain't the sausage that matters in this life. It's the sizzle.' "

Matthew's eyes narrowed as he nodded slowly to himself. That's what it is, all right. The *sizzle*.

After they finished the dishes, Matthew said goodnight to Mr. Kane, and Ruth Lillian lit a candle to accompany him down into the darkened store, where he picked up the food, soap, lamp, and lamp oil he had bought on credit.

"Just think, tonight I'll sleep in my new home. The marshal's office! Say! That sort of makes me marshal of Twenty-Mile." He pushed out a laugh, to show that he was only joking.

"Twenty-Mile ain't had any call for a marshal for donkey's years, so..." She opened a drawer and felt around for something. "If there's any spooks in the marshal's office, you can just arrest them and—Where *is* the

darned thi—Oh, here it is.'' She drew out a six-pointed
star. Matthew took it and hefted it in his palm. It was
heavier than he would have guessed, and each point of
the ball-tipped star reflected a minute candle flame.

''I don't think it'd do much good to throw spooks in
jail,'' he said. ''They'd just ooze out through the bars.''

''We never had a jail in Twenty-Mile. When a miner
got drunk and nasty, they'd lock him up in our storeroom
until he sobered up.''

''So your pa used to be the marshal, eh?''

''Marshal? Can you imagine my pa with a gun hanging on his hip? No. But he was Twenty-Mile's mayor.
Well—sort of. He wasn't voted in or anything. A bunch
of men just got together at the Pair o' Dice Social Club
and decided that the town needed a mayor, and that old
Kane would do well enough.''

''The Pair o' Dice Social Club?''

''That burned-out building across from the Traveller's
Welcome? That used to be the Pair o' Dice, where Mr.
Delanny worked his table. There wasn't any competition
between the two places, though. The one did gambling
and the other did women. So the miners—and there were
a couple hundred of them back then—they'd stagger out
of one place and across the street into the other and shake
hands as they was passing.''

''Who burned it down?''

''God.''

''...God?''

''It was struck by lightning during the worst rip-
snorter that ever hit us. I won't forget that night if I live
to be ninety-eight in the shade. The lightning came crashing down, four or five bolts, one right after the other!
And the thunder shook the whole mountain! Mrs. Bjorkvist ran around in the rain screaming that the fury of God
was descending on Sodom and Gomorrah! Pa was afraid
the roof was going to be torn off the Mercantile so he
was bundling me up in a blanket (I was just little) when

there was this terrific *crack!* and next thing you know the Pair o' Dice was burning like sixty, and the wind was snatching sparks out of the flames, but they didn't set anything afire because the rain was pouring off roofs in sheets and running down the sides of the buildings. Pa carried me out onto the porch with blankets wrapped around me, and we watched the Pair o' Dice burn down. It was the most wonderful thing I ever saw. And scary! The walls finally caved in, but we couldn't hear a thing, what with the wind screaming and the rain drilling down on the porch roof, and you know how they say lightning never strikes twice in the same place? Well, that's a lie, because while we were watching, there was this *crack!* and lightning struck right in the midst of the flames, and sent sparks and tongues of fire flying in every direction! It was beautiful. Truly beautiful.''

"I can just *see* it from the way you describe it, Ruth Lillian. You describe it as good as in a book.''

"You think?''

"Hoo-birds! It sure sounds like God had it in for the Pair o' Dice, hitting it with lightning twice like that.''

"Guess so.''

"And they didn't bother to rebuild it?''

"No. Mr. Delanny just installed himself across the street. The boom was already beginning to peter out and most of the prospectors had gone west. Pretty soon there was nothing left but the weekly gang of miners from the Surprise Lode. And anyway,'' she frowned heavily, and her voice dropped to an ominous note, "it's not wise to try to rebuild something that God has reached down and destroyed.''

Matthew nodded slowly. "Yeah, I guess you're— Hey, are you funning me?''

"Of course I'm funning! Jeez!''

He was silent for a moment. Then he spoke energetically to cover his embarrassment. "So your pa was the mayor, was he? Well, look at me, everybody! Here I am, talking to the mayor's daughter.''

"Like I said, it wasn't legal or formal or anything. The only mayoring he ever did was to marry folks every once in a while, and he always worried about it because he didn't think he had the authority to marry people. Then when the men at the Pair o' Dice decided the town needed a marshal to keep the Saturday-night mayhem down to size, it was Pa who had to pin the badge on the man they chose. And later on, when . . .'' She stopped and lowered her eyes. "Later on, when this marshal left town, he gave the badge back to Pa. He did it as a sort of slap in the face.''

"Slap in the face?''

She looked at him long and levelly, deciding whether or not to share this with him, and he could see miniature candle flames in each of her eyes, like those on the ball points of the badge. "I guess you better be getting to your new home,'' she said.

"All right. I'll see you tomorrow at dinnertime. Oh, here. You'll be wanting this marshal's star back.''

"No, you keep it.''

"Well . . . thanks! Gee. Well, I guess I better be saying good night, Ruth Lillian.''

"Good night, Matthew.''

BY THE LIGHT OF his new lamp that burned with that nose-tingling new-lamp smell, he began to unpack and arrange things. He had taken almost everything of value from his home—well, there hadn't been all that much, really. He not only had a blanket and his clothes, but also a kettle, a frying pan, a coffee pot, his ma's hand mirror and comb (genuine animal bone), a mixed assortment of mugs and knives and forks, three chipped enamel plates, and a tin wash-up basin and pitcher. These he arranged on a shelf by the stove to make himself a kitchen of sorts.

Think of it! Living in the marshal's office. The Ringo Kid, marshal. Hoo-birds!

From other deserted houses, he had scavenged a bed, a big table and a smaller one, three straight-backed chairs, and a bentwood rocking chair that squeaked like his ma's used to—not the same note, but just about the same place on the back-push. He wasn't sure what he should do with the awkward old shotgun he had carried so far and with such effort. He should get rid of it, really. He'd meant to do that right from the first. Maybe he should bury it. But it was dark out, so he hung it on two square-cut nails over the doorway. And as he was doing this, it occurred to him that the marshal had probably driven those nails in to put his rifle up there, where it would be handy to hand, should there be trouble out on the street. He took from his pack the canvas sack that held twelve handmade, wax-dipped shells for the shotgun along with his other treasures: a small blue glass bottle he had found buried in the back yard of one of their many temporary homes (What used to be in it? Who had owned it? And, most mysterious of all: *Why had they buried it?*), a marble with an American flag suspended in the middle (How did they *do* that?), a rock with gold flakes in it that his pa said was nothing but fool's gold (but which *might* be real gold because, after all, Pa didn't know everything). To these treasures he added the six-pointed marshal's star that Ruth Lillian had given him. A badge for the man living in the marshal's office. He looked around for a safe place to stash his treasures and ended up pushing the canvas sack far back under the bed.

After spreading out his blankets (Whew! He'd have to take the straw-filled mattress he'd scavenged and hang it in the sun to get rid of the mildew smell!), he arranged his collection of books on the small table. All but one of them were well-thumbed, cardboard-bound Ringo Kid books; the other was a broken-backed dictionary a

teacher had given him. He loved looking up words in his
dictionary and saying them over and over to himself until
they were his. That night, he looked up *chameleon*, but
it took him a while to find it because he began looking
under "k," then under "ca." When he was satisfied that
chameleon was forever his, he selected *The Ringo Kid
Deals Himself In*, and settled back into *his* rocking chair
in the middle of *his* house and began reading by the light
of *his* lamp. It had been a long day, and he was dozing
and dipping over the pages when he was jolted awake
by a sound out in the street. Somebody was moaning . . .
moaning and sobbing. His first fright-flash was that it
might be one of the ghosts Ruth Lillian had mentioned,
but the voice cried out in a whiskey-smeared voice that
it was a sinner! A fornicator! A slave to the appetites of
the flesh! Not worthy—No, Lord, not *worthy!*—to be a
vassal of the Risen Christ and a vessel of His Sacred
Word!

Matthew blew out his lamp, took the old shotgun
down, and quietly opened his door. A full moon hung
over the foothills, filling the street with a slanting slate-
blue light. And there, staggering down the street from the
direction of the Traveller's Welcome, was a tall, black-
clad figure wearing a round "parson's" hat. With each
stumbling step, his boots raised a little puff of dust into
the moonlight. A drunk! A stinking, slobbering drunk! If
there was anything Matthew *hated* . . . ! His hands tightened on the shotgun, and he forced himself to take slow,
calming breaths, like his ma used to make him do when
he was in a blind rage. Then he pressed his door closed
and hung the gun back up over it. With a convulsive
shudder he scrubbed his hands against one another to get
the feeling of *gun* off them. Why had he hung the
damned thing up there in the first place? He hated the
sight of it!

Without undressing—without even taking off his
boots—he lay down on his rustling straw mattress and

stared up into the darkness. The smell of mildew blended with the smell of just-blown-out lamp.

From far down the street: *Punish him, Lord! Chastise this foul and fallen sinner!*

And a little later, in a more distant voice: *... but forgive him, Lord! Oh, please, please, forgive him!*

Late into the night, long after the drunken voice had gone silent, Matthew watched the door through a small peek-hole in the blankets he had pulled up over his head.

THE NEXT MORNING, MATTHEW sat on the edge of his bed, his head throbbing, his blood thick, his eyes stiff. All night he had been pursued from one nightmare to another by ... he couldn't remember exactly what. But it had a slimy texture and it ... argh! He didn't want to think about it! He grunted to his feet and poured water into his basin and splashed it up into his face, snorting loudly to drive off the last clinging tendrils of dream.

As he slowly dressed, numb-fingered, he considered his situation in Twenty-Mile. So far, things had gone pretty well. He had wormed his way in; now he had to make himself indispensable. During a childhood spent moving from town to town and school to school, he had developed his own technique for gaining admittance into new "gangs," one based upon his gift for role-playing and his particular thirst for respect. It was a two-step system. Step One: break your way through the gang's tough protective membrane in any way you can: lie, cheat, flatter, fight, amuse ... whatever it takes. Step Two: once inside, you show yourself to be friendly, helpful, willing to play by their rules, and the gang will come to accept you, maybe even respect you. He never actually reaped the fruit of these tactics, because every time he started to settle in, his family moved on again. Mr. Delanny had assumed that Matthew's social ploys were devices for conning the marks; in fact, they were strategies for survival.

After dragging his ma's genuine animal-bone comb through his wet hair, he went forth to show the Twenty-Mile gang just how accommodating and friendly a man could be.

He found Jeff Calder in the hotel kitchen, cursing the Dayton Imperial stove and batting at the thickening smoke with a rag. Matthew's sunny "Mornin', sir!" was ignored as the veteran raged against goddamned-useless-sonofabitchin' stoves in general, and this goddamned-useless-sonofabitch of a stove in particular! And these new-fangled Diamond "book" matches! Either they don't strike at all, or the whole book burns up at once ...and your goddamned fingers with it!

"Say, now!" Matthew said. "That's an idea!" He set the flour, baking powder, and corn syrup he had bought at the Mercantile onto the drain board.

"*What's* an idea?" Calder growled.

"You were going to try opening that thingamabob—that grating at the bottom. And I think you're right, Mr. Calder. That just might do 'er."

Jeff Calder located the air vent and tapped it open with the lid-lifter, and instantly the fire caught with a soft pop, and started burning so vigorously that it sucked back into itself some of the nearby smoke.

"You got it!" Matthew said with unconcealed admiration.

"Yeah, well...one thing the army teaches a man is how to get things done."

"Thanks for giving me a head start with the stove, sir," Matthew said in a busy, bustling tone as he took off his jacket. "I'll take her from here. You said you wanted your breakfast set up at a separate table from Mr. Delanny's, is that right?"

"Ah-h...well...Yeah, that's right."

"You're the boss. Breakfast'll be ready in two shakes. Oh, by the way. Do you like biscuits?"

"Sure."

"Well, biscuits it'll be, sir. Just like my ma used to bake."

"I *THOUGHT* I SMELT biscuits!" Queeny cried when Matthew set the steaming plateful on the girls' table and, with a flourish, snatched off the towel covering them. Beside the dish, he placed a bowl of corn syrup and a spoon. "And you said I was crazy!" This last was directed to Frenchy, who cut open a biscuit, drizzled corn syrup over half, and popped it into her mouth.

"The biscuits was Mr. Calder's idea," Matthew said over his shoulder as he carried a plate of four biscuits to Jeff Calder's table. "He said biscuits might be a good idea, didn't you, sir?"

"Well...there ain't nothing wrong with having biscuits for breakfast!" the old man declared in a tetchy tone that dared anyone to suggest there was.

Mr. Delanny received his plate of two biscuits with a half-cynical, half-admiring shake of his head.

"Mr. Calder told me you usually only take coffee in the morning, sir. But I thought maybe...?"

"You're some piece of work, you are."

Matthew smiled. "That's the way it is with us chameleons. More coffee, sir?"

"To go with my biscuits? Sure, why not?"

Queeny grabbed Matthew's arm as he passed on his way back to the kitchen. "You know what you are, kid? You're a goddamned treasure, that's what. Biscuits! And bacon that ain't burned to a crisp...for once! You'd make some woman an A-number-one wife!" She hooted with laughter that produced a fine spray of biscuit.

"You keep this up, boy," Frenchy said, "and who knows? You might win my heart."

Although she didn't raise her eyes to meet Matthew's, Chinky was making fast work of her biscuits too, a blessed change for a woman with an oriental palate who had been obliged to stuff down bacon and cheese and other disgusting Western flavors and textures.

"It was my ma taught me how to make them. I used to help her around the kitchen when she couldn't manage on her own."

"O-o-o-o." Queeny's downward-plunging note reflected both the moist sentimentality of the drunk and the theatrical emotionalism of a woman who, as she would tell anyone who would listen, had earned more than her fair share of fame as an entertainer on the stage. "Well, you done right to help your ma. A body don't get but one mother in this life, and I don't care what anybody says. She's sickly, is she, your ma?"

"She passed on, ma'am. Just a few days ago."

"O-o-o-o-o."

"Yes, well . . . I keep reminding myself that she's beyond pain and trouble now. And that's a consolation."

"O-O-o-o-o-o. Ain't that the truth? I always say, if there's one thing in this world—Hey! You could leave a *few* of those for someone else, Frenchy! You don't have to cram them *all* down your gullet! Honestly! Some people is just *hogs!*"

———————

THENCEFORTH BISCUITS WERE A part of the morning routine at the Traveller's Welcome, as were a few minutes of bantering chat between Matthew and the girls. Frenchy had a wry, arid sense of humor, and his unconcealed appreciation of it caused her to try harder; Chinky would lift her eyes to exchange a fugitive smile for his facile one; and he always listened attentively to Queeny when she launched into her recollections of the good old days.

"Did I ever tell you about when I was a dancer, kid?"

"Only about two hundred million times," Frenchy muttered as she devoured a biscuit.

"You should of heard the men hoot and whistle when I did my Dance of the Seven Veils!"

"It'd take seven bed sheets to cover you now."

It amused Mr. Delanny to note how Jeff Calder, having reaped all the credit for the improvement in the quality of the breakfast, was willing to admit, albeit with reluctance, that the boy was "a quick learner." But even Mr. Delanny's eyes lost some of their habitual world-weary scorn when he looked up from playing two-handed solitaire with Frenchy and saw Matthew hard at work, humming to himself as he swept the floor or wiped up the tables with cheerful energy.

Matthew sensed that there was something between Mr. Delanny and Frenchy. She would occasionally sit at his table, and without a word he would sweep up the solitaire lay-out before him and deal out two-handed solitaire, which they would play in silence, a sharpness of concentration and a crispness of movement suggesting that each was eager to beat the other. They never spoke to one another, although a particularly unlucky run of cards might cause Frenchy to utter one of her succulently raunchy oaths that made even hardened miners blink and puff. When the game was over, she would leave the table, and Mr. Delanny would shuffle and lay out another game. No one else in the hotel ever dared to sit at Mr. Delanny's table. What was between them wasn't physical. It wasn't even friendship, in the ordinary way. But Matthew noticed that Frenchy always sat a little sideways at the card table, keeping the scarred side of her face away from Mr. Delanny. One night while he was pondering this strange relationship, muttering to himself as he always did when he was thinking things out, he decided that Frenchy and

Mr. Delanny were like strangers passing time together while they waited for a train. "Strangers who are going in the same direction, but not to the same place." He was proud of that wording, and he remembered a teacher—the one who had given him her dictionary—once saying that he had a natural way with words. "Two people going in the same direction, but not to the same place," he repeated aloud. "Now *that* makes a body think. It's . . . deep. You know, maybe one of these days I'll get myself some paper and a pen and write myself a book. Something like Mr. Anthony Bradford Chumms. But I'll make my hero different from the Ringo Kid, so's people won't think I'm copying. My hero will be *left*-handed, and he'll cross-draw. And he won't be from Texas, like the Ringo Kid. He'll be . . . Canada! That'd make him a foreigner and *totally* different. And he'll ride a pinto, rather than Ringo's big gray. And he'll . . ."

Matthew's daily life soon assumed a rhythm. His morning work at the hotel turned out to be his principal source of income, because cleaning out the tubs and doing the barbershop was only a once-a-week chore, and the make-work jobs B. J. Stone and Coots scratched up for him never occupied more than five or six hours a week. Although his work at Kane's—the heavy tasks that Mr. Kane protested grumpily he could perfectly well do himself, but really couldn't because of chest pains—required only a couple of hours a day, the Mercantile became the hub of his life. He regretted that Mr. Kane never again talked about his early years as he had on that first night. Instead, soon after supper, he would say he was tired and would go to his bedroom while Matthew and Ruth Lillian were doing the dishes. Then the young people would sit on the porch for half an hour or so, looking out at the night sky above the foothills, enjoying the evening breezes, sometimes talking quietly, sharing vagrant wisps of thought that drifted into their minds, only rarely glancing at one another.

It was during one of these rambling chats that Matthew learned enough about Reverend Hibbard's weakness of the flesh to arm himself against their first encounter. He was surprised at the matter-of-fact way Ruth Lillian spoke of the hotel as a "whorehouse."

And impressed, too.

———————

THE NEXT MORNING, AFTER he had tugged his mother's comb through his wet hair, winking and flinching each time it stuck in a tangle, Matthew swilled his wash-up water around the basin, bumped his front door open with his hip, and threw the water . . .

. . . right onto the boots of Reverend Leroy Hibbard, who was standing with his fist raised to knock at the door.

"Hey! Watch what you're doing, boy!"

"Oops, sorry! Didn't know you were there."

"That ain't no excuse! I ought to box your ears for you!"

Matthew looked up at the preacher for a moment, then answered in his soft Ringo Kid voice, "Well, sir, maybe it ain't an excuse, but it's an honest explanation. I'm truly sorry I got your shoes wet. But as for getting my ears boxed? That ain't going to happen. It just naturally ain't going to happen. You hear what I'm saying to you?" His experiences of being the new boy in school after school had left him with an instinctive recognition of the bully, and this preacher was a bully. Matthew had learned that backing off from bullies only whets their appetite for abuse. He could feel himself slipping into what he called "the Other Place," his habitual retreat from danger and aggression. While in this Other Place he remained aware of everything going on around him, but events took on a dreamlike vagueness that stripped them of their menace. Matthew felt the profound safety of the Other Place begin to rise within him, as though drawn up through his spiritual wick.

When the Reverend snapped, "What are you doing here, boy?" Matthew's eyes softened even more, and he smiled.

"Well, right now I'm fixing to go to work."

"No, I mean what are you doing in the marshal's office?"

"I live here."

"Oh, so you just moved in and took it over, is that it?"

"Yes, sir. Same as you did down to the depot."

"Say what?"

"You took over an abandoned building. Just like me."

"But I *belong* here."

"So do I. This town's my home now." He smiled. "Well, sir, it's mighty kind of you to come wish me welcome, but I'm afraid I have to be getting to work. So if you'll excuse me?"

But the preacher stood firm, his feet rooted in the puddle of his shadow. His gaunt body was rigid both with an affected dignity and a genuine hangover that was manifest in nicks on his concave cheeks caused by shaving with an unsteady hand. For all the Reverend's stiff aridity, most of his details were liquid: watery eyes laced with angry blood vessels, a wet, drooping lower lip, beads of sweat on his brow, a phlegmy baritone voice decorated with that false tremolo preachers use to lend gravity to the Sacred Word. Even his diction was moist, in part because of the slackness of his mouth, and in part because of the absence of back teeth. Having gained no edge over this young interloper on the issue of residence, he shifted to more familiar ground. "Tell me, boy. Have you been born again into the ways of righteousness?"

"I can't rightly say. But my ma used to read the Bible every night, if that's any help."

"The Devil hisself can quote scripture!"

The smell of stale whiskey caused Matthew's stomach to tighten. "I hope you ain't saying my ma was a devil."

"What I'm saying is that quoting the Bible don't make a sinner into a saint."

"You got *that* right."

The Reverend scowled. Was that a dig at *him?*

"But Bible reading sure didn't do my ma much good. She used to say the meek would inherit the earth. But after a lifetime of being meek, the only earth she inherited was a six-foot hole."

"Don't you *dare* talk against the Book, boy! It's blasphemy! And blasphemers are damned to twist and scream in rivers of fire!"

"That so?" Matthew looked into the Reverend's hooch-whipped eyes with a chill calm that caused them to flicker uncertainly. "What about drunkards, Reverend? Are they going to twist and scream too? And what about Bible-pounders who sneak into whorehouses at night? They do much twisting, do they? I know they do their share of screaming, 'cause I heard one of them the other night, stumbling down the street, bawling and blubbering."

The Reverend's lips compressed. "You're brewing all kinds of trouble for yourself, boy! Who sows the wind shall reap the whirlwind!"

Matthew looked at him long and levelly, then he allowed the Ringo Kid to say on his behalf, "If there's a storm brewin', mister, you can bet I won't be the only one to get wet." With which, the Ringo Kid turned on his heel and walked away, his gait loose and confident, although an uneasy Matthew could feel the Reverend's eyes boring into his back.

As he approached the Traveller's Welcome to start making breakfast, he felt himself emerging from the Other Place. Weight returned to his legs, and objects around him began to lose their smeared halos of light.

He drew in long breaths of cool morning air to dilute the angry acid that was etching into his stomach, like it used to every time he was obliged to face up to bullies at a new school.

He knew he had made an enemy of the Reverend, and he knew that wasn't smart, because experience had taught him that the best way to manage people was to keep them buttered up and off balance with his special blend of joshing and sudden sincerity.

... But that smell of whiskey on his breath!

Tie Siding, Wyoming

THERE WAS A TRICKLE of drool at the corner of the old man's mouth because a recent stroke had left him with a slack lower lip and one drooping eyelid.

The biggest of the intruders, the one with the bullet-shaped head that sprang neckless from his shoulders, and the lips that were permanently drawn into a tight little pucker, sat at the at the old man's table, ripping chunks off the loaf of sourdough bread and dipping them into the honey pot, then wedging them into his mouth. As he chewed, he hummed with infantile pleasure, and this seemed to annoy the second intruder, a diminutive barrel-chested man who kept watch on the street from behind the lace curtains.

The old man searched the pale gray eyes of the third intruder, who sat patiently before him, his fingers toying absently with the slide of his braided leather lanyard. Why had these men pushed their way into his snug little house? Who were they?

"Oh, come on now, Mr. Ballard," the gray-eyed one said. "Think back! I cannot believe you don't remember me, 'cause I remember *you*. Oh, I remember you very well indeed. I even remember those fancy waistcoats you always wore.'' He reached over and felt the silky lapel of the old man's green-and-gold brocade waistcoat between the pads of his fingertips. ''I am sorely pained to see you so crippled up, Mr. Ballard. May I have that, please?'' He took the old man's cane from between his knees. ''For weeks now me and my followers have been hiding in ditches and barns, while men with guns searched everywhere for us. And all that time I dreamed of catching up with you in your schoolhouse, after everyone had gone home. Just you and me, all alone. Like when you used to keep me after school.''

''You were one of my pupils?'' Mr. Ballard asked, his numb lip making the p's puffy.

''There you go! Now let's see if you can come up with my name. Think back. Think back.''

But over the years, Mr. Ballard had taught so many children in his one-room school in Tie Siding, a town that had sprung from the red dirt of the Wyoming/Colorado border to provide the Union Pacific railroad with the pitch-soaked ties it needed in its land-grabbing race against the Central Pacific. It wasn't long before ancient high plateau pine forests were plundered to extinction, and the town rapidly declined from its zenith when it had boasted two general stores, three hotels, a post office, the biggest saloon south of Laramie, and a stone jail, the only stone building in this town of wood. Of all this, there remained only one store whose keeper doubled as postmistress. By the time Mr. Ballard had his stroke, only a dozen students were left at the school, so few that his place could be taken by a recent widow who had once been his pet student, and who now combined her teaching duties with the task of bringing him meals and keeping his clothes clean and tidy. Mr. Ballard frowned and pressed his fingers to his lips in an effort to envision which of the half-forgotten parade of little boys that had passed through his school could have grown into this

man with the dead, ice-gray eyes. His fingertips felt the
drool that his lips were unable to feel, and he wiped it
away with a little shudder of disgust. He had always been
meticulous about his dress and his diction, and the effects
of his stroke on both these carefully cultivated social at-
tainments caused him intense embarrassment. "I'm sorry,
but I'm afraid I don't remember you."

"Oh, now, please try real hard to think, Mr. Ballard,"
the pale-eyed intruder implored. Then he suddenly
smashed the tabletop with the cane. "*Think back, goddamn it!*"

This eruption of violence brought a sudden epiphany
of recognition, and Mr. Ballard's left eye widened in terror.

Lieder grinned. "Ah, now you remember! I can see it
in your eyes. Well...in the one eye, anyway. Yes, it's
that no-account Lieder kid, back like a biblical scourge!
You thought you'd seen the last of me when you had me
dragged off to that home for wayward boys, didn't you?
Didn't you, Mr. Ballard? But you didn't reckon on this
force I read about in a book. Karma. And what Karma
means is this: As you dish it out, so will you get it
crammed down your own throat, sooner or later! And you
sure could dish it out, Mr. Ballard. Oh, Lord how you
could dish it out! For some reason, you set yourself
against me from the first day I came to your school."

"I doubt that I set—"

"*You set yourself against me!* I was a smart kid, and
I had questions to ask. But you set yourself against me.
Do you remember that first day?"

"I've had so many pupils. I can't remember any one
particular—"

"Oh, you're going to remember. Don't you worry
about that, Mr. Ballard. I've risked my neck just to jolt
your memory. I've come back to this one-dog town,
when I knew they might be waiting to drag me back to
prison."

"... I really don't—"

"The first day I came to school, I tried to let you know that I was smart and worthy of your attention and praise. I raised my hand time after time, but you only called on your *pets*. Then when you were telling the class about Indians, I leant over and whispered to a boy about how I'd once seen a Indian with a patent medicine huckster, and I described how he'd done the Rain Dance right there in front of the Price Hotel. You slammed that switch of yours down on your desk and snarled at me to shut up. I tried to explain that I was just telling this boy about Indian dancing—but you said if I knew all that much about dancing, then I'd better come up to the front and dance for everybody. Are you telling me you don't remember *that?*"

"I *don't* remember! I swear to God I don't." There was a whimper in his voice, and the drool flowed freely.

"You don't remember, huh? Well, let me paint the picture for you. I was eight years old. Skinny little barefoot kid in short pants. You told me to dance for the class, but I told you I didn't want to. I was dying of shame, but you got me by the hair and you started hitting the backs of my legs with your willow switch, and I started dancing. Dancing and whooping. And the harder you hit, the higher I danced and the louder I whooped!" Hard tears filled Lieder's eyes, and his jaw muscles rippled. "And you said: 'Well, well, it seems our little Indian can sing as well as dance.' And everyone laughed. And that willow switch of yours came down across my bare legs again and again and *again!* And I danced for you, Mr. Ballard! And I sang for you!"

Both the followers stood, their mouths open with rapt attention. They were entranced by the way their leader could flow words out like that!

"I assure you, young man, that I never meant to—"

"And your pet, that Polish girl with the yellow curls? The one that was always dressed up in pink and white?

She laughed till the tears ran down her cheeks! And there
we were, that girl and me, both of us with tears running
down our cheeks!''

''I don't remember any of that. But if I did what you
say, it was wrong. I admit that. But please don't—''

Lieder brought the cane down across the side of the
teacher's head with such force that it tore the top of his
ear. The old man's eyes rolled up as he slipped toward
unconsciousness from shock, but Lieder grasped his hair
and snatched his head up.

The big bullet-headed man stopped eating and looked
on, grinning, as the honey dripped from his bread and
made a little puddle on the table. The small barrel-chested
man at the window stepped over to where he could see
better.

''And from that day on, Mr. Ballard!'' Lieder thrust
his rage-contorted face to within inches of the old man's
half-paralyzed one. ''From that day on it was war between you and me. You'd beat me every chance you got,
and I used to raise hell in the back of the class, and hurt
kids during recess. I even snuck over to your house one
night and shit in your well. You been drinking my shit
ever since! But our war wasn't a fair contest, Mr. Ballard,
because you were a man and I was only a kid. And you
had the stick. You always had the stick! Then one day
you dragged me up to the front of the class and whipped
me so hard that you broke your stick on my ass. Broke
the goddamn stick! You wanted me to beg for mercy,
but I wouldn't! I wouldn't, 'cause I was all through singing and dancing for you, Mr. Ballard! I clamped my jaw
so tight to keep from crying that I broke this tooth. Look!
You see? *You see?* All the kids laughed. They never did
like me 'cause I was smarter'n they were and I used to
make them play games *my* way. That little pink-and-
white polack pet of yours, she laughed hardest of them
all! And do you wonder if I was humiliated, Mr. Ballard?
I was *humiliated!* Well, guess whose turn it is to be hu-

miliated now, Mr. Ballard. Bobby-My-Boy? Grab this old turd and bend him over the table.''

The bullet-headed giant stuffed his bread into his mouth and dragged the old man to the table and bent him over the edge until his cheek lay in the puddle of honey.

''Snatch his pants down!'' Lieder ordered. ''I'm going to whup his ass! Who knows? Maybe he'll sing and dance for us.''

Grinning, Bobby-My-Boy undid Mr. Ballard's belt and pulled down first his trousers then his flap-seated drawers, and Lieder began methodically to rain blows on the shrunken old buttocks. With each of the first half-dozen clouts, the old man's body convulsed as he whimpered into the honey, then suddenly his muscles sagged, and he lay still and silent, but Lieder's rage fed off his exertion, and the blows came ever swifter and harder until the buttocks were the color and texture of currant jelly. ''Don't die on me! Don't you dare die on me, you son of a bitch!'' he cried through bared teeth. ''Don't you cheat me! I got revenge coming! *I got years of revenge coming!*''

The small barrel-chested man hissed from the window, ''Somebody's coming!''

Panting, sweat running from his hair, Lieder blinked his way back toward reality. ''Wh—? What are you saying?''

''*Somebody's coming!*''

Lieder went to the window and looked out through the lace curtain. There was a woman approaching from the far end of the long dirt lane, carrying a metal lunch pot.

''Looks like she's bringing the old man his dinner,'' the short man said. ''We better slip out the back and push on into Colorado.''

''We ain't going to Colorado. We're heading north, up into the Medicine Bow country. There's gold and silver up there. Precious metals to finance my crusade.''

"But...but if we were going north, why'd we come south in the first place? Don't make no sense!"

"Don't you tell *me* what makes sense and what don't! I came here because I had business to attend to. Now that account is closed and my mind can rest easy. We're heading north. So you two better start looking around this place. Fast! Take anything you can carry: guns, clothes, money, food...anything."

But the small one couldn't believe what he was hearing. "We're heading back toward Laramie and the prison?"

"You heard me. The last place they'd look for us. We'll slip around Laramie and head for the high country. I got two rules. Always do what they don't expect. And always do it real sudden. They'll find out what happened here, and they'll think we slipped down into Colorado. So either they'll chase after us or they'll—Hey, I *know* her!"

"What?"

"That woman! I remember her blond curls and her pink-and-white dresses! Now look at her, will you? All grown up, plump and proper."

"We better get going. She's almost here!"

"N-no. No, I think we'll just sit tight and let her come. Pass me that cane, Bobby-My-Boy."

"You're going to whup her?" The neckless giant asked, his nostrils flaring in anticipation.

"I'm not exactly sure *what* I'm going to do to her." Lieder's eyes became soft and distant. "But one thing's sure. She won't laugh at me this time...not even a little snicker."

Bobby-My-Boy smiled and sighed, contented.

———————

FRIDAY MORNING, AFTER ATTENDING to his chores and exchanging with the hotel girls the half-joshing, half-flirting banter that had become ritual, Matthew had a couple of hours on his hands before dinner with the Kanes, so he drifted up to the only grassy spot in Twenty-Mile, the triangular, up-tilted little meadow crossed by a rivulet running off from the cold spring that provided the town's water. This meadow belonged to the livery stable, and half a dozen of its donkeys lazily nosed the grass while, at the far end, a scrawny cow stood in the shade of the only tree in Twenty-Mile, a stunted skeleton whose leafless, wind-raked branches stretched imploringly to leeward, like bony fingers clawing the clouds. The meadow couldn't be seen from any part of the town except the Livery, so Matthew felt comfortably secluded as he sauntered along, intending to investigate the burial ground that abutted the donkey meadow, but B. J. Stone called to him from the Livery, so he turned back and began the chore they had found for him to do: oiling tools.

While Matthew applied himself to a task he knew was invented to give him some wages, B. J. and Coots continued their ill-tempered game of whist, slapping down the limp, greasy cards with cries of victory for each trick taken or sullen growls at each trick lost.

"I saw you exchanging social niceties with our local sin-merchant yesterday morning, Matthew," B. J. Stone said as he tentatively tugged a card from the tight fan of his hand...then tapped it back into place with his forefinger...then gnawed on his lower lip and hummed an uncertain note...then—

"Are you going to play or not!" Coots snapped.

"Hold your bladder," B. J. advised. "Problem is, I can't quite remember. Whether or not you've played the queen of clubs?"

"That's for me to know and you to find out."

"Hm-m-m." He looked over at Matthew. "What was going on between you and Twenty-Mile's version of Billy Sunday—except that unlike the inexhaustible William Ashley Sunday, our Hibbard never played professional baseball, and God knows he isn't a fulminating proponent of prohibition—or maybe he *is*. No depths of hypocrisy would surprise me.''

''What's a preacher doing in a little place like Twenty-Mile?'' Matthew asked.

''What are any of us doing here?'' B. J. Stone replied.

''Not playing cards, that's for damn sure,'' Coots grumbled.

''I'm thinking! Now, let's see . . . I led with the seven, and you took it. But did you take it with the queen? That's my question.''

''I ain't telling. That's my answer.''

''Hm-m-m.'' B. J. turned to Matthew. ''The Surprise Lode is owned by Boston merchants, descendants of folk who came over on the Mayflower, not in search of religious freedom like the history books tell us, but in search of a place where they could impose their own brand of religious intolerance. You'd think that once the oppressed got the upper hand, they'd banish oppression from society. But no. No, human nature being what it is, as soon as the oppressed manage to snatch a little power, they use it to oppress their erstwhile oppressors . . . or anybody else handy.''

''Who gives a big rat's ass?'' Coots wanted to know. ''Are you going to play cards or not?''

''These pious Bostonians dismiss the maiming and death of workers in inadequately reinforced mine shafts as an unfortunate by-product of the need to maximize profit, but their moral sensibilities insist that their wage slaves be exposed to the word of the Lord God Almighty at least once a week. So the manager of the mine had to find somebody willing to go up there and threaten the poor bastards with eternal damnation every Sunday. And what kind of preacher would live in a place like Twenty-Mile and tend to that reluctant flock up at the Lode? The Reverend Hibbard, that's what kind.''

"Are you going *ever* to play?"

"Patience, patience. *Aequam memento rebus in arduis servare mentem*, as old Horace says."

"I don't care what the old whore's ass says! What *I* say is you should either shit or get off the pot!"

"So you see, Matthew, Reverend Hibbard does what everyone else in Twenty-Mile does. He serves the mine. Even poor old Coots and I work for the mine. They use donkeys in the shafts, and we bring the lame and sick ones down to tend to them and feed them up, and we keep a few backups out in the meadow yonder. You must have seen them, along with the beef."

"The beef?" Matthew asked.

"Every week the train brings a live beef up from Destiny to supply the boardinghouse. Usually a stringy old cow that's gone dry. We let the Bjorkvists keep it in our meadow in return for a few 'steaks.' Sometimes the poor old cow arrives with a broken leg, because no one's taken the trouble to tie it up properly in the train. But, thank God, it only has to suffer for a few days, until Bjorkvist and his dim-witted son butcher it. Not proper butchering, just cutting it up into slabs that mostly get eaten by the miners, but the Bjorkvists sell some to their fellow townsmen. A couple hours of butchering each week is the only contribution the male Bjorkvists make to our economy, but without their 'steaks' we wouldn't attract the miners for the Kanes to sell things to, and for Professor Murphy to bathe and shave and perfume, and for Delanny to provide with whiskey and poontang—which, come to think of it, could be considered another aspect of the meat-selling business. So you see, son. Serving the silver mine is what everyone in Twenty-Mile does!"

"What we *don't* do is play our goddamned cards!"

"Twenty-Mile is a community of has-beens and never-wases. Misfits all. Once in a blue moon, a prospector climbs up out of the ravines and stumbles across that meadow into town, craving some of Delanny's whiskey, or a little relief from one of the girls. But pretty soon he drifts back into the mountains in search of the big strike that'll put him on Easy Street.''

"Crazy old fools!" Coots grumbled.

"Maybe they're not so crazy,'' Matthew said. "Maybe they're just looking for the sizzle."

"Looking for *what?*" B. J. asked.

"...the sizzle?"

The men exchanged dubious glances.

"Ah...what sizzle is that, Matthew?''

Embarrassed, Matthew applied himself energetically to oiling the pincers he was working on.

"Maybe you're right," B. J. conceded. "Maybe the prospectors are no crazier than those of us who've let ourselves get marooned in this butthole of the Western Hemisphere.''

"Why do you stay if you don't like it?" Matthew asked, remembering that he had asked Mr. Delanny the same thing.

"Why *do* we stay, Coots?"

"Beats my two pair. Maybe because we're just too old and worn out to move on.''

B. J. Stone nodded thoughtfully. "Yes, I guess that's it. And at least they leave us alone here. I'm not saying we're welcome. Hell, we're not even accepted. But we are left alone, and that's something."

Matthew didn't understand this, and he was wondering how he might ask why they weren't accepted without seeming too nosy, when Coots suddenly cried out, "All right! All right, goddamnit! I played the queen of clubs! I played it! I played it! Now can we *please* get on with the goddamn game?!''

"Ah! That's all I needed to know," B. J. said. "Because if you played the queen, then my jack, ten, eight are good. And that bleeds out your trump. Which makes my hearts good." He laid down his cards. "Looks like I win again.''

"That's it!" Coots slammed his cards onto the barrel. "I ain't never playing cards with you again! *Never!*"

"I'm sorry you have to witness this peevish behavior," B. J. confided to Matthew. "It's an ugly sight: a grown man being such a bad sport."

Matthew didn't let himself smile. He wasn't going to take sides.

"I take it you and the Reverend had words about your setting up in the marshal's office?" B. J. went on in a calm, conversational voice he knew would irritate the silently fuming Coots. "He wanted to live there himself when he came to town, but Mr. Kane told him it was town property and he couldn't have it."

"How did you know me and the preacher had words?"

"There was tension and anger in the way you were standing, facing one another. From the way you sauntered off, it looked like you won. That may not have been smart, Matthew."

"You're saying I should have let him win?"

"No, no, but you should have let him *think* he'd won. You see, Hibbard's a coward, and cowards are dangerous because they strike from behind. There's an old Spanish proverb—"

"Oh, shit," Coots groaned. "Here we go!"

"—a proverb that says, 'Beware the man who knows but one book.' And that's especially true if that one book is 'sacred.' The man-of-one-book will slit your throat without a moment's hesitation or an ounce of remorse, confident that he's done it in the service of all that's good in this world and rewarded in the next."

"Well?" Coots asked impatiently.

"M-m-m?" B. J. asked, his face spread in innocent inquiry.

"*Are you going to deal or not?*"

The second game had no sooner begun then a pitiful bellowing brought the three of them out to the donkey

meadow, where they were reluctant witnesses to a
botched job of slaughtering the weekly beef. The Bjorkvist man and his son had failed to stun the animal properly with their sledgehammer before hanging it up on a
tree branch by its hind legs to slit its throat. And now
the cow dangled upside down without struggling, nar-
cotized by panic. Oskar Bjorkvist took out his butchering
knife and looked over toward Matthew as he tested the
edge with his thumb. He bared his teeth as he drew the
blade across the cow's throat. The beast died a messy,
gurgling death.

"Bjorkvist!" Coots snapped.

The father shambled over to them, his sledgehammer
in his fist, while his son began cutting up the beef and
putting the joints onto the barrow they had pulled over
with them. "Ya? Vat y'vant?"

"Do that right, or don't do it at all," Coots said.

"No old man tells me how—"

But Coots pointed a forefinger at the middle of
Bjorkvist's chest. "Don't you sass me! Just do like I
say."

Bjorkvist's fist tightened on the neck of his sledgehammer. Coots was unarmed, and his wiry sixty-year-old
body was slight by comparison to the Swede's broad
frame. Bjorkvist looked into Coots's Cherokee eyes and
recalled the stories about this man's past as a gunfighter.
To save face, he sniffed and flipped up a hand dismissively, then he returned to his son, whom he slapped on
the back of the head for being so *goddamned stupid!*
Making a mess of slaughtering the beef, *like dat!* Can't
you do *nottin'?*

Matthew followed Coots and B. J. back to the livery
stable, anger and disgust sour in his stomach.

———

EVERY SATURDAY, TWENTY-MILE PERFORMED the rituals of preparing itself for the arrival of the miners. Jeff Calder and Mr. Delanny would take their breakfast at the usual time, but the girls would sleep late in preparation for a long night's work that would extend well into the next morning. It was eleven o'clock before they descended, puffy-eyed, loose-robed, tangle-haired, and spiky-tempered. While Jeff Calder stumped around behind the bar, making sure everything would be swift to hand when the thirsty horde came crashing in, the girls grimly downed what Frenchy had come to call their "4-Bs," beans, bacon, biscuits, and black coffee, responding to Matthew's buoyant greetings with only grunts or nods or, in the case of Chinky, a quick, fugitive smile.

One Saturday, while he was clearing the tables, Matthew saw Frenchy get a bottle of whiskey from the bar to bring up to her room. She intercepted his glance and explained with a shopworn laugh, "Just something to oil up my tired old ass." He nodded and smiled thinly, and for the first time in weeks he noticed the jagged, pouting scar that drew the corner of her eye down toward the corner of her mouth. But he supposed her clients wouldn't remember her face any more than she'd remember theirs.

The late breakfasts put him so far behind schedule that he had to rush through the dish-washing to get to the Kanes' in time for dinner, which was a heavier meal than usual because, as Ruth Lillian explained, she and her father would only be having cold corned beef and canned tomatoes for supper, and they would eat separately, during lulls in the trade, because one of them had to be in the shop at all times. Matthew would have to fend for himself.

In all the town's bustle of preparation there was nothing for him to do—evidence that he was still an outsider. So he returned to the marshal's office to take a nap because his sleep had been harried by recurring nightmares for several nights running, nightmares in which images wove bizarre yet dreadfully logical patterns, like Reverend Hibbard's red-rimmed eyes laced with angry veins when he reached out for Ruth Lillian, so Matthew pulled the trigger and Pa's old shotgun kicked him hard in the shoulder as it roared like a bony old cow snorting wetly through its frothy blood, but you don't sell the meat, you sell the sizzle, so Coots swore he'd never *ever* play cards with B. J. again, while Oskar Bjorkvist smiled and dragged the knife across the cow's throat, and the skin split open like the slit in a ripe watermelon running ahead of the knife, so of course Pa's old shotgun roared out again, and this time it was answered by the roar of another gun, and another, then three or four firing at the same time—

—Matthew sat up, gasping for air, his heart thudding in his chest! There was gunfire out in the street, the newly arrived miners shooting pistols into the air as they whooped their way from the train down to Bjorkvist's boardinghouse.

He put his head under the blankets and watched his door through a peek-hole, until he fell into a troubled sleep populated by slimy things, and ropy things, and Pa's old shotgun, and cows with slits throats, and . . .

One Saturday evening after the slopes of the distant wooded foothills had begun to tint with autumn, Matthew stood in the doorway of the marshal's office watching the tangled mob of hooting, laughing miners pass by, all bent on quenching the week's fatigue, danger, and boredom with great draughts of fun and hell-raising. He smiled on the invading horde with comradely affection. They were like the cowboys who come ripping into cattle towns in Anthony Bradford Chumms's books: a little wild sometimes, but good-hearted deep down. If a gambler cheated one of them, or if a professional gun tried to tempt a youngster into a face-off just to add another notch to his gun butt, then the Ringo Kid would intervene, speaking to the bully in his soft but strangely ominous voice, all the while smiling—except for his eyes—and the bad'un would back off, saying he wasn't up to anything and what's wrong? Can't anybody take a joke?

On impulse, Matthew stepped out into the human flow and let it carry him up to the Bjorkvists'. There was a contagious energy in the crowd and a diffuse fellow-feeling, even in the shoving and lighthearted tussling in the ragged line that developed at the Bjorkvists' door, everyone eager to get at those ''steaks'' and peaches. But Mrs. Bjorkvist stood at the entrance, allowing each to pass only after he had handed over his silver dollar. When Matthew worked his way up to her, he tipped his hat and said, ''Evenin', ma'am. I thought I might eat with you this evening. 'Course I don't need a bed, nor breakfast tomorrow, so what'll it cost for just supper?'' Mrs. Bjorkvist told him that the price was one dollar for bed and board. And if he didn't want to use his bed or eat his breakfast, that was his concern. Matthew might have tried to argue that this was a little hard on a fellow townsman, but the man behind him was pressing against his back, and several people farther back in the line were complaining about the slowdown, so with a sense of injustice, he paid his dollar and took his place at a table that soon filled up elbow to elbow with loud-voiced miners sawing away at slabs of rare, stringy meat, downing astonishing quantities of boiled cabbage, and quickly emptying each high-piled plate of biscuits that Kersti Bjorkvist dropped off at their table as she rushed to and from the kitchen. Her mother didn't give her a hand until the last of the miners had paid his dollar and she had stepped out and looked down the street to make sure there wasn't another dollar lingering out there. In the belief that table service was beneath menfolk, the Bjorkvist father and son took their dinner in the kitchen, but one or the other would occasionally come to the doorway to look over the crowd, just to make sure everything was going all right.

Matthew made the acquaintance of the miner to his right, a man in his late forties with creased, kindly eyes, when they both reached for the last biscuit, then both pulled back to let the other have it, then both reached again. The man laughed and broke it, giving half to Matthew. "That ought to hold us until the next batch comes along. Say, I don't think I've seen you around. My name's Doc."

"I'm called the Ringo Kid."

"Pleased to meet you, Ringo. You just sign on?"

"No, I'm not with the mine. I live here in Twenty-Mile."

"You don't say."

"Yeah, I'm the ... Well, you'd find me at the marshal's office up the street."

"You don't say! Shoot, I didn't know Twenty-Mile even *had* a marshal."

"Oh, I'm not exactly the marshal. I just sort of ..." He made a vague gesture.

"You just sort of look after things, is that it?"

"There you go."

"Hey, ain't you going to eat your steak?"

"... ah, no. No, I don't think so. You want it?"

"Do people in hell want ice water! Pass her over here! What's wrong with you, Ringo? Feeling bad?"

"No, no. I seem to have lost my taste for meat lately." In fact, ever since he'd seen the cow butchered by the Bjorkvists.

"Lost your taste for meat! Whoa, that sounds serious!"

A harassed Kersti Bjorkvist reached their table with the big two-handed kettle from which she was slopping coffee into the men's tin cups. After filling Matthew's mug, she leaned over him to fill two cups on the other side of the table, pressing her sweat-damp body against his back.

"Hey, how about some biscuits here, girl!" Doc said.

"Just hold your water! I ain't got but two hands and two legs!"

"There's something else you got two of," a wrinkled old miner across the table put in. "And they're mighty fine ones, too!" His pals hooted with laughter, because this fellow was the mine's self-appointed comedian. "Say, why don't you just bring them things over here so I can give them a little squeeze, see if they're up to snuff!"

"That'll be the day!" Kersti said, and with a toss of her thick blond hair she passed on to the next table, where she collected more of the suggestive remarks that were the only attention she ever got from men. It was true, Matthew noticed, that her breasts were big. But then, so were her ankles and her hips and her neck and her arms and her waist. But her hair was nice, you had to give her that. Not delicate and fine like Ruth Lillian's, but it was lush and golden, and it—

"Say, you're looking pretty hard at that girl, Ringo," Doc said. "And you said you didn't have any taste for meat! Get out of here!"

Matthew laughed to cover his blush.

"I guess you'll be going down to the hotel after you've ate," Doc said. "Which one's your favorite? I tried them all, and I guess for me it's a toss-up between Queeny and Chinky. Frenchy's a good old gal, but that scar of hers puts the heebie-jeebies up me. Maybe I don't drink enough first, eh?"

"Yeah, maybe that's it," Matthew said, immediately feeling disloyal to Frenchy, who had become his favorite of the girls.

"So, which one you got your mouth set for?" Doc pursued.

"Oh, I don't know. Maybe I'll just get on back to the office. There's work needs being done."

"Hey, that's right! You're here the whole week through! With all three to pick from! Some men's got all the luck."

"Ain't that the truth?"

A squabble broke out at the table over in the corner, and suddenly two men were on their feet, facing off. For a second, Matthew wondered if the marshal should step in and calm things down. He pushed back his chair to rise. Well...maybe not. After all, they're just a couple of young'uns letting off steam. And indeed, the marshal's instinct proved correct, because the peaches arrived just then, and the young men immediately set their differences aside to devote their energy to the serious business of slurping down peaches and syrup.

Following Doc's example, Matthew broke three biscuits into his plate before the arrival of the peaches, which Kersti ladled out with plenty of syrup that soaked into the biscuits to make what Doc described as "top-grade, high-assay *eatin'* food." And he didn't miss his chance to tease Matthew about how Kersti had pressed her hip against his shoulder while she was serving the dessert, or how she'd given him more peaches than anybody else.

"I do believe that girl's coming on heat for you, Ringo. Better watch yourself! Them big Swede gals have got needs that stretch from here to Wednesday! They can drain the juices out of a man and leave nothing behind but a dry husk!"

"Oh Lord!" cried the wrinkled old comedian across the table, affecting the trembling voice of a revivalist preacher in full salvation ecstasy. "Lord, let *me* be the one to suffer that draining! Let *me* become that dry old husk! I ask it in *His* name!" And everyone hooted, though a couple of the younger boys looked nervous, as though they expected the ceiling to come down.

Before long, the men started pushing themselves up from the table with satisfied grunts and complimentary belches. They drifted out into the street, some going across to Kane's Mercantile to make their weekly purchases, others up to the Traveller's Welcome to begin serious drinking and whoring.

But Doc sat back in his chair and drew a short-stemmed pipe and a tobacco pouch from his pocket. "No need to rush. Those gals won't be wore smooth before we get to them." He snapped a lucifer with his thumbnail and sucked the flame down into his pipe. "A body's got to learn to take life easy. After all, we all end up in the boneyard, and there ain't no prizes for getting there first. You want to borrow some tobacco?"

"No, I . . . I quit."

"You don't say! How come?"

"Well, smoking dims a man's vision. And in my profession . . ."

"Where'd you hear that smoking dims a man's vision?"

"I read it in a book by Mr. Anthony Bradford Chumms. You ever read him?"

"Can't say I have, Ringo. Writes about smoking, eh?"

"Yes, well . . . and other things. Like how a real man ought to act. And what's right, and what ain't. And how to get respect from people."

"All I ever read is operation manuals."

"About mining?"

"Sort of. I ain't a miner, really. I'm in charge of the crushing and dressing works."

"In charge? Well, now." And here Matthew had been eating and joking and smoking with a man who was in charge of something. And it was gratifying the way Doc called him Ringo, having accepted their introductory exchange of names without question.

Doc went on to say how the crushing and dressing

were done at the mine because transporting bulk ore down to Destiny would be too expensive. The dressed ore was nearly twenty percent silver. But while the quality of the ore was high enough, the quantity was steadily diminishing. "The works still make a profit, but not much. I reckon if those Boston bankers had known the ore was going to run skinny so soon, they'd never of laid out so much for the railroad line and the machinery. Just between you and me, I'd bet anything that if they ever find themselves facing a big investment to keep things going, that'll be the end of the Surprise Lode."

"What'd happen to the folks in Twenty-Mile?" Matthew wondered.

"Oh, I suppose most of them would move on. The girls, anyway. There's always a market for cheap poontang. The younger miners would probably drift up towards the Klondike, though I doubt any of them have saved enough money to put a kit together. As for us old-timers? Well, we got to face the fact that the boom days are all through booming. Prospectors, frontiersmen, pioneers, homesteaders—they belong to what you call your vanishing race. It's all merchants and bankers and brokers and salesmen now, and this country's become— Shoot, I don't know *what* it's become. Used to be that if you were poor or ambitious or just itchy-footed, you could always push on West. But there ain't no West anymore. We've used it all up. Maybe that's why we grabbed off Hawaii and the Philippines. I don't know what's become of this country, but it sure as hell ain't as much fun as it was back when I first paid my nickel and got on the ride." He stood up. "And speaking of cheap rides, you're certain-sure you don't want to go up to the hotel for a quick hunk of poontang?"

"No thanks, Doc. I'll just make my rounds then get back to my office."

"Well, been nice meeting you, Ringo. Don't work too late."

MATTHEW FOUND RUTH LILLIAN alone in the Mercantile, reading by a kerosene lamp. She explained that her father had gone up to take a nap.

"It's pretty late for a nap, isn't it? Or pretty early?"

"He calls it a nap because he won't admit that he can't work hard anymore. His 'nap' will last until morning."

"I've noticed how your pa has to stop to catch his breath all the time."

"It's his heart. It ain't much good."

"I'm awful sorry to hear that, Ruth Lillian."

She made a tight, resigned shrug; and her profile in the lamplight tugged at Matthew's heart. "He hides it," she said. "He's ashamed not to be healthy, like he thinks a man ought to be. That's why he didn't want to take you on to help with the heavy work. He thinks that being grumpy will hide the fact that he's sick. But everyone in town knows. And they're out there, circling like vultures."

"Circling? What for?"

"They want the Mercantile! Except for the weekly beef, everything passes through this store. Food, clothes, lamp oil, coal, tobacco—everything. The Bjorkvists would love to get their hands on it. And Professor Murphy, too. Sometimes I can almost feel them out there in the dark, hoping, and plotting, all greedy and mean and . . . *small!* But they're never, ever going to get this store. Pa's taught me everything about running it. How to order things and how to keep records and all that, so I'll be able to fend for myself as long as the mine holds out. If I have to, that is. I mean, if pa's heart . . ." She shook her head to banish the possibility.

A moth tapped plumply against the lamp chimney and circled over its updraft: intrigued, infatuated, baffled . . .

then suddenly incinerated. Ruth Lillian curled her hand over the top of the lamp and blew into her palm to put it out. She pushed open the squeaking screen door and went out onto the porch, where she stood resting her cheek against a pillar, looking out past the cliff edge to stars hanging in the matte-black sky.

Matthew followed her out, softly closing the screen door behind him. "But if you had the store, you'd need help with the heavy work. Lugging supplies up from the train on Sundays, and bagging the coal, and things like that."

"Oh, I'd find help."

"Where?"

She shrugged. Then her eyes took on a teasing glint. "Maybe I'd offer Professor Murphy a job as my shop assistant. Wouldn't that burn his tail feathers!"

"It'd burn mine, too."

"How come?"

"Why wouldn't you ask me to help you, instead of old Murphy?"

"You?" A sudden chill caused her to rub her upper arms, and she left her hands on her arms, as though hugging herself. Her voice slipped to a minor key. "You won't be around, Matthew."

"What makes you think that?"

"By the time my pa . . . By that time you'll be out in the world somewhere. Chasing after life."

Matthew nodded thoughtfully. Yes, that was probably true. He'd be out chasing after life. A loner. A drifter who went his own way and did what had to be done, like the Ringo—But, no. No, he couldn't leave Twenty-Mile. Not for a long time. Maybe never.

A burst of laughter from the Traveller's Welcome interrupted these musings. The bat-winged bar doors clattered open, and someone came hurtling out, arms flaying, and ended up sprawled in the dust. He got up slowly. Dusted himself off. Then calmly walked back in, as though he had just been passing by and had been attracted by the light and the laughter.

"Why don't you close up and go to bed, Ruth Lillian?"

"I can't. Every once in a while a drunk miner gets it into his head that he needs something from the store. Last week a man came crying and blubbering and saying he forgot his little girl's birthday and he just *had* to have a doll. And he wanted it right then! If we're not open, they'll break in and mess things up. So someone has to be in the shop day and night till the miners go back up to the Lode. Pa and me take turns."

"So you're going to stay up all night?"

"Looks like."

"You want me to stay with you?"

"No, thanks. I'll be all right."

"You're sure?"

She nodded vaguely, her eyes still on the scattering of stars along the horizon.

Matthew looked at her profile, and his heart expanded with feelings for her. He wanted very much to touch her, to hold her hand, maybe even...He surreptitiously scrubbed his palm on his trousers to make sure it was dry. Just as he reached out to her, she turned and took his hand...and shook it firmly.

"Good night, Matthew."

"Ah-h...well, good night, Ruth Lillian."

———————————

A COUPLE OF NIGHTS later, they found themselves again on the wooden front steps of the Mercantile, watching lightning blossom then fade in the clouds on the distant horizon, while thunder growled grumpily from mountain to mountain. Sitting side by side, they spoke in quiet voices about things they used to do, and think about, and believe, when they were kids. Now and then,

something they recalled was attached by hidden threads
of memory to some other event or moment, and their talk
would drift to that, like when Ruth Lillian said out of a
deep silence, "...The giants are moving their furniture
again."

"Huh?"

"Thunder used to scare me something terrible when I
was little. Then one stormy night Pa told me that thunder
was giants in the sky moving their furniture. A real loud
clap meant they'd dropped their piano. I was never afraid
after that."

Shortly before sundown, a brash of plump raindrops
had plopped dark spots into the dust of the street, but no
real rain had followed, only the cool winds that swirl at
the edges of a storm. And now the night air still carried
the exciting, nose-tingling smell of *storm*: that mixture
of electricity and dust.

"You were lucky to have a pa that cared about you
being scared," Matthew said. Then he added quickly,
"Of course, my pa was like that, too. Always explaining
things to me. He knew about everything. That's why
everyone looked up to him and respected him."

She hummed a vague note of agreement, but she
wasn't really listening because mentioning the night she
learned about thunder and the giants had somehow
evoked the memory of her vanity mirror, the vanity mirror her mother had given her. Her father had broken it
in a rage the night her mother ran off.

"I used to have this mirror," she said quietly. "I
would sit in front of it for hours, staring deep into my
eyes, until I got this funny feeling that the person in the
glass was a stranger who happened to look like me. That
was eerie enough, but then I'd start wondering: and
who's the *other* person, the one inside my head, looking
out through my eyes at the strange girl in the mirror?
Then I'd say my name aloud over and over. Ruth Lillian,
Ruth Lillian, Ruth Lil-li-an, until the sounds didn't make

any sense, and pretty soon I'd get the feeling that I was right on the edge of finding out something that was too scary to know. You ever felt like that, Matthew?''

"No. Just the Cracker-Jacks box.''

She turned to him and blinked. "Cracker-Jacks?''

"Cracker-Jacks is popcorn with caramel on it and a few peanuts. And there's a little toy in—''

"I know what Cracker-Jacks *are*, Matthew. But what do they have to do with anything?''

"Well, the box is something like your mirror. I mean, on a Cracker-Jacks box there's a sailor boy holding a smaller Cracker-Jacks box. And one day it suddenly came to me that there must be another, smaller sailor boy on that smaller box, and he must be holding another, even smaller box of Cracker-Jacks, and on *that* box, there must be a little teeny sailor boy holding a little teeny box of Cracker-Jacks, and on *that* box there must be . . . And it would go on forever! Everything getting littler and littler, *forever*. I felt dizzy thinking about it. And scared. Kind of like your mirror. See what I mean?''

Ruth Lillian did see what he meant . . . sort of.

"I once had this teacher that liked me? And when I told her about the Cracker-Jack sailor boys getting smaller and smaller, she said it was called infinity. And she made the sign of infinity on the blackboard. It looked like a Lazy-8 cattle brand.''

"What looked like a Lazy-8 cattle brand?'' Mr. Kane asked from the doorway, startling them. He had padded down from his bedroom to see why Ruth Lillian had not come up to bed yet.

Matthew stood up quickly, but immediately wished he hadn't, because that made it look like they were doing something they shouldn't, which they weren't. "Infinity, sir.''

"Infinity? You've been sitting out here all this time talking about infinity?''

"Yes," Ruth Lillian said. "And mirrors. And Cracker-Jack."

Mr. Kane shook his head wearily. "Go to bed. It's late."

"All right. Good night, Matthew."

"Good night, Ruth Lillian. Good night, sir."

"Hm...? Oh, yes. Good night."

DURING HIS FIRST WEEKS in Twenty-Mile, Matthew had seemed to be succeeding with the second phase of his technique for survival in new places: Once inside, be nice, and play by their rules. Everyone was impressed by his willingness to work hard for small wages. "Look at that kid go, will you?" But after the shine wore off, people came to take his good-humored hard work for granted. "That's just the way the kid is. He *likes* working hard. Guess it takes all kinds."

He couldn't rid himself of the feeling that he wasn't really respected by any of them. And in some cases it was worse than just lack of respect. While he was having his weekly meal with Doc and the other miners at the boardinghouse, he'd sometimes look up and see Oskar Bjorkvist staring at him from the kitchen door, resentment seething in his eyes. Oskar's mother constantly berated him for letting a stranger come into town and snap up all the jobs that were rightfully his—money he could be earning if he weren't such a *stupid!...lazy!...* She punctuated her fury by slapping his ears so hard they were hot and red for hours.

Nor had Professor Murphy reacted in a friendly way when, after the two-week trial period was over, Matthew had asked that his seventy-five cents for half a day's hard labor be doubled to a dollar fifty. Twenty-Mile's Tonsorial Maestro had rankled at having to come up with an additional six-bits, and he accused Matthew of having "roped him in" by offering to do the work for one price, then blackmailing him for more. Matthew admitted that the original arrangement was his way of letting the Professor see a sample of his work, but he didn't feel it was blackmail to ask for a buck fifty for a whole day's hard work when he got that much for doing odd jobs for B. J. Stone and Coots up at the Livery. Professor Murphy responded with a snort.

In the end, Murphy reluctantly compromised, offering a dollar and a *quarter*, but he warned Matthew that he'd be considering "other arrangements." And the following Sunday morning Matthew arrived at the barbershop to find Oskar Bjorkvist scrubbing out the bath barrels. But the viscous-minded boy used up two bars of Fels-Naphtha, broke the long-handled brush, and did such a poor job that Professor Murphy had to spend the next morning re-cleaning them, swearing and growling, his wig in constant danger as he grunted over the rims of the barrels that cut into his potbelly. So Matthew got his job back (at a dollar and a *half*), and Oskar Bjorkvist, who had received a proud maternal pat on the cheek only the day before, got such a slap on the ear that his head ached for hours.

ONE NIGHT, AFTER BEING irritable throughout supper because he'd had particularly sharp chest pains that afternoon, Mr. Kane went to bed early. After cleaning up the dishes, Matthew spent his customary half hour with Ruth Lillian out in the cool of the porch, she gazing out across to the foothills while he looked wistfully at her profile, just visible in the starglow of a moonless night.

"What you thinking about?" he asked.

"Hm-m? Oh, nothing really. I was just wondering what was the most important thing a person can have in this life. Beauty? Brains? Wealth?"

"Respect," Matthew said without having to consider. "*Respect?*"

"Respect may not seem important to you because you and your pa have always had it. But not me. And as for my *pa...*"

"But everyone likes you, Matthew."

"That ain't true, Ruth Lillian. And even if it was, liking ain't respecting. Mr. Anthony Bradford Chumms wrote that a man who don't command respect ain't but half a man. That's why I want respect, even from people like Professor Murphy, and the Bjorkvists, and the Benson brothers, and—"

"The Benson brothers?"

"Oh...they were just some kids who..." He shrugged, reluctant to explain. But after a while, he began telling her about how his family had drifted from town to town, so he was always, *always* the new kid in school. And that meant taking a lot of razzing from bullies. One of the things he got teased about was his name. Kids used to chant, "Dub-chek...chek...chek...chek," making the sound you make when you're calling chickens to feed.

"But...I thought your name was Chumms. Matthew Bradford Chumms."

"Well, yes...that's...my name *now.* But when I was little they used to call me..." He looked down and scrubbed one palm hard with the other thumb. Then he lifted his head and looked her straight in the eye. "Ruth Lillian, I lied when I said my name was Chumms. It's really...Dubchek."

"There's nothing wrong with Dubchek."

"Except that it's not a real American name!"

"Well, what about Kane? Kane's a Jewish name."

"It is? Yeah, but it *sounds* American. That's what counts."

"Is that why you fought with those Benson boys? Because they poked fun at your name?"

"No, it was more than that. We'd just moved to Bushnell, Nebraska, and right from the first I had trouble with the Benson brothers. They were bigger than us other kids 'cause they'd flunked twice. I hated school because of them, and I'd of played sick and stayed home, except there was this schoolmarm who took a shine to me and said I had the richest imagination of any boy in school."

Not wanting to make Ruth Lillian jealous, he didn't mention the secret, painfully intense love he had nourished for this pretty young teacher, nor the apple he had stolen from somebody's back yard and buffed on his shirt until it had a deep ruby shine, but then didn't have the courage to put onto her desk for fear the kids would ridicule him. In the end, he ate it behind his book to get rid of the evidence, but the teacher caught him and chided him for eating in class. But he did tell Ruth Lillian about the dictionary the schoolmarm gave him as a prize for a story he'd written. The dictionary wasn't new. It was better than new; it was her *own*, with her name written in it and all. He still had it, and he'd keep it for ever and ever.

When he went up to the front of the class to receive the dictionary, the Benson brothers had scowled at him and shown their teeth. And later in the school yard they called him a liar, because his story was about a boy who had a brave father who was hard to live up to, while *his* pa was a drunk who couldn't keep a job because he stole and lied and was nothing but a low-down *Dubchek...chek...chek...chek.*

"And they beat you up?" Ruth Lillian asked.

"They tried." Matthew told her how the Bensons gathered a bunch of younger boys behind the outhouses and described what they were going to do to the schoolmarm, when it was their folks' turn to board her. They told how they were going to sneak into her room when she was sleeping and—He stopped short.

"Something dirty, I suppose," Ruth Lillian said dully,

knowing what sewers most boys' minds were.

"Awful dirty. Too dirty for me to tell you."

"And you stood up for her?"

"Well . . . yes. So the oldest Benson pushed me against the wall, and the next thing I knew we were at it—me against all of them. Even the smaller kids joined in. I couldn't do much, what with all their hands grabbing at me and dragging me down. But I wasn't scared, because I'd gone to the Other Place, and I couldn't feel anything, so it didn't matter how hard they punched me. I got in a lucky shot and gave the younger Benson a cut lip. Then they really went crazy! They all started punching and kicking! And the older Benson got me around the neck and shouted into my ear, asking how I liked it: getting beat up, just like my ma got beat up every night by my drunken pa! And the next thing I know, I'd wriggled the kids off me and I had that Benson by his hair and I was banging his head on the ground! And his nose started to bleed! But I kept banging away until his teeth clicked and his eyes got glassy! And all the kids started screaming that I was killing him! But it didn't matter to me because I was in the Other Place, so I just kept banging away . . . banging away . . . banging away . . ."

Matthew stopped and swallowed hard several times, his heart thumping beneath his ribs. Ruth Lillian was looking at him oddly, so he forced his breathing to calm down before saying, "Well, there was this man who visited the schoolmarm during recess sometimes. Her beau, I guess. I think he was a teacher too, because he wore glasses and talked sort of refined. Well, he came running out of the schoolhouse shouting and slapping heads to break through the ring of kids, and he snatched me up and shook me and asked did I want to kill that boy? And the schoolmarm came pushing through and knelt down by the Benson kid and waved air at him until he gagged and spit and came to. Then she looked stern at me and told her beau that I was a new boy in town, and that new boys always caused trouble, trying to prove how tough they were, and then this beau of hers snatched me around some more and asked me if I thought I was tough, and all the kids were looking at me and grinning, so, naturally, I said, you bet! Plenty damned tough! And the schoolmarm said it wasn't my fault because my folks were . . . she didn't want to say what. But the smaller Benson piped up that my pa was a drunk and always beat up my ma! And the man said that was too bad, but it didn't excuse me being a troublemaker and pounding kids' heads on the ground until they were half-dead. And then he put his face up close to mine and said, 'If you think you're all that tough, little man, why don't you try to take a poke at *me?*' I could tell he was sure I wouldn't do it, and that he was sort of showing off for the schoolmarm, letting her see that he knew how to handle children. But all the kids were standing there, grinning, and the bigger Benson was sneering at me through his bloody nose, so what could I do? I mean, *what could I do?* I gave him my hardest shot. It broke his glasses, and he went down—from surprise, mostly. The schoolmarm knelt over him, dabbing his cut eyebrow with her handkerchief. She looked up at me and screamed, 'Go home! Go home, and never come back, you hear?' So I . . . I went home and never came back.''

The story had begun hesitantly, but the last of it gushed out, leaving him gripping the porch rail so hard that his fingertips were splayed flat. He swallowed to keep back the bitter tears that stung his eyes. When he could speak, he said, ''When I got home I took that dictionary of hers and threw it at the wall! It ended up on the floor, splayed open, with its spine broken. And I felt real bad, looking down on it . . . limp and broken-backed. All the rest of it—the kids pounding on me, the schoolmarm screaming at me—none of that hurt so bad as breaking my dictionary. It was the only thing I'd ever won.'' He closed his eyes hard.

Ruth Lillian was silent for a time. Then she spoke in a soft, healing tone. "I'm sorry, Matthew. I know how mean kids can be. You wouldn't think it now, but there used to be a school in Twenty-Mile. Thirty or more kids. Old B. J. Stone was the schoolmaster. The girls didn't like me because my ma always dressed me up in pretty clothes. And I was sort of stuck-up, I got to admit. They used to mix nasty things about my ma into their jump-rope rhymes. And sometimes they'd make a circle around me and scrape their fingers at me and chant: shame, shame, double shame! Everybody knows your name! So I know how mad and helpless you must have felt when those bullies made up lies about your pa beating on your ma."

Matthew looked at Ruth Lillian. "I guess I better be getting home."

He went down the four wooden steps to the street, where he stopped. Without turning back to her, he said in a toneless voice, "Fact is, Ruth Lillian, those kids weren't making up stories. My pa *was* a drunk. He used to come home smelling like whiskey and pee and up-chuck, and he'd beat on my ma something awful. Beat her till she was..." He drew a deep breath and scrubbed his face with his hands, then he sniffed hard. "I just hate the smell of whiskey!" Then, after a moment: "So it was true, what the kids said. That's why I couldn't stand it and had to fight them to keep their mouths shut. But I guess that when a person's pa always smells like whiskey and up-chuck, he can't expect to get much respect. Know what I mean?"

She didn't say anything. What could she say?

He went home.

MATTHEW'S CONVICTION THAT THE people of Twenty-Mile didn't respect him despite his hard work and his constant efforts to be biddable and cheerful was reinforced a week later when a slip of the tongue gave him reason to believe that not even Ruth Lillian really respected him. It was Sunday, and after the train off-loaded supplies for Twenty-Mile and took the miners back up to the Lode, Matthew made his usual two trips from the depot to the Mercantile, pushing a handbarrow loaded with new stock. That done, he went to the barbershop to do his barrel-scrubbing. He was late getting to dinner because Professor Murphy had piled on extra chores, saying that, by God, if he was going to be black-mailed into paying somebody an extra six-bits of his hard-earned money then, by God, he meant to get an extra six-bits' worth of sweat out of him! So Matthew arrived at the Mercantile late, and Mr. Kane, worn out by an all-night vigil behind the counter, grumbled about Matthew's letting his food get cold, then he said he thought he'd go to his room and lie down...not that he was tired. No, he was just...well, his back was stiff, that was all!

After they did the dishes, Matthew and Ruth Lillian walked down the Sunday-silent street, then turned up into the donkey meadow. He was careful to guide her away from the soggy patch beneath the tree, where the Bjork-vists had slaughtered that week's beef. Lost in their own thoughts, they strolled across the meadow, the uneven ground causing their shoulders to brush occasionally, un-til they reached the fenced-in burying ground with its weathered wooden grave markers, some already slump-ing in toward the settled graves. Matthew thought the burying ground was awfully big, considering the small number of wooden markers clustered in one corner; and Ruth Lillian told him the space had been set aside when Twenty-Mile was still growing and everyone expected the Surprise Lode to last forever.

"How come all the grave markers are the same shape?"

"The mining company had a whole lot of them run off at the sawmill down in Destiny. Most of them are still stored in Professor Murphy's shed. He's got the burying concession. He used to make a good profit, back before the bust, when lots of people got killed in fights and accidents. He still buries three or four a year, men killed by mine cave-ins, or by getting caught in the machinery." She shuddered at the thought of that.

They wandered among the markers, most of which bore only a name and the year of death, but a few of the older ones had epitaphs burned into the wood, and some were intriguingly enigmatic like: *Now it's her turn!* And: *Well, he'd tried just about everything else.* A relatively conventional epitaph, *Not Dead, Just Sleeping*, made Matthew frown and shake his head. He told Ruth Lillian that he'd rather think of people buried in a cemetery as dead, good'n dead, and not just lying down there *dozing*. As they walked along, he read some of the names aloud, and asked who they'd been. She remembered nearly all of them, her parents having come to Twenty-Mile when she was seven and the town not yet a year old. Him? He was the assayer. Her? She was a whore who got shot by another girl... something about a red dress. Him? He used to pull teeth and tell fortunes. I don't know what he died of. Whatever it was, you'd think he'd of seen it coming, what with being a fortune-teller."

A thought came to Matthew. "Ruth Lillian, is . . . is your ma here?"

"No," she said curtly. They walked on. He found a stick and used it to whip the heads off some weeds. After a time, she said dryly, "My ma's in Cheyenne. At least, that's where she went when she left here. Of course, maybe she's moved on by now. I don't know."

He didn't want to pry, but at the same time he didn't want her to think he didn't care. So he said a noncommittal, "Cheyenne, eh?"

"Yes. She run off with the town marshal."

"The man who used to live in my place? The one who wore the star you gave me?"

"That's the one."

"And she . . . run off? Just like that?"

"Just like that. The marshal was a big, handsome man. And Pa? Well, Pa was a lot older than her. And he worked all the time, trying to build up the business, so he didn't have time to go to dances over to the Pair o' Dice Social Club, and things like that. When they argued, she'd complain about him not being any fun, and he'd snap back that he worked day and night to keep her in fancy clothes, and she'd shout back that there were plenty of men who'd give her nice things, believe you me! She used to say that a lot: believe you me. I never say it."

Matthew nodded but remained silent, in case she wanted to tell him more. But after a time, he felt pretty sure she didn't, so he took the burden of the silence off her by reading aloud from another cross: *1889. Prospector. 60 years old—give or take.*

"There used to be lots of prospectors wandering these mountains in the early days," she said. "They figured if there was one Surprise Lode there must be others. But the 'surprise' was that there wasn't but one vein of silver in the whole Medicine Bow Range."

Matthew chuckled at this, then he turned his attention to battling a tall mean-tempered weed with his stick, finally winning with a parry and a deft slash.

"Matthew?" she asked in an offhand tone.

"Hm-m-m?"

"What's 'the Other Place'?"

He turned and stared at her. "How do you know about that?"

"You told me."

"I never!"

"Yes, you did. You were telling about your fight with the Benson boys, and you said you couldn't feel their punches because you were in this 'Other Place.' I didn't

ask you about it then, 'cause you were all worked up.
But I've been curious about it ever since.''

"Oh, it's just . . .'' In a gesture that had something of
embarrassment in it and something of irritation, he threw
his stick as hard as he could, and it whop-whop-whop'd
through the air, landing against the sagging fence that
separated the burying ground from the donkey meadow.

"If you don't want to tell me, forget it. I just thought .
. . Never mind.'' She walked on.

"It's not that I don't *want* to tell you. But it's . . . it's
hard to explain.''

She stopped and waited patiently.

"It's just . . . well, when I was a little kid and I was
scared—scared because Pa was shouting at Ma, or because I was going to have to fight some kid during
recess—I'd fix my eyes on a crack in the floor or a ripple
in a pane of glass—on anything, it didn't matter what—
and pretty soon I'd slip into this—this Other Place where
everything was kind of hazy and echoey, and I was far
away and safe. At first, I had to concentrate real hard to
get to this safe place. But then, this one day a kid was
picking on me, and just like that—without even trying—I
was suddenly there, and I felt just as calm as calm, and
not afraid of anything. I knew they were punching me,
and I could hear the kids yelling names, but it didn't hurt
and I didn't care, 'cause I was off in the Other Place.
And after that, any time I was scared, or if I was facing
something that was just too bad, I'd suddenly find myself
there. Safe and peaceful.'' He searched her eyes. "Does
that make any sense to you, Ruth Lillian?''

"Hm-m . . . sort of. It sounds kind of eerie.'' And she
added quickly, "But really interesting!''

"I've never told anybody about it. Not even my ma.
I was afraid to because . . . This'll sound funny, but I was
afraid that if other people knew about the Other Place, it
might heal up and go away, and I wouldn't be able to
get there when I really needed to. Crazy, huh?''

"A little. But remember, I'm the gal who used to stare into her mirror, wondering who was inside her head, looking out through her eyes. So maybe I'm not the one to judge who's crazy and who ain't."

"You know what worries me sometimes? This'll make you laugh."

"What?"

"Well, like I told you, at first I had to work hard to get to the Other Place. Then it got so as I could slip into it without even trying, any time things got to be too much. What worries me is this: What if, someday, I go off to the Other Place, and I can't get back? What if I get stuck there? Wouldn't *that* be something!"

She looked at him out of the corner of her eye and didn't respond.

"I'm glad I've told you, Ruth Lillian. You may think I'm crazier'n a hoo-bird, but I'm still glad I've told you."

"What's a hoo-bird?"

"Something I made up. A crazy bird that doesn't say anything but *hoo hoo.*"

"Sort of like an owl?"

"Yeah, but taller. Hey, look there!" A name on a slumping wooden cross had snagged his attention: *Mule. 1892.* "They buried a mule here? Alongside of folks?" he asked.

She laughed, relieved to be talking about something else. "Mule was a man! That wasn't his real name, of course. It's just what people called him."

"Who was he?"

"Nobody. Just an odd-job man. Strong as an ox and twice as dumb. He'd work like a Chinaman for just a nickel or a sandwich. People used to play tricks on him and laugh when he made a fool of himself. And he'd laugh along too, happy for the attention."

Matthew's voice dropped to a minor key. "Just an odd-job man, eh?"

"Yeah, he worked a little here and a little there, and

he'd—Matthew, he wasn't *anything* at all like you. Not a bit.''

"But nobody respected him. I mean . . . look what they did! They even wrote Mule on his grave, so's everybody could come and have a good laugh at the odd-job man!''

"They laughed at him because he was a fool. Not because he did odd jobs! Jeez!'' She was embarrassed, but angry too. Angry with herself for accidentally saying something hurtful, and angry with him for being so sensitive about it, so she said, ''All right, maybe you're right. Maybe people *didn't* respect poor old Mule. Who *cares?*''

Matthew cared.

―――――――――

KERSTI BJORKVIST SNORTED MOISTLY as she climaxed. Her strong body heaved in rapture, lifting him up on her wide pelvis. Then she settled back and hugged him to her chest, hard. ''Wasn't that *something!* I think there's nothing better in the whole world! What do you think?''

Matthew's thoughts were in great confusion at that moment. For one thing, Kersti smelled of old sweat. For another, this was sin. Sin of the Flesh. It was the first time he'd ever . . . done it. And it left him feeling empty and bad and embarrassed and ashamed. But most of all he felt sad that his first time had been with Kersti Bjorkvist, when all along he'd been thinking and dreaming about Ruth Lillian.

He had been in bed reading *The Ringo Kid Turns Tail*. (Of course, he didn't really turn tail, but he made everyone think he had, to give himself time to figure out how to thwart the slick-talking land-grabber who was scheming to get this orphan girl's ranch.) He must have dozed off because he was falling, falling, falling . . . when suddenly his head snapped up and he was full awake, his heart pounding. Was that a noise at his back door? No, no it was just something left over from his bad dream. He smiled at himself for being frightened, like some scaredy-cat kid. But maybe he'd better blow out his lamp anyway, just to be sure. He remembered how in *The Ringo Kid Places His Bet*, Ringo had heard footsteps outside his cabin (Mr. Anthony Bradford Chumms called them "footfalls" in his cultured English way), and Ringo immediately blew out his lamp, so he wouldn't have the disadvantage of being in the light while his enemy is in the dark. Matthew had paused over that passage and nodded with admiration at the Kid's savvy, and at how he had thought of it right off, just like that!

He heard the sound again, a scratching at the back door. Then someone whispered harshly, "Hey? Open up!" It was a girl's voice!

He got out of bed and unlatched the back door to ask what—But suddenly she was in and everything happened at once. She gave him a big wet kiss that half missed his mouth, and she fumbled around until she had it in her hand, and he could feel it getting hard, then she was sitting on his bed, snatching her dress off over her head, and there was a strong smell of sweat when she raised her arms, and she pulled him onto her. At first he didn't really want to. But then he did want to, and pretty soon he really *needed* to something fierce. She sort of growled, annoyed because he was fumbling around, so she put it in for him, and she came almost immediately, then he came, but she continued heaving and pumping and he stayed hard long enough for her to climax again . . . snorting . . . and then she settled back and hugged him to her, hard, and said, "Wasn't that *something!* I think there's nothing better in the whole world! What do you think?" He still lay on her thick, sweat-slippery body, feeling empty and embarrassed and sinful, but sort of wanting to do it again, and at the same time feeling disgusted with himself for wanting to. And vaguely sad, too.

She pushed him off and hugged him against her side, where he was close to the sweat smell. "Was that the first time you ever did a girl?"

"No! No, I've done lots of...But it's been a spell. A man forgets."

"*Forgets?*"

"Well, I don't mean *forget* so much as...well, you know..." He didn't go on with it. It wasn't going to get any better.

"I'm quick," she boasted. "Men like a woman who's quick."

"Of course they do. I mean...why wouldn't they?" His eyes had adjusted to the moonlight coming through the window, and he could make out her profile, the lush hair growing low on her forehead, the long meaty nose, the thick lips. And lower down, he could see the still-erect nipple of one heavy breast.

She threaded his arm around her neck and cuddled close to him, playing idly with his penis as she talked into the darkness above them. She didn't have her parents' chanting accent, which didn't surprise Matthew because most of the kids he'd gone to school with had parents with old-country accents, but the kids talked regular American—like Ruth Lillian, who had no trace of her father's brittle consonants. The thought of Ruth Lillian made his ears tingle with shame.

While Kersti babbled on, hungry for a chance to talk to someone, his arm, trapped beneath her neck, became numb, then it began to tingle painfully, but he didn't move it because he didn't want her to think he didn't like her.

"It wouldn't surprise me if you never done a girl before. You're still a kid. Me, I'm twenty-two years old. My brother's about the same age as you, and he does himself out in the back shed. Sometimes three, four times a day. He's *always* at it. Maybe that's why he's so dumb. But I don't think so. If you ask me, he's just naturally dumb. But I suppose doing himself all the time don't help any. There was this drummer come through town four, five years ago? The last drummer ever to come to Twenty-Mile. He was different from most drummers. He didn't have a big smile and a bright tie and tell jokes and all. He dressed in black, like a preacher, and he talked serious and deep, like he was feeling sorry for everybody? He read to my ma out of this book that said how it was dangerous for boys to do themselves 'cause it made them stupid and blind. Me and my brother was listening from behind the door, and we had to bite our knuckles to keep from laughing out loud, 'cause my brother was already doing himself regular and his eyesight was just fine. Well, this drummer said that parents who cared about their sons ought to stop them from doing themselves by feeding them plenty of a special flour invented by a preacher named of Dr. Sylvester Graham, and this Graham flour was what the drummer sold. You paid him in advance, and he'd have the Graham flour shipped to you, but my ma told him she wasn't born yesterday, and she wasn't going to give no drummer money in advance for flour he might ship and might *not*, and anyway she didn't have to worry about her son abusing himself, because she'd raised us kids as God-fearing Christians, and that made my brother and me snicker even more because the reason our family got chucked out of the settlement of Swedes my folks came to America with was because my pa got caught doing the prayer-leader's wife. And *that* was funny because the prayer-leader had been doing *me* on the sly for months. Not *really* doing me, 'cause I was too young and small down there to be done proper. But while he was giving me Bible instruction, he'd touch me and make me touch him and that sort of stuff. That's why they run us off from the settlement and we ended up in Twenty-Mile. From that day on, my ma wouldn't let my pa do her. I know 'cause I heard them arguing about it at night. And that's why my pa sneaks out sometimes to do one of the girls at the hotel.''

Matthew was both dumbfounded and fascinated by her talk. He'd heard older boys at school talking dirty and explaining things to younger boys—mostly wrong, as any farm boy with livestock would know—but he'd never dreamt that girls thought about such things, much less *talked* about them. Or *did* them. He admired Kersti's frankness. Too bad about her looks . . . and the sweat.

''How do you know that your brother . . . does himself?'' he asked.

''I watch him sometimes. You should see the stupid glazed look in his eyes, and the way his mouth hangs open when he gets close to squirting.''

''He lets you watch him?''

''Sure. When I was fourteen–fifteen and he was only ten–eleven, I used to sneak into his room late at night and have him do me—well, as best he could with his squiggly little thing. But I made him stop when he got old enough to start squirting, 'cause I don't want no baby with two heads like you get if you do your own brother. Did you know about that? About babies with two heads?''

''Ah . . . no. I didn't.''

''Well, it's true. And some pretty scary things can come from men doing cows and sheep, believe you me!''

This expression brought Ruth Lillian to mind, and he felt just rotten to be lying here with another girl.

''Have you done that uppity Ruth Lillian yet?'' she asked, almost as though she had penetrated his thoughts.

''No, of course not! She ain't the sort of girl to do—'' He stopped short, hoping he hadn't hurt her feelings. *Lordy, my arm is going to rot off!*

''Oh, she'd do it. Any girl will do it, if the time and the man is right. Everyone *wants* to do it, even if uppity people pretend they don't. I've seen you two sitting out on her porch at night, and I know what you're both thinking about behind all your talk. But you're wasting your time, what with her fancy airs and her hair piled up on top of her head, like she was somebody. Boy-o-boy, my brother really hates your guts! He's always saying how he'd like to cut you, and stuff like that? Partly it's because of the jobs you snatched up and the way our ma bad-mouths him and slaps him around for not grabbing them first. But mostly it's because of that Ruth Lillian. He wants her real bad. He always thinks about her whilst he's doing himself out in the woodshed.''

This notion disgusted Matthew. And angered him. "How do you know that?"

"He told me. He gets so mad about you that sometimes he cries. Just puts his face into his arm and blubs. And sometimes I feel so sorry about the way he hankers so hard for that Ruth Lillian that I do him with my hand, just as a favor. But my regular is old Murphy.''

"The barber?"

"Sure. I sneak out once a week and we do it. He gives me four-bits. He says he's afraid to do the girls at the hotel because they might have the clap, but I think he does me because the girls charge two bucks and he's a cheapskate. Did you know that he's bald as a coot under that wig? Well, he is. It makes me laugh sometimes, when he's pumping away on top, trying to hold his wig on with one hand! Lordy, my ma would pee bob-wire if she knew I was messing with old Murphy, considering that he got caught doing young girls back East. *Real* young girls. Used to give them penny licorice twists. He was stingy even then, I guess. A bunch of men was going to tie him to a tree and cut off his hose, but he ran away. If you ask me, he picked Twenty-Mile because there's still people wanting to cut it off, and this is the last place anyone would think of looking for him.''

"Gee. Do you do other men in town?"

"*Who*, for crying out loud? You think I'd want old peg-leg Calder on top of me? A gal could get splinters!''

"Well, what about Mr. Delanny?"

"Naw, he's too sickly to do anybody."

"Not even his own girls?"

"No, I'm pretty sure not. He seems to like that Frenchy the best—the niggra with the cut face?—but I'm pretty sure he don't do her. I'd of heard about it if he did. Everybody knows everything about everybody in a little hole like Twenty-Mile."

An icy thought chilled Matthew's stomach and wilted his penis, which had begun to respond to Kersti's idle handling. Did that mean Ruth Lillian would find out about tonight?

"And you don't think I'd do Reverend Hibbard, do you? *Please!* I wouldn't want him staring down at me with those sunk-in eyes of his! And just imagine how he'd go staggering down the street afterward, sobbing and bawling about sinning with me! And if my ma heard, she'd flay me alive!"

"Well, what about B. J. Stone and Coots?" Matthew asked. "They ain't sickly, nor one-legged, nor bald, nor drunkards."

Kersti convulsed with wheezing laughter that made her squeeze his penis hard enough to hurt. But her movement gave him a chance to slip his arm out. "Stone and Coots! You're joshing! Don't you know about them?"

"Know what?"

"They don't want women! They do *each other!*" Kersti went on to say that they were what her mother called Sodomites, and the wrath of God was upon them. That was why they stayed in this godforsaken town, where nobody cared who you were, or what you did . . . or *who* you did. "But you better not hang around them so much, if you don't want people to think you're one of them Sodomites too."

Matthew couldn't believe that B. J. Stone and Coots . . . I mean . . . how?

". . . and that's everybody. Except for old man Kane,

and he ain't been interested in doing anybody since his wife run off with the marshal and left him with little Miss Stuck-up, with her fancy dresses and her hair piled up on top of her head, like she was somebody.'' The flow of talk stopped as her thoughts turned inward. After a while she said softly, ''So you see, there ain't nothing or nobody for me in Twenty-Mile.''

''Well then maybe you shouldn't stay in Twenty-Mile, Kersti.'' He was thinking that if she left town, maybe Ruth Lillian wouldn't find out about tonight.

''Oh, don't you think for one minute that I'm staying in this stinking little town! Not on your life! No-sir-ee! I been saving up my two-bit pieces from old Murphy, and one of these days I'm going to up and leave! Get myself a job of work in some big city, and buy nice clothes, and have somebody do up my hair real pretty. . . . But not on top of my head, like a stuck-up.''

''What are you waiting for?''

''I *ain't* waiting! Don't say I'm waiting, when I ain't! Any day now, this town's going to look around and see nothing but dust settling where I used to be standing!'' She took a breath, and her voice went hollow. ''. . . It's just that . . .''

''It's just what?''

''Well . . . I don't know nothing but cooking and serving. What would I do down in the flatland, all alone? How'd I keep myself? I'd sure hate to end up like Mr. Delanny's girls. Done by anybody who wants you. Ugly old men, or men with disease, or just . . . *anybody.* I want to get out of here more'n anything in the world, but . . .''

Matthew felt her shrug, and suddenly he knew that Kersti would never leave Twenty-Mile and take his guilt away with her. In fact, she'd probably . . .

''Hey! You're getting hard again,'' she said with a conspiratorial giggle. ''Let me ride *you* this time.''

THAT NEXT FRIDAY, MR. Kane was feeling better than he had for weeks. All through supper he entertained them, telling about pranks the kids used to get up to in the New York tenement where he'd grown up, pranks like hiding in dark hallways and scaring old women who believed in ghosts and golems. Matthew laughed until tears stood in his eyes, and Ruth Lillian accused her father of "telling whoppers," which he denied categorically, totally, emphatically, and... "All right, so maybe I polish the truth a little."

"That's a kind of lying."

"Small-minded people might call it lying. But I say it's just decorating the truth so as to make it more interesting."

Matthew knew exactly what he meant.

Mr. Kane joined them out on the porch for a breath of fresh air before bed, and the three of them looked in silence at the stars above the foothills, bright and brittle in the chill mountain air. After a while he sighed and scratched his stomach and said that if they weren't going to have one of their mind-stretching talks about infinity and mirrors and such, he might as well get some sleep, because the miners would be coming tomorrow and they'd have to keep the Mercantile open all night. Ruth Lillian said she'd be up in a few minutes.

Matthew and Ruth Lillian sat in silence on the top step, their backs against opposite porch pillars, his long legs splayed out down the stairs, hers hugged to her chest.

"In just two years," she said over her knees, "we will be in the Twentieth Century. The Twentieth Century. Sometimes I try saying those dates out loud: Nineteen ought-five. Nineteen twenty-four. Nineteen ninety-eight. That nineteen just doesn't...doesn't *fit* in the mouth, somehow. The Twentieth Century! Lord, I don't belong in any Twentieth Century, but I'm being dragged into it, willy-nilly!"

"I don't see what we can do about it. I think a body should save his worrying for things he can do something about."

"What do you worry about, then?"

"I don't know." He shrugged. "Well, God and sin and hell, of course. But I suppose everybody worries about that."

"Not me."

"You don't?"

"No. I'm not even sure there *is* a hell. And even if there is, it can't be for little things like stealing cookies, or sassing your pa, or daydreaming about . . . you know, about loving and kissing and all. I mean, God just can't be that *small*."

Matthew wondered if she had mentioned loving and kissing because she'd heard about Kersti and him. Maybe somebody had seen her slipping out of the marshal's office. He had been worrying about that all day, unable to get his mind off it because he was still a little sore from their doing it three times. He had gone back to wash up for a second time before going to dinner at the Mercantile because he was afraid they might smell Kersti on him. And after dinner, he had gone back and lain down on his bed to think things over and figure out how he could explain to Kersti that they mustn't never, ever do one another again. He'd tell her that it was wrong, considering how he felt about Ruth Lillian and all. While he was working out the words he'd use to tell her, he fell asleep, probably because he'd been awake most of the night, either doing it or listening to her prattle on and on, like she'd been saving up her talk for years. He woke up too late to do his chores at the Livery, and maybe that was just as well because he needed time to mull over what Kersti had told him about B. J. Stone and Coots. He wasn't sure how he should act toward them.

"Penny for your thoughts?" Ruth Lillian said.

"Hm-m? Oh...I was just...wondering about things."

"Like what?"

"Well, you said you daydreamed about loving and hugging and...all."

"Doesn't everybody? Well, young people anyway. I don't suppose old Mrs. Bjorkvist daydreams much about kissing and cuddling. But now Kersti—"

"What about Kersti?"

"Well, everybody knows about her and old man Murphy. Everybody except her folks, that is. I don't blame her."

"You *don't?*"

"No. The thought of old Murphy touching *me* makes my flesh crawl, but I can see how maybe Kersti needs a little attention and affection sometimes, and the good Lord knows she doesn't get much of that from her folks. So she gets it where she can. You know what makes me sad about Kersti?"

"What?"

"The way she's sure to get cheated. She'll go with men to get some affection. To have someone to talk to. But the men take their pleasure, then they don't want anything to do with her. And that's *small* of them."

"You're right there! I don't know how a man could ...Well, I just don't know."

"My pa says men are a lot closer to wild animals than women are."

"Ain't that the truth. Say, Ruth Lillian? About your dreaming about loving and kissing and all? Do you have daydreams about...you know."

"Don't you?"

"Well...sure. But I'm a man, and men are closer to animals, like your pa says. But a nice girl like you..."

"Girls have feelings too. It's just that we keep them to ourselves."

"I've had daydreams about...." Matthew glanced

over to see how she would react. "...about you."

She nodded thoughtfully. "Hm-m. I'm not surprised."

"You're *not?*"

"Well, after all, I'm the only girl in Twenty-Mile—other than poor Kersti—so it would be sort of funny if you *didn't* think of me that way."

"And you? Do you ever daydream about me?...That way, I mean? Cuddling, and all?"

She lifted her head and looked at him, her eyes narrowed speculatively. "Well...yes, sometimes. It's only natural to wonder about things. But, of course, I'd never do anything more than wonder."

"No, no, of course not. No, me neither. No. But it's nice to know that you think about me sometimes...like that. And maybe even at the same time that I'm thinking about you...like that."

"Well!" Ruth Lillian stood up and flattened her skirts behind with her palms. "I'd better be going up."

He stood up quickly. "I didn't mean anything wrong."

"No, there's nothing wrong. I just think it's time to say good night." She turned back at the door. "And, Matthew? I don't think we should talk about this again. I'm not saying there's harm in it. But it's...it's sort of *on the road* to harm, if you know what I mean."

"I know exactly what you mean. Ruth Lillian. And I respect you for it."

"Hm-m...well. Good night, Matthew."

"Good night, Ruth Lillian. Sleep tight."

As he walked up the street to the marshal's office, Matthew promised himself that he would never do Kersti again. Nor let her do him, which was more like what had happened. It wouldn't be fair to Ruth Lillian, who was always having loving daydreams about him.

And later, as he lay on his bed looking up into the dark, he wondered what Ruth Lillian would think of him

if she knew he had committed sin. Not just what he had
done with Kersti, but ... *real* sin.

IT WAS SEVEN IN the morning, but it would be a couple of hours before the sun climbed high enough over
the mountain behind Twenty-Mile to let the pale autumn
sunlight work its way down the wooden façades of the
buildings on the west side of the street. Matthew walked
across to the Traveller's Welcome, his collar turned up
and his fists plunged into the pockets of his canvas jacket.
There was a snap in the air, but not the slightest breeze,
so when his breath made ghost cones, he could walk
through them, and they would brush his cheeks. His head
and ears were cold because he had wet his hair and raked
it down flat with his mother's genuine bone comb. October already, would you believe it? He'd been in
Twenty-Mile seven whole weeks! He'd have to get
himself a warmer jacket before the snow came.

  As usual on the day before the miners descended from
the Surprise Lode, the girls slept late and came down to
breakfast looking mottled and puffy-faced. As she
dunked a biscuit into her coffee, Queeny admitted that
she felt as though somebody had pulled her through a
knot hole—and not a smooth one neither! "Sometimes I
think I'm getting too old for this business!" And she
snorted a laugh before anyone could agree with her.
"Maybe I should go back to the theater! At least the
hours are better! Did I ever tell you I used to dance the
Dance of the Seven Veils?"

  "Only about two hundred million times," Frenchy
muttered into her coffee cup.

  Chinky raised her eyes to Matthew as he filled her
cup, and she smiled one of her hesitant, almost wincing,
smiles. When he smiled back, she quickly lowered her
eyes, as she always did.

Matthew approached Mr. Delanny's table to refill his mug from the big enamelled coffee pot, but the gambler waved him away irritably. He couldn't speak because his handkerchief was pressed to his mouth and he was wheezing and bubbling into it, and he hated to have anyone near him when his dignity was diminished in this way. His lungs had weakened so much in just the two months since Matthew's arrival that he now got through a dozen handkerchiefs a day, and consumed ever-greater quantities of Mother Grey's Patented Suppressant. Matthew occasionally sensed Mr. Delanny's eyes on him as he worked around the barroom. Their earlier one-con-man-to-another complicity had eroded, and now Matthew felt a blend of envy and dislike emanating from Mr. Delanny. Not for anything Matthew had done, or failed to do. Just for his being young and healthy.

And Jeff Calder had made a quick recovery from any gratitude he may have felt toward Matthew for taking over most of his work while always deflecting to him any praise he received from the girls. Not only did Calder assume the boy's accomplishments were the consequence of his own virtues as a watchful and demanding boss, but he shared with his occasional late-night bottle-chum, Mr. Bjorkvist, his suspicion that Matthew was either up to something, or "didn't have both oars in the water." What normal boy would work harder than he had to? And what normal boy would go around with a smile and a cheerful hello all the time?

Matthew was sweeping the barroom when Frenchy came down to pick up her usual bottle of whiskey to fortify herself against the night to come. She happened to glance over, and her eyes intersected his before he could conceal the disgust that whiskey always evoked in him. "What *is* the matter with you, boy?"

"Nothing. It's just . . ." He had wanted to talk to Frenchy about this, and now seemed as good a time as any. "Frenchy, I like you. I really do. But I've got to tell you that I just *hate* liquor. I've seen what it can do to a person, and I hate to see you putting that stuff inside you. I just . . . Well, I just wanted to tell you that.''

She allowed her yellow eyes to lie wearily on his for a moment before asking, ''That's all you got to tell me?''

''Yes, ma'am.''

''Uh-huh, well now let *me* tell *you* something, boy. As you don't know shit-all about life, you'd do better to keep your nose out of other people's business. You hear what I'm saying to you?''

He smiled a slack, inane smile and returned to his sweeping. After she brushed past him and padded back upstairs with her bottle, his embarrassment turned to bitterness. For crying out loud, he'd only said what he said for her own good! To shake off his feelings of unjust rejection, he applied himself energetically to his push broom, raising clouds of churning dust that first discovered, then defined, a shaft of morning sunlight that had climbed high enough to come in over the bat-winged bar door.

Lodgepole Creek Gully

EVENING WAS CLOSING IN when the prospector tied his riding mule and his two coffee-colored pack mules to scrub pine and started his cooking fire with pine cones and sticks of windfall. He had snared two nice fat jackrabbits, and he meant to have one for his supper.

A susurrous scurry of sliding scree drew his attention to three men climbing up the slope toward him. Well now! It had been a donkey's age since he'd had a good chin wag. By the time he'd added more windfall to the fire and blown on the ash-scabbed pine cones to get his coffee pot boiling, the men were closer. He answered their call with a cheerful wave of his hand. By God, he'd roast *both* jackrabbits! Have a little celebration. These flatlanders probably never ate jackrabbit in their lives. It'd be a treat for them. He could tell they were flatlanders from the elegant clothes of the one in front: that leather doohicky for a tie, and that fancy green-and-gold waistcoat.

LIKE EVERY SATURDAY, THE noonday meal with the Kanes was bigger than usual because Mr. Kane and Ruth Lillian would only have time for a quick sandwich that evening. Matthew was expected to follow his Saturday custom of taking supper at Bjorkvist's boardinghouse. Since he had the whole afternoon on his hands, he knew that he really ought to go up to the Livery to see if B. J. Stone and Coots had any chores for him, but he was still uncomfortable about them, and he was afraid that something in his manner might reveal that he knew their secret. The idea of men ''doing'' one another seemed to him—well, not exactly evil or repulsive, but *odd*. And sort of embarrassing, too: an embarrassment he felt on their behalf, something like the embarrassment he had felt on his parents' behalf when he first learned how babies are made, and pictured his folks doing it. He hadn't known whether to laugh, or shudder in disgust.

But he had been avoiding B. J. and Coots for a week now, and he made a firm resolve to see them soon. Tomorrow for sure!

. . . Or maybe the day after.

When evening brought the miners hooting and shooting their way down the street, he joined the queue, paid Mrs. Bjorkvist her silver dollar, and took his usual place at his usual table. When Kersti leaned over and pressed herself against him while serving the biscuits, Doc nudged him and pumped his eyebrows. ''I do believe

you've made yourself a conquest there, Ringo! And I'll
bet she *never* quits! As for her looks...? Well, hell's-
bells, all cats are gray in the dark, like the fella says.''
He nudged him again.

Matthew glanced up to see Oskar Bjorkvist staring at
him from the kitchen doorway, his bland face puckered
into a frown of intense hate. He felt a flash of anger at
the idea of that slack-mouthed idiot thinking of Ruth Lillian while he ''did'' himself out in the back shed.

That night he sat up in bed, reading *The Ringo Kid
Takes His Time* by the light of his kerosene lamp, while
from out in the street came the occasional yelp or hoot
of a miner raising hell. His attention kept sliding off the
page, not only because he had read the book more than
a dozen times already and it was not one of his favorites
because there was too much ''pink-and-silver sunsets''
and ''yellow-streaked dawns'' and ''purple-tinged des-
erts'' and such fancy truck between the interesting action
bits, but also because his ears kept straining toward the
back door, harkening for Kersti's arrival. Just before
leaving the other night, she had said something about
coming again Saturday, after she had cleaned up at the
boardinghouse. He had gone over in his mind half a
dozen times how he'd tell her that they couldn't do it
anymore—not because he didn't like her, he would has-
ten to say—but because it wasn't fair on Ruth Lillian,
who was his...well, he didn't know exactly *what* she
was, but anyway they couldn't do it anymore, and that
was that! But he'd tell Kersti that it wasn't because he
didn't like her! 'Cause that wasn't true! He *did* like her.
In fact, he thought she was...you know...just fine. And
he hoped someday she'd manage to get out of Twenty-
Mile and get a job in some city and find friends—and a
fella, too, of course!

What really troubled Matthew—and made him angry
with himself—was that even while he was remembering
Kersti's beefy face, thick body, and tangy smell, and

thinking about how terrible it would be if Ruth Lillian found out that he and Kersti had done one another, he felt himself getting hard, in spite of himself. He couldn't explain it. How could low feelings of lust get hold of a man when all his loftier aspirations were tugging him in another direction? Maybe Mr. Kane was right when he said that men were lots closer to the animals than women were. One thing was for sure, you could bet the Ringo Kid never found himself getting hard while he was talking in his polite, soft-voiced way to one of the pretty young women he met in his wanderings from town to town, looking for chances to do good.

It suddenly occurred to him that he shouldn't be lying in bed in his long johns when Kersti arrived, because that would give her the wrong idea. He was tugging his trousers on when he heard her scratch at his back door, and he was still stuffing in his shirt as he opened it and told her to come in and sit down, because there was something they had to talk about. She sat on the edge of his bed and made a little pouting face when he sat in the chair over by his reading table and began by saying, "Now look, Kersti. There's something we got to talk about. You and me, we can't—"

"Ain't you afraid somebody might look in the window and see me here, and you with your shirttail sticking out?" Kersti asked, cupping her hand over the kerosene lamp and blowing it out. "That's better. Now come sit over here by me, so's we don't have to talk so loud and risk being heard by folks."

With an impatient moan, Matthew crossed and sat on the edge of the bed as far from Kersti as possible, which wasn't all that far, as she was sitting in the middle. "You see, Kersti, the fact is . . . listen, we got to talk about—"

But she avoided the "lecture" she could feel was coming by the straightforward expedient of reaching out and grasping his penis, right through his trousers.

"I knew it! You're hard, and that means you want to do it. So what are we waiting for?"

He stood up. "No, now look, Kersti, we really—" But she pulled him down onto the bed and started fumbling with his belt.

And he didn't stop her. Lordy, he didn't stop her.

But as soon as they'd finished, he told her that they mustn't do this again. Never, ever. (It was somehow easier to tell her now that he was spent and soft.) She lay beside him, silent and heavy, and he could feel anger and hurt radiating from her. Then she began to cry. Great sobbing snorts...oddly like her snorts when she climaxed. Her voice was all wet and slippery when she blubbered that she knew it was because of that stuck-up Ruth Lillian Kane...with her piled-up hair and her orange-blossom water! But what about *her?* She didn't have nobody but old Murphy, with his falling-off hair!

In that overly patient tone of weary reasonableness that men use on women they've wronged, he reminded her that she intended to get out of town pretty soon anyway. And he went on to assure her that she'd find someone who'd love her, and take care of her, and always be—

Well, maybe she didn't *need* to be loved and taken care of! Maybe she didn't need him nor anyone else! Yes, and another thing! She'd just as soon he didn't come to the boardinghouse to eat on Saturday nights anymore! And if he did? Well then, she'd be damned if she'd serve him!

He asked if she was mad at him.

What did he think?

"Sh-h-h! Somebody'll hear you!" Her mention of the orange-blossom water that Ruth Lillian sprinkled on her handkerchiefs had reminded him that he should have said something nice about the vanilla extract Kersti had dabbed behind her ears and under her arms, largely eclipsing the smell of stale sweat. "You're not thinking of telling anyone about you and me, are you?'' he asked.

After a petulant silence that she maintained for a punitively long time, she finally said...no. No, she wouldn't tell, because if her ma found out she'd beat her into next Tuesday. So he needn't worry! She wouldn't tell his precious Ruth Lillian!

She turned away from him and lay there, brooding over her hurt. Then, to hurt him in return, she said that her pa had told Jeff Calder that he'd better hire Oskar to do the breakfast chores at the hotel and kick out this Chumms or Ringo or Dubchek, or whatever-the-hell-he's-calling-himself-*this*-month, because he was mighty friendly with those Sodomites up to the Livery, and everyone knows what *that* means.

''But I ain't been up there for a long time.''

''What does that prove?''

''Well, I can tell you that neither B. J. nor Coots has ever done anything wrong when I was around.''

''That's what *you* say.'' She was struggling into her dress.

''But it's the truth!''

''It don't matter what's true and what ain't. It's what people think that matters! *Now* look what you done! You made me rip my dress!''

''I didn't mean...I'm sorry.''

''Sorry don't get the barn painted!'' She stormed out, slamming the back door behind her.

He sat on the edge of the bed, shaking his head. ''...the barn?''

———————————

''AFTERNOON!'' MATTHEW GREETED. HIS jovial tone was calculated to make up for his failure to drop by for more than a week...or at least to deny B. J. a chance to comment on it.

''Mm-m...'' B. J. didn't look up from the two-month-old copy of the *Nebraska Plainsman* he had found at the bottom of the pile when he was desperate for something to read.

Matthew chafed his hands together vigorously. "Hoobirds! There's a nip in the air! Winter's on its way, and no mistake."

"You reckon?" B. J. turned the page and read for a third time an article written in succulently ghoulish journalese that fleshed out the headlines:

TRAGIC INCIDENT AT BUSHNELL
GORY SCENE GREETS CURIOUS NEIGHBOR

"Yes, sir," Matthew pursued with dogged verve. "Early this morning, I could see my breath in the air, and I was *indoors!*"

"See your breath, could you? Well now, how about that?"

Matthew couldn't help glancing thirstily at the tin mug of steaming coffee beside B. J.

"Where's Coots got to?"

B. J. carefully folded the paper, set it aside, and leaned back against the wall, his mind still on the article he had been reading. He regarded Matthew with a long, defocused gaze as he hefted various possibilities. Then he blinked and said, "I'm sorry, Matthew. What were you saying?"

"I was just wondering where Coots was."

"He took the donkeys up to the Lode by the back trail."

"Hey, maybe he'll run into Reverend Hibbard up there! Maybe he'll get a free sermon! A nice long juicy one, with plenty of hellfire and goddamnation!"

"That would be a real treat for him. Well, Matthew! I don't believe we've seen you around here for a spell."

"Yes, well...I've been...you know...real busy."

"I see." B. J. drew a breath as though to ask about something . . . then he decided to take a different tack. "Matthew?"

"Sir?"

"May I give you a bit of advice?"

"Yes, sir."

"There are two are things in this life that are easily squandered, and too late regretted: time and friends. The wise man either spends his time well or wastes it gracefully. But he never, never lets a friendship shrivel and die for lack of attention. Friendships are just too precious. Too rare. Too fragile."

Matthew knew he should try to explain why he hadn't been around, but instead he said, "I don't have to worry. I've got plenty of friends." And he instantly regretted the cocky sound of that.

"Have you?"

"Sure."

"Like Reverend Hibbard? Or Professor Murphy? Or the Bjorkvists?"

"I was thinking of the Kanes. And the folks at the hotel."

"The Kanes? Yes, probably. The hotel? Well, I suppose you might count on the girls as friends . . . in their way, and to their limits. One often finds a residue of sentiment in girls like that. The lees of love at the bottom of the bottle. But sentiment is to love what ethics are to morality, or what legality is to justice, or justice to compassion—all degraded forms of a loftier ideal. But yes, the girls might come to your aid, should you fall upon evil days. But as for Delanny and Calder . . . ?" B. J. made a dry three-note laugh. "Delanny doesn't care about people. Dying is a selfish business, Matthew. Ask anyone who's cared for an aging parent. And Jeff Calder is no one's friend. He's a man of prejudices, rather than values; of appetites, rather than tastes; of opinions, rather than ideas. He doesn't care who's right, only who wins.

There are millions of Calders out there. They elect our presidents, they fill our church pews, they decide our— What in hell are you smiling at?''

"The way you talk, sir. There's no doubting that you used to be a schoolteacher. Hoo-birds!''

B. J. Stone chuckled. "I guess I *was* waxing a little pedantic. Cup of coffee?''

"I'd like nothing better. No, don't get up. I'll fetch it.''

From the kitchen, he raised his voice to ask, "Ah... did you know Coots back when you were the school-teacher here?''

There was no answer. When Matthew returned, rolling his mug between his palms to warm them, he repeated, "Is that when you two met? Back when you were teaching school?''

"Why this interest in Coots and me?''

"Just curious.''

B. J. looked at him through narrowed eyes. Then he lifted his shoulders as though to say, "Well, why not?''

"No, I didn't meet Coots until what I thought would be my last day in Twenty-Mile. The town was dying and there weren't enough children left to support a teacher. The lawyer had already gone, and the blacksmith, and the town marshal—this last taking with him the wife of our principal merchant. The time had come for B. J. Stone, Esquire, to drift on to the next town and try to teach a love of books to a new batch of kids who'd give the world to be anywhere but in that schoolroom.'' He leaned toward Matthew and informed him in a mock-confidential tone, "Teaching, you understand, is not just a profession. It's a *calling*.''

"So how'd you meet Coots?'' Matthew perched up on the work bench with his cup of coffee.

"Coots had the misfortune to blow into Twenty-Mile just as the dried-up town was beginning to blow away. For a couple of weeks he worked here at the livery stable.

Then one morning, the owner told him he was fed up, and Coots could *have* the goddamned Livery, lock, stock, and unpaid debts. The lock didn't have a key, and there wasn't much stock, but there were *plenty* of debts. Luckily, the creditors had all left town, too.'' B. J. scratched his chin stubble with his thumbnail and lowered his eyes. ''I'd planned to leave a box of books at the Livery to be forwarded when I found a town that needed a burned-out teacher. We fell to talking, Coots and I. I don't remember about what. Just...talking. And that was it. Just like that. It's silly, really: two old farts in their fifties. Ridiculous. But...'' B. J. shook his head at the capricious vagaries of human emotion. ''Coots had known about himself for a long time. I, on the other hand, had not known. Oh, I'd *surmised*, but I had never let the truth get close enough to read its name.'' He drew a breath, and his attention focused back to Matthew. ''You understand what I'm talking about, don't you, Matthew?''

''Yes. Well...sort of.''

''And does it trouble you? Or upset you?...Matthew?''

But Matthew was looking past B. J.'s shoulder, out across the donkey meadow.

''About Coots and me? It's neither good nor bad. It's just...the way we are. You understand?''

''Somebody's coming.''

''What?''

''Three men. Look.''

B. J. turned and stood up. One of the men was on foot; the other two were mounted on coffee-colored mules that were so spent and stumble-footed that the men had to rib-kick them ceaselessly to keep them moving. They were crossing the donkey meadow, having worked their way up from the tangled labyrinth of cuts and blind ravines below.

''Prospectors?'' Matthew asked.

''No,'' B. J. said. They weren't dressed like prospectors, at least not the one wearing that fancy waistcoat. And mountain men know how to treat mules. All three men had pistols stuck into their belts. No holsters. B. J. recognized this to be a bad sign.

The men threaded their way toward the Livery, but it wasn't until they were almost at the shoeing yard that B. J. stepped out from the shadow of the lean-to into the sunlight.

"Nice-looking herd you've got there!" the one in the waistcoat said, flicking his thumb toward the scraggly beef standing forlorn in the empty meadow. "Need many ranch hands to look after it?"

"Looks like you've lost a mule," B. J. said in a tone bereft of either friendliness or curiosity.

The man in the waistcoat slipped down from his mule and stepped forward, grinning. "That we did, friend! Couple of hours back. The poor beast just balked and wouldn't go another step. I tried reasoning with it, but we were on a narrow cut with sheer rock on one side and a whole lot of nothing on the other—a real awkward place for a mule to get ornery. Well, I gave that mule a tug or two, sort of inviting it to have second thoughts about its uncooperative behavior. But, no. No, the poor old beast had made up its mind that it was going no further. So I did what any reasonable man would do when friendly persuasion fails. I sent a slug into his stubborn head and pushed him off into the ravine. He made a fair splat when he hit the bottom, I got to give him credit for that. As a comfortable ride and a willing companion, that mule was no great shakes, but when it came to splatting...! Well, that just goes to show that all God's creatures have their own special gifts. Some are strong; some are wise; some possess the ability to comfort and console. And that mule? He was a natural-born splatter." Lieder grinned, and B. J. could tell that he took pleasure in his ability to turn a colorful phrase.

The man who had come on foot chortled, a gnarled

gnome of a man with a barrel chest and facial features that were flattened and askew, as though someone had pushed the heel of his hand into the face of a soft clay statue and given it a twist. Lieder turned and raked him with a theatrical glare. "Don't you dare laugh at that poor beast, Tiny! That poor mule was one of God's creatures, and its journey to the great pasture up yonder is not to be laughed at!" Then he turned his eyes to B. J. and winked. "...But it *did* make a fine splat."

B. J. spoke dryly. "If you're thinking of buying a fresh string, we don't have any mules. We only keep donkeys. And they're all on their way up to the mine."

"I see. Well then, I guess we'll have to make do with horses."

"We don't keep horses."

"But wait a minute, here." He stepped back and squinted up at the weathered sign over the barn door. "Doesn't that say livery stable? And yet you stand there telling me you don't have any horses. I'm confused. I don't understand how a livery stable—You! Boy! Don't you hang back in the shadows where a man can't see you! Step out here!" Then his voice suddenly returned to its tone of honeyed menace. "Just be so kind as to step out here and tell me how come a livery stable doesn't have any horses. I seek to be enlightened upon this point." The two followers grinned; they had come to delight in their leader's slick flow of talk.

Matthew stepped out into the autumn sunlight. "There's no use for horses up here. The only way in or out of town is by the mule track you come up."

"And the railroad! You weren't going to forget to mention the railroad, were you, boy?" He turned to his followers. "I fear that this boy was not going to mention the railroad that brings a load of silver down to Destiny every week, regular as clockwork. Now, why do you imagine he'd try to baffle a weary traveler thataway? Is it not written: baffle *not* the weary traveler, nor seek to deceive the humble passerby?... Paul to the Georgians: 7, 13.''

The third stranger, a long-faced giant with a fleshy little bow of a mouth that was puckered into a permanent kiss, slid off his mule and pulled down the crotch of his trousers to ease the irritation of his long ride. ''I'm hungry,'' he complained in an incongruously thin, high voice.

''All things in their season, Bobby-My-Boy.''

''Those mules are finished,'' B. J. said. ''You've ridden them too hard.'' Their backs had been rubbed raw; they suppurated at the edges of their saddles, and constant heel kicks had opened the skin along their rib cages. They stood with their heads low, long threads of saliva hanging from open jaws.

''Do I detect recrimination in your tone, friend? You shouldn't be hard on us. We're just three poor sick boys doing the best we can in a cold, harsh world. Ain't we, Tiny?''

The gnome with the smeared face showed a big yellow grin.

''There's something strange about Tiny's name. Mostly people called Tiny are big strapping fellas, just like most men called Curly are bald. But our Tiny is... tiny. Now, ain't that fascinating? But you were right, friend, when you pointed out that these poor old mules are broke and useless. I guess there's no point wasting good feed on them, is there? Tell you what I'll do. I'll just leave them with you, and you can have them as a free and complimentary gift. A memento of our meeting.''

''I don't want them.''

''Oh-oh! *Now* look what you've done. I just got through telling you what I was going to do, and there you come sassing back, telling me that I can't do it. That's the kind of thing that just frustrates the living hell out of me. But I'm a reasonable man. You say you don't want them? Well then..." He drew the pistol out of his belt and shot first one mule, then the other. They both dropped onto their knees, snorting and blowing wetly in their agony. The leader turned to B. J. and raised his palms. "Now look what you done! Your bickering and contradiction has brought pain and suffering to these poor dumb beasts. But you have my permission to put them out of their misery, if that's your desire."

B. J. stared at the man, his disgust undisguised. Then he turned to Matthew. "Go fetch Coots's old rifle."

"You do that, boy," Lieder said. "You fetch this old coot's rifle. Say, I got an idea! It might be interesting to see if our new-found friend here has any guts. What's your name, new-found friend?"

"Stone."

"Stone, eh? I like to know a man's name. Permit me to introduce my followers. The little one's called Tiny, like I said. And the big one, that's Bobby-My-Boy. They're both pretty ugly, as you can see, but they try to make up for it by being mean and low-minded. *Real* mean. And *real* low-minded. Me? My name's Lieder. L-i-e-d-e-r. It's a Pennsylvania Dutch name. When I tell people my name, they sometimes think I'm claiming to be a *leader*. And you know what? Maybe there's something to that. I don't believe in coincidence. I think our lives are directed by forces 'beyond our ken'—as they say. Those forces chose to call me Leader for a good reason. And I'm pretty sure I know what that reason was. So your name is Stone, eh? Now, *that* is what I call interesting! Anyone can see you're a hard man, Mr. Stone, the way you talk so mean and harsh to strangers. You're a Stone who's *hard*. That's like Tiny being small, or like me being a leader, if you see what I mean. Funny old world." He turned to his men. "You know, boys, I'm curious to find out just how *hard* Mr. Stone is. I wonder if he's hard enough to use his gun on me, rather than the mules, 'cause I can tell from the way he looks at me that he thinks he's an altogether higher and nobler example of mankind than this poor contemptible creature standing before him.'' He turned back to B. J., still smiling. ''I've got that right, haven't I, Mr. Stone? You do find me contemptible, don't you? Come on, fess up.''

Matthew emerged from the kitchen with Coots's rifle and a box of cartridges.

''Well, look there, will you?'' the leader said. ''I haven't seen an old rimfire Henry in a coon's age. You cut a good deep cross on the nose of that Henry's .44 slug, and you've got yourself a real *stopper!* It'll blow everything out of a man but his bad intentions!''

The mules were still snorting in pain, but Lieder spoke comfortably and easily as his followers grinned along, spectators to the fun. ''You know how to load that Henry, boy?'' the leader asked, his eyes never leaving B. J.'s.

''Yes, sir.''

''Do it, boy. *Do it!* We are about to learn something. We're going to find out how hard the stones on this barren old mountain are. Ain't that right, Mr. Stone?''

B. J. didn't answer.

While Matthew was loading the gun, the man with no neck and lips in a permanent pucker complained again that he was hungry.

''Patience, Bobby-My-Boy, patience. First I got to sort out what's what in this town, and...'' He turned to B. J. ''...and who's who. Then we'll eat, drink, and make merry. Make merry! Hey, wouldn't it be something if in your den of vice—the Traveller's Welcome, if I'm not mistaken—one of the girls turned out to be named Mary? That'd make what I said about 'making Mary' pretty goddamn witty! And as the Book so truly tells us: Laughter colors our lives and lightens our burdens...Paul to the Virginians: 7, 13. *Give that gun to Mr. Stone, boy!*'' he spat out, in a sudden rage. ''*Give it to him! Go on, give it to him!*''

As Matthew numbly passed the rifle to B. J., one of

the mules died. Died with pathetic simplicity. It stretched its neck and looked back toward its wounded flank, its white eye huge with sorrow, then it lowered its head to the ground and, with a sound like a human sigh, died.

The instant B. J.'s hands touched the rifle, the leader grabbed its muzzle and pulled it into his own stomach, burying more than an inch into his navel. "Now, Mr. Stone, all you got to do is pull the trigger! Just *squee-e-e-eze* the trigger, and I'll be dead and gone. What an opportunity for a noble and superior being like you to rid the world of low-down garbage like me . . . but!" He held up one finger in front of B. J.'s face. "But, but, but, just a second! Just one teeny little second before you shoot. It's only fair for me to tell you what will happen when you do." His face took on an expression of intense sincerity, and his voice dropped to a sober tone. "What will happen when you pull that trigger is this: I will shit." He grinned, and his followers sputtered with laughter. "Oh, I'll die, don't worry about that. A man shot point-blank in the gut has very little choice other than to die. But I will also shit. You see, when a fella gets gut-shot, he almost always shits. It's some kind of convulsion thing. Well, Mr. Stone? You going to pull that trigger and make me shit? I'll try to shit real good for you. Cross my heart and hope to . . . oh-oh. Maybe I shouldn't say that. Bad luck."

B. J.'s jaw muscles tensed.

The leader watched B. J. through a tight-eyed smile. "Oh, and there's one other thing that will happen when you pull that trigger, Mr. Stone. My devoted followers here will shoot you dead. Who knows, you might get it in the gut, and you'll shit too. Just picture it! You and me, lying side by side on the ground, the righteous man and the low-down sinner, both all shitty-pants and shame, shame on us!" He grinned.

B. J. swallowed.

"So it looks like if you want to take my life, you've

got to be willing to sacrifice yours. Nothing in this world comes free, Mr. Stone, for verily it is written that those who would attend the barn dance must pay at the door. I believe that's Paul to the Oklahomans: 7, 13, but I could be mistaken.'' The grin collapsed, the eyes hardened, and he pressed the muzzle deeper into his stomach. ''Well? Shoot, if you're not yellow! *Shoot! Shoot!*''

B. J. snatched the barrel out of the leader's grasp.

Tiny and Bobby-My-Boy reached for their pistols.

The gun roared.

A glob of mule brain splattered onto one of Tiny's moccasins.

Matthew noticed this disgusting detail with sharp-edged clarity, but it didn't upset him, for he had slipped into the Other Place.

The gnome with the twisted face made a retching sound as he tried frantically to wipe the glob of brain off on a clump of grass. ''Look what you done! You ruin't my shoes! They're ruin't!''

''Now, Tiny, don't you go getting mad at poor old Mr. Stone. He didn't mean to be disrespectful to your shoes. He's shown us that he doesn't have any guts. But still he's a lofty and noble sort of being, and not the kind to go around dirtying other people's shoes without due cause. Here, I'll just take that rifle, Mr. Stone. *And* the ammunition, if you please. You got any more guns hid away inside there somewhere?''

''No.''

''You sure? I do hope you aren't trying to mislead a poor stranger. Bobby-My-Boy, maybe you'd better go look around. Just in case there's a gun or two in there that Mr. Stone's forgot all about.''

''I'm hungry.''

Lieder slowly swung his gaze to Bobby-My-Boy's face. ''What did I just tell you to do?''

With a whimpering growl, Bobby-My-Boy brushed past B. J. and went into the stable.

"Lord love and bless us," Lieder said with a long intake of air between his teeth. "I do truly hope you aren't lying to me about there being no guns in there, Mr. Stone, because if there's anything that makes me mad, it's people lying to me, and there's just no limit on what I do when I get mad. I'm like a little kid that way, I guess. *Tiny! Will you stop fiddling with that shoe!*"

From within the kitchen they could hear Bobby-My-Boy snatching drawers open and tipping things over in his search. Then he moved into the house proper, and there was the sound of boxes being thrown onto the floor and furniture being pushed over.

"You know what else makes me mad, Mr. Stone? The sneaky way the government in Washington D.C. is taking away—*I'm talking to you, Mr. Stone! Don't you look away when I'm talking to you!*" Then he flashed a grin and continued with fatal calm, "...the way the government in Washington D.C. chips away at our constitutional rights, bit by bit... bit by bit. Take for instance my constitutional right to the pursuit of happiness. I once wrote a letter to the president of the United States, telling him how they'd locked me up and denied me my constitutional rights, and you know what the president replied? *Not a word!* He never even had the manners to answer my letter! And me a freeborn white citizen of these United States of America! Oh, sure, niggers can swank down the street, elbowing white women into the gutter, and foreigners can come swarming over in cattle ships to steal Americans' jobs, but a real American can't exercise his constitutional right to the pursuit of—What does that mean?"

"What does what mean?" B. J. asked.

"The way you're looking at me!"

"I wasn't looking at you any special way."

"The hell you weren't! I've seen that look before. You're thinking to yourself, this here man's crazy. Ain't ya. *Ain't ya?*"

"I was only wondering why you've come to Twenty-Mile."

"Is that what you were wondering, Mr. Stone? You're sure you don't have any idea at all? You can't think of anything around here that a person might want? Maybe something that comes down the mountain on the train every week? Something sort of shiny and valuable, hm-m? *Bobby-My-Boy! Will you hurry up?*"

"I'm looking!" came the muffled response from the second floor of the house.

"The train that brings the silver down from the mine also drops off about sixty miners," B. J. said calmly. "And most of them have guns."

"I told you how I feel about people who lie to me."

"Sixty of them," B. J. repeated. "With guns."

Lieder measured him with a long look. Then he suddenly grinned. "Sixty, eh? And all of them with guns? Well, well! But, the Lord will provide the way, if I provide the will. And I got *tons* of will. I got enough will to put an end to the terrible things happening to these United States of—*What the hell's wrong with you, boy? Why are you staring right through me with that silly-assed smile on your face?*"

Matthew blinked and pulled himself back from the Other Place. It took him only a second to run what Lieder had just said to him through his mind. "I didn't mean to stare, sir."

Bobby-My-Boy burst out through the side door, slapping dust from his trousers and grumbling to himself. "No guns. Nothing but *books.*"

"Books? *Well*, now! I'm pleased to discover that you're a bookish man, Mr. Stone. During the long, weary years when I was unjustly deprived of my freedom, I read morning, noon, and night. That's how I developed a vocabulary that a warden once described as 'out of the ordinary.' *Out of the ordinary!* Would you believe that I have read more than a thousand books? More'n a thousand! Books on every subject. Even an interpretation of the Book of Revelations that nobody had ever read before me, because the pages were still uncut. Do you know what 'the Seventh Seal' *really* means? Bet not. And once I came across a dog-eared little pamphlet telling about what happens to juicy young novices in convents when a pack of horny old nuns get ahold of them. More'n a thousand books! How many books have *you* read, Mr. Stone? Nowhere near a thousand, I bet.''

''Mr. Stone used to be the teacher,'' Matthew offered in the hope that this would inspire some respect in a man who liked to read books. ''He reads about Romans.''

Lieder sucked his teeth. ''Well, well. A teacher, eh? I've always had a special place in my heart for teachers. There is no higher calling than the shaping of young minds. I had a teacher who helped to shape mine. And through the long and difficult years, I never forgot his contribution. Not for one minute.'' He examined B. J.'s face with leisurely, amused eyes. ''You know what I bet, teacher? I'll bet you're wondering how come I know all about this town, and the silver shipment, and the whores working at the Traveller's Welcome, and how there's only a handful of townsfolk living here. Well, I learned all about Twenty-Mile from an old prospector we met up with. A good Samaritan, he was. Not only eager to lend his mules to poor weary travelers, but he even gave us his guns and the little bit of gold dust he had ripped from the unwilling womb of Mother Nature—ain't that a colorful way to put it? I thought maybe this prospector had more gold stashed away somewhere, so while we were feasting on jackrabbit, I asked him about it in a conversational sort of way. He wasn't very forthcoming at first, but I managed to convince him to tell me everything he knew. I think it was the *smell* that convinced him. Did you ever smell feet roasting in a fire? It's an *unpleasant* aroma and there's no use trying to deny it. And when the skin starts to char and blister and burst . . . ! Oh, my! But there's something about that smell that makes a man eager to tell you everything he knows. It turns out the poor fella didn't have any more dust stashed away after all, so he died for nothing. Just goes to show, doesn't it? Now, then!'' He raised one finger, his eyes glittering. ''The question is this: Why am I telling you all this? Why am I opening my heart to you? You're an educated man, Mr. Stone. Suppose you tell me why.''

B. J. unclenched his jaw to speak. ''Because you want me to know what lengths you'll go to if you're crossed.''

Lieder turned to Bobby-My-Boy and Tiny, his eyes wide with admiration. ''Did you hear that? Mr. Stone here has penetrated my devious intent to the very *core!* There's the advantage of dealing with educated people.'' He turned back to B. J. ''Well, I hate to lose the pleasure of your refined conversation, but I want to look around town a little. Get to know my neighbors. Maybe have a bite to eat. Just generally relax and pleasure ourselves after our many travails.''

Although both frightened and repulsed, Matthew couldn't take his eyes away from the man's face: the sharp nose, the feverish pale gray eyes, the network of fine lines that worked and wove in response to his rapid shifts of mood and intent. Suddenly Matthew realized that Lieder was looking directly into his eyes, a penetrating stare that seemed to scour his soul. Matthew returned the gaze, unable to unlock eyes. Then Lieder smiled and winked, as though all this were some kind of joke, and only the two of them were in on it. ''I guess I better take this old Henry along with me, don't you think, boy? It is evil to leave temptation in the hands of the young.'' He turned to B. J. ''*And* the cowardly.'' With a little flip of his forefinger along the brim of his hat, he turned and walked diagonally across the yard toward the street, followed by his men.

B. J. Stone and Matthew looked after them in silence.

"Wha..." Matthew had to clear his throat. "What are we going to do?"

His eyes still on the departing men, B. J. shook his head slightly and spoke in a lipless whisper. "I don't know."

"I'll bet he made up all that about the prospector just to scare us. I mean, half the time he seemed to be sort of joshing."

B. J. was still shaking his head. "No, he wasn't joshing. He did exactly what he said he did."

"You think he's really that mean?"

"He's worse than mean. He's insane." He watched the three men stop in the middle of the street and look up and down, before walking past the Traveller's Welcome, down toward Kane's Mercantile. "They're looking for guns and ammunition. They probably intend to collect all the guns in town."

"So...what should we do?" Matthew asked.

B. J. drew a long breath and pressed his fingertips into his eye sockets. "Wait for Coots to come back. He'll know what to do. You and I have to get rid of these mules. We don't have time to bury them. We'll take them across and push them into the ravine. Fetch the barrow."

"Yes, sir, but *then* what are we going to do?"

"Just fetch the barrow, boy! I need time to think."

While Matthew was pulling the barrow out of the shed, B. J. sat on the bench beside the wall and tried to clear his mind so he could work out some plan of action. His eyes fell on the two-month-old copy of the *Nebraska Plainsman*. Just a few minutes ago, he had been pondering what—if anything—he should say to Matthew about the killing of that man and his wife in Bushnell, Nebraska, and about the mysterious disappearance of their son...possibly kidnapped, the reporter had suggested.

But there were more-immediate problems and dangers.

———————

ABOUT AN HOUR LATER, Matthew eased open the back door of the Mercantile and tiptoed into the storeroom, where he paused to listen for voices.

Silence.

He called in a strained whisper. "Ruth Lillian?" Then: "Mr. Kane?"

No answer.

His pulse throbbed in his ears as he tiptoed toward the door to the shop and pushed it open slowly. "Mr. Kane?"

The old man gasped and pressed his hand against his chest. "What's the matter with you, boy! Sneaking up on a man when he's working!" Actually, his nib had long ago stopped scratching in the account book he had opened automatically, seeking to calm himself by returning to numbing routine after his encounter with the three strangers. But he had been staring through the columns of numbers, so totally absorbed in worry that he hadn't heard Matthew's soft calls.

"Sorry if I gave you a start, sir. Where's Ruth Lillian?"

"Up taking a nap. She's got a sore throat. Wore herself out, minding the store over the weekend."

"I saw those men head down this way. What did they want?"

"They asked—"

"They didn't see Ruth Lillian, I hope!"

"No. She was up in her bedroom."

"That was lucky."

Mr. Kane nodded vaguely, as though stunned. "Yes ... lucky. They asked if I had guns for sale. I told them no, I didn't keep guns in stock, but I could order anything they wanted from Destiny. But the boss, the one with the strange eyes, he said he didn't plan to be in town long enough, but thanks all the same. And he smiled at me. That smile of his was . . .'' He shook his head.

''They're real nasty men, Mr. Kane. B. J. Stone thinks they're lunatics, maybe broke out of prison.''

''Yes.'' Mr. Kane agreed in a gray note. ''Yes, that's possible. There was cruelty in his eyes. And . . . amusement.''

''What did he say when you told him you didn't sell guns?''

''He asked if I kept a gun for my own protection. I told him no, I hated guns. All I had was a few boxes of ammunition I stock for the miners. Then he said something strange.''

''What was that?''

''He asked what kind of accent I had. I made some joke about the Lower East Side. But he didn't laugh. He looked at me with those pale eyes and started talking about immigrant hordes descending on the United States to batten on our riches. I'm afraid we're in for trouble, Matthew.''

''Yes, sir, that's for sure. That boss told B. J. and me about an awful—I mean really *awful* thing he did to a prospector. They're killers, Mr. Kane. I think Ruth Lillian better stay out of sight until they're gone.''

''Yes. Yes, of course.''

''B. J. and me talked things over, and he said we should get together and decide how to protect ourselves.''

''The whole town?''

''No, just him and you . . . and me, I guess. He doesn't trust the others. He told me to keep an eye on those strangers. Then I'm supposed to come here after dark and meet with you and him.''

''Yes, yes. I'm . . .'' Mr. Kane's attention seemed to drift away. Then he blinked and said, ''Yes, I'm sure that's a good idea.''

''Do you know where they went from here?''

''One of them kept saying he was hungry. The boss

asked if they could get something to eat at the hotel, and I told him no, they'd have to go to the boardinghouse across the street. And that's where they went.''

''Are they still there?''

''No. They left and went up to the Traveller's Welcome. One of them was carrying two rifles and a couple of pistols. The Bjorkvists' guns, I assume.''

''And they took Coots's rifle away from us. Looks like B. J. was right. They're rounding up all the guns in town.''

Mr. Kane nodded thoughtfully. ''Which puts us at their mercy.'' He closed his eyes and pressed his hand against his chest, where strangely pleasant ripples had been fluttering ever since his tense encounter with the three men. ''. . . At their mercy,'' he repeated. ''And how much mercy do you think those men have, Matthew?''

Matthew raked his lower lip with his teeth and looked through the store window up the street toward the hotel. ''Not a whole heck of a lot, sir.''

———————

MATTHEW HAD PLACED HIS chair so he could keep watch on the front of the hotel diagonally across the street from his marshal's office. The westering of the sun had caused the shadow of the hotel's false front to wriggle most of the way across the rutted street by the time Bobby-My-Boy slammed out through the bat-winged bar doors and lurched down towards the Mercantile. Clearly he'd been drinking, and Matthew worried that Ruth Lillian might disobey her father's instructions to stay upstairs. He was trying to decide between following B. J.'s orders to keep an eye on things, and obeying his impulse to run down there to make sure she wasn't in danger, when Bobby-My-Boy came back out onto the street clutching to his chest a toppling stack of small boxes hooked clumsily beneath his chin. That would be the ammunition Mr. Kane kept for the miners. Bobby-My-Boy returned to the Traveller's Welcome, and for the next hour Matthew heard and saw nothing out of the ordinary.

He was watching the sun melt, dull red and plump, onto the foothills, his eyes gritty with staring toward the brightness, when his breath suddenly caught in his throat. Lieder was crossing the street, heading directly for the marshal's office. Matthew barely had time to drag his chair to beside the table and snatch up a Ringo Kid book before the door banged open and Lieder was standing on the threshold, silhouetted by the setting sun. Matthew looked up from his book, blinking and shielding his eyes with his hand. "What is it? What do you want?"

"So you're the marshal, are you? Well, how about that!" His tone was yeasty with derision.

"Shoot, no, I'm not the marshal!" Matthew said with a dry chuckle. "This place was abandoned when I come to town. Its roof looked pretty tight, and the privy hole hadn't caved in, so I ... well, I just moved in."

"I'm awful disappointed. I was looking forward to an epic face-off: me against that famed and feared lawman, the marshal of Twenty-Mile."

Matthew forced a deprecatory laugh. "Twenty-Mile ain't had a marshal since heck was a pup. So ... ah ... have you decided what you're going to do?"

Lieder glared at him for a moment, then he laughed aloud. "That's a pretty subtle way you've got of prying information out of a man, boy. You'd make one hell of a spy." He chuckled. "No, I haven't decided ... other than to make myself comfortable until that silver shipment comes along to fill my war chest. Meanwhile, I'll just gather up all the guns in town, because I am concerned for the welfare of my fellow man. Everybody carrying weapons inevitably leads to dispute and conflict. But once all the guns are in my hands, the weeds of dispute will blossom into cooperation, and the tares of

conflict will flower into obedience. Chapter 7, verse 13,
Paul to the Democrats.'' He winked.

Matthew's eyes flinched from the sunset halo behind
Lieder, but he didn't allow himself to glance up toward
the big shotgun, hanging directly above Lieder's head.
''The fact is, sir, there ain't much call for guns in
Twenty-Mile. It's a peaceful place, and there's no hunting worth talking about. The blasting up at the Surprise
Lode has scared off all the game. But heck, I don't know,
there *might* be a few guns around. Maybe Mr. Kane down
to the Mercantile keeps guns to sell to the miners.''

''I already had a little talk with Mr. Kane,'' Lieder
said, stepping into the room. ''He doesn't keep guns.
Says he hates them. Now, isn't that a funny thing for an
American to say, considering how our forefathers fought
and died for our constitutional right to bear arms? But
then of course... Mr. Kane ain't a true-born American,
so I suppose we've got to expect him to scorn and ridicule all the things that made this land of ours great.''

''You're right. Mr. Kane *is* kind of strange. If you ask
me, it comes from living all alone like he does.'' Suddenly Matthew realized that when Lieder turned to leave,
he would see the gun hanging over the door. He stood
up. ''Sir?''

''What?''

Matthew sucked air in through his teeth. ''Gee, I hope
you won't get mad.''

''Mad about what?''

''Well, I just realized that I've been lying to you.''

''Lying to me?''

''Yes, sir. Fact is, I *do* have a gun. The granddaddy
of all guns, you might say. But it slipped my mind because... well, because it can't be shot. There ain't no
shells for it. But if you want it, there it is, hanging over
the door right behind you.''

Lieder turned. ''Well, I'll be damned! Look at that

monster, will you?'' He took the antique shotgun down.
''I ain't never seen the likes.''

''It's handmade. The only one like it in the world.''

''Where'd you ever find a thing like this?''

''It was my pa's. He got it from his grandpa. I don't
know where *he* got it. From Methuselah, maybe.''

''Just look at this thing, will you? It's a wonder that
hammer doesn't get blown back into someone's face.''
He broke it open and looked into the breech. ''Lord love
and protect us! If a man fell into there, it'd take a search
party to find him!'' He shouted down into the breech,
''Hello! Hello-o-o!'' Then he cocked his head as though
he were listening for an echo. ''You say there's no shells
for this cannon?''

''No, I'm afraid not. They was handmade too, and my
pa shot off the last of them years ago.''

''Too bad. Wouldn't you love to walk down the street
with that thing over your arm? The citizens would take
one look and they'd know they was dealing with a force
of nature!'' Lieder snapped the gun shut. ''Damn thing
must weigh a ton.''

''You don't have to tell me! I lugged it here all the
way from Nebraska.''

Lieder looked at Matthew, and the amused glitter in
his eyes faded out. ''How come you lugged it all that
way, if it can't be shot?''

''Well, sir, the truth is ...'' Matthew lowered his eyes.
''That gun's all I've got to remind me of my pa.''

''Yeah? Well, count yourself lucky, boy! When my
pa died, I had *lots* to remember him by. A broke collar-
bone, welts all down my back from his razor strop, a
busted nose. I wish I'd of had a cannon like this when
he was beating on me. You shoot a man with this thing,
and you don't have to worry about burying him. You can
just dab him up with a cloth and toss it into the stove.
You're cross-my-heart-and-hope-to-die *sure* there ain't
no shells for this gun?''

"I only wish there was!"

"So's you could shoot me and become the town hero?" He grinned.

"No, sir. I wish there were shells for it, so's I'd be able to sell the damn thing. Boy, if I could scrape together a little money, I'd be out of this town so fast that all you'd see was the dust settling where I used to be standing."

"I take it you ain't overfond of this town."

"No, I ain't. Nor of the folks that live here. They pay me next to nothing for my work, and they don't respect me."

"Why'd you come here in the first place?"

"No reason. I just drifted west along the Union Pacific line, looking for a place where people wouldn't come looking for you. I didn't have nothing special in mind."

"Just like me! I left prison and attended to some business, then I drifted up in this direction because I needed riches to finance my struggle. I'd never even *heard* of Twenty-Mile before that old prospector told me about the silver train. But I'm convinced there's no such thing as coincidence. There is a great plan behind everything that happens. I have been sent to Twenty-Mile for a reason. Why were you looking for a place to hide, boy? What did you do?"

"Well...the fact is, I run off. My pa was pretty free with his fists, like yours. That's why I took his gun. To spite him."

"I see." He settled his eyes on Matthew, then he said quietly, "I thought you said your pa was dead."

"No, sir. What I said was that the gun was all I had to remember him by. Say, *you* wouldn't want to buy it by any chance? I mean, you travel around a lot. Maybe you'd run across some ammunition for it. I'd sell it real cheap. I'd only ask...oh, say about—"

"If I wanted this gun, boy, I wouldn't buy it. I'd just take it. That's how I do business. I don't only cut out the middleman, I cut out the wholesaler and the retailer too! But the last thing I need is a ten-ton chunk of useless hardware to weigh me down. Here!'' He tossed it to Matthew with such force that it stung his hands when he caught it. As he was hanging it back over the door, Matthew thought of the canvas sack under his bed containing the last dozen of his pa's handmade shells. He'd better draw Lieder out of the marshal's office before he got to snooping around. So he nonchalantly stepped out onto his porch as though to take in the sunset and said over his shoulder, ''Tell me, mister. Where you planning to go after you—?''

''Well now! What's this I see?''

''Sir?'' Matthew returned to the room, his stomach cold.

''As I live and breathe! A Ringo Kid book! They all got the same gaudy covers.''

''*You* read the Ringo Kid?''

''Time hangs heavy when you're locked up in a stinking punishment hole. A man'll read just about anything.'' He tossed the book aside and stretched out on Matthew's bed, dangling his boots over the edge and tipping his hat down over his eyes. ''I've read more'n forty books a year for twenty years. A thousand books!''

''You were in prison for twenty years?''

''Give or take. Not all at one stretch, of course. I used to take little vacations. Just to break up the monotony, you know. But my prison years are behind me. I'm out for good, and the world better practice trembling!'' He laughed as he scratched his nose with his thumb.

''How'd you get all those books in prison?''

''The screws gave 'em to me,'' Lieder said, his hat still over his eyes. ''They gave 'em to me because of my warm and winning manner, and also because they were scared of what I might do to them. Sugar 'n spice. That's how to handle people, boy. Keep them off balance with sugar and spice. Sweet and smiling one minute, and the next thing they know you're holding the jagged top of a tomato tin to a guard's throat and asking him if he's ever seen the foam and bubbles a man makes when he tries to scream through a slit gullet. That's how I got books. By being the baddest thing those guards ever met. That's the way it works in this world, boy. If you're just a little bad, they beat you and punish you. But if you're *huge* bad, then they back away in awe and ad-mir-a-tion. It's the same way with stealing. If you're going to steal, steal big. A man who steals bread for his kids ends up on a chain gang, making big rocks into little rocks. But if you steal big, *really big*, then you are praised and emulated, like the Rockefellers and the Morgans and the Carnegies of this world. Of course, men like that don't break the law. They *make* the laws, so their stealing is called 'enterprise' and 'high finance.' When it comes to stealing or being bad, you got to do it big to be respected." He chuckled. "But I'll tell you one thing. You won't get much respect reading that Ringo Kid garbage."

"Garbage?"

"Shit like that will rot your brains, kid."

"Mr. Anthony Bradford Chumms is the best writer there ever was."

"Is he the one that pissed out the Ringo Kid books?"

Matthew's jaw tightened. "Mister, I better tell you that I particularly like the Ringo Kid books, and I really hate to hear anybody bad-mouth them."

Lieder tipped his hat up with his thumb and looked out from under the brim with a menacing scowl. "Well now! Is that so?"

Matthew straightened his shoulders. "Yes, sir, that's so."

Lieder's scowl flattened into a grin. "Well, I'll be damned! I will be god-good'n-damned! You remind me of myself when I was your age! You got guts, boy!" He let his hat fall back over his eyes and lay back. "But I'd sorely hate to see you end up sitting in the middle of the street, trying to hold those guts in with your hands, all because you'd made the mistake of crossing a crazy, vicious old bad-ass like me." He lifted his hat again and winked.

"I ain't meaning to cross you, sir, but I . . . well, I don't want to hear any bad things about the Ringo Kid books."

Lieder's eyes flicked from one of Matthew's eyes to the other. Then he laughed and sat up on the edge of the bed.

Matthew couldn't help glancing down to assure himself that the canvas sack wasn't sticking out, then he turned away, as though still angry, and went back out onto the porch. He could feel a tingle up his spine when Lieder didn't immediately follow him out as he had hoped he would, so he lifted his voice to be heard inside the office. "You say you're out of prison for good this time. How do you know they won't catch you again?"

"I can't let 'em catch me again," Lieder said from the bed. "There's been people killed, so if they get their hands on me . . . But the forces that brought me to Twenty-Mile won't let 'em catch me. And you know why?" A grunt in his voice revealed that he was rising from the bed. "Because I have a mission to fulfil. A sacred Mission. Did you ever hear tell of a book called *The Revelation of the Forbidden Truth*?" He was standing in the doorway behind Matthew.

"No, sir."

"Now *there's* a book. It changed my life. It illuminated my path and gave my days a purpose. That book made me—" He stopped short and changed the subject. "Tell me, boy. Have I met everybody in this fine, prosperous town of yours?"

"I couldn't say. I don't know who you've met."

"Well, there's you, fine young man that you are, despite reading garbage—whoops, sorry! And there's that all-mouth-no-balls schoolteacher. And the four Swedes down at the boardinghouse. And that Jew over at the store.'' He stepped out onto the porch and sat next to Matthew on the step. ''Then there's that snide-mouthed pimp who runs your whorehouse.''

''Mr. Delanny?''

''That's the one. A lunger, from the look of him. And there's his peg-leg helper. And the three holes he keeps for the miners. That's all I've met. Is that the whole town, son?''

''Just about. Except for Professor Murphy. He sells hot baths and shaves to the miners when they come down.''

''*Professor* Murphy! Well, now! You figure the good Professor keeps any guns?''

Matthew shrugged. ''Beats my two pair. You can ask him yourself when he comes to the hotel for his dinner. He always eats at the hotel.''

''Is that so? You know, I'll bet anything that the Professor is going to insist on turning over his weapons in the cause of peace and public order. And, who knows, he might also insist on heating me up a nice deep bath. Oh my, do you wonder if a long hot soak will feel good? It will feel *good*. Hey, you know something, kid? I like you. You're smart and you got grit. I took a shine to you right from the first. This sorry excuse for a town ain't no place for a smart kid with grit. You play your cards right, and maybe I'll take you on as one of my apostles. What do you say to that?''

''Well...I don't rightly know...''

''I ain't promising anything, y'hear? But if you keep your eyes and ears open and let me know anything that might interest me and...well, who knows? You just might get a chance to kick the dust of this one-dog town from your heels and follow me into the glittering world of frolic, adventure, and sin! How do you keep yourself, boy?''

''Sir?''

"How do you earn your bed and beans?"

"I help Mr. Kane up to the Mercantile. And do chores for Mr. Stone over to the Livery. And I clean up Professor Murphy's place. And I make breakfast for the folks over at the hotel, and sweep up and stuff."

"Lord bless and console us, it sounds like you do *all* the work in this town!"

"You can say that again," Matthew said with bitterness.

"Well, tomorrow morning you can make three extra breakfasts. Big 'uns! But not too early. It's been a long, *long* time since my followers had any woman-meat, and do you wonder if we're going to indulge ourselves tonight? We are going to *indulge! In*-dulge and *out*-dulge and *over*-dulge! That's one reason why I'm collecting all the town's hardware. A man ain't his most alert when he's indulging, and I would be sorely embarrassed to have someone kick open a door and catch me in midindulge, if you see what I mean. Picture me! Butt-naked and nothing in my hand but my hose! I'd have to point it at the intruder and say, 'Bang-bang, you're dead!' Oh hey, here's a hoot! What if this intruder shot the gun out of my hand!? Whoo-ee! Now wouldn't that *sting!*" He spluttered with laughter. "Sting! Sting! Sting! *Oooo!*" After he caught his breath and wiped tears from his eyes, they continued to sit side by side on the steps, looking across the street toward the mountains without talking. Almost like two friends.

"You know, Mr. Lieder, you're a real scary man."

"That's true," he admitted, pressing the last tear out of his eyes with the heel of his hand.

"I'm surprised Mr. Delanny let you stay at the hotel."

"Oh, he wasn't exactly tickled pink. But his druthers don't matter, because I have chosen him to be my Example Nigger."

"Sir?"

"I read this article in a *Harper's Monthly Magazine*

called 'Arab Slave Traders of the Congo'? The screws had been passing it around 'cause there were pictures of a nigger woman naked from the waist up. A young woman she was, with pert little titties. A high-quality magazine like *Harper's* would never offend its readers by offering them peeks at a white woman's titties, but somehow black titties are understood to be educational and uplifting things. Well, this article described how Arab slave-traders used to control a whole village of niggers by collecting all the weapons before anyone knew what was happening, then they'd choose one person from the village to be an example of what would happen to anyone who gave them trouble. They'd take this Example Nigger out in full view of the village and they'd give him a taste of what the writer called 'most excruciating and humiliating tortures.' After that, they didn't have any trouble. I read that article over and over till I'd memorized it. Those Arabs knew their business! That's the way to control a town. So Mr. Delanny's going to be my Example Nigger. I'll bet that sounds sort of cruel to you.''

''It does, and that's a fact.''

''Uh-huh, well, actually it's just the opposite of cruel, because in the end it saves a lot of unnecessary pain and punishment. Making decisions like this is not pleasant, but it's part of being a leader. And it's necessary . . . for the greater good. The same kind of thinking made me choose Tiny and Bobby-My-Boy to bring along when I busted out. They're not very smart—hell, let's face it, they ain't even normal!—and they don't give a damn about my Sacred Mission, but they're the sort of mean, ugly bad-asses that gets the local yokels' attention. You follow me?''

Matthew didn't answer.

''Of course, scum like them could never be leaders in my Army of Liberation. For that, I need bright young men with grit and brains and bone-deep patriotism. I need

someone to be my sword and my shield! My eyes and
my ears! Someone to take over, if I fall a martyr to the
cause . . . as I am likely to do. A prince regent is what I
need! And you know what, son? *You* just might be that
prince regent.'' He moved his hand across the space before him, as though envisioning the print on a big poster.
''Wanted: Prince Regent! Reasonable hours! Opportunities for travel and advancement! Dummies and yellow-
bellies and foreigners need not apply!'' His voice
dropped to an earnest register. ''You know why I chose
you?''

''No, sir.'' Matthew inched his bottom over, making
more space between them on the step.

''I chose you because we're the same sort, you and
me. I saw it in your eyes. You know what we are, kid?
We're damaged boys. Damaged boys! And if you damage a boy before his spirit has set strong, you end up
with one of two things, either a spineless slave that lets
the world trample him and smear his face in the mud, or
a dangerous Force of Nature with an unquenchable rage
boiling inside him! And when that rage is harnessed to
a noble cause . . . well, then you've got something awe-
inspiring and dreadful!'' He turned and looked into Matthew's eyes with searching solicitude. ''Who damaged
you, son? Me, I was damaged by my pa, then by a man
teacher, then by a warden in a home for boys. But I can't
be damaged no more. From now on, it'll be me who does
the damaging. So tell me, boy. Who damaged you? Was
it your pa?''

''I wasn't never damaged.''

''Now that's just pure bullshit, boy. You got damage
writ deep in your eyes! You're either going to end up
nothing at all in this world, or something awe-inspiring
bad! That's the way it is with us damaged boys. It's what
they call our Karma!'' He grinned and winked.

Matthew was glad for the chance to change the subject
that came when he looked past Lieder and saw the Rev-

erend Hibbard step off the tracks down at the end of
town, having walked back from the Surprise Lode after
preaching at the miners. Matthew snapped his fingers.
''Oh, there's one other person living in town. I plum
forgot about him.''

''Who's that?''

''A preacher name of Leroy Hibbard. He goes up to
the Lode every Sunday to give the miners a dose of brim-
stone. But he usually gets back before sundown on Monday.''

''A preacher, eh?''

''Well . . . not much of a preacher. He drinks whiskey,
then he reels down the street late at night, yammering on
about how he's a sinner and vile and worthless and all.
Mr. Stone agrees with him about his being worthless. He
says Reverend Hibbard ain't worth the powder to blow
him to—Hey, talk of the devil.''

Lieder grunted up from the step and stood awaiting
the approach of the preacher, the cup of his right hand
resting on the butt of the pistol stuffed into his belt.
''What'd you say his name was?'' he muttered out of the
side of his mouth.

''Hibbard.''

''Well now, if it ain't Reverend Hibbard!'' Lieder
greeted. ''As I live and breathe! Welcome home, Reverend! I've been keeping your flock safe for you!'' He
thrust out his hand, which the confused clergyman took
tentatively, only to have the bones of his clammy fingers
crushed in Lieder's strong grip. ''Now, here's what we're
going to do, you and me, Reverend. We're going to your
place and have a chin-wag, in the course of which you
can give me any guns you might have lying around. Who
knows? I might even suddenly feel a great urge to testify.''

Throughout the dusty six-hour walk back down from
the mine, Hibbard had been tormented by visions of the
back door of the Traveller's Welcome, where he habit-

ually bought his bottle from Jeff Calder, so he was reluctant to turn back and accompany the stranger up the street to the old depot. But Lieder's handclasp tightened painfully as he smiled into the Reverend's eyes and told him that if he didn't take him to his house—*right now!*—he'd likely get his kneecaps shot off and have to hobble around for the rest of his life, a useless cripple, and it would be on his own head "... for he who tempts a man to violence is *himself* guilty of that violence ... Paul to the Chippewas: 7, 13. I'm sure you're familiar with the passage."

Matthew sat on the steps, watching the two men go back up the rutted street toward the last embers of the sunset, Reverend Hibbard's thin, black-clad body followed by a snake of a shadow that slithered after him.

Matthew returned to the marshal's office and sat heavily on the edge of his bed, his eyes fixed on a crack in the floorboards as the gloom deepened around him. Some time later ... an hour, maybe more ... he emerged from the Other Place, blinked, and slowly stood up to take the shotgun down from above the door. Then he fished the canvas sack out from under his bed and spilled his treasures over his blanket, including the marshal's badge and the homemade shells. He broke the gun open and pushed in a shell. The tight fit scraped off a thin curl of the candle wax that sealed the shell. Argh! He shuddered with disgust as he snapped the curl of wax off his fingernail! He clawed the shell back out of the gun and threw it into the sack, as though it were something organic and loathsome, then he wiped his hands on his shirt to scrub off the feeling of the waxy shell.

When his heartbeat returned to normal, he tried to sort out his thoughts. In about an hour, he had to go to the Mercantile to meet with B. J. Stone and Mr. Kane. But first he'd better slip over to the boardinghouse to see if the Bjorkvist men were game to join them in fighting against these ... What the hell *were* they?

As he turned back from hanging the shotgun above the door, his eyes fell on the book Lieder had tossed aside.

He really hated the thought of a man like that reading the Ringo Kid books!

STANDING IN THE DEEP shadows close to the Bjorkvists' woodshed, Matthew could see through the screen door into the kitchen of the boardinghouse, where Kersti was working by lamplight, ladling stew out of a big iron pot on the stove into the bucket that she would carry over to the Traveller's Welcome to feed the usual residents and those three strangers. Mrs. Bjorkvist had prepared enough for her own family as well, but at the last minute she decided to send it all over to the hotel, so the strangers couldn't complain that there wasn't enough. And as for her son and husband? Well, they'd pretty much lost their appetites anyway, after what those men did to them.

Matthew crept up the back steps. "Kersti?" he whispered, his lips almost touching the screen.

She let out a half-stifled yelp of surprise. "What is wrong with you?! Scaring a body like that!"

"Sorry, but I—"

"I almost spilt the stew! There'd a been hell to pay!"

"Sh-h-h, keep your voice down, *please*. Come over to the door. I got to talk to you, but I don't want to step into the light, just in case one of them's wandering around."

Sniffing with annoyance, the girl carried three large tins of Beechnut brand peaches (extra-thick syrup) to the stone drain board and began opening them, working the can opener up and down with angry energy, her lips compressed in stubborn refusal to talk to him. He could see her clearly because she was on the lamp side of the screen; she could barely make him out because he was on the dark side. "Well?" she hiss-whispered, after he had stood there in silence for fully a minute. "What do you want?"

"The men that came here? Mr. Kane said he saw them leave carrying guns."

"That's right. They took all Pa's guns. Even Oskar's squirrel rifle."

"Did they get every last one? Wasn't your pa able to hide something from them?"

"*Hide* something! Are you crazy?"

"Sh-h-h."

She lowered her voice, but there remained a tense squeak of irritation in it as she hissed, "There wasn't no way my pa could of hid anything! Not hurt like he was."

"They hurt him?"

"The boss one, he said they had come to collect weapons to distribute to the heathen Chinee. Pa told him to get the hell out of here. And Oskar stood up beside Pa, like he was ready to fight. But the big one with the long arms and the puckered-up lips—you know the one I mean?"

"They call him Bobby-My-Boy."

"Well, he goes over to my pa and punches him in the stomach. Hard. Then he grabs both him and Oskar by their hair and he smashes their faces together. Three— four times! Then he lets go of them and they slump down and sit there on the floor with their noses bloody and their eyebrows cut. Then the boss tells my ma in a real sad voice how sorry he is that her menfolk needed to be done thataway, but she better give them all the guns in the house, because if he finds out that we've kept one back, then he'll get *real* mad. Well, you can bet Ma gave him every single gun. You can't blame her, can you?"

"No, but we sure could use a couple of guns."

"Who's *we?*"

"Well there's..." He almost named B. J. Stone and

Mr. Kane, but he thought better of it. "... you know, the folks that are getting together to fight these men."

"*Fight* them! Are you *crazy?*"

"Sh-h-h-h."

"Sh-h-h-h your own self! You can't stand up to men like that! You'll get us all killed! Ma says they only want the silver from the mine, and the smartest thing to do is just let them take it. It ain't our silver! It ain't no skin off'n our butts."

"But they're not just robbers. They're crazy. I got this terrible feeling, Kersti, that if we don't—"

"*You're* the one that's crazy! And there's no use you trying to talk Pa and Oskar into any crazy plan. They're busted up too bad. And Ma wouldn't let 'em anyway." She poured the last can into a tin pail, the slippery peach halves making clumpy splashes. "Now you get away from here, y'hear me? I don't want them men thinking any of us Bjorkvists are trying to do something against them, especially now that they've took Pa and Oskar up to the hotel."

"What?"

"They came and got them just a while ago."

Matthew was surprised that he hadn't seen them come out of the hotel and go down the street. Then he realized that it must have happened while he was sitting on the edge of his bed, off in the Other Place.

"If my ma knew what you was up to, you know what she'd do?" Kersti said. "She'd tell on you, hoping to get on the good side of those men, so's they wouldn't hurt Pa and Oskar no more."

"But Kersti, there ain't no good side to those men. They *like* hurting people. It's fun to them."

"Just so long as they don't hurt us Bjorkvists! So you just stay away from here! And stay away from *me!*"

Matthew closed his eyes and pressed his lips against the screen. "All right. I'll go." He moistened his lips, and he could taste the dirty-screen-door taste that sent him for an instant back to his childhood. "Kersti? You wouldn't tell those men that I been here trying to find guns, would you?"

"I don't have no reason to do you any favors, Matthew Dubchek. Not after the way you treated me."

"I know that, Kersti. And I'm real sorry if I hurt your feelings. But you won't tell I was here, will you?"

She threw the empty peach tins into the trash barrel, intentionally making a clatter that caused Matthew to wince and look around into the darkness. She stared hard at him. Then she sighed. "No, I won't tell. Now you just . . . just get out of here!"

―――――――――

"WAIT A MINUTE, MR. Stone. Let's take it one step at a time. We can't afford to make mistakes." Mr. Kane's voice was hushed but urgent: urgent because they had to make a decision soon; hushed because they had not dared to light a lamp, and the only people who speak loudly into the darkness are drunks and those who are afraid of being thought afraid.

"You're right," B. J. Stone said. "I was getting ahead of myself. It's just that we don't have much time."

A few minutes earlier, Matthew had slipped silently through the back door of the Mercantile and sat at one end of Mr. Kane's worktable with B. J. Stone and Mr. Kane to his left and right, facing one another. As his eyes adjusted to the dark, he could make out their profiles, lacquered at the edges by moonglow that came in the store windows, making greasy highlights along their brows and down their noses, and causing one eye of each to glow against the black shadows of the store's interior. Ruth Lillian sat opposite him, her back to the window. Her face was in shadow, but myriad minute granules of moonglow were captured in her copper hair. Dim re-

flected light made faint smears in her eyes when she
glanced from her father to Mr. Stone.

His sudden plunge from full moonlight to the absorb-
ent darkness of the store, the hushed tension in the voices
of these two one-eyed men discussing the menace brewing down in the hotel, Ruth Lillian sitting across from
him, faceless, her hair aglow—it all felt to Matthew like
some daydream place, some nightmare place. He had to
remind himself that this was really happening . . . was really happening . . . really hap—

"I realize we haven't much time, Mr. Stone. But we
must consider our options carefully," Mr. Kane said.
"You may think I'm too plodding and cautious, but . . ."
He lifted his shoulders in a tight shrug, a gesture that
revealed his origins as much as did his slight accent.

Although these two men had been residents of
Twenty-Mile almost from the town's chaotic beginnings,
they had never exchanged more than the utterances of
commerce and rote politenesses, but each had always recognized discernment and compassion in the other, and at
moments of intellectual loneliness, each had vaguely
wished that they had become friends.

"All right," Mr. Kane continued, his repressed voice
making his slightly dental final *t*'s more pronounced.
"Let's begin with what we know for sure. These men
have come to steal the silver shipment. Right?"

"Right. But of course they'll never get it. Not with
sixty miners coming in on the train, most of them
armed."

"Ah, but these men don't know about the miners."

"They do know. I told them."

"You told them?"

"Yes. I was trying to persuade them that it was no
use their staying in Twenty-Mile. But there's no reasoning with them. They're insane."

Mr. Kane recalled Lieder's pale, suddenly empty eyes
when he asked about his accent. "Yes, all right, let's

assume they're insane. What does that mean we should—What's that? What's going on?''

From the hotel across the street came male voices singing ''Rock of Ages'' in a hesitant, lurching way. But the voices strengthened as they repeated the first verse, then repeated it again, and again . . . stronger each time.

With the first note, B. J. had lifted his hand for silence as he leaned toward the sound. ''That's funny. There's four—no, five men's voices. Who's over there with them?''

''The Bjorkvists,'' Mr. Kane told him. ''And maybe others.'' He went on to say that he had seen two of the strangers pushing Mr. Bjorkvist and Oskar ahead of them up to the hotel. Their faces looked as though they'd been beaten.

Matthew nodded, wanting to lend support to this version of what had happened, without revealing that he'd been speaking to Kersti.

''But, why did they want them at the hotel?'' B. J. wondered aloud. ''And why in God's name are they singing?''

''I don't know,'' Mr. Kane said. ''Maybe they're drunk. Or maybe . . .'' His hands flapped.

The hymn abruptly stopped. Then came loud applause.

''Is it possible they're being *forced* to sing?'' B. J. asked. ''That leader has a twisted sense of humor.''

Mr. Kane digested this in silence before saying, ''It seems to me there are two possibilities open to us. We can either sit tight and hope things blow over, or we can embark on some kind of action. The risks involved with each course are obvious. The benefits . . . not so obvious.''

From the hotel came a gush of player-piano notes: a syrupy ballad, its long dragged-out notes sustained by octave-wide trilling. Matthew half-knew the song: something about a girl in a cage. The male voices were joined by a wobbly soprano. ''That's Queeny,'' Matthew said.

And when the others looked at him questioningly, he added, "She...ah...she used to be in show business."

B. J. turned to Mr. Kane. "I don't think we have the option of sitting tight and doing nothing. It's our bad luck that they came just after the miners went back up to the Lode. That means we'd have to hold out for six whole days."

"Too long," Mr. Kane agreed. "Much too long. So what do you suggest?"

"Well, I've concocted half a dozen plans, but they all come down to the same thing in the end. We have to band together to protect ourselves. And particularly to protect..." His lit eye disappeared as he glanced over at Ruth Lillian.

Mr. Kane nodded.

A burst of ribald laughter came from the hotel, and the player piano began "She's Only a Bird in a Gilded Cage" again, this time without the singing.

B. J. continued. "One possibility would be to barricade ourselves here in the Mercantile, or we could—"

"Why in here?" Mr. Kane asked.

"Because there's food here. And the gun you keep in case of robbers."

"Food yes. But no gun. I used to keep one behind the counter, but no longer. To tell you the truth, I'm afraid of them."

A long sigh escaped B. J. "Well, I'll admit that's a blow. I naturally assumed you had a gun under the counter or somewhere."

There was a flutter of laughter from across the street. Someone whistled a piercing note between his teeth. The player piano continued grinding out the soupy ballad.

"Well, maybe it's just as well that we don't try to hold out here, after all," B. J. said. "That would only draw their attention toward the Mercantile when—thank God—they don't yet know that Ruth Lillian exists. That leaves us only one way to go. We'll have to get the men of the town together and drive them out.''

''Kill them, you mean?''

''Mr. Kane, I'm not a violent man. And my pacifist principles are reinforced by a generous portion of cowardliness. But when you're dealing with men like that...''

''But if we face them down, *we're* the ones likely to get shot. After all, they have all the guns.''

''Not *all* the guns. The Bjorkvists have hunting rifles, and if they join us, we can—''

''No, sir,'' Matthew interrupted. ''The Bjorkvists don't have any guns. Those men came and took them. And they beat up Mr. Bjorkvist and Oskar. Bashed their faces together and broke their noses.''

''How do you know this?''

''I snuck over to talk to...them.'' His eyes flicked to Ruth Lillian and back. ''I was trying to find out what was happening. After getting beat up so bad, the Bjorkvists wouldn't dare do anything to make those men mad.''

''I see.'' There was a silence during which Matthew could hear the squeak-squirt of B. J. Stone swallowing. ''Well...!'' He sucked at his teeth. Then: ''All right. But that still leaves the people over at the Traveller's Welcome. Now, I know for a fact that Jeff Calder has his Civil War rifle. He waves it around when he's drunk and yammering on about what a hero he was. And surely Delanny packs some kind of gambler's weapon, a derringer, or a pepperbox. That's two guns. And it's possible that—What is it? What's wrong?''

Mr. Kane was shaking his head. ''What makes you believe they haven't taken Calder's and Delanny's weapons as well? And even if they haven't, what chance do you think a consumptive gambler and a one-legged old man would have against three insane killers armed to the teeth? I don't mean to belittle your—''

The player piano came to the end of its ballad with a

climax of two-fisted chords, then a woman's voice
snarled out a string of abuse the vituperous intent of
which could not be mistaken, even if the words were
smeared by her whiskey-thick tongue.

A harsh laugh.

A scream and a crash of glass that made the four sitting in the Mercantile catch their breaths.

The doors of the bar flapped against the sides of the
hotel.

Mr. Kane crossed to the window and looked obliquely
down the street to where lamplight spilled from the door
of the Traveller's Welcome. "My God, she's..." He
returned to the table and sat heavily. "They've stripped
her naked and thrown her out into the street."

"Who?"

"The old one."

"Queeny?"

Mr. Kane nodded.

From within the hotel the music-roll ballad began
again, and the drunken voices rose...*for her love was
so-o-o-old, for an o-o-old man's go-o-o-old*...

After a silence, Matthew felt he should try to take their
minds off Queeny lying out there, naked. "Ah...Mr.
Lieder came to see me over to the marshal's office a
couple of hours ago."

"What did he want?" B. J. asked.

"He was looking for guns. He talked a lot, but I
couldn't tell when he was joking and when he wasn't.
He said I reminded him of himself when he was a kid.
And he asked if I wanted to become one of his gang. He
said something about me being his sword and his shield
and his apostle—you know how he talks."

"And what did you say to him?"

"I didn't know *what* to say. I just sort of played
dumb."

"That's good," Mr. Kane said. "If he's taken a liking

to you, maybe he'll take you into his confidence, and we'll know what they're planning to—"

They all jumped convulsively at the sound of a gunshot from the hotel.

B. J. went to the window and peered down the street.

"What is it?" Mr. Kane hissed.

"She's all right. I was afraid they'd...But she's still there on the steps, her head hanging between her legs. Dead drunk, from the look of her." Then, in an optimistic tone meant for Ruth Lillian: "Chances are they were just shooting into the air. You know...making noise just for the sake of making noise."

Mr. Kane rubbed his fingertips across his forehead and closed his eyes. Then he said quietly, "What about poison?"

"Poison?" B. J. asked. "How would we poison them?"

"I don't know! The possibility just came to me. Matthew here will be making their breakfast tomorrow. Maybe...I don't know...something in the coffee or...?"

"But, Pa!" Ruth Lillian said. "That'd kill *everyone*. Mr. Delanny. The girls. Everyone!"

"But we've got to do *something!*" Mr. Kane stood up, knocking the table with his knee. "We can't just sit here while they—!" He grunted and grasped his left arm as though to pinch off the pain that swelled in his chest and streaked down to the elbow.

"*Pa!*"

"It's all right," he said between clenched teeth as he slumped back into his chair. "It's only..."

Ruth Lillian took her father's hand, and Matthew saw her slim fingers crumple under the strength of his grip. He knew it must hurt to have her knuckles crunched together like that, but she didn't make a sound.

Mr. Kane gasped twice, each time emitting a little chirp of nasal sound as he drew himself up tight in an effort to stay above the chest pain. Finally he let out a long wheezing sigh...gingerly, as if he were testing for a final stab of pain. Then... "It's passed," he whispered. "Thank God."

"You're all right?" B. J. Stone asked.

"Yes. Yes, I'm fine now. I'm...sorry." He released Ruth Lillian's hand and patted it, as though to soothe any pain he might have inflicted.

After a silence, B. J. said, "Well, at least there's one thing in our favor."

"Tell me," Mr. Kane said, forcing a smile. "I could use a little good news just now."

"They don't know about Coots. When they came, he was off bringing a string of donkeys up to the Lode. I expect him back early tomorrow morning."

"Does he have a gun, Coots?"

"Yes. He always carries his old flat-top Colt when he's on the trail. He's afraid of snakes. It's about the only thing in this world Coots is afraid of."

"So that's *two* things in our favor," Mr. Kane said. "We have Matthew on the inside...more or less. And tomorrow morning Coots will be coming back, and we'll have an armed man they don't even know about."

"They don't know about me either," Ruth Lillian said.

"Yes, and that's how we're going to keep it," her father responded sternly.

"But wait a minute!" Matthew said. "What if they see Coots coming down the trail? I mean, he doesn't know what's going on. He's got no reason to sneak into town."

"You're right," B. J. said, his stomach sinking at the realization that he had overlooked something so important. "I'll have to go up-trail before dawn and let him know what's going on."

"And if those men come looking for you and you're not at the Livery?" Mr. Kane asked.

"I'll go warn Coots," Ruth Lillian said simply.

"You'll do nothing of the—!"

"But, Pa! Who else can go? You've got to stay here in case they want something from the store. Matthew will be over making breakfast. And you just said Mr. Stone mustn't be away from the Livery."

"Listen to me. You are not leaving this—"

"She's right, you know," B. J. interrupted. "She could sneak out first thing in the morning and go up-trail to meet Coots. If I keep a lookout through my back window, I'll see them coming around Shinbone Cut about a quarter of an hour before they get to the meadow." B. J. had often watched for Coots's return so he could have a hot cup of coffee ready for him. "When they get down, they can slip—"

"I am not going to let my daughter run the risk of being caught by those—"

"Mr. Kane?" B. J. interrupted again. "Ruth Lillian is a smart girl. She won't take any foolish—"

"No," Mr. Kane said with finality. "No."

"Sir?" Matthew said. "What about if Ruth Lillian sneaks real careful behind the buildings and goes up to the Livery before dawn? Then at first light she could start up the trail, and when she meets Coots, she warns him to make his way down as quiet as he can. Then she could—"

"I will not have—"

"No, just a minute, sir. Then she could go on *up* the trail to the Surprise Lode, and she could tell the miners what's going on down here. That way she'd be out of town and safe, and Coots would be warned, and—"

"—and the miners could come down and surprise those men!" B. J. continued. "They could arm themselves to the teeth and take the train most of the way, then come the last mile or so down the track on foot, quietly . . . at night, maybe. That's it!"

Mr. Kane could see that this plan made sense, but he

was still reluctant to let Ruth Lillian run any risk. "Are you sure she can make it up the trail? I've never been higher than Twenty-Mile myself."

"It's steep and rough," B. J. admitted. "And when it rains it gets pretty treacherous. But so long as it's dry, she can make it." He turned to her. "You'll just have to take it easy. Don't push yourself. Expect to take a good nine, maybe ten hours getting up to the lode. Until the miners arrive, it'll be our job to make sure we don't give those madmen any reason to start hurting people. Well? Do you agree, Mr. Kane?"

Ruth Lillian touched her father's arm. After a brief internal struggle, he closed his eyes and nodded. "Yes, yes, anything that gets her out of town."

"Good," B. J. said. "Then tomorrow morning, after I see Ruth Lillian off up the trail, I'll keep a sharp lookout. And when I see Coots come around Shinbone Cut, I'll go over to the hotel and have a few words with the boss. I'll tell him he hasn't got a chance of getting the silver, and I'll say that—hell, I don't know what I'll say. I'll just make it up as I go along. But one way or another I'll make a diversion to give Coots a chance to get down to the Livery unnoticed. So! That's it. Now I guess we'd all better get some sleep. Make sure you wear something warm and rough tomorrow morning, young lady. Matthew? You'll have to do something about Queeny."

"Me? Ah...do what?"

"Well, we can't leave the poor old thing sitting out there, naked. Bring her to your place."

"But, I—"

"Ruth Lillian, can you find something for Matthew to put around her?"

"Sure." She took a Hudson Bay blanket down from the shelf. "Will this do?"

"That'll do fine," B. J. said. "Well, then!" He pushed his chair back. "Is there anything else we should talk about, Mr. Kane?"

"No, I think that's about it," Mr. Kane said. "And I don't mind telling you that I feel much, much more assured than I did a while ago."

Aware that Mr. Kane's false confidence was for Ruth Lillian's benefit, B. J. reached up and gripped the girl's forearm. "Are you all right?"

"Sure." But she had been shivering involuntarily.

"Not too scared?"

"No, sir. I'd say I was scared just about the right amount," she said with a faint smile. Then, more seriously, "Don't worry about me, Mr. Stone. I'll do what has to be done."

"There you go! Now, Matthew? You'd better get back to the marshal's office."

"But what about Queeny?"

"You should walk across to her from your place. I don't want you seen coming from here."

"Oh, I see. Sure."

"You'd better go to bed now," Mr. Kane said to his daughter.

"I won't be able to sleep."

"Maybe not, but you can keep out of sight."

"But, Pa . . ."

"Ruth Lillian!"

". . . All right, Pa."

"Now you two get going," B. J. said.

At the foot of the stairs, Ruth Lillian gave Matthew the blanket. In reaching for it, he found her hand and pressed it briefly. Then he left.

The two old men sat in the darkness, drained and sour-stomached, the aftermath of prolonged emotional tension. When Mr. Kane spoke, his voice was husky. "Do you really think we have a chance?"

"Oh, sure!"

"Hm-m. And even if you didn't think so, you'd pretend you did."

"Yes."

Mr. Kane nodded. "We're asking a lot of young Matthew. Giving him the dangerous task of spying on them."

"He's a bright kid."

"Oh, yes, he's bright. But there's something..." Mr. Kane lifted his shoulders and shook his head.

B. J. recalled the graphic description in that two-month-old *Nebraska Plainsman*. How much emotional elasticity could a boy have left, after finding his parents ...like that? He considered offering Matthew a chance to talk about what had happened. But what if making him remember unraveled the fabric of forgetfulness and fantasy that was holding the boy together? Well, he was too tired to make an intelligent decision tonight. He really should get back to the Livery and—

But Mr. Kane began speaking quietly into the dark, his gaze focused on the moon-glossed surface of his battered worktable.

"I told you I got rid of the gun I used to keep behind the counter because guns frighten me. Well, that's true, but also..." He shrugged, then he lightly rubbed his fingertips over the edge of the table worn smooth by years of doing his accounts there. B. J. sat patiently until Mr. Kane continued, "I was working. Right here at this table. It was late at night, and my wife was out visiting a sick friend. Oh, I knew there was no sick friend, but..." He puffed out a long sigh between slack lips. "I sat here with my account book open, trying to keep my mind occupied...trying not to imagine her...well! Then I heard him walking up the steps to the porch. The footsteps of a strong, confident man. You remember our town marshal?"

"Yes."

"A strong, confident man. Well, he came in and tossed his badge onto this table, and he said the town could have the job back. I didn't look up at him. He told me he was leaving because Twenty-Mile was a dying town. Then he added—almost incidentally—that he'd be taking my wife with him. Do you remember my wife, Mr. Stone?''

''Yes.''

''A beautiful woman.''

''Yes. Beautiful.''

''Much too young for me, of course, but . . . beautiful. Ruth Lillian is so much like her. Well, after he left, I sat for hours, here at this table. In my hand was the pistol I kept to scare robbers off. I had always thought I could never actually kill a living human being, but that night . . . that night I came within minutes of taking a life. If my little girl hadn't cried out in her sleep . . . if I hadn't considered what might become of her, alone in a place like Twenty-Mile . . . So I eased the hammer back down, and I got up and walked out into the night. It was almost dawn, still and cold, and I . . .'' He compressed his lips and shook himself. ''I walked across the railroad tracks to the edge of the cliff, and I . . . I threw that pistol as far as I could! You see, Mr. Stone, getting rid of the gun was the only way I could be sure my daughter wouldn't become an orphan the first night I felt swamped by loneliness and depression.'' He looked up and smiled thinly. ''Since that time, the Twenty-Mile Mercantile Emporium has not stocked guns. Not because I have any high-minded objection to violence. But only because, like I said, I'm afraid of them.''

B. J. let the silence soak into the darkness for a time. Then he nodded and stood up to leave.

Mr. Kane stood and shook his hand. ''Good night, Mr. Stone.''

''Good night, Mr. Kane.''

THE LOW-HANGING FULL moon drenched the street with a pale but penetrating light, so to keep out of sight of anyone watching from the hotel, Matthew passed behind the ruins of the Pair o' Dice Social Club on his way back to the marshal's office. Through a gap between two abandoned buildings, he glimpsed Queeny sitting on the steps of the hotel, naked in the moonlight, rocking herself in drunken misery.

He slipped in through the back door of the marshal's office, and took a moment to think out how he would deal with Queeny. He decided it would be best to go across the street boldly, so that if one of the men saw him, he could act irritated and say the noise and shouting had awakened him, and he'd come to see what the hell was going on. He lit his lamp and turned it up bright so no one could claim he was sneaking around in the dark, then he took the blanket Ruth Lillian had given him and was about to step out into the street when he remembered to pull his shirt out of his trousers and muss his hair up.

"Queeny?" he whispered hoarsely.

She half-sat, half-sprawled across the hotel steps, her flaccid, fish-belly–white legs splayed wide.

"Here. Put this around you." He draped the Hudson Bay blanket over her shoulders, looking aside to avoid seeing her glaucous flesh.

She shivered and drew the wool blanket around herself. "That wasn't no way for a gentleman to do," she muttered slushily. "No real gentleman would say those things to a lady!" Her right eye was almost closed with swelling.

"No, he surely wouldn't, Queeny." He tried to draw her to her feet, but she was too heavy, too limp. "It was mean and low-down of him to say those things," he said in the honeyed, agree-with-anything chant that his ma used to affect when his pa was drunk and balky. From somewhere in the lagan of his memory, he recalled a wet spot on the hearthstone where his pa had drooled while lying there in a stupor. "Come on now, Queeny. You got to help some. I can't heft you."

She heaved herself up and stood, unsteady. "Where

we going, honeybun?'' Her whiskey-sour breath and the smeared hint of coquetry in her voice tightened his throat.

He half-supported, half-herded her through the door of the marshal's office and over to his bed, onto which she collapsed as though her bones had suddenly melted. He cupped his hand over his lamp and blew it out. The sudden plunge into darkness seemed to alert the half-conscious Queeny, who rose up onto one elbow and said, ''...I told them I didn't want any more to drink, thank you kindly, but the big one with the kissy lips pushed me back onto the table and poured it down my throat! Down my...!'' She began to sob, great slobbery blubs shaking her body. ''Then they made me dance. Tore off my clothes and made me dance! With everyone looking. And laughing! That ain't no right way to do a lady, is it?''

''No, it surely ain't, Queeny. And I'm sorry.''

''O-o-o-o, are you, honeybun? Are you really and truly sorry?''

''You said *everyone* was looking at you.''

''And laughing. I used to be a real good dancer when I was on the stage. Light as a feather. Everybody used to clap and whistle and...But as a girl gets older...'' Lush, hot tears swamped her voice.

''Who was this *everyone* that was looking at you, Queeny?''

''...light as a feather, I was. Ask anyone. I used to dance the Dance of the Seven Veils. But, you see, honeybun, when a gal gets older, she gets a little...well, a little hefty. No use denying it.''

''I'll bet you were a real *fine* dancer, Queeny. Who'd you say was laughing at you?'' He imitated his ma's gentle persistence, when she was trying to pry a bit of information out of her drunken pa.

''All of them! They was *all* laughing! And passing remarks! That barber, old Peg-leg, the preacher, those no-'count Bjorkvists. And *drunk?* The boss, he made them

all down whiskey till they was stumblin' and giggling.
But that ain't no excuse for them to...Honeybun? Poor
old Queeny's just burning up with thirst. You got some
nice cold water for your poor old Queeny?''

Matthew dippered up a mugful from his water pail and
brought it to her. She sucked it down greedily, swallowing some air and coughing a spray back at him. ''But
that ain't no excuse, is it? Just 'cause they was drunk
ain't no excuse for passing remarks about a person being
...getting a little hef—hefty.''

He sat on the edge of the bed. ''What were all those
men doing in the hotel?''

''I just told you! They were laughing and passing remarks!'' And she began to blub again.

''Yes, but why did they come there in the first place?''

''He made them come!''

''Mr. Lieder?''

''Sure!''

''But why did he do that?''

''Don't ask me. I don't...I don't...'' She fell silent
and her breathing deepened.

''Queeny? Queeny! Tell me about Mr. Delanny.''

''Wha...? Huh?''

''When those strangers came into the hotel, didn't Mr.
Delanny do anything?''

''No, of course not! Mr. Delanny ain't the kind to
laugh and pass personal remarks about a lady. He's a
professional. Like me. Could you give old Queeny another little drink, honeybun? She's just *parched.*''

Matthew refilled the tin mug, returned to the bed, and
held it to her lips as she drank greedily. ''Queeny, you've
worked for Mr. Delanny for a long time. Tell me, does
he have a gun?''

''He's a real professional,'' she said hollowly into the
mug. ''Firm but fair...like me.''

''Yes, Queeny, but listen to me. Does...Mr...De-
lanny...have...a...gun?''

"Of course!" She threw the mug onto the floor. "I told you he was a professional! Can't you punks understand anything?"

He waited for her muddled fury to subside before asking patiently. "And what kind of gun does Mr. Delanny have?"

"A little teeny-tiny one. In his boot. A derringer with a little teeny-tiny barrel. No bigger'n a little boy's pecker." She giggled... and gagged. "Uh-oh! I'm afraid ...the cold water...makes the whiskey come back up. I'm afraid I'm going to..." She dropped back onto the pillow.

"Queeny?"

"I just got to sleep, honeybun," she slurred. "I really *got* to, or I'll be sick."

"Queeny? *Queeny?* Do you think Mr. Delanny will use his gun on those men who laughed and passed remarks on you?"

"No, I don't...wha...? Can...get up..."

"What?"

"He's...can't...chair..."

"Queeny?"

"He can't get up, I'm telling ya!"

"What? Why can't he get up?"

"They made him sit on a chair. And he don't dare get up. They won't even let him talk, and he—Oh, honeybun, I...I think I'm going to be sick. Why'd you make me drink that water?"

"You want to go outside to be sick?"

"Yeah, maybe I better. Help me up. Oh-oh. No, I... can't. I can't lift my head. I'm too..."

"You'll be all right, Queeny. Just sleep. You'll be just fine in the morning."

"Will I, honeybun? You think old Queeny's just fine, don't you? You wouldn't pass remarks about old Queeny, would you?"

"No, Queeny, I wouldn't pass remarks."

"O-o-o-o, ain't that sweet? I know you wouldn't pass remarks, 'cause you were good to your ma and helped her make...biscuits. I just...I can't...'' A short, moist snore, and she was asleep.

Matthew tucked the blanket up around her, then he sat in his chair in a dim shaft of waning moonlight. A sudden chill ran up his spine. He scrubbed his goose-bumpy arms. And took his canvas jacket down from its nail and put it on backwards, the collar under his chin to keep his throat warm. He scrunched down in the chair and decided he'd just sit there and wait for morning.

Well, maybe he'd rest his eyes, then come morning, he'd...

...He snapped awake, his heart beating and the base of his spine sore from the hard chair. The smell of whiskey and sweat from Queeny was thick in his throat, like the smell of his pa when he came home late and collapsed on the floor. That whiskey stench had somehow filtered into his nightmare about spongy red stuff...no, it was about his pa's face, all bloated with anger...no, about a roaring gun and...no, something about damaged boys and apostles and...no, he couldn't remember. The dream elements were rapidly dispersing and disguising themselves.

From down the street, came the sounds of laughter and splashing and shouting and...

...Splashing? He rose from his chair and, rubbing the base of his spine, went to the window. The moon had set, leaving the street matte black except for a dim glow of red-gold from behind Professor Murphy's Tonsorial Palace, where the wheezing old coal boiler was heating water. There came a loud whoop and another splash, then a snort, and a high-pitched yap. Someone had poured cold water on someone. Those men must be having baths in the wooden tubs out behind the barbershop. There was something weird, something repugnant about the thought of those men sitting up to their necks in wooden tubs of skin-scummy bathwater, splashing and horseplaying like kids in a swimming hole.

Matthew turned back from the window and decided to light his lamp and read until the clinging fragments of his nightmare withered and dropped away from his memory. He would seek calm in the uncomplicated, righteous world of Anthony Bradford Chumms, like he used to do when the sound of his parents fighting downstairs left his stomach all twisted.

So as not to waken Queeny, he drew the lucifer slowly along the bottom of his table until it hissed into a flat, puffing flame.

Just before dawn, his chin dropped into the collar of his jacket, and *The Ringo Kid Plays His Last Ace* slipped from his numb fingers into the pool of lamplight on the floor.

———————————

EARLIER THE PREVIOUS AFTERNOON, Mr. Delanny had been in the barroom playing two-hand solitaire with Frenchy when the three trail-stained strangers sauntered in. He had looked up, made an instantaneous evaluation, and told Jeff Calder to give them a drink. "One drink on the house, gentlemen, then I must ask you to be on your way."

Lieder blinked in a burlesque of befuddlement. "Well now, I am confused. The sign outside proclaims this to be the Traveller's Welcome. And here we are, three travelers on the weary road of life. But you don't seem to be offering us genuine and heartfelt welcome. How come that is, friend?"

Mr. Delanny arched a disdainful eyebrow and spoke in his tight, precise way. "This is a private hotel. I reserve the right to choose my clientele."

Lieder grinned. "Oh, I see. And we don't come up to snuff, is that it?"

"That is it exactly, friend. And furthermore—"

"Nope! No furthermore!" Still grinning, Lieder slipped his gun out of his belt and cocked it. "And *please* don't call me friend. Matter of fact, I don't think I want to hear another word from you of any kind. *Not one more word!* And you know why? Because I don't like your fancy shirt, nor your spindly wrists, nor your lily-white hands, nor your uppity-man-looking-down-upon-scum attitude. I purely hate it when people talk to me in a tone of voice! This place of yours ain't nothing but a low-class whorehouse. And you ain't nothing but a pimp. And I ain't going to take sass from any slimy clap-merchant. So here's what is going to happen. *Listen up!* You are going to sit right there in that chair and not say another word. Not...a...word! Because if you move your ass out of that chair, or if you so much as open your mouth just *one* time, I shall be obliged to punish you. And you had better believe that I am a most-vigorous and imaginative punisher. You understand what I'm saying to you? Just nod."

Mr. Delanny started to reply, but Lieder lifted his eyebrows and the barrel of his pistol warningly, so he lowered his eyes to the cards on the table.

"Now, that's more like it. You play your cards just right, and you might escape being punished. But to tell you the truth, Mr. Pimp, I don't think there's much chance of that. You remind me of somebody I loathe and detest. Someone who used to talk to me in a tone of voice. Hey! You, there! Stand up and step away from him, unless you want to share his punishment."

Frenchy's yellow eyes met Mr. Delanny's. He gestured with a lift of his chin for her to leave his table. She glanced at Lieder, then slowly rose from the table and moved back to against the wall, where she stood, her eyes on Lieder's face.

"You behind the bar! Peg-leg! Do you serve the drinks around here?"

Jeff Calder was caught swallowing nervously, so his voice squeaked when he said, "Yes, sir."

"Well then, get to serving!"

Jeff Calder reached down for glasses.

"Whoa there, old man! When your hands come up from under that bar, they better not have anything in them but a whiskey bottle. Or I'll blow your ass into next week, and that's a promise."

"I wasn't going to—"

"You keep any iron under there?"

"Just my old army rifle. But honest to God, I wasn't going to—"

"Tiny, you go upstairs and look around. Bring everybody down to join in the festivities. Bobby-My-Boy, I think you better take Peggy's old army rifle from him. Unless he objects, of course. Do you object, Peggy?"

"No, sir, I don't object."

"That's the kind of eager and cheerful cooperation I like to see. Where you keep your ammunition?"

"I ain't got but half a box. It's right here under the bar with the rifle."

"Get the ammunition too, Bobby-My-Boy." He slapped the bar top. "Now, let's have a little service here, Peggy! It's been a long time since last my followers was in a saloon."

After handing over his battered old rifle, balancing it on wide-splayed hands to show that he had no intention of trying anything, Jeff Calder set up three thick-bottomed glasses and started pouring rye, but he was shaking so hard that he chipped one of the glasses with the neck of the bottle. He reached under the bar for another glass, then froze and said, "Now, I'm just reaching down to get a glass, mister! That's all I'm doing! They ain't no other guns down there!"

"Calm yourself, friend. Just take it easy." Lieder's tone suggested that he was the only reasonable man in a panicked world. "You've got to learn to lean back and let things happen. Nobody's going to get hurt around here. Not so long as they do what they're told. And do it quickly. Don't you bother about getting another glass, Peggy. I can drink out of the broken one. I ain't no fragile dandy like that pimp sitting over there so nice and obedient. I've got what you call your 'common touch.' I'm a Man of the People, risen from the ranks of the downtrodden to—*Why you staring at me like that, woman? I don't need no dime-a-go nigger whore staring at me!*"

Frenchy let her heavy-lidded gaze linger on him for a moment before dragging it lazily away to look out the window. For the rest of the evening she kept the scarred side of her face toward Lieder, in part as a punishment, and in part to deter any appetites he might develop.

As Tiny and Bobby-My-Boy slapped back their drinks, Lieder held his glass of rye up to the light, but he didn't drink. "You know what I'll bet you're wondering, Peggy?"

"I ain't wondering anything! Honest!"

"I'll bet you're wondering why I let your boss sit in that chair of his own accord, rather than tie him down to make sure he doesn't move."

"It ain't none of my affair, sir," Jeff Calder said.

"Are you telling me you don't want to know?"

"No, no, I'd be glad to know. I just meant...well, you know...I ain't one to poke my nose into other people's business."

"Well, since you're so eager to learn, I'll tell you. I spent some time in an institution for wayward boys, where there was this warden. And every time this warden he talked to me, he used a tone of voice—just like our pimp over there. When a kid acted up, this warden would have him brought to his office and tied into a chair that faced the corner, like a dunce stool in school—Hey, pour out another round here, Peggy! And have one yourself! Hell, it's on the house! This warden, he earned my respect, because he knew how to punish. He *really* knew how to punish. I found that out when the guards caught me being high-spirited like any normal American boy, and they brought me into the warden's office. He smiled at me and waved his hand toward the chair. I sidled over and sat down, smiling and sassy, the way a kid has to be to show the world he can take anything they can dish out. The guards came over to tie me into the chair, but the warden said no. 'No, don't tie young Master Lieder. I'm going to trust him to sit right there until nightfall of his own free will. There'll be no ropes to bind him. But to bolster Master Lieder's willpower, I'll give it a little support. If he says one word, or moves so much as a hair, I shall chastise him. Oh, and there's one other thing. Master Lieder. There won't be any going to the toilet.' And he went back to doing his desk work while the guards sat by the door, grinning because they'd seen this punishment before. So I sat there facing the corner. And the time went by. And I could hear the scratch of the warden's pen on paper. But before long I had to piss something fierce. That was when it dawned on me that the real punishment wasn't being made to sit in the corner. It was being made to piss yourself, like a little baby, with guards looking on and snickering. Now pissing yourself because you're tied to a chair and can't do anything else is bad enough, but to piss yourself when you aren't bound by anything other than the warden's warning not to move...that's *humiliating*. Well, finally I couldn't stand it no longer, so I whipped it out and started to piss on the wall. And the guards grabbed me and pinned me against the wall with my pecker still hanging out, and this warden came over to me with a ruler in his hand, shaking his head sadly and saying, hadn't he asked Master Lieder nicely to sit in that chair and not move a muscle? And hadn't he been kind enough not to tie Master Lieder to the chair? And look how Master Lieder had disappointed him. And he brought that ruler down on the head of my pecker! Hard! Five times! He counted them out! And his face was all puffed up and purple with rage, and with a kind of . . . joy! After a while, he got control of himself and calmed down. He told me to tidy up my clothing, and not just stand there revealing myself like that. He had the guards put me back in the chair, and he told me that if I moved again from that chair, it would be ten strokes with the ruler, and *I'd* have to count them out. I sat there. And do you wonder if my pecker hurt? It *hurt!* All the way up to my belly, it hurt. But the funny thing was, I didn't have to piss anymore. That warden had scared the piss out of me. *Scared the piss right out of me!*'' And Lieder roared with laughter.

Tiny laughed so hard he had to slap the bar until his palm stung to stop, and Jeff Calder laughed along, shaking his head and wiping his eyes with his knuckle as he forced out a string of breathy, high-pitched he-he-he's.

When Lieder's laughter subsided, he turned to Mr. Delanny, mirth still damp in his eyes, and said, ''I don't intend to take a ruler to you, Mr. Pimp, because that's a degrading thing to do to a person. If you disobey me by talking or getting up from that chair, I'll just . . . shoot you. You see, I have chosen you to be my Example Nigger, so the town will know what a dangerous and stupid thing it would be to cross me. You probably wonder why I have selected you for this honor. Well, fact is I'm not exactly sure. I think it's the way you talked to me. I really hate people to use a tone of voice on me.''

Mr. Delanny looked up, heavy lidded, from the solitaire he had begun defiantly to lay out, then he returned his attention to his cards. His glance had been intentionally slow and indifferent, and his hands were steady, but Frenchy was uneasy, because he failed to put the red nine on the black ten, and Delanny never missed a play.

His amused eyes never leaving Mr. Delanny, Lieder asked Jeff Calder, ''What's your boss's name?''

''Mr. Delanny, sir.''

''Delanny, eh? I like to know a man's name. Gives

you something to hang your hate on. Doesn't it bother you, Peggy, to work for a slimy pimp who talks to weary travelers in a tone of voice?''

Jeff Calder showed his teeth in an uncertain attempt at a smile.

"Yes, Mr. Delanny acts all refined and superior. But he won't be refined and superior for long, because sooner or later the need to piss will rise within him, as it must for all men born of woman. And that's when we'll find out what Mr. Delanny is made of. Either he will just sit there and piss his pants like a little baby, in which case he won't seem nearly so refined and superior. Or he will try to get up from that chair to relieve himself, in which case he will be dead, because I've promised to shoot him if he moves, and I'm a man of my word. It'll be interesting to see which path he chooses, don't you think?''

As Jeff Calder swallowed, the sound of a door slamming upstairs was followed by a slurred snarl from Queeny, as she and Chinky were herded down the stairs by Bobby-My-Boy, the Chinese girl wearing only a camisole and her everyday cotton knee-length culottes, Queeny in a frayed old wrap, her orange, gray-rooted hair a tangled nest over her sleep-puffed eyes. They had been sleeping late after yesterday's work.

"You took your own sweet time rounding these holes up!" Lieder accused. Then in a "naughty, naughty!" tone, he said, "Bobby-My-Boy? Have you been sampling the merchandise? Fess up, now!''

Tiny laughed and slapped the bar, and Jeff Calder snickered, while Bobby-My-Boy protested petulantly that he hadn't done nothing!

"Well, just so's you don't try to get a head start on your friends." Lieder turned to Jeff Calder. "You got any sarsaparilla back there, Peggy?''

"No, sir. There's a couple old bottles of birch beer, but I don't know if they're still good. They been around a spell."

"Pour me out one and we'll test 'er. You see, I don't drink anything hard, 'cause I don't need drink to get my blood churning. It's *always* churning."

Calder wiped the dust off one of the bottles, snapped up its wire-clamp seal, and poured some into a glass.

Lieder sipped cautiously, then pursed his lips and narrowed his eyes like a connoisseur. "Well now, that ain't *half*-bad. I'm more partial to sarsaparilla, but this'll do." Then with one of those sudden shifts of topic designed to keep the other person off balance, he said, "So tell me, old timer. Where did you leave your leg?"

"Ah...I lost it in the Battle of the Wilderness," Jeff Calder said.

"Ah! A veteran of the South's struggle for its constitutional right to self-de-ter-min-a-tion!" His voice swung from syllable to syllable in the manner of a tent revivalist. "The bankers and mill-owners of the North told the stupid Yankee cannon fodder they were fighting to free the slaves. Free the slaves, my butt! The owners of those cotton mills didn't give a shit for slaves, neither black field slaves nor white wage slaves! They just wanted to keep the South from deciding its own destiny. Free the slaves to do *what?* To wander the countryside hungry and out of work? To swagger drunk down the street, pushing white women into the gutter? Did they free black women so they could end up in low-class whorehouses— like Miss Slashy-face yonder—selling their ass to all comers? *Free the slaves!*"

Jeff Calder saw no reason to mention that he had fought in blue, or that he had left the army informally on the eve of the great battle, slipping into an empty boxcar of a departing supply train. It was an accident in the switching yard that had cost him his leg.

"What do they call you, bartender?"

"Name's Jeff Calder....Sir."

"Well, Mr. Calder, fill those glasses to the brim! And don't forget the ladies. We want them in a generous and frolicsome mood for their night's labors. Drink up, ladies and gentlemen! Let our rejoicing be unbounded!'' But when the rye bottle approached his glass, he put his hand over it and scowled, and Calder quickly refilled it with birch beer.

For several minutes Frenchy had been concentrating on Mr. Delanny with all her might, trying to project from her mind to his the image of the over-and-under derringer he kept in his boot. She knew he couldn't take out three men with a two-shot derringer, but at least he could act like a man and—! Delanny looked up from his cards, having felt Frenchy's concentration on him. She stared at his boot and slightly lifted her chin in an effort to tell him to *use it. Use it!* She was sure he understood, but he pursed his lips and lowered his eyes with a ghost of a shrug, and she realized that he was going to accept his humiliation. Just as greed for a few more years of life, however empty and dull, had caused him to stay in this dead town for the sake of its clean mountain air, so he would swallow the indignity of sitting in cowed silence in his own barroom. And when he could hold it no longer, would he just sit there and piss himself? Or would he take his chance? She thought she knew. She turned and looked out the window, feeling pity for him but also, for the first time, contempt.

With the approach of evening, Lieder decided to meander down the street "to get the lay of the land." He crossed over to the marshal's office and had a long talk with Matthew, during which he told him that if he played his cards right, he might become one of his army, maybe even his prince regent. Then Reverend Hibbard returned from preaching up at the Surprise Lode, so he walked him down to the old depot to collect the pistol he kept in his bedside table beneath his Bible.

Kersti kicked open the hotel's kitchen door and heeled it shut behind her. As her hands were occupied with two cast-iron pots, one full of stew and the other containing beans with salt pork and onions, she had to duck under the sodden underwear the girls had hung up on lines looping around the kitchen. Annoyed at getting some drips down her neck, she banged the pots onto the stove just as Jeff Calder scuttled in. "Here's your grub," she said curtly. "Ma says there's plenty for all." The two of them began to dish up the food.

"Never mind the high-and-mighty Mr. Delanny," Lieder said from the doorway, having returned from collecting the Reverend's gun. "He won't be dining this evening. He's far too refined and uppity to eat with us riffraff. And anyway, the poor fella appears to have lost his appetite. He just sits in his chair, pouting. You're the girl from over to the boardinghouse, ain't you? What's your name, darlin'?"

"Kersti Bjorkvist," she said sullenly, not pausing in ladling out the stew onto tin plates.

"Well now, just look at you, Kersti Bjorkvist! My, but you are one healthy piece of girl-meat, and that's no lie! You're no decorative bit of fluff. No, sir! You're built for long wear and rough use. *Look* at those shoulders, will you? And those hips! You are destined to bear children easily, girl. You'll just grunt 'em out in the morning and be back digging in the fields by afternoon. And it looks like you won't have much trouble feeding them either. But Lord love us, Kersti my darling, for all your big udders and that fine thatch of straw hair, you are the *plainest* thing these weary eyes have seen in a long, long time! Were you hiding behind the door when the angels was dishing out the looks? But hey, don't you worry about it. Ugly ain't as bad as dirty, and neither one is as bad as having the clap. Matter of fact, ugly can be thought of as a gift from God, 'cause it makes it easier for a girl to maintain her virtue!"

Tightening her jaw, but refusing to look at Lieder, Kersti told Jeff Calder that she'd want the pots back after they'd eaten. Her ma'd need them for tomorrow's noon meal. Then she left, slapping the wet laundry out of her way and banging the door behind her.

Lieder laughed and went back into the barroom just as Professor Murphy, having slept all day, entered through the bat-winged front doors for his supper. At the sight of the strangers, he froze, still holding the doors open.

"I'll bet a shiny new silver dollar against a kick in the ass that this is the famous Professor Murphy!" Lieder strode toward him, his hand outstretched. "Come right in, Professor! Make yourself to home! I've been informed that you eat your meals here at the hotel, and I've been looking forward to your company." He squeezed the barber's soft, hesitant hand and drew him to the bar. "But first things first. I see you ain't wearing a gun. But surely you keep a gun somewhere in your shop? For protection against mean and vicious people?" He grinned. "... Like me, for instance?"

Murphy blinked and looked over at Mr. Delanny, who was folding his linen handkerchief to hide the smear of red he had spat into it. Frenchy was leaning against the wall, watching him from beneath half-closed eyelids; and two rough-looking strangers, one big and one little, were sitting at a table with Queeny, who was downing a glass of rye and wiping her mouth with the back of her hand, while Chinky was turning her head from side to side to avoid the whiskey Bobby-My-Boy was trying to force on her. Murphy's worried eyes returned to Lieder just as Jeff Calder came in from the kitchen, carrying two steaming tin plates.

"Set 'em right over here, Mr. Calder," Lieder said. "The professor and me'll eat at the bar. Excuse me, Professor Murphy? I didn't quite hear you. Was that 'thanks a lot' you said?"

"Ah ... thank you ..."

"You're entirely welcome, I assure you! And those guns you keep to protect yourself from us mean and vicious people? Just exactly where are they?''

"I . . . ain't got but one. An old double-action Colt.''

"Now, don't you feel bad about having only one gun
to offer. It's the spirit of the gift that matters. Tiny, go
over to the barbershop and gather up Mr. Murphy's do-
nation. Where'd you say it was, Professor?''

"Ah . . . it's . . . under my pillow.''

"O-oh, now! That is a dangerous place to keep a gun!
Say you was having a nightmare, and there you are,
pounding at your pillow, trying to fight off some monster,
and all of a sudden *bang!* and you got an extra eye right
in the middle of your forehead. Tiny, are you going to
stand there gawking like a stupid moonberry, or are you
going to get that gun?''

Tiny left through the bat-winged doors.

"Give us that food while it's hot, Peggy. Tell me,
Professor Murphy, just what are you a professor *of?*''

"Oh, it's . . . you know. Barbers always call themselves professor . . . it's just . . .''

"Ho-no-ra-ry,'' Lieder pronounced. "It's what they
call a ho-no-ra-ry title. Murphy. Now, that's an Irish
name, ain't it?''

"Ah . . . yes?''

"Dig in! Eat up, Professor! Down the hatch! And I
suppose your folks came to this country to escape the
potato famine?''

"Ah . . . well . . .''

"And why not, for crying out loud? All the riffraff
and scum from the old world comes swooping down on
America to gorge themselves on the richness produced
by the sweat of my forefathers, so why shouldn't the Irish
join the feast? The more the merrier, I say! Get your
snouts into the trough!'' As though accepting his own
invitation, Lieder began to down the food on his tin plate,
gripping his spoon in his fist like a child, and talking
while he ate. "You've heard of the Statue of Liberty,
Professor Murphy? It sits out there in New York Harbor,

a beacon for the world's garbage to come gobble up this beautiful land's bounty! Well why not, eh? Why the hell not? Streets paved with gold! You can say what you want about niggers, but they ain't as bad as the immigrants. It ain't their fault they're over here, loafing and stealing and raping our women. It's our own selves that's to blame. We brought them here and we made them breed for the auction block, and now we got to pay the price of our folly.'' He choked on the food he was shoveling in, but as soon as he regained his breath, he pursued, ''And what does Washington D.C. do to protect native-born Americans from these European locusts? Not a goddamned thing, that's what! Come on over, they say! Just push your way up to the trough! And do you know *why* the government wants all them immigrants over here? You ought to know, if you're a professor, but I can see you don't have the slightest idea, so I'll tell you. It's so's the rich factory owners will have cheaper labor than they can get from real Americans. But don't you worry, Professor. The immigrants ain't going to get this country without a fight. Fate has brought me to this town, where there's silver a-plenty to buy arms for my American Freedom Militia, and we shall battle against the plague of immigrants come to infest this blessed land. Hey! Eat and drink, everybody! We are celebrating the Second American Revolution!''

Tiny had no sooner returned with Professor Murphy's revolver than Lieder announced that he would be pleased to have that preacher Hibbard join their celebrations. ''And fetch along those men down at the boardinghouse. Take Bobby-My-Boy with you.''

''But I ain't ate yet!''

''Well shovel it down! Then go fetch our neighbors for a night of joy and ju-bil-a-tion. I'd a hell of a lot rather have them in here drinking and singing than out there skulking around in the dark, plotting to do me hurt!''

While Bobby-My-Boy gulped down his meal, Tiny

asked if they should bring in the Bjorkvist women, too.

"No, let's just have a stag party. Only men and whores."

"What about that kid? And the old fart at the Livery? And the one over to the store?"

"Don't mess with the kid. He's all right. He's got grit. As for the old farts? No danger there. One of them ain't got guts enough to pull a trigger, and the other's nothing but an old Jew, sitting there counting his coins and having fantasies about white women."

MR. BJORKVIST AND OSKAR stumbled in through the bat-winged bar doors under the impetus of a shove from Bobby-My-Boy. They stared around, cowed and frightened, but Lieder greeted them robustly, telling them they were in for a rare old good time with plenty of singing and drinking and all-purpose hell-raising.

When, a short time later, Reverend Hibbard was projected into the barroom, the neck of his black alpaca coat up to his throat in result of having been hustled down the street by the back of his collar, the Bjorkvist men had already brought in the weathered loafers' bench from the hotel porch and were sitting on it sheepishly, their hands folded in their laps, one with a split left eyebrow and the other with a split right one in result of having had their faces clapped together like cymbals. Lieder beckoned Reverend Hibbard and Professor Murphy to join the Bjorkvists on his "deacons' bench." "Now! To loosen things up, I'm going to offer you some spirituous refreshment, and you are going to drink it right down. Peggy?"

"Sir?" Jeff Calder stood to arthritic attention. For some reason, he had escaped inclusion among the townsfolk to be browbeaten and terrorized, and he had no intention of jeopardizing this advantageous position.

"Bring glasses and a bottle of rye for my deacons

here, and fill those glasses up to the rim! Let the spirits flow so that the spirit may rise! Mr. Delanny doesn't mind if we drink up his rye, do you, Mr. Delanny?''

Without responding, Mr. Delanny snapped a card from the pack and placed it on top of another. Only Frenchy was close enough to see his hand tremble.

''Down the hatch, boys! Bottoms up!''

The four ''deacons'' drained their glasses of raw rye, but tears stood in Oskar Bjorkvist's eyes, and his Adam's apple worked hard to keep it down.

''Fill 'em up again, Peggy! Can't you see that my deacons are still thirsty?''

The second glasses went down with difficulty for everyone except Reverend Hibbard, who had often struggled with Demon Rum at close quarters. But even he had trouble draining the third.

''Five glasses is our target, gentlemen. Two more to go! Tell you what, let's make a game of it. Anyone who can't finish his five glasses will have to pay a penalty. Now, what would be an interesting penalty? Hey, I got it! Whoever doesn't finish his five glasses, Bobby-My-Boy gets to cornhole him while the rest of us look on. And you better believe that Bobby-My-Boy will do a first-class job of reaming you. Back in prison, he used to break in all the new young prisoners, and it was truly wonderful to hear those boys yelp and whimper, and to see the tears of gratitude standing in their eyes.'' Lieder grinned. ''So I guess it's bottoms up, boys!...one way or t'other.''

Tiny and Bobby-My-Boy burst out in moist nasal plosions of laughter.

Downing five brimful glasses of rye in quick succession left the ''deacons'' slack-mouthed and gray-skinned, and young Oskar could breathe only in shallow oral pants.

''Now then, gentlemen!'' Lieder announced, assuming the role of master of ceremonies. ''Let us begin our evening's fellowship by raising our voices in what has always been one of my favorites, and I hope is one of yours: 'Rock of Ages.' '' He raised his hands to lead the choir. ''And let's put some feeling into it, shall we? Ready? *And...*''

After a thin, ragged beginning, the hymn increased in volume, if not in melodic refinement, because each of the deacons wanted to be heard contributing his share under the forceful conducting of Lieder, whose florid gestures and rapt facial expression were mocking imitations of the choir leader at his parents' strict fundamentalist church, where he used to get whipped for daydreaming when he should have been devoting his attention to the words of the Redeemer. The Bjorkvists didn't know this English hymn, but they mouthed and muttered their way along. Professor Murphy only knew the words to the first verse, which he repeated with such dogged determination that the Reverend was forced to follow his lead. At the fourth verse (actually, the first verse sung for the fourth time), Tiny felt inspired to lead Queeny out onto the floor to dance to the lugubrious rhythm. He was still wrestling her around when Lieder brought the hymn to an end with a theatrical gesture and turned to bow, his arms spread wide as he harvested the applause to which everyone contributed fulsomely, except Frenchy and Delanny, who exchanged hooded glances, and Chinky, who didn't understand what was going on.

It was this singing and applause that had caused the four sitting in the dark, across the street in the Mercantile, to wonder what was going on over in the Traveller's Welcome.

As he made his way back to his table, drawing the thoroughly drunk Queeny along by her wrist, Tiny passed behind the deacons' bench. He snatched off Mr. Murphy's wig and with this trophy he crowned Bobby-My-Boy, who let it remain there, cocked forward over one eye, as he continued trying to force whiskey on Chinky, but she turned her face from side to side to avoid drinking from the glass that clicked against her teeth. Lieder advanced on the table and asked what was wrong. Did this yellow-skinned sperm-spittoon think she was too high-and-mighty to drink with one of his apostles? Without raising her eyes, Chinky answered in a voice so low that she was obliged to repeat twice that she didn't like whiskey. It made her sick. "O-o-o-h, now that's too bad," Lieder said in a tone dripping with compassion. "She doesn't *like* whiskey! Well, now." He turned and announced to the assembly that once his American Freedom Militia had crushed the combined forces of the immigrants and the Wall Street barons, freedom of choice would become a basic constitutional right...even for slanty-eyed spunk buckets. And, by God, he was going to grant her freedom of choice right now! "Peggy, bring us a glass. Tiny, I want you to fill this glass with piss." When Tiny had accomplished this task, the wincing barber being obliged to hold the receptacle while straining his face away in an effort to avoid the effects of Tiny's unsteady aim—this to the general amusement of his fellow deacons—Lieder set the glass of cloudy liquid beside Chinky's glass of clear whiskey and said, "There you are, my dear. You're free to choose which one you drink. But you are *going* to drink one of them, you hear me?"

She gagged down the whiskey. Then a second glass. And a third.

While the fourth glass was being filled, she suddenly rose and stumbled out through the kitchen into the back yard, where she vomited onto the railroad tracks. The deacons' bench rocked with laughter; the loudest was Reverend Hibbard, who had by then thoroughly drowned the demon within him.

When Chinky returned, pale and fragile, her vulnerability must have touched some cord of feeling within Bobby-My-Boy, for he grasped her wrist and led her back into the kitchen, where he bent her over the drain board and used her, as she twisted her neck to keep her face out of the dirty water. When he was done, he called for Tiny, who came and took his turn.

They brought her back into the bar, and she slumped into her chair, where she sat shivering, her eyes riveted to the tabletop, while beside her Queeny smiled with dazed, slack-lipped benevolence upon the world.

Eager to provide fun for his guests, Lieder's eyes next settled on Frenchy, who glared back with narrowed menace. He snorted derisively, but nevertheless he decided to choose Queeny for their further amusement. "Does that player piano yonder work?" he asked.

"Sure does!" Jeff Calder said eagerly. "But somebody's got to pump the pedals. I'd be glad to do it, but what with me having only one leg, the piano only plays every other note!" He cackled at his oft-repeated joke and looked around for appreciation.

"Then you pump the pedals for us, Professor. Unless being bald hampers a man's pumping, too."

Murphy sat at the ornate if battered player piano. "What do you want to hear?"

"What you offering?"

"Well..." He reached into one of the storage slots. "...ah...what about 'Silver Threads Among the Gold'?"

"Well now, ain't that a coincidence? Silver! Like the silver that comes down your railroad track every week. I take that to be a good omen. But it's a rotten song all the same. What else you got?"

"Ah...here's 'There'll Be a Hot Time in the Ol' Town Tonight.' The Rough Riders' song. No? Well, let's see...ah...here's 'She's Only a Bird in a Gilded Cage.' "

"There you go! Something sentimental to soften our hearts and mist our eyes. You thread that on and start pumping. And you, old woman! You'll sing for us. Together we shall make a joyful noise unto the Lord...as

Paul enjoined us to do in Seminoles: 7:13.''

"Me?" Queeny pressed splayed fingers against her chest. "You want *me* to sing? Well, I ain't no Jenny Lind, but when I was a young girl on the stage—"

"That must have been a fair piece back," Lieder interrupted. "Judging from appearances, I'd guess you were already well past your prime when you were selling ass to the pharaoh's soldiers! Now start singing! And, deacons? I want you to accompany her!"

The choir members struggled to find a compromise key. *She's only a bird . . . beautiful sight . . . gilded bird . . . in a gilded cage, a byoo—tee—ful sight to see-e-e-e . . .* Their combined volume was topped by Queeny's wobbly soprano. . . . *for her love was so-o-o-o-old! For an o-o-o-ol' man's go-o-o-old, she's a bird in a gilded—*

"Whoa!" Lieder shouted, and there was sudden silence. "Now *that*, ladies and gentlemen." He shook his head and laughed helplessly. "That, folks, is what I would call . . . *terrible!* And I can't permit myself to embarrass an old woman any further by making her sing when she's got a voice that would shatter a spittoon at fifty yards. So instead, I'll tell you what. You can *dance* for us, grandma. Tiny, give her some more whiskey. And to make it more interesting, grandma, I think I'm going to have you dance . . . naked. I cannot *wait* to see all that tallow a-wobbling and a-jiggling! A sight to make a man swear off woman-meat forever! Gentlemen of the choir! Give this little lady a big welcoming hand! Professor Murphy? Music, if you please."

The choir applauded, and Jeff Calder put two fingers into his mouth and whistled an ear-splitting note.

"Take it off!"

"Let's see what you got!"

Queeny's pudgy fingers hesitated at the ties of her wrap. Drunk though she was, she was loath to reveal the not-excessively-clean underwear she wore during the week, when there were no customers. But Tiny overcame her show of reluctance by ripping the wrap off her, snatching her drawers down, and pushing her out onto the dance floor. Her feet got tangled in her drawers, and she stumbled against Bobby-My-Boy, who pushed her back into the center of the room, where she stood beneath the big overhead oil lamp, her crossed arms scooping in her breasts, her drawers puddled around one ankle. Professor Murphy pumped away at the player piano, his head glistening with sweat, and she began to shuffle from foot to foot, at first awkwardly, miserably, ashamed of her age and weight. But . . . but every eye was on her! She was the focus of all attention! She was on stage again! A sultry grimace creased her cheeks as the whiskey transported her back to happier times. Responding to her public's whistles and slurred suggestions, she began a grotesque imitation of her old Dance of the Seven Veils, using her hands to conceal, then coyly reveal, tantalizing glimpses of her bulbous nipples and her shaggy pudenda. Rivulets of sweat lacquered the rolls of fat beneath her underarms. Her pendulous breasts swayed and jiggled. Each time a pelvic bump made her audience hoot and whistle, she shook a finger at them, and her mouth made an o-o-o of naughty admonition.

Show business!

Only slowly . . . and with growing bewilderment . . . did she become aware that they weren't cheering. They were saying cruel, wounding things about her body. Why, they were passing personal *remarks!*

Queeny stopped jiggling from foot to foot and stood beneath the big kerosene lamp, sobbing into the hands that now concealed only her face. The ballad ended with a crescendo of chords; the piano roll flapped within the mechanism; and the room was silent.

Suddenly Queeny's head snapped up, and her eyes flashed within their tear-smeared sockets. A string of snarled abuse poured out of her. She called them every nasty thing that came to mind, while tears worked their way down her cheeks to the corners of her mouth, and the overhead light caught patches of slippery wet on her naked flesh.

Lieder laughed and told Tiny to pour the old gal a drink. She'd earned it! But Queeny snatched the bottle from Tiny and hurled it at Lieder, who ducked as it shattered against the wall near his head. His eyes suddenly emptied, and his lips curled back from his teeth. "Get your fat ass out of here before I kill you," he snarled. "*Get out!*" Then his voice dropped to a tense, breathy timbre. "And if you come back, old lady, I'll arrange a little romantic encounter between you and a broken bottle. It'll be a night of love you'll *never* forget. Bobby-My-Boy, stop grinning and show the lady out."

Bobby-My-Boy grabbed Queeny by her hair, slapped her face, and propelled her through the bar doors, which flapped against the walls as she stumbled out into the darkness and fell to her knees, skinning them on the rough boardwalk. She tried to stand, but whiskey sloshed through her senses, and she sprawled across the steps.

Across the street in the darkened Mercantile, Mr. Kane crossed to the window and looked down the street to where lamplight spilled from the door of the Traveller's Welcome. "My God, she's—" He returned to the table and sat heavily. "They've stripped her naked and thrown her out into the street."

In the Traveller's Welcome, Lieder stood beneath the big oil lamp, his eyes lost in the shadow of his brows. He searched the faces of the silent deacons, seeking the slightest sign of amusement at his having been obliged to duck the bottle. There was none. "Everybody sing! Pump that goddamned piano, Curly! Fill up those glasses, Peggy!" He punctuated his orders by pulling out his pistol and firing into the ceiling, which caused Mr. Delanny to twitch and crimp the card he was laying out. Notes gushed from the player piano, lush and syrupy, and everyone sang, heads thrown back, mouths open wide.

. . . for her love was so-o-o-old, for an o-o-old man's go-o-o-old. . . .

After obliging them to down two more glasses of rye "for the road," Lieder escorted his guests out. "And mind you get plenty of sleep, 'cause we'll be fetching you tomorrow night for more jollity and fellowship. Whoa, there, Professor. I want you to stoke up your boiler and fill us three tubs. Up to the brim and steaming!"

"Tonight?" The bleary-eyed, nauseated barber looked wistfully after his fellow deacons, who were stumbling home along the moonlit street.

"Yes, tonight! We ain't none of us had an all-over bath since I don't know when. And do you wonder if we're going to have a wallow? We're going to have a *long, long* wallow. And I want that water hot enough to melt the marrow out of our bones!" He told Tiny to collect their "arsenal" and take it over to the barbershop, so they could keep an eye on it while they were soaking in their tubs. "We mustn't leave temptation in the way of these good people. They're too weak to fight against it. Ain't that right, Mr. Delanny?"

Delanny did not look at him.

"Of course we all know the urge to do something brave and dangerous isn't very strong amongst pimps, but just to be on the safe side . . . Peggy, you go cut some of that clothesline in the kitchen and tie Mr. Delanny into his chair." He walked to the table on which Mr. Delanny was laying out solitaire with ostentatious lassitude. "I don't think Mr. Tone-of-Voice would mind being tied into his chair . . . just to help strengthen his resolve to be a coward. What do you say, Peggy?"

"No, sir. I mean . . . yes, sir." To cover his confusion, Jeff Calder went quickly into the kitchen, where he snatched down the wet underwear and cut off a length of clothesline.

"And I'd cinch that rope down real tight if I was you,

Peggy," Lieder said, "because if I come back from my bath and find this pimp's got away..." He let the bartender imagine the consequences.

Calder snatched the rope tight and tied it off. Delanny smiled thinly to cover the pain in his skinned wrists.

As she looked from the window to Lieder's face, Frenchy's glance fell to Delanny's right boot. If the chance came to get at his gun...

Tiny returned from carrying the "arsenal" over to the barbershop, where he left Bobby-My-Boy guarding it. "You know what I saw?" he asked Lieder.

"What?"

"That kid was helping the old whore into his place, the one who tried to bash you with that bottle."

"Let him be. He's just what you call your good Samaritan. Generous to a fault. He's like me in that way. Now, I want you ladies to take off your shoes and give them to Tiny. That's so you won't take it into your heads to run off up to the mine or down to Destiny." Frenchy kicked off her shoes as Tiny approached her, but he had to twist the shoes off Chinky's unresisting feet.

"Go upstairs and collect *all* the shoes," Lieder said. "We'll stuff 'em into the barber's boiler to help heat up our bathwater. That way they'll serve a useful purpose."

As Tiny disappeared up the stairs, Lieder looked at Frenchy, who returned his gaze with her eyebrows arched over half-closed eyes. "What do they call you, girl?"

When she didn't answer, Jeff Calder volunteered, "Frenchy's her name."

"Frenchy, eh? I suppose that means you used to sell ass down New Orleans way, right?" Frenchy didn't answer. Lieder smiled and shook his head. "You have got real sassy eyes, girl. *Real* sassy. But I'll get you. Don't worry, Frenchy. I'll get you. That's a promise." He grinned, then he turned, to Jeff Calder. "Peggy, I'm putting you in charge of these good people. You can handle that responsibility, can't you?"

Calder squared his narrow shoulders. "Yes, sir."

"And to show how much I trust you, I'm going to leave your army rifle and one round...so you can enforce your will on these folk. But..." He held up his finger. "But if anything goes wrong while I'm off enjoying my nice long bath, guess who I'm going to gutshoot first."

Jeff Calder swallowed.

Lieder nodded, "That's right." He left the barroom.

A moment later, Tiny came clumping down the stairs carrying a pillow slip lumpy with shoes.

The bat-winged doors were still oscillating behind him when Frenchy stepped toward Mr. Delanny to get...

Lieder pushed the doors open again and stood on the threshold, smiling and shaking his head. "Did you *really* think I was just going to leave like that, girl? Come on now! I've known all along that Delanny probably had some sort of sneak-gun up his sleeve or in his boot. His kind usually do. I've been watching him out of the corner of my eye, wondering if he'd go for it. But I was pretty sure he wouldn't have the guts to draw down on me. But you, girl...? O-o-oh, you're a different kettle of fish. Peggy, go find Mr. Delanny's gun. Feel around until you come up with it. Yes indeed, you are a different kettle of fish altogether. You're the sort that could do a man real harm—and I don't just mean by giving him the clap or scaring him to death with that ugly face of yours." He accepted the over-and-under derringer that Calder had found in a small holster stitched into the lining of Mr. Delanny's boot. "Well now, look at this. A .41 Remington double. Isn't that just the kind of shooter you'd expect a pimp to pack? A healthy man can piss further'n that thing can shoot, but its slug starts tumbling as soon as it leaves that dinky barrel, so it can tear an awful hole in a fella. Tell me the truth, Frenchy. When you thought I'd left you within reach of your pimp's gun, didn't a little thrill of hope tingle down deep in that black heart of yours? Come on, fess up! And when you saw me walk back in here, didn't that black heart just shrivel up? Admit it! Your hopes were lifted, then they were crushed. That's what they call the Torture of Hope, and it's the worst torture of all, because tantalizing hope keeps you from taking the easy way out and killing yourself. It's hope that holds your face down in the mud. It's hope that keeps you nailed to the cross. It's hope that turns the knife in the wound.'' He shook a finger at her and said in a singsong tone, ''I *told* you I'd get you, Frenchy. I told you.'' He left to have his bath.

———————————

MATTHEW JOLTED AWAKE, HIS heart beating, the base of his spine sore from the hard chair. The whiskey stench coming from Queeny had filtered into his nightmare about some spongy red stuff...no, it was about his pa's face, all bloated with anger...no, about a roaring gun and...no, something about damaged boys and apostles and...no, he couldn't remember. The dream elements were rapidly dispersing and disguising themselves.

From out in the street came the sounds of laughter and splashing and shouting and...

...Splashing?

He heard a loud whoop and another splash, then a snort, then a high-pitched yap. Someone had poured cold water on someone. Those men must be having baths in the wooden tubs behind the barbershop. And there was something repugnant about the thought of those men sitting up to their necks in wooden tubs of skin-scummy bathwater, splashing and horseplaying like kids in a swimming hole.

Matthew decided to read until the clinging fragments of his nightmare withered and dropped from his mind. So as not to waken Queeny, he drew the lucifer slowly along the bottom of his table until it hissed into a flat, puffing flame, then he lit his lamp.

Just before dawn, his chin dropped into the collar of his jacket, and *The Ringo Kid Plays His Last Ace* slipped from his numb fingers into the pool of lamplight on the floor.

———————

HE WOKE TO FIND his book on the floor, but the pool of lamplight had been diluted by, then absorbed into, the wan light of dawn seeping in through the window. He blew the lamp out and dragged his fingers through his hair, then he tiptoed out to avoid waking Queeny. It was not until he was standing in the chill of the empty street that he realized his jacket was still on backward. As he was taking it off and putting it on right, he noticed that the spreading dawn light was strange ... greenish and oily. And there was a dirty smell to the unnaturally still air. Back in Nebraska those signs would have meant that a big storm was on its way in. But the sky was bell-clear and the far foothills were gold-crusted by the first rays of an autumn sunrise. If there was a storm brewing, it was hidden behind the mountain that loomed over Twenty-Mile. He thought of Ruth Lillian, who must have gone up to the Livery before dawn, then started climbing the trail toward Coots as soon as it was light enough to find her footing. He could picture B. J. at his back window, watching for Coots to appear around Shinbone Cut, a pot of coffee simmering on the stove to greet him.

He eased open the back door of the hotel kitchen and crept across to peek into the barroom. Tiny, Bobby-My-Boy, and Chinky were not there. Upstairs, probably. Frenchy was sitting at a table by the wall, her head down on her arms. Mr. Delanny was near her, his back to Matthew, but there was something strange in his stiff, awkward posture. Lieder was in a chair tipped back against the wall, facing the bat-winged doors, a rifle cradled across his lap. Matthew could only see his profile, but his chin was down on his chest, and his breathing was deep and regular.

If only Coots was here right now with his pistol. He could get the drop on him and ...!

But Coots wasn't there, so Matthew tiptoed back into the kitchen to light the stove and begin making breakfast, doing everything as quietly as he could, but each little unavoidable noise he made caused him to pull in his neck and suck air through bared teeth.

After carefully sliding the first batch of biscuits into the oven, Matthew sliced bacon and put it into a big two-handled frying pan on the middling-warm part of the stove, then he filled the tin pot with water, dumped in a good handful of coffee, and put it on the hot center ring. When the first batch of biscuits was done, he put them under the warming hood and started a second.

"Hey there!"

Matthew gasped and almost dropped the bag of flour he was pouring into the mixing bowl.

"Colder'n a witch's tit this morning!" Lieder said from the doorway to the barroom.

"I thought you were asleep!"

"I *never* sleep, boy. Just quick little catnaps. I don't seem to need sleep, like ordinary men do. And I never drink liquor. I require neither rest nor stimulation."

"I don't like liquor either," Matthew said. "Just the smell makes me want to urp."

"Speaking of stuff to make a body urp, *please* don't tell me you dipped your wick into that old whore I threw into the street last night! You can do better'n that, boy! Hell, even Old Lady Fist is better than that sorry old worn-out hole. And a hell of a lot cleaner, too."

The coffee boiled over, sending drops hissing and dancing over the surface of the Dayton Imperial. Matthew grabbed up a rag and dragged the big pot over to the edge of the stove. "You want a cup, sir?"

"A cup of coffee'd go down real good on a cold morning like this. The air smells like there's a storm brewing."

Matthew poured and passed it over, and Lieder sat down on the kitchen steps and took a noisy sip. Matthew put a couple of biscuits onto a plate along with an open tin of corn syrup and set them on the step beside Lieder, then he returned to mixing up the second batch of biscuits.

"So!" Lieder said, warming his hands on the speckled enamel cup. "You say you didn't ream old... whatshername?"

"No. I just brought her to my place so she wouldn't have to sit out in the cold."

"There you go! I *told* them you were just doing a good deed and not meaning to go against me. I admire kindness more than any other quality... except for patriotism. The only reason I threw that old hole out into the street was because I could see right off that she was nothing but dregs." Lieder dunked a biscuit into his coffee. "And I don't let my apostles accept dregs. You want to know why?" He held the dripping biscuit up and ate half of it from beneath to catch the drips.

"Why?"

"Because once a man starts accepting dregs, that's all he ever gets. For the rest of his life, it's nothing but dregs and leftovers that other people don't want! Shoot, even Tiny and Bobby-My-Boy didn't want to stick that jiggling pile of lard! And they've been inside so long that they'll stick 'most anything that's warm... even one another! Now ain't *that* a picture to gag a maggot!" He laughed and finished his biscuit.

Matthew concentrated intensely on dropping spoonfuls of biscuit dough onto the tray.

"Lord, that bacon smells *good!*" Lieder continued. "I been smelling it for a quarter of an hour, and do you wonder if my mouth's been watering? It's been *watering*.''

Matthew slid the second tray of biscuits into the oven and closed it. ''You really think you've been awake since I started the bacon?''

''Like I told you, boy. I don't need sleep like an ordinary man.''

Matthew shrugged.

''I ain't lying to you, boy!''

''I didn't say you're lying, but people sometimes think they're awake when they ain't.''

''I was awake! Don't you contradict—I heard you come into the kitchen, pussyfooting it. Then you stood at the door, looking around the barroom.''

''But...how could you see me? You had your back to me.''

''I can *feel* when people are looking at me. It's a gift been bestowed on me as a sign of favor. A kind of armor to protect me against my enemies so's I can fulfil my mission. Shoot, I can even see through closed eyes! You don't believe me, but it's true! Sometimes when I'm reading late at night, I get so sleepy that I can't keep my eyes open, but I still read. Right through my closed eyelids! I spend a lot of time on one page, that's true, but I'm reading! I'm reading!'' His eyes softened, and his tone shifted to one of gentle wonder. ''Did you ever notice how a mess of bacon frying sounds like rain on a tin roof?''

''No, sir,'' Matthew said, his mouth suddenly dry, because if this man could see through closed eyes, it was a good thing Coots *hadn't* been standing there with him in the doorway of the barroom.

''Me, I notice things. Like how bacon frying sounds like rain on a tin roof. Poetic things like that. It don't hurt a man to be sensitive to the beauties around him.''

''Have you thought about what you're going to do, sir?''

"What do you mean, *do?*"

"When the train comes and you find yourself facing all those miners."

Lieder leaned back on his elbows and blew out a long jet of breath. "Yeah, I been giving it some thought. And I've decided that maybe those miners ain't a threat. Maybe they're an opportunity."

"Opportunity?"

"I'll talk to them. Tell them about what's happening to this country of ours. Chances are they'll want to join my cause! Something brought me to Twenty-Mile. Maybe it was the opportunity to enlist those miners into my militia. Hey, wait a minute. Those miners are of Aryan blood, ain't they?"

"What's that?"

"People who come from healthy northern European stock. You can tell just by looking. Those Mediterraneans, they're mostly small and dark and shifty-eyed. And those slavs, they're mostly flat-faced, and their nostrils point right at you, like a shotgun."

"I don't know what kind of people the miners are. Just *people.*"

"There ain't any Chinee among 'em, is there?"

"Not as I've seen."

"That's good, 'cause The Warrior has prophesied that the Chinaman is this nation's final enemy. The Yellow Peril. There's *millions* of them over there, all waiting to come swarming over in search of white women, 'cause they've killed so many of their own girl babies to keep from having to feed them that they're running out of women. Did you know that Chinamen cripple their girls by binding up their feet, so's they can't run away when they're raping them? It's true! And rich old Chinamen pay big money to have rhinoceros and tigers killed so's they can eat the horns and balls to make their withered old peckers strong enough to screw a few more times before they die. And if there's anything this poor old world doesn't need, it's more goddamned Chinamen! Well! Let's get to that breakfast!'' Lieder turned back into the barroom and shouted, ''Everyone up! Breakfast!'' He pounded on the bar with the flat of his hand. ''Everyone awake! Reveille! Reveille! Up and out!''

Mr. Delanny's neck muscles twitched with each shout, but he did not turn toward Lieder. Frenchy shuddered and lifted her head from her arms, blinking as though uncertain of where she was. Then she saw Mr. Delanny tied to his chair, and she knew that her bad dreams had not been dreams.

Lieder went to the bottom of the stairs and shouted up in the taunting, brassy tones of a sergeant who enjoys tearing men from the temporary haven of sleep. ''All right, men, get down here! Breakfast! Breakfast! The last one down gets nothing to eat!''

Jeff Calder crawled stiffly out from behind the bar, where he had bedded down on the floor, dead drunk. He was suffering from a hangover so bad that the roots of his hair hurt.

When Matthew came in from the kitchen carrying the coffee pot, its hot handle swathed in a rag, and a bouquet of tin cups threaded through the fingers of his other hand, Tiny and Bobby-My-Boy were coming down the stairs, their eyelids raw and sticky and their slept-in clothes smelling of sweat, whiskey, and sex. Tiny drew Chinky behind him by her wrist, like a pull toy. She followed numbly, barefooted and shivering in her chemisette and pantaloons. Her face was ashen and her mouth puffy and bruised. They had used her often and roughly during the night.

''Well, looky there!'' Lieder said. ''The blushing bride and her two tuckered-out bridegrooms. Now, ain't that a picture?''

After refilling Lieder's cup, Matthew served the table where Chinky sat between Tiny and Bobby-My-Boy. She didn't lift her eyes when he set her cup before her, so he

pushed it toward her and said, "Here you go, Miss
Chinky. It'll do you good." She didn't respond. Dropping Jeff Calder's cup off on the counter, he served Frenchy, who drew a long, thirsty sip off the surface of the
coffee, despite its heat. It was not until he turned to serve
Mr. Delanny that he saw what a terrible state he was in.
Because his arms were tied to the arms of his chair he
had been unable to use his handkerchief throughout the
night, and there were crusts of blood on his chin and
down his usually snow-white frilled shirtfront. His fingers were fat and purple because, in his eagerness to
show himself obedient and willing, Jeff Calder had
cinched the rope up as tightly as he could. Matthew could
feel how those blood-bloated fingers must have throbbed
with pain before they became numb, and he empatheti-
cally splayed his own fingers wide apart as he said, "I
could hold the cup for you, Mr. Delanny. Or maybe
you'd like a glass of water?"

"No, Mr. Pimp here won't be having any coffee this
morning," Lieder said from his chair tipped back against
the wall. "He's doing penance for having overindulged
himself last night. Not with whiskey like my choir members did. Drunk as pigs, they were! A disgrace to the
good name of Twenty-Mile! No, Mr. Delanny overindulged himself in sassy uppityness and snotty-nosed
finer-than-thou-ness. But I'll grant him one thing. He sure
can hold his piss. Lord-love-us; his bladder must be
stretched tighter'n a virgin's hole! I am impressed. Mr.
Delanny. Truly impressed."

Matthew couldn't help glancing down. In fact, Mr.
Delanny had not been able to hold his piss. When he
looked up, Mr. Delanny's eyes caught his and held them
in an intense glare that dared him to say a word.

Matthew gave Mr. Delanny a little helpless shrug and
went back into the kitchen. After he had distributed plates
of bacon and biscuits, he returned to Mr. Delanny's chair
and used a wet cloth from his tray to wipe away the scabs

of blood on his mouth and chin. The muscles of Mr. Delanny's chin worked, and his mouth tightened to a thin line. He stared at Matthew, his eyes almost spitting hate at this witness to his helplessness and humiliation. He started to say something, but he coughed and began to raise blood, so Matthew held the rag to his lips, looking away so as not to embarrass him. His glance intersected Frenchy's. Her yellow eyes were brittle, and her jaw was set tight. Matthew wondered if she had seen the dark stain of piss. He hoped not.

"Hey! *Hey!* What do you think you're doing there, boy?" Lieder asked.

"I'm tending to Mr. Delanny," Matthew said quietly.

"Did I say you could do that?"

"No, sir, you didn't." He continued wiping away the water-softened scabs of blood.

Lieder scowled at Matthew. Tiny nudged Bobby-My-Boy in anticipation. After a silence charged with menace, Lieder said, "Well . . . you just get on with it, boy. You have my permission to follow your Christian impulses. Caring about other people is one of the differences between natural-born Americans and these immigrants that don't give a frog's fart about nobody but themselves and their own spawn. But be careful, boy, less'n they take advantage of your kindness."

Bobby-My-Boy and Tiny were disappointed . . . and jealous.

Lieder turned to them and spoke with mock gruffness. "Now I hope you two treated your bride with the same Christian charity that this boy is showing toward our sassy-mouthed pimp."

They blinked in confusion.

"What I mean is, I hope you gave her plenty of opportunities to turn her other cheek."

After a moment of baffled incomprehension, they both spluttered with biscuit-clogged laughter. *Turn her other cheek!*

His eyes glittering with pleasure at the effect of his wit, Lieder dipped a biscuit into the bowl of corn syrup and turned it back and forth adroitly until the syrup had coated most of the surface before putting it whole into his mouth. Chewing and swallowing around his words, he explained for Matthew's benefit, "Now me? I seldom require the pleasures of the flesh. I save my strength for the crusade I have been chosen to lead. But I am a mere mortal, a son of man, and I admit that I sometimes feel a powerful urge for that spiritual relief that only a chunk of poontang can bring. But I would never, *never* permit myself to use that Chinee or that nigger gal." He washed down the biscuit with the last of his coffee and held out his cup for Matthew to refill. "I could never be a party to the mongrel mixing of the races. Did you ever see a dog mount a cat? Of course not! And why? 'Cause the mixing of races is both unnatural and unholy. Don't you agree, Mr. Delanny?"

The gambler didn't respond.

"No, boy," Lieder continued, "I would never let my good American seed fall upon alien ground, but pretty soon I'm going to have to let it fall *somewhere*. What I'm looking for is a beautiful young virgin to serve as a vessel for my seed. Upon her body I shall produce a manchild to complete my work on this earth, and she will be accounted blessed among women. But in the meantime..." He cocked a mischievous eye and grinned as Matthew felt a wave of relief that Ruth Lillian was safely out of town. "...while I'm waiting for my virgin vessel, I sure could use a piece of standard, all-purpose poontang. It's been a long, *long* time! And it ain't healthy for a man to go dry too long 'cause all that pent-up sap clogs his mind and messes up his thinking. I've been considering that Swede girl that brings the food from the boardinghouse. Now, she ain't no oil painting, that's for damn sure, but she's got nice thick hair to get your fingers into, and big udders to rest your weary head on. All in all, I believe she'd make pretty fair utility-grade poon-tang. Tell me, boy, have you ever stuck that Swede girl? What's she like?''

Matthew shrugged his shoulders and muttered nega-tively as he busied himself with filling cups around.

"Yes, I better look into that. Just a little something to hold me over until Fate delivers unto me the immaculate virgin destined to carry my seed. Hey, how about some more biscuits? Come on, everybody! Eat, drink, and make merry. Hey, wouldn't it be funny if that Chink's name was Mary? Eh? Eh?''

"You already cracked that one,'' Tiny said.

Lieder wheeled on him. "Don't tell me what I already cracked and what I ain't! Don't you ever do that again! *You hear me?''*

Matthew was washing dishes in the kitchen when Frenchy slipped in without a word and took a drying rag to help. He began to speak to her, but she shook her head curtly, so he continued swishing the cold water with the wooden-handled wire basket filled with left-over slivers of soap. Frenchy reached through the meager froth he had raised and drew out the slim boning knife he had used to slice the bacon. She slipped it into the waistband of her camisole, then settled her yellow eyes on him with icy calm. He didn't say a word.

From the barroom, they heard Lieder's voice. "Well, as I live and breathe! The schoolmaster's come to pay his respects!''

Matthew followed Frenchy into the barroom, feeling a quickening excitement because B. J.'s arrival meant that he had spotted Coots coming around Shinbone Cut, and had come to occupy Lieder's attention while Coots worked his way down to the donkey meadow.

Lieder was sitting with his chair tipped back against the wall, smiling brightly at B. J., who stood in the door-way, holding the bat-winged doors open. "Come on in, schoolmaster! Boy, fetch our guest a cup of coffee.''

"I don't want any coffee," B. J. said curtly.

"Well, if you haven't come to be neighborly, then to what do I owe the honor of your august presence? Or maybe I should put it this way—what the hell you want?"

Tiny and Bobby-My-Boy grinned to their gums. Ain't he a card, though!

"I've come to talk a little sense into you."

"Have you, now? Well, so long as it's only a *little* sense, go ahead. Give her a try."

"There's no way in the world you're going to get that silver."

"And who's going to stop me? You? That Jew store-keeper? Everybody else in town seems happy to have me here. I bring color into their drab lives."

"But sixty armed miners might slow you down some. And the train doesn't come down until Saturday. That's five days away."

"I'm a patient man. And if I get bored, well, don't you worry. I'll find something to amuse myself."

"But why just sit here for five days, when you know perfectly well that the law's on your trail and has probably found that prospector by now? You could get down the track to Destiny in half a day."

"Half a day, eh? I see. So you're advising us to walk down the railroad track, right into the arms of a whole townful of men with guns." He rocked back on the legs of his chair and looked up at the ceiling, as though he were giving this option serious consideration. "Well now, I suppose we *might* do that. On the other hand, we might just stay right here having our meals served regular, drinking free whiskey from Mr. Delanny's hospi-tality, and ripping off a chunk of poontang whenever we feel the urge. Gee Whitakers, it's hard to choose between getting shot by a whole townful of angry men, and sitting around here loafing and having fun. Tell me, schoolmaster. Which would *you* choose, if you were in my place?''

Something occurred to B. J. for the first time. "How do you see the silver that's coming on that train? The silver you mean to finance your 'struggle' with?"

"How do I see it?"

"Are you envisioning bars of silver? Bags of coins? Well, it's nothing like that. It's just ore. Ore that's been crushed and dressed for smelting down in Destiny. There's no treasure of silver for you on that train. There's only sixty miners with guns."

The darkening of Lieder's face revealed his disappointment at learning that his treasure of precious metal was just...crushed rock! He glared at B. J. as his mind ransacked the possibilities. "All right! All right! But... but maybe the treasure I seek is the miners themselves! Eh? You didn't think about that, did you, schoolteacher? No! Maybe I'll talk to those miners. Make them see the Light and the Way. And they'll join me in driving the foreigners back to where they came from!"

"And if you can't convince them?"

"Well, then...then there'll be one hell of a battle! It'll be Armageddon with spurs on! Just picture it! On one side, there's me and my apostles, the defenders of everything that made these United States great. And on the other side, those miners of yours, men who make their livings raping this country of ours, ripping the gold and silver out of her womb to line the pockets of Wall Street bankers! If I win, I get a whole trainload of silver ore!"

"And if you lose?"

"Lose? Lose? Well then...just think of the stories they'll tell about me! And the songs they'll sing! They'll be slapping up three-color posters about my martyrdom from Maine to California! Generations yet unborn will glorify my struggle against a corrupt government!" His eyes narrowed, and he asked, "You're a book man, Mr.

Stone. What do you know about a book called *The Revelation of the Forbidden Truth*?''

''Never heard of it.''

''No? Well, *The Revelation of the Forbidden Truth* was written by a man who only dared call himself The Warrior, because The International Conspiracy was trying to assassinate him for turning the spotlight of truth onto their plans. He had to print his book privately because all the publishers are in on The Conspiracy. And clever? He even misspelled some words to throw his enemies off the track by making them think his book was nothing but ignorant trash. By the time I'd read half a dozen pages I knew—I could feel in the marrow of my bones—that this book had been *destined* to come into my hands. I read it till the words flowed in my blood and echoed in my brain. It wasn't always easy to understand what The Warrior was trying to tell me. There were mysteries. Some things didn't seem to make sense although I read them over and over. But then one night...one night I was lying on the floor of my prison cell, reading by the light that came in under the door, and suddenly ...there was this...'' His voice softened with awe. ''...it was like a blaze of blue light in my brain! All at once I understood everything. *Everything.* I saw how The International Conspiracy was jealous because America has become the greatest Aryan nation on earth, and so they've all gotten together to destroy us, not by facing us on the battlefield! No! They're too cowardly for that! Instead, they're sending the scum of their gutters and ghettos to weaken our national spirit, to dilute our pure stock with their diseased blood! With every immigrant those countries send, they grow stronger and richer by ridding themselves of their vermin, while we grow weaker and poorer with every one we take! You see how it works? You see how it works?''

B. J. closed his eyes and shook his head, as though in pity.

"*The Revelation of the Forbidden Truth* tells how the majority of stupid, trusting Americans have never even *heard* of The International Conspiracy, because all the newspapers are being blackmailed and don't dare print the truth. Why, most Americans don't even know that the pope in Rome has given instructions to the Irish and the Jews and the Mexicans and all the rest of them, ordering them to breed hard and fast. Multiply! And do you wonder if they're out there multiplying? They're *multiplying*. Pretty soon they'll outnumber us, and they'll vote one of their own kind to become president of these United States! Think of *that!* White Protestant Americans will find themselves in the minority because we're being *outfucked!*"

Bobby-My-Boy and Tiny exchanged appreciative nudges. They loved it when Lieder was in a preaching frenzy like this, the words just *gushing* from him like music.

B. J. Stone controlled his impulse to walk away from this rancorous blend of hatred and ignorance, but it was his task to hold Lieder's attention while Coots got into town, so he continued to argue, "But everyone in America is an immigrant, even the Indians, if you go back far enough."

"Oh, that old song! 'We're *all* immigrants! We're *all* immigrants!' That's what The Conspiracy wants us to believe, but it ain't true. Our forefathers were *colonists*, not immigrants! And there's a world of difference between a colonist and an immigrant. The Warrior explains how colonists came to clear the forests and seed the wide prairies. They mingled their blood and sweat with the rich earth to create the greatest nation on earth. But the immigrants? They come to reap what we have planted. To prey on hard-working men! To steal our jobs by working for nigger wages. To drive us out of business by conniving amongst themselves and underbidding us. They attach themselves like leeches to the breast of our country and suck all the goodness out of her. The Warrior gives the example of the Jews. You listen up, boy,'' he said, glancing sharply at Matthew, who was making himself small beside the kitchen door. ''You listen up, because you got to know about these things if you're going to be my apostle.'' He turned back to B. J. ''Tell me something, schoolmaster. How many Jew farmers have you met? How many Jew miners? Or Jew fishermen? Or Jew lumberjacks? *None*, that's how many! And why? Because miners and farmers and fishermen and lumberjacks, they *create* the wealth of the nation. But the Jews are here to *feed* on that wealth! Now I have to admit that before reading *The Revelation of the Forbidden Truth* I had lived man and boy without ever noticing that simple fact.''

''Simple?'' B. J. said. ''Simple-minded, you mean. All this 'international conspiracy' is nonsense! It's a fiction created by the envious and the lazy to justify their failures. It would be laughable if it weren't so pitiably ignorant. And dangerous.''

''You better believe it's dangerous!'' Lieder snarled, rising to stand face to face with B. J. ''Dangerous to all enemies of my country!'' He drew back his fist, and B. J. raised his elbow to protect himself.

Lieder laughed. ''Still all mouth and no balls, eh? But we know that, don't we? Otherwise, you would have shot me when you had the chance.'' He winked at Matthew and sat down again, chuckling. ''Actually, you couldn't have shot me, no matter how hard you'd tried. And you know why? Because I can't be killed. Not until I've accomplished my mission. The Warrior prophesied that a leader would rise and free the common people from the threat of the foreigners and the oppression of the government Washington D.C. And as I read those words I suddenly . . . knew that *I* was that leader! Suddenly I saw *everything*. I looked about me and I could see what was right and what was wrong, what was true and what was false. All was revealed to me. Everything was illuminated.''

''By that blue light in your head?''

Lieder's mouth closed and his lips compressed. He stared at B. J. for a long moment before saying very slowly, very clearly, ''You really shouldn't take that tone with me, schoolmaster, because there is nothing—*nothing!*—on God's green earth more dangerous than ridiculing me.''

B. J. unflinchingly held Lieder's eyes with his own, although his mouth was dry with fear.

''Oh, I know what you're saying inside your head, schoolteacher! You're saying, this man is insane.'' He sniffed. ''The Warrior warned us that the unenlightened and the cowardly would call us patriots insane. All right, maybe I *am* a little bit insane. I'm what they call an enthusiast! Do you know what that word really means, schoolteacher? Ever look it up in the dictionary? An enthusiast is somebody who has God inside him.''

''And you think God's inside *you?*''

''Well, there's sure as hell something inside me, old man. Something gnawing at my guts!'' His eyes flicked from B. J. to Matthew and back again. He smiled. ''Maybe it's just something spicy I ate.'' He winked at Matthew. ''You think maybe that's it, boy?'' He laughed. ''Come on! Can't anyone take a joke?''

B. J. turned away, and noticed for the first time how stiffly Mr. Delanny was sitting at his cards. He had been so intent on distracting Lieder's attention that he had no more than glanced at the other people in the room. ''You all right, Mr. Delanny?'' he asked. The gambler didn't speak. ''Mr. Delanny?'' Still the gambler didn't answer. ''What's going on here?''

''Now, now, schoolteacher,'' Lieder said, wagging his finger in warning, ''you mustn't tempt our pimp to talk. I've ordered him to keep quiet, and if he disobeys me, I'll have to punish him. And it'll be all your fault. Remember those poor mules? That was your fault, too.''

B. J. crossed to Mr. Delanny, who turned his head aside to hide the blood-froth on his lips. He looked down at the rope that bound Delanny's arms to the chair so tightly that his fingers were plump and the skin taut and shiny. ''His circulation's been cut off. He could get gangrene.''

''Gangrene, eh?'' Lieder asked in a tone ripe with concern.

''I'm going to untie him.''

''Whoa, there, schoolteacher, not so fast! Maybe Mr. Tone-of-Voice doesn't *want* to be set free, because he knows that if he stirs from that chair, I am going to hurt him bad. Now, you can free him if you're willing to take the consequences. But maybe you better ask Mr. Delanny. He isn't permitted to talk to you, but he can nod his head. Go on. Ask him.''

Tiny and Bobby-My-Boy glanced from Lieder to B. J. Stone to Mr. Delanny, mischievous anticipation in their eyes.

B. J. lifted his eyebrows at Mr. Delanny. The gambler's eyes flickered, then he closed them and lowered his head.

''There, you see?'' Lieder said. ''Mr. Delanny doesn't want to be free. Freedom imposes certain responsibilities and risks, as The Warrior tells us. Maybe those ropes pain Mr. Delanny and corrupt his flesh, but at least he's alive. Most men will suffer any amount of humiliation just to keep on breathing. Oh, not superior, book-reading men like you and me. We'd rather die than be degraded and humiliated. But pimps and other sorts of bottom-feeders, they cling to life for all they're worth . . . however little that might be. I can see in your eyes you don't believe me. You think Man is a noble creature, occasionally brought low by misfortune. But the fact is, Man is essentially evil, sniveling, whining, cringing, disgusting, and unworthy of the good Lord's mercy . . . nor mine

either, for that matter.'' Lieder rose from his chair with
sudden energy. ''You know what? I think it's time the
teacher was taught a lesson, for a change. I'm going to
show you what a disgusting, cringing thing a man can
be. You watch this too, boy. It's your first lesson as my
apostle. Listen up, Delanny! I am giving you permission
to speak. In fact, I am *commanding* you to answer the
question I'm going to put to you. Watch carefully,
schoolteacher. Tiny, take out your gun and put the barrel
into Mr. Delanny's ear. Now cock it. Oh, now don't you
worry about the noise, Mr. Delanny. You won't hear a
thing. The bullet will get to your brain before the sound
does. Now! We're going to play a little game. Here's
how it goes. You have two choices, Mr. Delanny. If you
want to...and only if you really and truly *want* to...
you can ask Bobby-My-Boy to punch you in the face as
hard as he can. Chances are he'll break that fine-boned
nose of yours, but every game has its penalties and for-
feits. Your other choice is this. You can manfully *refuse*
to ask Bobby-My-Boy to punch you as hard as he can.
If you do that, then Tiny will shoot you in one ear and
out the other. It's your choice. But there's one thing I'd
better make very, very clear. Don't make the mistake of
thinking that I wouldn't go through with this. I've told
the schoolteacher that I'm going to teach him a lesson,
and you *know* I'm not going to accept the humiliation of
backing down. All righty, everybody! Lesson time! I'm
going to count to twenty inside my head, Mr. Delanny.
And when I get to twenty. I'm going to nod, and Tiny
will pull the trigger, and you will be instantly dispatched
to the great whorehouse up yonder—*but*...but...you'll
have the consolation of knowing that you've proved me
wrong and proved that mankind is basically dignified and
noble. On the other hand, if you can say 'Mr. Bobby-
My-Boy, please hit me in the face as hard as you can.'
And if you say those exact words—loud enough for me
to hear them over here!—then Bobby-My-Boy will do

what you ask, and I'll stop my count, and the lesson will
be taught and learned. Is that all clear, Mr. Delanny? Say
yes or no.''

Mr. Delanny's voice was hoarse from lack of use for
he hadn't uttered a word since he was ordered not to. He
made a thin, clogged sound.

"Speak up! Do you understand or don't you?"

"...Yes..."

"Now just a minute—!" B. J. began.

But Lieder cut him off. "I'm already counting. Don't
waste his time, schoolteacher. He ain't got all that much
left....four...five...six..."

Mr. Delanny muttered something.

"I can't *hear* you!" Lieder chanted in a school-yard
singsong. "...eight...nine..."

Over behind the bar, Jeff Calder stopped wiping the
glasses and watched, his mouth agape, fascination and
fear in perfect stasis.

"Yes," Mr. Delanny said in a half-whimper.

"Are you saying that you want Bobby-My-Boy to hit
you?"

"Yes!"

"Hard?"

"Yes!"

"Well then, you better tell him. Say it in words. Say,
'Bobby-My-Boy...'"

"...Bobby-My-Boy..."

"Will you hit me in the face as hard as you can,
please?"

"...hit me in the face...as hard as you can..."

"Please!"

"...please...*please!*"

"Come on now, don't make the man beg and grovel,
Bobby. Give him what he's asking for."

The blow would have knocked Mr. Delanny out of his
chair if he hadn't been tied in. He slumped against his
ropes swooning with the pain and shock of having half

his upper teeth loosened and the cartilage of his nose crushed against his cheekbone. Blood gushed from the corner of his mouth and oozed from his nose and his ear.

"For the love of God!" B. J. cried.

Matthew felt himself rushing toward the Other Place ... then he was gazing soft-eyed out through the bat-winged doors into the glaring brightness of the street ... deep into, and beyond, the blurry glare.

"That's enough!" B. J. said.

"*I'll* say when enough's enough," Lieder told him. "You just tell me who was right, you or me? Do you see now what a low, cringing thing your ordinary human being is? Now you and me, we wouldn't have acted like that. We'd of spit in their eye and let them do their damnedest. But then, we're superior beings. We read books and have ideas—Hey! I just got one of those ideas. And it's a honey. Listen up, Mr. Delanny. Maybe tonight I'll treat the townsfolk to a little show for their entertainment and edification. And you will be the star of the show. I'm going to have Bobby-My-Boy and Tiny bugger you, taking turns, one doing the buggering while the other holds the gun to your ear, and you'll be sobbing and whimpering and begging them to bugger as hard as they want, but please, please, please don't shoot me! For the love of God, don't shoot me! I think that will make an enlightening demonstration of human frailty. What do you think, schoolmaster?" He grinned.

"I think you're insane."

"You reckon? Well, maybe it ain't my fault." His eyes twinkled. "Don't be hard on me, mister. I been made into a monster by a cruel childhood! Nobody ever loved me or praised me, and they made me sit at the table until I'd downed all my greens!" He grinned. "Anyway, schoolteacher, I don't give a big rat's ass what you think one way or the—Hey! Get away from him, girl!"

But Frenchy had already slipped the boning knife between Delanny's ribs. He made a slight, almost apologetic grunt, and slumped against the restraining ropes. There wasn't much blood. Only a spreading stain on his ruffled shirtfront.

"Take that knife away from her!"

She dropped it at Bobby-My-Boy's feet and settled her eyes on Lieder's with insolent calm.

"Look what you have done, girl!" he said, approaching her with menace. "You've killed a white man! I'd be in my rights to string you up!"

"She didn't kill him," B. J. said. "She just put him out of your reach."

Lieder dismissed this with an irritated snap of his head. His pulse throbbing in his temples, he searched the depths of Frenchy's arrogant stare, his pupils flicking from one yellow eye to the other. Without looking toward it, he gestured at the corpse. "Tiny, you and Bobby take that thing out of here!"

"Take it where?"

"I don't care! Dump it over the cliff! Just get it out of here! Peggy!"

Jeff Calder tried to swallow and speak at the same time. "Sir?"

"Get a bucket and clean up this blood and . . . everything. This is no way for things to be!"

Calder sprang into rheumatic, stump-legged action.

Tiny and Bobby-My-Boy waddled out the front door with Mr. Delanny's slack body between them, Tiny backing out with the feet, and Bobby-My-Boy following with the bulk of the weight. They crossed the line of Matthew's vision without altering the soft intensity of his gaze out the barroom door into the glare of the street. He was aware that Frenchy had killed Mr. Delanny as one is aware of a fact of history. Nathan Hale had only one life to give for his country, and Frenchy killed Mr. Delanny. Frenchy . . . Mr. Delanny . . . Nathan Hale. He drew a sigh and settled deeper into the cosseting void.

Lieder continued to search Frenchy's eyes with a blend of revulsion and admiration. "I said you were a different kettle of fish, and you certainly are! You are something special, girl. Slip a knife into a man just as cool as well water." His eyes chilled. "You better get out of my sight. And for as long as I'm in town, you'd better make yourself scarce, 'cause if I catch one glimpse of that ugly face of yours, I will kill you. And not in any fast way, neither."

She didn't move.

B. J. stepped forward. "Come with me, girl. Matthew, there are chores to be done up at the Livery.... Matthew!"

Matthew blinked and returned, smoothly and simply. "Sir?"

"You have chores to do!" B. J. said with false severity.

"Wait a minute," Lieder said. "Maybe he ain't finished his work here."

B. J. detected a tone of rivalry for Matthew's allegiance. He avoided a confrontation by asking Matthew, "Are you done here?"

"What? Ah... well... pretty near. Just the dishes to wash up."

"All right, you do the dishes, then come over to the Livery. I don't pay you for standing around here gawking. You come with me, Frenchy." When Frenchy didn't move, B. J. took her by the arm and drew her out into the street and across to the Livery.

MATTHEW WAS IN THE kitchen, washing the last of the dishes, humming in tuneless misery.

"Hey, how's things going, boy?" Lieder asked from the doorway.

Matthew tugged the old tablecloth he used as an apron

out from under his belt and dried his hands on it. "I got
chores to do over to the Livery."

Lieder sighed and abandoned the breezy tone with
which he had hoped to transcend what had just happened.
He sat on the step. "I heard that schoolteacher call you
Matthew. Well listen...Matthew. I want you to understand what I'm doing here, because you and me, we're
the same thing. We're both damaged boys." Lieder's sincerity was so intense that there seemed to be tears just
beneath his words. "And we love this country, you and
me! We love every twig and pebble and mud hole, because damaged boys don't have anything to love but their
country. They don't have family and friends and all that,
you see what I mean? And it's only because I love this
country of ours so much that I sometimes have to do
things that may seem cruel. But what's really cruel is the
way this government is turning our land into a pesthole
of stinking foreigners. You see that, don't you, Matthew?"

"And you figure that gives you a right to torment
people and kill them?"

"Whoa there! I didn't kill that pimp! It was that nigger gal!"

"No, sir. No, it was like B. J. said. She didn't kill
him, she just put him out of your reach."

"Goddamn it, boy, you could do a whole lot better
than going around quoting some gutless, penny-'n'-
nickel teacher!" He glared at Matthew...then he lowered his eyes, suddenly diminished. "No, you're right,
boy. You're absolutely right. I let things get out of hand.
But you've got to humiliate your Example Nigger; that's
the only way you can control people. But I got carried
away, I admit it. I shouldn't have let Bobby-My-Boy hit
him like that. I don't care what the others think about
me, but you and me, we're the same sort. Both damaged
boys. So I'm asking for your understanding. And your
forgiveness."

Matthew felt miserable and embarrassed. "I guess you'll be leaving town, now that you know there ain't no silver...just ore."

"This town ain't going to get rid of me as easy as that. Maybe I'll just take that trainload of ore down to Destiny and make them refine it for me. Hell, boy, I am a Force of Nature! There's nothing I can't do! I can make people do whatever I tell them! They say I can talk the birds down from the trees! Matthew, I want to hear you say you forgive me for not preventing what happened to Delanny."

"The forgiveness ain't mine to give. It wasn't me you hurt."

"So you're refusing to forgive me?"

"I...really got to get going."

Injury and recrimination filled Lieder's eyes. "All right. Go, then. But remember this. I asked for your forgiveness, and you refused it. You just remember that."

"Yes, sir, I'll remember." Matthew hung his apron on its nail and eased himself past Lieder, who sat on the step, staring down at the floor.

As Matthew was crossing the barroom, the bat-winged doors opened, and Queeny entered wearing his Hudson Bay blanket around her shoulders, like a squaw. Her face was pasty, her hair matted, and her eyes bleary, but she stood in the middle of the room and looked around with a dazed hauteur, dazed because of the quantity of rotgut she had downed the night before, and haughty because she had wakened with no memory of the humiliation she had suffered the night before, but with fragmentary recollections of having performed her Dance of the Seven Veils to the applause of an admiring audience. The selective memory that had become essential to the survival of her self-esteem did not provide her with any clues as to how she had ended up in a strange bed, naked beneath the blankets, but she assumed that one—maybe several—

of her audience had been carried away with passion by her provocative dance.

She had sat up in Matthew's bed...then slumped back, beaten down by jagged pain behind her eyes that throbbed with each beat of her pulse. Lord-God-a-mighty, she was thirsty! She sat up again, this time more cautiously, and walked to the window, dragging one of the blankets behind her. There was the Traveller's Welcome diagonally across the street. Where was *she*, then? She looked around the sparsely furnished room: a couple of chairs, a rickety table with a row of dime westerns. Where the hell...? Her eyes fell on Matthew's genuine bone comb-and-brush set, and she made a couple of slack, patting passes with the brush over her matted hair before gathering the Hudson Bay blanket around her and stepping out into the street—Lord-God-a-mighty, that daylight cuts your eyes like ground glass! She crossed to the hotel, her dogged dignity only slightly diminished by the absence of shoes.

It was not until she got out in the street and looked around that she realized she had slept in the marshal's office, where that kid camped. Well, she'd be damned! The little *devil!* And him acting like butter wouldn't melt in his mouth, and always talking about his ma! But then, kids of that age are hot-blooded and easily carried away. The little scamp! Well...that's show business for you.

And now she wagged her finger at Matthew and gave him a knowing leer. "Fetch old Queeny a cup of coffee, will you, honeybun? You owe her that much. And make it strong. My tongue feels like the whole Apache nation walked over it...barefoot."

"I'm sorry, Queeny, there ain't no coffee left. And I'm late for my chores over at the—"

"Well, well, well! Look what the cat dragged in!" Lieder said from the kitchen doorway.

Tiny and Bobby-My-Boy came pushing in behind Queeny, having seen her crossing the street as they were returning from dumping Delanny over the cliff. They looked at Lieder eagerly, anticipating his fury, because he had warned her that she'd better never let him see her fat ass again.

Lieder shook his head slowly. "I'll be damned. I will be God-good'n-*damned!* I don't know if you got lots of grit or just lots of stupid. Whichever it is, you sure like walking close to the edge, old lady."

"You said you'd use a broken bottle on her," Tiny reminded him. "You going to let her just thumb her nose at you like that?"

"Aw, the poor old bitch was too drunk to remember what she did. She doesn't have the slightest idea of the danger she's running, sashaying in here like this."

"Yeah, but . . . you ain't just going to let her get away with it, are you?" Disappointment compressed Tiny's voice to a whine.

"No, let her be. And anyway, I got sweeter fish to fry." He grinned and winked. "I'm going a-courtin'! Go on upstairs, old woman. Wash yourself up and get some clothes on. No one wants to think of you, bare-assed under that blanket. We just ate, for Christ's sake!"

With an imperious gesture Queeny flung the flap of her blanket over her shoulder and walked past him and up the stairs, where she found Chinky sitting on the edge of her bed, her face in her hands. "Hey, where's Delanny?" Queeny asked. Chinky shook her head: she didn't know. "Well, where's Frenchy then?" Chinky didn't know and didn't care. "What is *wrong* with everybody this morning?" Queeny wondered as she went to her room, where she took her red dress from the wardrobe to air it . . . just in case she was called on to dance again that night.

On his way out to go courting, Lieder stopped beside Matthew, who was standing on the porch, watching two angry little dust devils weave their drunken ways down the street, one chasing the other. They crossed the train tracks and approached the cliff edge, where they were suddenly sucked over into oblivion. "There's one hell of a storm brewin'," Lieder said, pulling his hat brim down tight. "It's going to rain like a cow pissing on a flat rock."

Matthew was silent.

"You're on your way over to the livery stable, huh?" Matthew nodded.

"Well...that's good. That's good, Matthew, 'cause it's exactly what I want you to do. And keep your eyes peeled, hear? That schoolteacher might be foolish enough to try something, and that'd be the biggest mistake he *ever* made." Lieder squinted up at the sickly yellow-green sky. "Yes-siree-bob, we're in for one hell of a storm. Hey, I hope you noticed how I let that Queeny be, even though I'd promised her a whole lot of hurt if she ever came back. A true leader is above spite and revenge. He's big enough to forgive people. I've learned that lesson, Matthew." He paused a moment before adding, "It's a pity you haven't."

MATTHEW ARRIVED AT THE Livery to find the shoeing yard empty, but the pair of donkeys Coots had led down were out in the meadow, nosing around the old cow the train had brought up from Destiny. He looked into the kitchen. Nobody.

"Up here, boy," Coots called huskily.

He climbed the stairs to find himself for the first time in the bedroom Coots and B. J. shared. Coots was sitting on the edge of their double bed, and B. J. was in a Lincoln rocker, his head against the back and his eyes closed, looking much the more worn of the two. The strain of facing up to Lieder and distracting his attention while Coots descended into town, then having to witness

Mr. Delanny's humiliation and death, had sapped his energy and left his nerves frayed.

"I didn't hear your steps until you were in the kitchen," Coots said. "Must be the wind."

"Stand by the window and keep your eye on the street, Matthew," B. J. said without opening his eyes. "We can't let one of them sneak up on us."

Matthew established himself at the window that gave a view across the burying ground to the far end of town. "So Ruth Lillian found you on the trail?" he said to Coots.

"That's a narrow trail, son. She couldn't hardly miss me." He had known that something was amiss when he found the Kane girl standing in the middle of the trail, shortly before he got the brace of worn-out donkeys down to Shinbone Cut. It had been a steep, unnerving descent, and the donkeys were skittish because they could smell the incoming thunderstorm that Coots had seen roiling angrily all along the northern horizon when he was up at the Lode, but that was not yet visible in the sky above Twenty-Mile. "There's a real ripper coming in. And that may be to our advantage. They'll be stuck inside tonight, and they won't be able to hear anything, what with the rain and thunder and all."

"What you planning to do?" Matthew asked, confused. "I thought we were going to wait for the miners to come down tomorrow morning before dawn."

Coots glanced at B. J., who nodded, his eyes still closed. "Tell him."

"Fact is," Coots said, "they won't be coming down, boy. Not before Saturday night as usual."

"But...why not? I mean...as soon as Ruth Lillian tells them how things are down here, they're sure to—"

"Ruth Lillian won't be telling them anything. I brought her back with me."

"*What?* But the whole point was to get her out of here!"

"She'd never of made it up to the Lode, son. When it rains, that trail's a death trap. All slimy and muddy, with patches falling away into the ravine. The wind would of snatched her right off one of those exposed bends. Oh, she was willing to give it a try. That girl's got more grit than sense. But I couldn't let her do it."

"Where is she now?"

"Up in the loft out of sight. With Frenchy."

Matthew raked his fingers through his hair and pulled on it. The only good thing in all this trouble had been the knowledge that Ruth Lillian was safe. But now...

"She's in terrible danger. That Lieder's looking for a virgin girl to carry his seed."

"She'll be all right," Coots said. "I'm going to deal with 'em tonight. That's already been settled." His quick glance toward B. J. said that it was Coots who had settled it over B. J.'s objections.

"What are we going to do?" Matthew asked. "What's your plan?"

"Plan? It's hardly a plan at all," Coots admitted. "Those men don't know about me or my gun. That gives us an edge. B. J. tells me that all the men in town will be in the hotel tonight, singing and drinking. And that's just fine. I'll lie low until the storm's at its fiercest, then I'll make my way down to the train track and come back up behind the hotel. Its kitchen door ain't locked, is it?"

"Can't be. There's no lock."

"Good. How will I recognize the boss?"

"He's strange-looking," B. J. said, and Matthew could see his eyes move behind their closed lids, as though he were examining Lieder's face in his memory. "Sharp features," B. J. continued. "Almost refined. But his eyes are opaque. Like porcelain. You can't see what's going on behind them."

"A big man?"

"Middling."

"How old?"

"Hard to say. Anything from thirty to fifty. His face is all covered with fine lines. He looks like a man riven through with hate and malice. A man who means to get even . . . with everybody."

"Do you know what happened to Mr. Delanny?" Matthew asked Coots.

"Yeah, B. J. told me. I'm glad that Frenchy's on *our* side."

"It was my fault. . . . partly, anyway."

"How you figure?"

"It was me let Frenchy take the knife. I thought she was going to use it on Lieder."

"Maybe that's what she had in mind," B. J. said, opening his eyes. "But when she saw how Delanny was being treated . . ." He lifted his shoulders.

"And Ruth Lillian? Did you tell her that Mr. Delanny is dead?"

"No reason to worry the girl more than we have to. All I told her was to keep out of sight upstairs."

"What about you, Mr. Coots? Shouldn't you keep out of sight too?"

"I'll be staying right here until it's time to go." He set his coffee cup on the table, pulled the old thick-barrelled Walker-Whitney Colt from his belt and put it beside the cup, then he lay back with a sore-muscled grunt, and for the first time ever, B. J. didn't make a fuss about his goddamned *boots!* Coots blew a long sigh toward the ceiling. "We sure have got ourselves a shitload of trouble."

"Yes sir, that's true." Matthew stared at the floor before asking, "So what are you going to do?"

"What do you mean?"

"When you get into the hotel, what are you going to do? Call him out?"

"Do *what?*"

"Call him out?"

"Oh, my. You read too many of those Ringo Kid

books. No, Matthew, I'm not going to call him out, or do anything else stupid. What I'll do is sneak up as close as I can, then shoot him. In the back, if I can. I'm going to put him down like you would a mad dog.''

"Just...shoot him?''

"Just shoot him.''

"But he's had lots of trouble and misery in his life. He's been...damaged. Oh, I know he's mean and dangerous! But still he's...'' Matthew shrugged.

"But still he's what?'' B. J. asked, exchanging a glance with Coots. "What are you trying to say, Matthew?''

"I don't know. It's just that...well, people aren't always to blame for things they do. Sometimes things just *happen*. People get damaged, and things happen without it being anyone's fault!''

B. J. recalled what he had read in the *Nebraska Plainsman*: that man and woman found in a farmhouse outside Bushnell. "Tell me what you think we should do, Matthew.''

"Well, maybe we could...we could...I don't rightly know!''

"But you *do* understand that this man is insane, don't you? And you realize there's no reasoning with him?''

"Look, boy,'' Coots said. "A rattlesnake kills. Not because it's evil, but just because it's a rattlesnake, and killing is what rattlesnakes do. So when you find one in your bedroll...''

B. J. could sense Matthew's misery of indecision, so he took the pressure off him by asking Coots, "If you get a clear shot at the boss, and if you hit him, then what will you—''

"If I get a clear shot, I'll hit him. Don't worry about that.''

"All right. But what about the other two?''

Coots nodded. "Yeah, I been thinking about that. I been picturing just what I'll do and just what'll happen.

That's what you got to do—picture it all beforehand, step-by-step, so there won't be no surprises. The minute I squeeze off the first shot, all hell's going to break loose, with the townsfolk and the girls scuttling for cover and crossing my line of fire, so dropping those other two could be messy. Some people might get hit by strays. The important thing is to drop the boss with the first shot. You snap off a snake's head, and the body might coil and twist for a while, but it ain't going nowhere.''

Matthew nodded, savoring these matter-of-fact details, coming as they did from an experienced gun.

''If we had another gun, I could back you up,'' B. J. said.

Coots lifted the brim of his hat and regarded him with an alarmed frown. ''Benjamin Joseph Stone, you're an educated man and you're a fair-to-middlin' partner— even if you can't cook for shit. But in a fight the only thing more dangerous than a gun-smart enemy is a gun-dumb friend. No, taken all in all, it's probably just as good we *don't* have another gun.''

''But, I ...'' Matthew began.

''What is it, boy?''

''Well ... you seem to have forgot my pa's gun. Maybe I could—''

''That antique shotgun?''

''Yes, sir.''

Coots sniffed. ''That ain't no weapon for close-in fighting. Especially at night.''

''But maybe I could go over there in daylight—''

''Just sashay across the street carrying that cannon? Boy, you'd never even get *close*. They'd drop you before you could ... no, forget it. I know what I'm doing. And it's best if I do it alone. At least I can't get into my own line of fire.''

''Look, you better go down to the Mercantile, Matthew,'' B. J. said. ''It's dinnertime, and you always eat there. We don't want to raise any suspicions that might bring those men snooping around. Tell Mr. Kane that his daughter's here, and she's safe. Explain about the storm. Try to reassure him. He's an old man and he's bound to worry.''

Coots chuckled dryly. ''He's no older'n you. Maybe even younger.''

''And Matthew?'' B. J. pursued, ignoring this.

''Sir?''

''Tell Mr. Kane that we'll keep his girl here out of sight until after dark. He's not going to like hearing that she didn't manage to get out of town, so you'll have to try to ... you know ... reassure him.''

''Yes, sir. Shall I come back here after I talk to Mr. Kane?''

''No, don't draw their attention to this place any more than you have to. You just hang around the marshal's office.''

''Yes sir. Maybe first I'd better go up and see if there's anything Ruth Lillian wants me to tell her pa.''

''If you want.''

When Matthew lifted the trapdoor to the loft, he found Ruth Lillian and Frenchy staring down at him, each holding her side of a back issue of *Harper's Illustrated*. They had been paging through it to pass the time, carefully peeling apart pages that had been stuck together by the damp, when the sound of Matthew climbing the steep loft ladder made them catch their breaths and freeze.

''I'm just ... going down to the Mercantile,'' he said half-apologetically. He felt he ought to have something to tell Ruth Lillian to justify startling them, but the only thing he could think of was, ''Is there anything you want me to tell your pa?''

''Just tell him I'll be back after nightfall. And not to worry. Coots is going to take care of everything.''

''All right.'' He felt stupid, standing there on the ladder, with half of his body sticking up into the loft, and them sitting side by side on the iron cot that occupied most of the space, looking down at him. "Anything else you want me to tell him?"

"Just that I'm fine."

"All right." He started to descend. Then he pushed the trapdoor back up. "Looks like we're in for one of your rip-snorters."

"Yes."

Matthew nodded. "Well, then...I guess I'll be getting."

"All right."

He started to descend, then: "You okay, Frenchy?"

"Yeah, I'm all right."

"Anything I can do for you?"

"No, I don't think—Well, you could tell them downstairs that I could use something to eat...and some shoes."

"Shoes?"

"Yeah. Any kind of shoes. I don't care."

"Oh. Well then...I'll tell them about the shoes and ...well, I guess I better be going."

"All right," both women said at once, and before he had closed the loft trapdoor over his head, they were paging through the magazine again, their hair touching.

He stood for a moment at the bottom of the ladder, feeling swamped by reality vertigo. It seemed so strange, those two sitting together up in that close space smelling of dust and old things. Small white girl, tall black woman. Virgin and whore, smooth cheek next to scarred cheek, both looking at pictures of smiling, urbane young men and women parading their fashionable clothes in last year's Easter Parade down New York's Fifth Avenue. Just a short time ago, one had been prepared to risk her life in a storm; and less than an hour ago, the other had slipped a knife between a man's ribs.

———————

MATTHEW FOUND MR. KANE sitting at his table, where he had been the night before, and he had the odd feeling that he hadn't moved since then. But that couldn't be, because he had seen Mrs. Bjorkvist leaving as he arrived, and she was carrying some purchase.

"Ruth Lillian must be almost up to the Lode by now," Mr. Kane said before the spring bell over the door had stopped jangling. "I hope she doesn't get caught in the rain."

"Well, no, sir. You see, she—"

"What's wrong? What happened?"

"Now don't worry, sir! She's fine. Fine. She met up with Coots and warned him, but there's a terrible storm on its way in, and Coots thought it would be too dangerous for her to try to make it up the trail. So he brought her back with him—But don't worry. She's hidden away up in B. J.'s loft. She said you're not to worry one bit, and she'll be here as soon as it gets dark. B. J., he said her going up there to warn Coots was just about the bravest thing he'd seen in all his born days, and that she was safe and...everything. So you're not to worry."

"Do you know how many times you've said 'Don't worry'? When you're told that often not to worry... there's reason to worry." Mr. Kane lowered his eyes to his ledger book and blinked. "So...she's back. Back, with those men in town." He squeezed his eyes shut and shook his head slowly.

Matthew noticed that Mr. Kane hadn't shaved. He always shaved, even when his heart was playing him up. "What did Mrs. Bjorkvist want? She hardly ever buys anything."

"...Hm-m? What?" It was almost as though Mr. Kane had dropped off for a second. "Oh...bicarbonate of soda and headache powders. Her men drank too much last night, and they have to go again tonight."

"Oh. Well, I guess I better close up for dinner, huh?"

"What? Oh...yes, I suppose so. But I...I

haven't . . ." He didn't finish. He closed his account book and lightly rubbed his palm over the cover, frowning as though he were puzzled by something. Then he looked up at Matthew, blinking. ". . . ah . . . I haven't made anything for dinner."

"I'll do it, sir!" Matthew locked the front door and turned the Open at One sign so it could be seen from outside. "I'll just open us a can of tomatoes and fry up some . . . whatever there is. Don't worry, we'll make do." Mr. Kane dully followed him upstairs to the living quarters, where Matthew started putting a scratch meal together, like he used to when he got home from school and found his mother too beaten up to cook . . . or just too down in the dumps to care. As he bustled around the kitchen, he ransacked his imagination for something to talk about so he could avoid mentioning Mr. Delanny's death. And he certainly wasn't going to tell Mr. Kane that Lieder was looking for a virgin beauty to carry his seed! "Boy-o-boy, the weather sure feels eerie."

"What do you mean, eerie?"

"Well, it's sort of like holding its breath. There's no breeze at all. One minute the air feels warm, and the next it's sort of clammy. And you can *taste* it . . . the air, I mean. I guess one of your rip-snorters is coming in. Ruth Lillian told me about the time the Pair o' Dice Social Club got hit by lightning, and how you wrapped her in a blanket and brought her out on the porch to watch it burn down, and how the rain was pelting down so hard that you couldn't hear the flames roaring and crackling. Boy, that must of been one heck of a—"

"What is it, Matthew?" Mr. Kane said irritably.

"Sir?"

"Why are you babbling on like this? You're trying to avoid telling me—Something's wrong with Ruth Lillian! I know it!"

"No, sir! No, she's fine. She's sitting up there, reading a magazine, just as pert as can be. No, it's just . . ." He spooned their dinner from the frying pan into two plates.

"It's just *what?*"

Matthew carried to the table the "stew" he had made from canned beans mixed with canned tomatoes into which he had chopped an onion, to give it "crunch." "There you go, sir! It's not much but, like my pa used to say, it's better'n a poke in the eye with a sharp stick!"

"Tell me what's happening!"

"All right, sir, I'll tell you. B. J. and Coots wanted me to explain our plan to you, so you'd know how we're going to protect Ruth Lillian. What we're going to do is this. When it gets good'n dark, and the storm's ripping and snorting, Coots is going to sneak across to the hotel and slip into the kitchen. And while they're all singing and drinking, he's going to keep back in the shadows and take careful aim and drop that boss. Then he'll have to do the best he can with the other two, what with all the confusion and scrambling around. B. J. wanted to back him up, but we decided he wasn't cut out for gunplay. And anyways, they don't have but one gun. There was some talk about using my pa's gun, but I don't believe a big old double-load shotgun like that is the right thing for close-in work. Especially in the dark. What I've got to do is figure out how to tote that old cannon across the street in broad daylight without them starting to blaze away at me. I haven't thought up a way yet, but I'm working on it."

Mr. Kane took up his spoon and dully pushed the beans and tomatoes around in his plate, then he put his spoon down. "I suppose there's no other way? No other way than killing?"

"No, sir, there ain't. With rattlesnakes, you got to keep them out of your bedroll, and that's all there is to it."

Mr. Kane blinked. "*What?*"

"After all, it ain't us that started the killing." Having made this slip, Matthew decided he'd better tell Mr. Kane about Delanny. "There's something you ought to know, sir. Mr. Delanny is dead."

"They killed Mr. Delanny?"

"Well . . . yes . . . well . . ." and he told what had happened in the Traveller's Welcome, omitting the nastier details of Lieder's taunting and baiting, and winding up with: ". . . and B. J. said it wasn't really Frenchy that killed him, she had just put him out of Lieder's reach, so's he couldn't torment him anymore and . . . well, that's pretty much what happened."

Mr. Kane shut his eyes. "Oh, God." He scrubbed his face hard with his palms. "So, what did they do to Frenchy?"

"Mr. Lieder said that if he ever saw her ugly face again, he'd kill her, so we got her out of there, B. J. and me, and now she's hiding out. I wish you'd try to eat something, sir. I know my cooking ain't much compared to yours, but . . ."

"THIS IS THE BEST cup of tea I've had in all my born days, ma'am," Lieder said, carefully setting Mrs. Bjorkvist's cup back on its blue-and-white saucer, the only two pieces of family china that survived the trip from Sweden to provide testimony to her respectability. The fragile wicker armchair was too tight at his hips, but he was perfectly at ease as he smiled and told her that it wasn't every day that a traveling man like himself was greeted with such hospitality, and he appreciated it.

Mrs. Bjorkvist was sitting nervously on the edge of her chair; Kersti stood by the window twisting the hem of the curtain insensibly; and the Bjorkvist men hovered in the archway with a blend of sulky menace and cowed diffidence. Lieder sipped his tea.

Unable to stand the tension any longer, Mrs. Bjorkvist asked if he was satisfied with the food she'd sent over to

the hotel for their dinner. It was just fine. She knew it
wasn't fancy, just everyday cooking, but—he *preferred*
everyday cooking. Well, that's good. But if there hadn't
been enough to satisfy everybody, she could make more
come sup—No, it was just fine! If there was one thing
she liked to see, it was men tucking in hearty, and no
one could say she was stingy or—"Mrs. Bjorkvist? I
think I'd better explain why I've come calling. First, I
wanted to invite your husband and son to participate in
fellowship over to the hotel again tonight."

"Vell, I don't tink dey feel—"

"And second, I wanted to tell you how bad I feel
about the way my followers punished them yesterday.
Oh, it's true that your menfolk were disobedient and disrespectful, but having their faces banged together like
that...well, I wanted to apologize and tell you that I'll
do everything in my power to see it doesn't happen
again."

"Vell, dat's—"

"But I got to be honest with you, ma'am. Those boys
of mine aren't what you'd call civilized. They tend to
hold grudges something fierce. Of course, I'll do what I
can to keep them from coming over here and busting
things up, but—"

"Busting tings—!"

"Into smithereens, ma'am. Smithe-r-*reens*. Lord love
us, I remember when they took a grudge against this one
family? You'd think they'd be satisfied with smashing up
the menfolk and making a bonfire with the furniture. But
no! No, those animals had to grab the womenfolk and
drag them out into the barn, where they...well, I won't
describe how they used those poor women every-which-
a-way a woman can be used, but..." He sucked his teeth
and shook his head.

"But...but...why *us?* We ain't done notting."

"It doesn't seem fair, does it? But then, life is seldom
fair, and justice is rarer than virtue in a brothel, as Paul

told the Iowans in 7, 13. Well, ma'am . . ." He stood up. "I better be getting back. The good Lord only knows what those savages are up to at this very minute." He started toward the door; both the Bjorkvist men backed up clumsily to make room for him, treading on one another's toes. At the archway he stopped and touched his fingertips to his forehead. "What's *wrong* with me? I am getting so forgetful!" He turned to her and smiled. "I declare, I'd forget my own head, if it wasn't screwed on tight. There was something else I wanted to ask you, Mrs. Bjorkvist. My men, they've been relieving their needs with the help of that Chinee girl over at the hotel. You know the one? Now me, I can't do that, because I don't think it's right for a white man to give his sap to women of the lower races. Don't you agree, Mrs. Bjorkvist?"

She pursed her lips and puffed. "Dose girls over dere! But, no, it ain't right for white men to—"

"But I'm a man. Mrs. Bjorkvist. A frail thing of flesh, bone, and gristle. And I too have needs that must be relieved. So here's what I've been thinking, ma'am. I've been thinking that—with your permission—I might give my sap to young Kersti here, because she's a strong, healthy, well-brought-up girl, and a credit to her family. But of course I'd only take her if she was willing, and if her family agreed, 'cause I am not a man to force himself on a girl, and I know you wouldn't let your daughter have anything to do with the sort of man who would. I'm pretty sure those animals of mine wouldn't *dare* come over here and hurt your men and bust things up, if they knew that Kersti and me were upstairs in the hotel comforting one another. Now, I want you folks to talk things over and do whatever you think is right. Just follow your consciences. A body never goes wrong following the dictates of his conscience, that's my view of it." He put on his hat, tugged the brim to Mrs. Bjorkvist, and turned again to go. At the front door he stopped and said over his shoulder, "I'll be wanting her in about an hour."

MATTHEW LAY ON HIS bed with his fingers laced behind his head, listening to the wind that had begun to moan in his stovepipe. While walking back from the Mercantile, he had seen the first dark-bellied cloud come pressing over the mountain, its leading edge churning wrathfully.

...How could he get close to those men carrying that gun, without them...?

He took the shotgun down from above the door and held it. But his grip went limp with disgust, so he hung it back up and sat on the edge of his bed for a time, staring defocused at the floor. In time, he shook himself and reached far under his bed to pull out the canvas sack and spill its contents over his bed...his treasures. Twelve oversized handmade shells, the six-pointed star Ruth Lillian had given him, the small blue glass bottle somebody had buried (why?), the marble with an American flag suspended in the middle (how?), the rock crusted with glittering flakes that his pa had scoffed at and called fool's gold (but who knows?...maybe not).

...How to get that shotgun over to...?

He took one of the Ringo Kid books from the neat row on his table and hefted it in his hand, as though it might inspire him osmotically, then he put it back and pressed his thumb along the spines of the books, lining them up exactly.

Twice he went to the window and looked across to the Traveller's Welcome. Then he threw himself across his bed and examined the ceiling, his eyes narrowed, searching for inspiration.

The rising wind fluted in the stovepipe and wuthered

at the corners of the marshal's office, pleading for entrance.

...How would the Ringo Kid...?

TINY WAS BORED. HE leaned against the sill of the hotel's front window, watching the wind scurry dust swirls down the street. Bored...bored...bored. Lieder had taken that Swede girl upstairs more than an hour ago, and Bobby-My-Boy was sitting in the corner with Chinky, making her play with his pecker. Bored! He aimed the hunting rifle he had taken from Sven Bjorkvist at the heart of a dust swirl and squinted down the sights, tracking it until it got momentarily caught in the corner of a building, then he tightened his finger on the trigger and made a keesh sound in his cheek. A movement to the left of his sights caught his attention, and he lifted his cheek from the stock.

"Well, I'll be damned!"

It was that kid, the one the boss had taken a shine to. He was coming across the street carrying one huge sonofabitch of a gun! He had it over his shoulder with the barrel in his fist and the butt sticking up in the air, like it was a club.

Tiny cocked his rifle and moved to the bat-winged bar doors, over which he shouted, "You can stop right there, kid!"

Bobby-My-Boy left his table, his flies unbuttoned, and came over to the door. He pulled the pistol from his belt. "You can stop right there, kid!"

Tiny gave him a weary glance.

Matthew smiled and waved and said something that the wind snatched away as he continued to walk toward them.

"I said you better stop right there!" Tiny shouted.

Bobby-My-Boy cocked his pistol.

Lieder called down from above, asking what the hell was going on? Tiny shouted up that the kid was coming across the street lugging a gun! And he wouldn't stop when he was told to!

Lieder pulled Kersti up from her knees by her hair and pushed her aside. He was just about fed up with her whimpering and whining, anyway. Pressing against the wall, he peeked around the edge of the window, down to the street where Matthew was standing with his weight on one leg and his pa's shotgun over his shoulder. The wind billowed out his jacket and snapped the collar against his neck. Matthew shaded his eyes, looked up at Lieder, and shouted something into the wind. Then he shrugged in broad pantomime and grinned foolishly. Lieder laughed and called down the stairs for them to let the kid come on ahead.

"But what about his gun?" Tiny wanted to know.

"I guess you boys are going to have to figure this one out for yourselves." He chuckled, and returned to Kersti.

Tiny waved for Matthew to come into the hotel, but he shouted into the wind that he'd better keep his finger away from the trigger of that gun!

Matthew cupped his hand behind his ear and shrugged. "Can't hear!" he shouted. "Are you saying it's okay for *me*...?" He pointed to himself. "...to come *there?*" He pointed to the hotel.

"Come on ahead!" Tiny shouted. "But don't try nothin'!"

"Don't try nothing!" Bobby-My-Boy said.

Tiny gave Bobby-My-Boy a withering look.

Matthew approached the hotel doors, smiling easily, one fist gripping the barrel of the shotgun, the other hand splayed wide open in front of him to show there was nothing in it. As soon as he crossed the threshold, Tiny snatched his shotgun away.

"What do you think of her?" Matthew asked. "She's handmade. Only one like it in the world. To make ammunition for it, my pa had to use the powder and shot from two ordinary double-ought shells. And do you wonder if it can kick? It can *kick*." He hadn't expected Lieder to be upstairs, away from the other two. That was a disappointment.

Bobby-My-Boy took the gun from Tiny and hefted it. "Heavy."

Tiny snatched it back. "Is this thing loaded?"

"No, sir. There ain't no shells for it, and I can't get any in this godforsaken hole. That's why I'm willing to sell it. At a real good price, too."

"What do you hunt with a thing like this? Barns?"

Matthew laughed and allowed as how that was a good one. "It's only a single-shot, but it makes one hell of a hole. Well? Either of you interested?"

"A gun without ammunition ain't worth a fart in a whirlwind," Tiny said.

"That's true," Matthew agreed. "But you're traveling men, and I bet you could find someone to make ammunition for her."

"Naw, that heavy old thing ain't for traveling men," Tiny said. "Hell, you'd need three men and a boy just to tote it around for you."

Matthew laughed again, even harder. "I thought the fella upstairs had all the brains in this outfit, but you've got off three good'uns in a row! First about hunting barns, then about a fart in a whirlwind, and now about three men and a boy!"

Tiny's face twisted yet further in an expression of self-satisfaction as Matthew turned to Bobby-My-Boy and asked, "How about you? Figure you're big enough to hold this gun down."

"Sure!"

"Then you want to buy it?"

"No."

"Look, I'll tell you what. I'll make you a price

that'll—'' A heavy hand descended on Matthew's shoulder from behind.

"Matthew? The funniest idea just popped into my head." Lieder had come silently down the stairs, stuffing his shirt into his pants. "I was upstairs funning, when this terrible thought came to me." His fingers tightened on Matthew's shoulder. "Can you guess what that terrible thought was?"

"No, sir. I was only asking your men if they wanted to buy my pa's shotgun. I didn't think you'd mind, because I already offered it to you and you said you didn't—"

"I asked you if you could guess what that terrible thought was!"

"No, sir, I can't."

"Hm-m. Well, I was standing there, receiving what you might call homage, when this voice inside my head said to me, what if that big old gun *ain't* unloaded?"

"I don't under—But I already told you there ain't no shells for it. My pa shot off the last ones back a coon's age."

"I know you told me that. And I know you wouldn't lie to me. But what if you honestly thought it was unloaded, but you were mistaken? What then, Matthew?" He smiled. "You wouldn't mind if I put you to a little test, would you? A man that wants to be one of my apostles shouldn't be afraid of a little test."

"What . . . sort of test?"

"Bobby-My-Boy, you keep your gun on Matthew here. (Don't you fret, boy. It's just part of the test.) Now Tiny, you give him back his shotgun." He put his arm around Matthew and pressed him close to his side, too close for him to be a target for the long-barrelled weapon. "I'll just stand close to you, boy, so's not to be in your way. Now, I totally believe you about that gun being unloaded, but you know what they say . . . it's usually the unloaded gun that kills somebody. Here's how the test goes. You and me, we're going to walk back here to where the blushing bride is sitting, all excited and panting with anticipation.'' He drew Matthew along with him to where Chinky sat. She looked up dully as they approached. ''Now Matthew, cock back the hammer of your gun. *Do it!*''

''Honest to Pete, sir, this gun ain't—''

''Just cock the gun, boy!''

Matthew thumbed back the hammer until it clicked.

''There you go. Now point it at the bride there. Oh, anywhere in the middle will do, because if that thing turns out to be loaded—by some miracle or other—it'll blow away everything from appetite to asshole.''

Chinky's eyes searched Matthew's in confusion, then they widened with dawning terror. She rose and put her hands, palms out, in front of her chest, as though to catch the blast.

Matthew swallowed. ''Don't worry, Chinky. It ain't loaded. We're just . . . funning.''

''Squeeze the trigger, boy.''

Chinky's mouth opened, and she shook her head, her eyes locked on Matthew's in silent supplication.

''Squeeze the trigger!''

To save Chinky from further torment, Matthew jerked the trigger, and the hammer fell.

The blood drained from Chinky's face. Her knees buckled. And she sat down hard.

''You see?'' Matthew said. ''I *told* you there wasn't any shells! Gosh, I'm terrible sorry, Chinky.''

Lieder roared with laughter, and his grip on Matthew's shoulder became a gruff squeeze. ''I knew it! I just *knew* you were made of the right stuff! I knew in the marrow of my bones that no apostle of mine would betray me! But I *had* to test you, 'cause premonitions and such can be messages from God, and the man who ignores them is asking to get his ass kicked by Fate. I hope you understand, Matthew. And I hope you forgive me—oh, I forgot. You ain't much given to forgiving, are you?'' As he chuckled and tousled Matthew's hair, Matthew noticed that his knuckles were bruised.

WET TO THE SKIN and shivering beneath the blanket draped over his shoulders, Matthew sat in the gloom of the marshal's office while rain rattled down on his tin roof. He had been crossing the street back from the hotel, his pa's gun slung carelessly over his shoulder, when the air went suddenly chill and the sky darkened. The first plump drops of rain kicked up little craters in which they lay for an instant, skinned with dust. Before Matthew could run, the torrent came pelting down; and by the time he arrived, heel-skidding, at his door, the dust of the road had been whipped into frothy mud.

His stomach was still tight, and there was an acid taste in the back of his throat from the narrow game he had played over at the hotel. It had never crossed his mind that Chinky might get involved, and there was no way he could have told her that he hadn't loaded the gun. After long cogitation earlier that afternoon, he had worked out that this was the way the Ringo Kid would play it. The hardest part of the "ploy" (that's what Mr. Anthony Bradford Chumms called Ringo's tricks) had been fighting off his urge to slip into the Other Place when that hand had descended suddenly on his shoulder. But the ploy had worked; the next time they saw him with the gun, they would be relaxed and off their guard.

He decided it wasn't worthwhile to start a fire in the potbellied stove, considering that in half an hour he would be going to the Mercantile for supper; following his usual routine, as B. J. had instructed him, to avoid suspicion. As soon as it got dark, Ruth Lillian would sneak down behind the buildings to the back door of the store, and both he and Mr. Kane would learn if there'd been any changes in Coots's plan. Matthew clutched the blanket to his throat and went to his table to light his lamp because, although it was only five o'clock, the street beyond his window was already storm-dark. He had trouble lighting the wick because his shivering made the lucifer tremble. The wick caught; he lowered the chimney; and the expanding yellow light pressed back the darkness, revealing his pa's gun standing against the wall where he had left it. He knelt beside his bed and dragged out the canvas bag, then opened the shotgun and took one of the thick shells from the bag. Matthew tried to load it into the gun ... but he couldn't do it! The wax-slimy feeling of the shell made him shudder and drop it onto his bed. He scrubbed his palms hard on his trouser legs to get rid of the feeling and cleared his throat harshly to relieve the panicky constriction. He took several long, deep, slow breaths and, clenching his teeth, forced himself to reach out for the shell again and touch ...

His back door burst open!

Kersti stepped through the sheet of rain falling from the roof. She was drenched to the skin, the dark of her nipples visible through her sodden dress.

"Kersti!" He crammed the shell back into the canvas bag and shoved it under his bed, then he crossed to the door and reached out through the glistening curtain of rain to pull it shut, wetting his shirtsleeve from elbow to cuff. Closing the door altered the sound of the downpour, subtracting the crisp sound of rain whipping up lather on puddles from the deeper drill on the metal roof. "Here." He put his blanket around her shoulders. "What is wrong with you, coming out in a storm like this? Your ma is going to tan you good and prop—" He stopped short. She had been hit in the face. There was a bruise on one cheekbone, and her upper lip was swollen. "What happened?" She stood whimpering with cold and misery as rainwater dripped from her disheveled hair. "Here, sit down. I'll get a fire going." He pulled his soap-stiff "other shirt" down from the string line on which it had dried a couple of days before. "Here, use this to wipe your hair. What happened, Kersti?"

"My ma, she..." It was hard to speak because when she unclenched her teeth they began chattering. "...she won't have me in the house! Told me to... go back... to the hotel."

Matthew was lighting a little tepee of dry wood in his stove, splinters ripped from the walls of the derelict buildings that served the whole town as a source of kindling. "Here, sit by the stove. What do you mean, go back to the hotel?" While she explained in a voice broken by cold and emotion, he knelt at her feet, feeding the stove first with bigger kindling, then with small chips of railroad coal. She described how Lieder had told her folks that he wanted Kersti to come over and do him, and if she didn't, then those men would beat her pa and Oskar up again, and wreck the place, and do nasty things to her and her ma. Then Lieder had left, telling her folks to think it over and follow their consciences. So her ma, she... Kersti fell silent.

Without looking up from tending the fire, Matthew asked. "Your ma told you to *go?*"

"No. No, she didn't tell me to go. She just..." Kersti sniffed back a runny nose. "She just..."

"Here. Put your hands on the stove. It's starting to warm up."

She laid her palms on the tepid stove top then carried the warmth back to her cheeks.

"She just... what?" Matthew asked.

"She said it was up to me. I should do what I thought was right. But she wasn't sure that Pa and Oskar could take another beating up. They might fight back, then they'd get killed for sure... but it was up to me. And it would break her heart to see everything she'd worked and slaved for all these years broken up and burned... but I should do what I thought was right. Then she just stared into the corner... crying without making any noise. Then she..." Kersti shrugged and sniffed.

"She what?"

"Well, she said that if I didn't give myself to that boss man, then his men would come and rape both me and her, and since I was going to lose my virtue no matter what... but it was up to me."

"So you went to the hotel?"

She nodded, then her face spread flat as she began to cry, hiss-sobbing between clenched teeth.

The top of the stove was too hot to touch now, but the sides were not, so Matthew put his palms against them until they were as warm as he could stand, then he put them around her throat... like his ma used to do when he came back from school wet and cold. "It's okay, Kersti," he said in his ma's singsong, comforting tone. "Don't you worry. Everything'll be okay." But he remembered how, even as a little child, he had known that was a lie; everything wouldn't be okay. Now that the stove had caught well, he opened the door and threw in the rest of the coal he had scrounged from around the old railroad depot. "There now! You'll be warm as toast in no time!" He could hear his mother's false and helpless optimism in his voice, and he knew he was babbling on because he didn't want to learn what had happened to her in the hotel. Somehow he felt this was all his fault because of the way he'd treated Kersti.

But Kersti needed to talk about it. Staring hard at the flickering glow behind the heat-wrinkled mica of the stove door, she gingerly touched her split lip with the tip of her tongue. Then she began to speak in a drained monotone. "He brought me upstairs and he sat me down on the bed and began talking to me... talking crazy, but real sincere, you know what I mean? He said he knew I wasn't worthy to receive his seed, but considering that the only other women in town were my ma and the hotel's whores, he'd have to make do with me. So he... he

made me play with him, but his pecker wouldn't stand
up . . . well, it'd stand up, but it wouldn't *stay* up, and that
made him mad. Just crazy mad! Every time he'd push
my legs apart and start to put it in, it'd shrink to nothing,
and he'd swear and grit his teeth, and I felt pretty sure
he had never done a woman . . . not in the regular way,
anyhow. Then he . . . he grabbed me by my hair and
snatched me around and told me that if I ever . . . *ever* . . .
told anybody about him not being able to do a woman,
he'd flay the skin off'n me! And do it real slow! And I
started to blub because I was scared and because he was
just about pulling my hair out! And it was like my crying
made him get hot, 'cause he got hard again, but as soon
as he tried to put it in, it went soft, so he raged and
punched the wall until his knuckles split, and there was
tears in his eyes, and he said it wasn't *his* fault his pecker
wouldn't stay up! Somebody once beat it with a ruler!
Hard! And ever since then . . . but he said there was something I could do to help him, and he dragged me off the
bed onto my knees, and he got me by the hair and told
me to get to work, so I . . . I . . .'' She made a tight noise
at the back of her throat. ''What could I do?'' Her eyes
searched Matthew's. ''I mean . . . *what could I do?*''

He closed his eyes and shook his head. . . . All his
fault.

She didn't speak for a time, but he could hear her
swallowing back tears. ''. . . then his men started shouting
from downstairs, saying you were coming across the
street with a gun, and I was glad because I thought you
were coming to get me out of there. But you weren't.
After he . . . you know . . . did his business . . . he told me I
better not make a sound if I didn't want to get the shit
beat out of me, then he went tippy-toe down the stairs.
Pretty soon he comes back up, laughing, and he starts
with me again, and the storm breaks and the rain starts
pelting down, and that kind of excited him, but it still
wouldn't stay up, so he got *real* mad, and he slapped me

in the face and said I'd tricked him! I wasn't no pure virgin! *That's* why it wouldn't stay hard! And I screamed at him that he was right! I wasn't no virgin! If he wanted a virgin, then why didn't he get that Ruth Lillian Kane with her hair all piled up, and I—!'' Kersti broke down in sobs.

Matthew was stunned for a moment, then he put his arms around her awkwardly and patted her back, in part to comfort her, in part to make her stop crying so he could think things out. His mind had hung up on one terrible fact. ''You . . . you told him about Ruth Lillian?''

''It just slipped out! And anyway, it ain't right for her to be all safe and hidden away while I'm there getting beat up! *It ain't fair!*'' Matthew was rigid, and she felt his mute accusation. ''It wasn't my fault! I was being slapped around and forced to do him thataway!''

But Matthew continued to shake his head, his eyes fixed wretchedly into the corner of the room.

The stove was radiating heat by now, and she turned to warm her other side. He stood and walked to the window. The wind seeping in through the ill-fitting panes made his shoulder cold where it was damp with Kersti's tears and saliva. Through the tattered screen of rain from his roof, he could see the street's shallow chocolate-colored ponds, their surfaces dancing beneath the torrent of drops.

He had to clear his throat to ask, ''How'd you get away?''

''The boss sent his men to round everybody up for the night's party. When he went down to join in, he locked me in the room. I waited until I figured they couldn't hear anything down there, what with the storm and their singing and all, then I went out the back window onto the shed roof, and I slid down from there. I went home and started to blub, telling my ma what had happened to me, but she said there wasn't no use crying over spilt milk, and maybe I should of stayed at the hotel where I'd be handy to that boss man. She wasn't saying it was my fault. But damaged goods is damaged goods, and there's no repairing them. The last thing she wanted was to have that man coming around looking for me. I got mad, and I told her that if she wanted me to go to the whorehouse, then fine! That's what I'd do! I'd go be a whore! And as for her, she could go to hell. Go straight to hell! And I walked out and slammed the door, and there I was in the rain, and up at the hotel everybody was singing and laughing. So I come here. I didn't know where else to go. I mean . . . where could I go?''

Matthew told her she was welcome to stay there until she got warm. But then she'd be safer up in B. J.'s loft, with Frenchy and . . . with Frenchy. He knew that Ruth Lillian would soon go over to her pa's store. ''I got to go down to the Mercantile in a while. You better keep my blanket, lest you catch your death.''

''Matthew?''

''Hm-m?''

''You're mad at me for telling about Ruth Lillian, ain't you?''

''No, not mad, I just . . . Lord God, Kersti! How could you tell him? What were you thinking of?''

''I ain't to blame!''

He stared at her hard. Then closed his eyes and shook his head.

''And anyway,'' she said with a defensive hitch in her voice, ''that sonofabitch was so het up he probably didn't pay me any mind. I'll bet he didn't even hear me.''

Matthew looked at her sadly. ''No, he heard.''

———————

WITH THE COMING OF darkness, lightning could be seen blooming within the bellies of storm clouds all along the horizon, but the continuous mutter of disgruntled thunder was barely audible beneath the din of the heavy diagonal rain that kept up a relentless assault on tin roofs and wooden walls. As Matthew made his way down to the Mercantile by short dashes from one abandoned building to the next, he got glimpses of the Traveller's Welcome through the rain. All the lamps were lit, and the windows shone through the rain, making wriggly golden smears in puddles that simmered with drops. He couldn't hear singing or the player piano, but shadows loomed and lurched across the windows; the "deacons" were enjoying another night of gruff fellowship.

Matthew found Mr. Kane upstairs in the kitchen, still sitting in the dark before his untouched dinner.

"Ruth Lillian's not here yet?" Matthew asked.

Mr. Kane shook his head.

"Well, don't worry, sir. She'll be here in no time." He lit the oil lamp on the kitchen table, and Mr. Kane blinked at the light that intruded on his somber ruminations. "I'd better heat something up for Ruth Lillian," Matthew said. The concoction of canned beans and canned tomatoes (with onion for "crunch") was still on the back of the stove, half-congealed and crusted at the edges. Matthew was able to blow a few ash-scabbed coals into a glow, and it wasn't long before he had the fire going. He scraped Mr. Kane's plate into the pot to avoid waste, then he opened a tin of corned beef, broke it up with a fork, and added it, together with another can of tomatoes. Mr. Kane watched these preparations with bewilderment. By the time the stew began to simmer, thunderheads had advanced across the lowlands beyond the cliff and were booming, deep-throated and angry.

They heard the back door of the store bang open, snatched from Ruth Lillian's grasp by the wind. "Pa?"

As his daughter rushed up the stairs, Mr. Kane stood to take her in his arms, but the table was in the way, so the embrace was clumsy, as were most gestures of affection for this essentially verbal and rational man. The awkwardness was increased by the voluminous, dripping-wet parka she had borrowed from Coots.

"I've been...so worried..." Mr. Kane said brokenly. "I imagined...all sorts of...terrible..."

"I'm all right, Pa," she assured him as she took off the parka and put it over in the corner. "I'm just fine."

"She is *not* just fine. She's splendid!" B. J. said, coming up the stairs, having had a struggle trying to close the door against the wind. He had decided to come with her because he couldn't abide waiting around for Coots to go out to face...Christ only knew what dangers. "She saved Coots's hide by alerting him. But it's a good thing he made her turn back. This rain would have turned that trail into a death trap."

"Yes, I suppose so. But still..." Mr. Kane returned to his place at the table, while Matthew found a plate for B. J. and served up his stew. Ruth Lillian ate with appetite, B. J. with caution, and Mr. Kane not at all.

"Does this *substance* have a name?" B. J. asked, gingerly prodding a lump with the tip of his spoon.

"Yes, sir," Matthew said, reading B. J.'s intention to distract Mr. Kane from his worries, "I call it 'Twenty-Mile Stew.'"

"Hm-m. Well, perhaps twenty miles is a sufficient distance. Provided you're upwind of it."

"I think it's delicious," Ruth Lillian averred loyally, offering her plate to be refilled by Matthew.

"Well, *de gustibus non disputandum est*, or so those who lack taste are constantly telling us." He turned to Matthew. "Kersti Bjorkvist came up to the Livery just as I was leaving. She said she'd been at your place."

"Did she tell you about...anything else?"

"Just that her mother threw her out. I wonder why?"

"Oh...some sort of fight." Matthew knew that Mr. Kane mustn't find out what had happened to Kersti over at the hotel.

"She and Frenchy are keeping the lamps lit and the

fire going in the Livery office, in case those men look across.''

"When is Coots—"

"Any time now!" B. J. snapped. Then he tightened rein on his nerves. "He'll go pretty soon, I guess. He said he'd wait until the storm breaks over the town. He figured it would cover any noise he might make."

"He's very brave, your friend," Mr. Kane said.

"Yes." B. J. said simply.

"There's no alternative, I suppose? No way other than . . . ?"

"Not with those men. Matthew told you about what they did to Mr. Delanny?"

Mr. Kane nodded and glanced apprehensively at his daughter, who looked down at her plate. Frenchy had told her what she'd done. And why.

"No," B. J. said. "With men like that, there's no other way."

"I suppose you're right, but . . ."

"But what?"

"It's all so complicated. I know that man is vicious and dangerous, but on the other hand, Matthew told me how he let Frenchy go. Just let her walk away, after she had deprived him of his prey. Why would he do that?"

"I don't know," B. J. said. "Maybe like dogs can smell fear on people, some men can sense panic on their victims, and it sends them into a frenzy of violence. But if you're not afraid—if they can't see it in your eyes— then they won't attack, because all bullies are cowards down deep. I remember an Indian tale about a young buck off alone on a purification fast. He emerged up from his meditation to find himself surrounded by hungry wolves, but he survived by locking his concentration on a mental image of his beloved mother, and he was able to walk slowly through the wolves, who couldn't smell fear on him. Maybe the fact that Frenchy stood up to Lieder . . . looked him straight in the eye and defied him..." B. J. shrugged. "While poor Chinky is shy and submissive...the perfect victim. Her terror excites her tormentors."

"Maybe you're right," Mr. Kane said. "But what about Matthew here? That leader seems to have taken a shine to him. Why?"

"No idea," B. J. admitted. Then to Matthew: "What happened when he came over to your place? Did you stand up to him? Refuse to back down?"

"Not as I remember. We just talked about...oh, yes! He made some remark about Mr. Anthony Bradford Chumms—the man who writes the Ringo Kid books?— and I told him that I wouldn't stand for any bad-mouthing of Mr. Chumms. I guess that was standing up to him...sort of."

"And maybe he sees something of himself in you," Mr. Kane suggested. "There's more vanity in our affections than we like to admit."

"I don't see that we're *anything* alike," Matthew replied testily. "He said that his pa used to beat him. And kids probably razzed and ragged him at school."

"Like you?" B. J. asked, glancing quickly at Ruth Lillian, with whom he had spent an hour that afternoon discussing Matthew.

"Like *me?* My pa never beat me. And you can bet that no kids ever razzed *me* at school. I wouldn't of stood for it!" He felt Ruth Lillian's eyes on him, and he recalled telling her about how the Benson boys had ridiculed him because his pa was a drunk and beat his ma. He kept his gaze averted, not wanting her eyes to touch his. He felt betrayed by her. He couldn't see anything he and Lieder had in common! He didn't know *why* Lieder had said they were both "damaged boys"! It didn't seem to him that they—

Blinding light leapt from the windows. A deafening peal of thunder shook the walls of the Mercantile. Two flash-*cracks* in close succession left the acrid, nose-tingling smell of ozone in the room, while the imprinted shapes of the windows lingered on their eyes, but with lights and darks reversed.

At the flash, a gasp escaped Mr. Kane, who now sat rigid in his chair, drawing short quick breaths through his open mouth, not daring to exhale completely for fear of chest pains. Ruth Lillian reached over and grasped his hand, but his breathing was already beginning to slow, and soon he was able to smile weakly and say, "God enjoys His little jokes, scaring people like that. What next, I wonder? A little buzzer that gives you a shock when you reach out for His helping hand?" Everyone laughed a little, but Mr. Kane's face was still ashen and beads of cold sweat stood on his forehead.

"There's no reason for you to sit up any longer, Mr. Kane," B. J. said. "God can scare you just as well in your bed."

"That's true," Mr. Kane said with a half chuckle. "Even better. He'll be able to mix his little jokes into our nightmares."

Everyone laughed a little again. Mr. Kane squeezed his daughter's hand to say he was all right now, then he rose and went to his room.

THE STORM WAS AT its height, and Coots estimated that the party over at the hotel was probably thoroughly lubricated by now. The time had come. He slipped a sixth cartridge into his revolver. Like most experienced gunmen, he always left the chamber under the hammer empty when he was doing physical work because, as he had once explained to Matthew, if the hammer should snag on something, a man could shoot off a toe...or something worse. He put a handful of cartridges into his jacket pocket as a matter of habit, but he knew that if he didn't do the job with the first six shots, he'd be unlikely to get a chance to reload. Frenchy stood at the bottom of the loft steps, watching these simple preparations. "You be careful, y'hear?"

He nodded.

"You're pretty old for this business."

"God knows *that's* true."

"Why you doing it then?"

"Beats my two pair." He pulled his hat down tight and went out into the storm.

THE THREE OF THEM sat around the lamp in tense silence, anticipating the next volley of thunder and lightning.

"It's getting late," B. J. said for something to say.

"What time you figure it is?" Ruth Lillian asked.

"Near midnight. I don't know exactly. My watch broke three-four years ago but, considering how slow things are in Twenty-Mile, I didn't bother to—"

"Ruth Lillian?" Matthew interrupted. "I think you better start getting your truck together, in case you have to leave town."

"What are you talking about?"

"I've thought it all out. You can follow the railroad track down to Destiny. It'll be tricky, what with the rain and slippery rails and all, but you've got to go, storm or no storm."

"I can't leave Pa! Not sick like he is, and weak."

"You *gotta* go, Ruth Lillian. There's things you don't understand. Mr. Lieder, he..." Matthew swallowed. "He wants a virgin girl. To carry his seed. He wants a son to continue the battle after he's gone."

"Continue what battle?" B. J. asked.

"Some kind of battle against foreigners and Washington D.C. and—I don't know—something about Jews not being lumberjacks, and other stuff he got out of that book of his. The point is, Ruth Lillian, he's meaning to have a virgin girl."

"But he doesn't even know I'm in town."

"He does now."

"How'd he find out?" B. J. snapped.

"Kersti told him... but it wasn't her fault! It just slipped out. She was being slapped around and treated rough. I mean *real* rough. And he'll be looking for you next, Ruth Lillian. I just know it. Probably not tonight what with the storm and all, but tomorrow for sure. That's why you got to get out of here. You understand?"

She was silent for a beat. "Yes. Yes. I understand. But Mr. Coots means to get him tonight."

"Yeah but... what if something happens?" Matthew said. "What if Coots don't get him? You got to be ready to go!"

"What do you mean, *if* Coots doesn't get him?" B. J. asked with offense. "Coots will get him! And if something happens that he can't... Well then, we'll just have to protect Ruth Lillian. You and me."

"*How?*"

"I don't know, Matthew! We'll find some—What about that gun of your father's?"

"That ain't no good! I can't use it! I tried to load it just a while ago, but I couldn't! I couldn't even touch the... shells! My hands wouldn't...!" Matthew's eyes began to flicker back and forth.

"Whoa there, son! Take it easy."

"But I can't even... touch... can't even... can't even..."

"Matthew? *Matthew!*"

His breathing calmed; his eyes softened; he released a long sigh and gazed past them toward the rain-streaked window on which the lamps of the hotel made smudgy glows. The storm slackened for a second, and the sound of men singing along with the player piano emerged through the moan of the wind.

"...Matthew?" B. J. said again.

Ruth Lillian laid her hand on his sleeve. "Matthew?"

Matthew blinked and swallowed, then he settled his eyes on her. "What is it? What's wrong?"

She forced a little laugh. "You just went off."

He frowned, perplexed. "Went off?"

"That 'someplace else' you told me about? I think you just went there."

He looked from her to B. J. Stone and back in confusion. "What are you trying to...? I don't understand what you're..."

"Matthew?" B. J. said.

"Sir?"

"I'm concerned about how you're going to bear up, if things get tough."

"What do you mean?"

"Well...when a person has gone through bad things, sometimes it's hard for him to...to keep himself together under pressure."

Matthew looked from B. J. to Ruth Lillian with a blend of confusion and wariness. What was this all about?

"This afternoon while we were over at the Livery," B. J. pursued, "Ruth Lillian and I passed the time talking about things."

"What sort of things?"

"You mostly."

"Me?"

"Well, it's something we have in common. We both like you. And we're both worried about you, and we wonder...if..."

"Worried about *me?*"

Ruth Lillian took up the task of explaining. "Mr. Stone told me about what happened in Nebraska. He showed me a newspaper. And he thought—we both thought—that maybe, you know, sometimes people need to talk about things to get them off their minds. And because we're friends, you and me, and we've talked about everything under the sun—about Cracker-Jacks and infinity and everything—I thought maybe . . .''

"You thought maybe what?"

"Well, it must have been awful when you were a kid. With your pa always beating on your ma and all."

"But it wasn't his fault!"

"Whose fault was it?" B. J. asked, sitting back in his chair so as to take himself out of the lamplight.

"It wasn't nobody's fault. It was just bad luck. Pa was always full of ideas and plans, but he never had any luck. People saw him like he was at the end, staggering around, drunk and sick. They never thought about what he might have been, if he'd only had a little luck. One night when Ma was sick, I sat up to change her mustard plasters, so I was still awake when Pa came home crying-drunk . . . which was a heck of a lot better than mean-drunk. We sat by the fire, him and me, and he started talking about how it was when he was young. I guess he wanted someone to understand why he was like he was. Like you said, sometimes people need to talk about things to get them off their—"

A flash-*crack* of thunder was followed by a strange splitting sound from lower down on the mountain, as though the lightning had blown something off its flank. For a moment, the drilling din of rain on the roof abated as the storm seemed to inhale. Then it came back with redoubled force, the wind sucking at the windows, rattling them in their loose frames as it alternately moaned and shrieked.

———

COOTS'S NECK MUSCLES FLINCHED when the flash-*crack* of thunder was followed by the splitting sound from lower on the mountain. He pressed against the back wall of the Traveller's Welcome, avoiding the gush of rainwater that fell from a broken downspout, but was snatched by the wind into spume before it reached the ground.

Teeth bared in a wincing grimace, he eased open the kitchen window just as—bad luck—the covering sound of the rain and wind abated, as though the storm had inhaled, and for a moment he could hear the thumping rhythm of the player piano from the barroom beyond. As he waited for the storm to regain its fury, Coots took off his boots and left them there beside the wall. Then, with the feline sinuosity of the Cherokee, he slowly hoisted himself up and disappeared into the pitch-black kitchen, carefully pressing the window closed behind him.

"PA JUST SAT THERE staring at the fire, tears running down his cheeks. He told me how he'd meant to bring me back a book, but somebody had cheated him out of his money. It was Pa that brought back my very first Ringo Kid book after he'd been away on a long binge. He started talking about how someday he was going to strike it rich and everybody would respect him. But he never had any luck, not a single drop! Chasing after luck was why Pa came to America in the first place. He met a what they call a 'labor-broker' back in the old country, a man who would pay Pa's way to America and find him a job in return for so much a month until the debt was paid off. Well, Pa was only seventeen years old, but things were sort of hot for him in his village because of some girl, so he jumped at the chance. When he got to America, they took him right from the dock and put him on a train—forty men to a boxcar—and the train brought him to the job the labor-broker had found for him. A slate quarry up in Vermont. It was hard work, and dangerous...the kind of work native-born Americans wouldn't touch. After he'd slaved for a whole winter, getting only a few dollars a month over and above his room and board, he found out that he had only worked off *seventeen dollars* of what he owed the labor-broker. All the rest had gone for interest and 'special charges.' At that rate he would have to work at the quarry for *six years* before he was free to look for another job. Well, Pa wasn't going to put up with *that*. He ran off, and for the next few years he drifted west, roaming from place to place, but never finding that one little nugget of luck he was looking for. People would lie to him and cheat him and underpay him, so he'd steal from them, just to get even. Every business deal he ever figured out turned sour through no fault of his own. Just no luck!''

Matthew went on to tell how his father met a girl at a charity social in Tarkio, Missouri; a plain, religious girl. She was not at all the "easy" sort he usually chased after, but someone told him the girl's father was old, and she would inherit the farm. Young Dubchek immediately envisioned himself as a farmer. He would plant corn— or whatever—and bugs—or something—would come along and wipe out everybody's crop but his, and they'd all go bust while he made a bundle, so he'd buy up their farms for a song, and become a big landowner. He'd hire others to plant and harvest for him, then he'd expand, go into the grain and feed business, not just your paltry little feed store in some whistle-stop tank town, but *big-time*. He'd corner the market! That's the way to do it! Work out the percentages, then corner the market! All you need is that first little bit of luck.

He joined the Bible circle of this girl's church, and the very first day he asked her if she'd have the kindness to help him with passages he couldn't quite make out, what with his English not being so good.

The farmer didn't like the look of this Dubchek—to say nothing of his slick ways and his funny-sounding name. He ordered him to stop hanging around his daughter. During their last meeting out in the barn, Dubchek pleaded for a parting proof of her love, and the weeping daughter was unable to refuse him. After that, he hung around doing odd jobs until, a couple of months later, the farmer came to town in his trap with a horsewhip, and ordered him to marry his daughter, or else!

When the farmer died a year later, Dubchek discovered that his wife's inheritance consisted of a web of mortgages and re-mortgages. Once again, he felt cheated, this time by a woman who had dangled a useless, debt-riddled farm in front of him to lure him into marriage. The child was born; the farm was repossessed; and the three of them pushed on west, drifting from job to job, each ending with Matthew's pa being accused of loafing or stealing or drinking or sassing back. Between jobs, there were wild schemes for getting rich quick. One time, Dubchek had a chance to get in on the ground floor with a red fox farm. Red fox furs that were all the rage among rich woman back East, who would pay a hundred dollars to hang one pelt around their necks, its tail in its mouth. A hundred dollars! You multiply that by a thousand, and you've got *a hundred thousand dollars*. And that's just for starters!

For almost a year, he gave up drinking and held down two jobs, working day and night, in rain and sun, through sickness and health, saving every penny. By spring he had enough for a down payment on a badly eroded farm with a half-ruined house. What did it matter if the land wasn't no good? He wasn't no stupid dirt farmer! He was going to raise red foxes, which only required a few knocked-together hutches out behind the house. Then the bad luck started coming. He had difficulty finding foxes to raise. None of his neighbors had even *heard* of raising foxes. They thought fox pelts came from trapping. Well ... well ... well, all right, he'd get some wild foxes and raise them in hutches, and they'd breed and pretty soon the place would be teeming with foxes! He managed to buy three foxes from a trapper, one with a chewed-up leg from the trap. They all died in the hutches, the one with the bad leg lasting the longest . . . which just proves how everything depends on luck. After a long, cold winter and a long, sodden spring, they had to let the farm go back to the bank . . . more bad luck to feed Dubchek's bitterness. He started drinking again. Well, why not? What was the use of trying when everyone was against him, and everything was keeping him from making something of himself!?

The wind rose to an insane screech, clutching at the windows of the Mercantile, and slashing at the wide sheets of water that poured from brimful guttering, ripping them into ribbons of froth.

THE DARKNESS WITHIN THE hotel kitchen was intensified by an eye-baffling contrast with a trapezoid of bright light pouring in from the barroom beyond. His flat-topped Colt in his hand, Coots inched toward the blinding swath of light, rolling his weight from heel to toe of his bare feet so as not to make a sound. Queeny—good luck—was singing to the player piano. *She's only a bird in a gilded cage, a byooo-ti-ful sight to see-e-e.* He inched forward, feeling his way with his bare feet rather than with his eyes. . . . *for her love was so-o-old, for an o-o-o-old man's go-o-old! She's a bird in a gilded ca-a-a-age.*

B. J. STONE SAT DEEP in his chair, his face out of the lamplight that glowed in Ruth Lillian's cupric hair. He had listened sympathetically to Matthew's explanation of why nothing was his father's fault, because he never had any luck. But his mind had slipped from time to time to Coots . . . out there in the rain . . . in danger.

Matthew's head was bowed, his eyes lost in the shadow of his brow. B. J. had hoped that Ruth Lillian's honest and obvious concern would tempt Matthew to talk about what had happened in that farmhouse in Nebraska. But he had parried her questions by talking about his father rather than himself, and after the last crash of thunder and lightning, he hadn't continued his story. So B. J. cleared his throat and began in a gentle, measured voice, "I...ah...read this article in a Nebraska paper. There was this man and woman who lived on a farm. With their son. A passing neighbor heard their cow bellowing to be milked, so he banged on the door and looked in through the window. Then he ran off for help. They found the woman dead. A broken neck. The man had been shot. Almost blown in half." He paused, but Matthew didn't respond, didn't even raise his head; his eyes remained lost in the shadows. "The neighbor described Mrs. Dubchek as a decent, God-fearing woman, and the husband as a violent ne'er-do-well who was 'no stranger to the bottle.' The son was nowhere to be found. The paper suggested that he might have been kidnapped by the murderers. Or maybe killed and buried somewhere. When he was asked about the boy, the neighbor couldn't give any useful description. 'Just a boy,' he said. 'Nothing special.' " B. J. leaned forward into the light. "That neighbor was wrong, Matthew. The boy was very special indeed. And my heart goes out to him when I think of how he must have felt when he found his parents...like that. Or, even worse, maybe he actually witnessed the murders. What a burden of pain and horror he must be carrying inside him."

Matthew lifted his head and looked into the space between B. J. and Ruth Lillian. He reached up and touched his temple with his fingertips, then his lips, then his hand fell into his lap. He swallowed dryly. When he spoke, he started in midstream, as though he had been talking for some time, but the words hadn't come out. "...so Ma, she'd spent the day with a neighbor lady because Pa'd beat her up real bad, and she wanted to get looking better before she came home because it used to make Pa mad to see her face beat up. Well, I . . . you know . . . I didn't want to be there alone with Pa, all drunk and smelling of whiskey and up-chuck so I . . . you know . . . I walked into town, just to get away for a while. But I didn't have any money, and it was getting dark and starting to rain, so I came back. And Ma was lying there on the floor with her head sort of sideways and . . . wrong. And he was standing over her, sobbing and clawing at his cheeks. What was going to happen to him? What would they do to him? He hadn't meant to hurt her! He'd just given her a little shake! He got ahold of my collar and pushed his face up close to mine and asked me what was he going to do? But I wouldn't look at him, so he let go of me and fell on his knees beside Ma, and he started moaning and rocking himself. He wasn't crying because Ma was dead! Only because of what they might do to *him!* And the smell of whiskey and up-chuck! I couldn't breathe. I couldn't see or breathe. He knelt there beside her, rocking and moaning. He didn't hold my poor broken mother and rock her. No, he just rocked himself! So I just . . . you know . . . I took his shotgun down and I said, 'Pa?' But he didn't look up, so I said, 'Pa?' again. And he still didn't look up, so I just . . .'' Matthew swallowed so hard that Ruth Lillian could hear it. His voice was full of tears, but his eyes remained dry . . . distant . . . empty.

This was not what B. J. had expected to hear.

PRESSING BACK INTO THE deep shadow of the kitchen, Coots cocked his pistol and eased his head out toward the trapezoid of harsh light from the barroom. Two reflector storm lamps stood on the bar, their light directed toward the open kitchen door. They were so bright that it was hard to see past them, but he could make out Jeff Calder standing behind the bar, half-asleep on his feet. By stretching his neck a little more, Coots could see the backs of Bobby-My-Boy and Tiny sitting at a table on either side of Chinky, each with a hand in her lap. The "deacons" were on their loafers' bench near the player piano, where Professor Murphy sat with his body twisted to avoid contact with Queeny, who leaned over his shoulder searching through the piano rolls, looking for a song that—

Wait a minute. The storm lamps! Why were they set up on the bar, pointed toward—?

"They tell me you're called Coots," Lieder whispered, his pistol pressed into the soft spot beneath Coots's ear. "I like to know a man's name."

———————

"YOU ACTED ON THE spur of the moment, Matthew," B. J. explained. "The shock of seeing your mother lying there on the floor, and knowing that your own father had...*Anybody* might have done what you did. You've got to understand that, and you must try to forgive yourself. Oh, it's going to take a long time to get over what happened. Maybe you never will. But believe me, son, in time you'll find a way to live with it...or live around it. And any time you feel that talking things out might help, well, we're here and we—"

"After I...did it, I dropped the gun on the floor," Matthew continued. Nothing B. J. had said had penetrated his mind. "I couldn't pick it up. I tried, but I couldn't make myself touch it."

"But you did pick it up," Ruth Lillian said, hoping to guide him back to reality. "You brought it here with you."

He blinked and looked at her with a confused frown,

as though realizing that fact for the first time. "You're *right*. I...I brought it with me."

"Why?" B.J. asked. "Why'd you do that, Matthew?"

"I don't know. Maybe because it was Pa's. And because he never had any luck."

Ruth Lillian repeated his words in a wondering whisper. "Because your pa never had any luck... that's why you carried that gun more'n a hundred miles?"

He settled his eyes on her without answering. The storm was fleeing southeast as quickly as it had roared in from the northwest. The wind had suddenly fallen, and the last of the departing lightning billowed dimly within horizon clouds, followed at a long interval by the distant mutter of weary thunder.

"Matthew?" she repeated gently. "Is that why you brought it?"

"I hate that gun, Ruth Lillian. I really and truly hate it. I don't ever want to see it nor touch it again!"

"And you don't have to," B.J. assured him. "You'll never have to touch that gun again. If you want, I'll go over to your place with you and we'll—*What was that!*"

A gunshot from across the street. Followed by five more shots, the rounds squeezed off at regular, unhurried intervals.

B.J. rushed to the window.

Having emptied his gun into the air to attract attention, Lieder was standing on the porch of the hotel, lit from behind by a tombstone-shaped slab of light formed by the open bat-winged doors.

The wind had died away, but that heavy, soaking rain that follows the trailing edge of mountain storms continued to drill down vertically, making such liquid din on glistening roofs and in mud-lathered puddles that Lieder had to cup his hands around his mouth and shout, "I know you're out there, schoolteacher! Come out, come out, wherever you are! All-ye, all-ye ox-in-free!"

B. J. could make out two figures standing behind Lieder . . . his lackeys. And between them there was a tall—
"Oh, God," B. J. whispered. "Oh, *God!*"

"What is it?" Ruth Lillian asked.

They had Coots. His arms were bound to his sides, and he was standing on a chair beneath the central beam of the hotel porch. B. J. couldn't see clearly, but he knew from the way Coots was standing—up on his toes to relieve the pressure—that there was a rope around his neck, running tight over the beam. And there were other men crowded along the wall of the porch. Lieder's "deacons". Witnesses.

Lieder shouted again, but some of his words got lost in the noise of the rain. ". . . Coots here . . . guilty . . . assassination! You . . . last words with . . . ?"

With an agonized cry, B. J. rushed from the window and pounded down the stairs to the darkened shop, stumbling at the bottom and ending up on his knees. He scrambled up and staggered on through the dark, catching his hip on the counter and upsetting a stack of cans. He reached the front door, which he shook until the spring bell above complained, but it was locked! "Wait!" he cried. "*Wait!*"

"Come out, come out, wherever you are!"

B. J. barged blindly through the store to the back door, clawed it open, and lurched out into a puddle being excavated by a thick rope of water falling from guttering overburdened with rain. "*Wait!*"

Lieder had expected to see B. J. coming from the direction of the Livery, so he was surprised to see him emerge from between the Mercantile and the ruins of the Pair o' Dice Social Club, slithering in the mud.

"Well, now! What were you doing over at the Jew's? Come on, schoolteacher! Run! You can make it! Hurry up, there!"

"Wait!" B. J. rasped, his lungs screaming for air.

"Run!" Lieder set his foot against the chair on which

Coots stood on his toes. "Come on! Go it, schoolteacher! Attaboy! You can make it!" He kicked the chair out from under Coots. "O-o—oh. Too late." The crack of his neck was audible through the rain; his body jerked twice with such convulsive force that he broke the cotton clothesline that bound his arms; then he hung still, turning slowly, his hands cupped, knuckles forward, his toes turned inward. There was an eternity of human suffering in those bare, gnarled old feet...turning.

B. J. stumbled up the steps of the hotel and grasped Coots around the knees. He tried to lift the body to take the weight from the rope, but he couldn't: the knees and waist were limp. "Help me!" he begged Tiny and Bobby-My-Boy, who looked on, interested. "Somebody help me!" There was a nervous stir among the deacons, but no one stepped forward. B. J. hugged the knees to his chest and moaned.

Matthew came running across the street, slipping in the mud. But before he got to B. J., Lieder grabbed him by the collar and snatched his face up close to his own. "Did you know about this, boy?! Did you know they meant to shoot me in the back?!"

Confused, frightened, Matthew cried, "What? What do you mean?"

"I knew it!" Lieder cried into the rain. "I knew it! I have always been a good judge of horse-flesh and man-flesh, and I just *knew* that one damaged boy couldn't never turn on another. They didn't tell you they planned to shoot me down in cold blood. No! They used you, boy. You let them use you just as bad as if you'd been a new boy in prison. *Now* maybe you know who your real friend is!" He looked down at B. J., who had slumped to his knees still hugging Coots's legs to him. "Oh for Christ's sake, old man! He's dead! All your sobbing and whimpering won't change that. He's dead, and it was your sneaking and plotting that killed him! Killed him just as sure as if you'd kicked that chair out from under him yourself. So stop slobbering on like an old woman!''

B. J. muttered something wetly into Coots's legs.

''What?''

''I want...take him down.''

''Take him, then! *Take him!* I don't need no back-shooting nigger hanging around my front door! Go on! Take him!''

B. J. looked up at the beam and the rope, confused, tears streaming from his eyes and nose and mixing with the rain on his face. ''Matthew...?''

Matthew fished his Barlow knife out of his pocket and held it out. B. J. climbed up on the chair and sawed at the rope, while Matthew did his best to lighten the strain by lifting Coots, but the legs were too limp, and when the rope parted with a dull twang, Coots slumped across Matthew's shoulders, the lifeless weight buckling his knees and making him stagger, but none of the deacons came forward to help him; they remained close to the wall, scared and drunk. B. J. peeled Coots's weight from Matthew's back and sat across the bottom step in the rain, holding Coots in his arms, the dead face buried in his neck.

''Now ain't that a picture?'' Lieder asked, stepping out into the rain and standing before B. J. and Coots to occupy the center of attention. ''Now, this here's what I call a picture of true friendship,'' he told his men and ''deacons'' with grave sincerity, the rain running from the brim of his hat onto Coots's chest. ''You may not believe it, schoolteacher, but I appreciate how you must be suffering, knowing that you caused the death of your friend with your treachery and schemes. Friendship and loyalty are two qualities I admire...'' He looked back up to his audience on the porch. ''...just as I detest sneaks and tattletales. And one among you is just that, a sneak and a tattletale. One among you is a Judas. Schoolteacher?'' Lieder placed his palm on B. J.'s head. ''Shall I tell you how I found out about your nigger friend?"

B. J. didn't respond.

"No, maybe I shouldn't tell. After all, I gave my word. But then, I do *loathe* a tattletale. Always have, ever since school. I gave my word, so I cannot divulge who told me in hopes of getting in good with me. But I can say this much: he was a man of the cloth."

B. J. lifted his head, and his eyes found those of Reverend Hibbard among the silent onlookers.

Hibbard's eyes flickered, and he pressed back against the wall of the hotel, shaking his head in denial and lifting his palms in helplessness. "Yes but...but..." he babbled into the rain. "I only did what I had to do. I saw your Coots up at the Lode! I knew he'd be coming back down today. It wasn't hard to figure out he'd be trying something!"

B. J.'s eyes remained heavily on Hibbard: there was neither hatred nor anger in them, only infinite sadness, infinite pain.

"Don't blame *me!*" Hibbard cried. "What if your Coots had failed? Eh? Mr. Lieder would have thought we were all in on it! You didn't care what would happen to us, did you?"

B. J. closed his eyes and lowered his head to Coots's, but Matthew continued to glare at the preacher with cold loathing.

"Don't you look at me like that, boy! I did what I had to do! I acted for the greater good!"

"Oh now, don't piss yourself, Reverend," Lieder said. "Nobody's going to hurt you. After all..." He smiled. "...you enjoy my personal protection."

"Matthew?" B. J. said quietly. "I've got to get him home."

Matthew looked around for something to carry Coots on, then he decided to fetch the handbarrow he used to bring supplies up from the train. He hurried back across to the Mercantile, and he was dragging the barrow out

of the shed when Ruth Lillian opened the back door.
"Matthew...?" But he shook his head and plodded back
through the rain.

They lifted Coots into the barrow as gently as they
could, but his legs and arms dangled over awkwardly.
B. J. grasped the handles and pushed Coots home, rain
washing the tears from his upturned face, his arms
stretched straight from his shoulders to the handles, his
boots slipping on the mud through which Coots's bare
heels dragged.

———————————

DAWN. AND THE RAIN had thinned to a chill mist
that condensed in opalescent beads on the rusted wire
fence between the donkey meadow and the burying
ground. The gritty scrape of B. J.'s spade cutting into the
yeasty earth was uncannily sharp and clear, as sounds are
in mist. Unused to such heavy work, B. J.'s breathing
soon became a rasp that galled his lungs, so he didn't
object when Matthew took the spade from him and continued digging at the same rhythm.

B. J. sat on the ground beside Coots and placed a comforting hand on his blanket-wrapped chest, too deep in
grief and pain to notice Matthew's peculiar expression as
he dug: faraway eyes and a vague half-smile.

The handle of Matthew's spade stung his hands when
the blade rang on the shelf-rock that lay about four feet
beneath the sodden surface. He turned and began to bring
the other end of the grave down to the same level. It
wasn't until he stood up to take off his hat and wipe the
sweat from his forehead that he noticed Frenchy standing
behind B. J. and Coots. Without a word she hitched up
her skirts and tucked the hem into her waistband until
her cotton-stockinged legs were free up to her knee-
length pantaloons. She stepped to the edge of the grave
and held out her hand with an authority of gesture that

dismissed argument. Matthew gave her the spade and watched her dig with the economic hip-swing of a woman who had done her share of field work as a girl, before she escaped to the glittering world. He was on her "scar side," and the immobile, dispassionate ugliness fascinated him.

He became aware of a soft humming behind him... an old Negro spiritual. He turned his head, and Lieder was standing there, his hat in his hand, his head bowed.

Without looking at Lieder, B. J. rose and took another turn, then he gave the spade to Matthew, who had struck shelf-rock from end to end before Frenchy's turn came again. And all the time, Lieder continued to hum in a soft, plaintive voice, his hands folded on the butt of the cocked pistol in his belt. The grave was only a few inches longer than Coots, so it wasn't possible to lower him in gracefully. Matthew stood in the hole with Coots's feet between his boots, while B. J.'s straddled his head. The face had become uncovered in the handling, so B. J. covered it up again, folding the fabric over tenderly. They climbed out and stood on the edge of the grave until B. J. said, "I guess I should..." But then he shook his head miserably. "No words." He pushed the spade into the newly dug earth and stood with it, but he was unable to dump it onto Coots.

Frenchy took the spade from him and led him back to the Livery, leaving Matthew to fill in the grave.

Lieder stopped humming and followed the departing B. J. with his eyes. "Just look at him. That schoolteacher is a broken man. Broken by suffering and loss. You saw how he couldn't even try to take his revenge on me? That poor old man's so full of grief and self-pity that there's no room left for hate. And a man needs hate. Sometime hate's all that keeps us going. Oh, it's all the old fool's own fault, of course, but still..." Lieder shook his head and sucked at his front teeth. "I hate to see a man's innards all scooped out like that. He won't be any good to anybody until the suffering burns itself out, and that'll take a long, long time. And you know what that means, Matthew? It means you're all alone now. You can thank your lucky stars that you and me, we're cut from the same cloth.'' He chuckled. ''Rough old burlap! That's the kind of cloth we were cut from, right? Eh? What do you say?''

Matthew stood stiff and unresponsive, his eyes defocused, not even feeling the hand that Lieder had laid on his shoulder.

''It wasn't my fault that jig tried to back-shoot me, Matthew. I *had* to punish him. I didn't have any choice. But you can believe me when I tell you that I wish to God it hadn't happened. I didn't want to harm anybody in this sorry excuse for a town. But people just won't *leave me alone!*''

Matthew didn't respond. His eyes were fixed on the space where Lieder was standing.

''You listening to what I'm telling you, boy?''

Matthew blinked and brought Lieder's face into focus. ''I got to bury Coots,'' he said dryly.

''All right then, you do that. We'll talk about things tomorrow. I've got plans for you, boy. A shining future!'' And he left, humming the old spiritual that he found so comforting.

Matthew reached down until the loaded spade almost touched the blanket, because he wanted to sprinkle the dirt softly over the head and shoulders, but it was sodden and clotted, so chunks fell in, making him wince. Only after the head was covered with a thick layer could he shovel in the rest of the pile at a slow, regular rhythm, his eyes calm and distant.

———————

PROFESSOR MURPHY FELT MISERABLE, both drunk and hung over at the same time. He would have swapped his front seat in hell for a chance to lay his throbbing head down...but no! No, they wanted hot baths...those two stupid animals!...and he had been obliged to fire up the boiler. The big one had soaked himself for half an hour before climbing out and returning to the Traveller's Welcome. But this little one had demanded more hot water. And now he was wallowing in the tub, the rising steam blending with descending mist.

The Professor rolled his bloodshot eyes and wondered how much longer he would have to stay there, waiting for this damned—*Now* what?

He watched that Dubchek kid—or whatever his name was—step out from the marshal's office and walk toward the barbershop, a six-pointed badge pinned to the breast pocket of his canvas jacket, and that big old shotgun over his shoulder, barrel in his fist, stock in the air.

Tiny had bent his knees until the water was level with his lower lip and he was blowing bubbles across the scummy surface. He looked up to see Matthew standing between his bath barrel and the wheezing boiler. "You still trying to get shed of that old cannon, boy? I already told you that nobody wants no ten-ton antique that don't even have...any...ammu..." His voice trailed off as he saw Matthew cock back the hammer. His eyes flicked over to the chair where the Colt he had taken from that nigger lay on his pile of clothes, then back to Matthew's face. A weary smile bent Matthew's lips, and his eyes looked gently upon Tiny...or rather, upon the place where Tiny was. When he spoke, it was with the soft burr that Mr. Anthony Bradford Chumms had described as "carrying more menace than any angry snarl."

"I'm sorry, Tiny, but there ain't no other way."

Tiny's twisted face started to spread flat, as though he were going to cry. "Ma-a-a?" he pleaded in a curling whine.

The shotgun roared, blowing the barrel staves asunder,

and for a fraction of a second the water retained the barrel's shape with Tiny standing in the middle of it, then pink foam blossomed from Tiny's exploded chest and the water dropped away, leaving him standing alone and naked for an instant, before he crumpled dead to the ground.

Matthew's soft gaze climbed slowly from what was left of Tiny to the façade of the hotel while his hands mechanically broke open the gun, clawed out the shell, wet with molten candle wax, took another from his pocket, and thumbed it in.

He snapped the gun shut and walked toward the hotel, his wrists throbbing from the recoil of the shotgun.

Bobby-My-Boy stumbled out through the bat-winged doors, levering a round into his rifle. "What the shit . . . ?"

". . . exploded . . ." Matthew muttered.

"What exploded?"

"The boiler, I guess. Your pal's a mess. All over the place."

Now, that was something Bobby-My-Boy had to see. He pushed past Matthew on his way to the barbershop.

"Hey?" Matthew said.

Bobby-My-Boy turned back. He never heard the shot that took off his head.

Matthew didn't look at the thing that shuddered convulsively on the ground. Again he had been obliged to shoot from the hip, and he had heard his right wrist pop with the wrench of the recoil. It didn't hurt yet, but it was numb, so he had to cradle the gun over his arm while he snatched the hot shell out and pushed another in.

He snapped the gun shut and mounted the steps to the hotel porch. Pressing his back to the weathered wall beside the door, he wet his lips with his tongue and took two long breaths. Lieder was probably in there, covering the door. But where? In his chair against the back wall? Behind the bar? Kneeling on the kitchen steps, aiming up from the floorboards? The shotgun would blow away a three-foot circle at the distance to the back wall, so he didn't have to hit dead center, but there wouldn't be time to put in another shell if he missed. How would the Ringo Kid—? The kitchen screen door slapped shut on its spring stop! Lieder had gone out the back! But which way? Was he slipping behind the abandoned buildings, up toward the tracks and Reverend Hibbard's depot? Or down the other way, down toward the boardinghouse and the Mercantile?

...Or maybe he was inching around the side of the hotel!

Matthew rushed down the steps and rolled in under the hotel porch, where he could look out between the broken skirting slats and survey the street from one end to the other. He wriggled farther back until his shoulders were against the stone foundation. He faced ahead, but his concentration was on the fuzzy peripheral extremes of his field of vision, hoping to catch any motion.

And what if Lieder had slipped back into the hotel and would soon come out onto the porch overhead? Well ...well, then he would do what he did in *The Ringo Kid Takes a Chance*: he'd shoot up through the floorboards. That hadn't been as "square" as meeting a man face to face in the street, but he'd been lying under that porch badly wounded, and a woman's honor was at risk, so there hadn't been any altern—

A blur of movement in the corner of his right eye! Lieder dashed across the street and up the steps to the door of the Mercantile, whose spring bell jangled faintly as he snatched it open and burst in.

Ruth Lillian!

Matthew rolled out from under the porch and stood up in the middle of the street. What should he do? Quick! What should he do? "Here I am!" he shouted. "It's me you want! I shot your men, and I'm going to shoot you!" As he walked toward the Mercantile, he fired the shot-

gun into the air to draw Lieder's attention away from
Ruth Lillian and toward him. "Here I am!" He opened
the gun and scrabbled in his jacket pocket for another
shell, but the fingers below his sprained wrist had swollen
to tight-skinned claws that fumbled and dropped the shell
into the mud. He kept walking toward the Mercantile,
changing the gun to a left-handed grip and clumsily pushing in a shell with his right thumb. When he reached the
store, he stopped and called, "Come out here!"

"I don't want to hurt you, boy!" Lieder shouted from
within. "You're my crowned prince! The future of the
movement!"

"Come out here, you yellow son of a bitch!"

"Now you listen, boy! If I come out there, there's
only one way things can end. And that would be a terrible
waste."

"I'm coming in!"

The door of the Mercantile slapped open, and Ruth
Lillian appeared on the threshold. Her neck was twisted
awkwardly because Lieder had the fingers of his left hand
tightly entwined in her hair and was keeping her in front
of him. "No point in this little virgin getting shot, boy!
We got better things to do with her, you and me! Now,
I admit that when that Swede girl told me about Miss
Kane here, I was mighty put out. Trying to keep this nice
piece of girl-flesh all to yourself! Shame on you! But then
I got to thinking things out and here's the way I see it.
I killed your nigger friend, and you got revenge by shooting my followers. I'm willing to call that even-steven.
And because I've always had a tender spot in my heart
for young love, you can have this little girl all to yourself.
What do you say?" He pushed Ruth Lillian out onto the
porch and followed her, keeping her back tight against
his chest.

Matthew's glance flicked from Lieder's face to Ruth
Lillian's. Her eyes shone with tears, and they looked almost oriental, drawn back at the corners by the tightness

of Lieder's grip on her hair. Her lips were parted and her teeth stubbornly clenched to keep from crying out at the pain. "What did you do to Mr. Kane?" he asked.

"He ain't hurt all that bad. Well, what do you say, boy? I don't want to kill you, and I know you don't want to shoot holes in this virgin girl. That'd be a terrible waste." He grinned. "Now, this may look like your classic Mexican standoff, but it ain't. It ain't, and you know why? Because I hold all the aces. You're standing there in the open, and I'm here behind this girl's *fine* young flesh." The grin faded from his lips. His pale gray eyes chilled. "And we both know—*we both know*—that you are not going to shoot this sweet young girl to get at me." He cocked his pistol. "So what you'd best do is this, Matthew. You'd best just lay that gun down on the ground and step back. And you'd best do it now, right now! 'Cause I'm through talking, boy, and the messy business is going to start a lot sooner than you think."

"You better look at my gun, mister," Matthew said in that softly menacing burr Anthony Bradford Chumms had so often described.

Lieder glanced down. The trigger was depressed, and the only thing keeping the shotgun from firing was the crook of Matthew's thumb holding back the hammer.

"You're right when you say that I could never shoot first," he said quietly. "But I don't have to. You shoot me, and this old gun goes off. And you're dead."

"And this girl's dead too."

"She'd rather be dead than have you messing with her."

"You're...you are crazy, boy." He started to ease back toward the door.

"One...more...inch, and I drop the hammer." The calm fatality of his voice gave Lieder pause. "And you better know something, mister. I hurt my wrists pretty bad shooting your animals, so I can't hold this hammer back much longer."

Lieder looked over his shoulder, estimating the distance between him and the door. Two long strides. Too far. And this girl's little body wouldn't absorb much double-ought at this range. He glared at Matthew, standing there with that silly-assed badge on his chest, holding that *stupid gun!*

He grinned.

"Well, I'll be damned," he said with a philosophic shake of his head. "I will be god-good'n-*damned!*" He raised his hand, letting the pistol dangle from his finger in the trigger housing. "You know, I knew it right from the first. Yes sir, the first time I set eyes on you, I knew you had enough grit and smarts to be my right-hand man."

"Let her loose."

"You bet." His grip on her hair slackened, but strands were still entangled in his fingers, so she had to snatch her head away with pain. She stepped toward Matthew.

"Lie down!" he ordered. And she instantly sank to the porch floor.

Lieder's grin widened. "That was smart, boy. You are really *something*, you know that? You and me, we're going to make—"

"Just let that gun fall off'n your finger!"

"Well now, if you're going to shoot me anyway, I might as well make a fight of it. And if you don't intend to shoot me, well then..." He started to walk slowly forward toward the porch steps.

"You better drop that gun."

"You reckon? Me, I'm not all that sure. And I'll tell you why."

"Don't come any closer!"

"...I'll tell you why, Matthew. If you really meant to shoot me down in cold blood, I'd already be dead. Now, just a bit ago... when you were trying to save this girl from what you call your 'fate worse than death'... you might of shot me then. Yes you might of. But she's safe now—honey, you go back inside and take care of your pa, like a good girl.'' Ruth Lillian looked up at Matthew for affirmation. He nodded curtly without taking his eyes off Lieder, and she crawled away from between them, then rose and ran into the Mercantile. ''There now! Now it's just me and you standing here looking at one another in the eyes, and I don't think you're the kind of person who could shoot a man who's shown you nothing but friendship and respect. A man who—''

''Don't come down those steps!''

''...a man who respects you enough to make you his successor in the great struggle to save these United States of America from—''

''Don't come any closer. I'm warning—!''

''All right! I'm dropping my gun. There she goes, Plop, right into a puddle. Ain't it a crying shame to treat a gun that way? And now here I am, standing in front of you, feeling naked as a jaybird with no gun to protect myself. But that's all right, Matthew. That's all right. And do you know why? Because this little face-off between you and me is already over. It's over, and I've won. I've won because you are confused and uncertain, weary of heart, and broken of spirit, and I have all the control. That's what happens when you stand against a man who can talk the birds down from the trees. At this moment, Matthew, right at this *very* moment, you're not exactly certain what's happening, are you? You're not even sure what I'm talking about, or why I'm talking this way, but you sense deep down inside that there's something dangerous in it. Well, don't you worry about it, 'cause I couldn't bring myself to hurt you. Look how I'm holding my empty palms out to you, Matthew. A gesture of peace and submission. And the wrath of Jehovah will descend on the man who offers harm to one who comes in peace and supplication.'' He grinned boyishly. ''As you probably recognize, that's from Paul to the Montanans...7, 13.'' He laughed, a thin note. ''Oh my, now I almost wish you *were* going to shoot me, because wouldn't it be thrilling for schoolchildren reading my biography to hear how I joked right up to the end? What a man! And you know what? You're going to become quite a man too, Matthew. You and me, side by side. There ain't nothing or no one in the world that can stop us. Now, boy what I'm going to do is reach out and take the shotgun from you. So I suppose if you really intend to let that hammer drop, this is the time to do it.'' Still smiling, he reached out and grasped the barrel.

But Matthew held tight.

Lieder glared. ''I'm taking the gun, boy!''

Matthew shook his head, his teeth clenched. He growled deep in his throat.

Suddenly, Lieder released the gun. ''All right...all right...you win! Keep the goddamn gun! I mean, after all, it has sentimental value, what with being your pa's and all. As for me? Well, I guess there's nothing for me to do but turn around and walk out of Twenty-Mile.'' He put his fists on his hips and regarded Matthew. ''You really *are* something, boy! Stubborn. Tough. Ornery.'' He grinned. ''Just like me when I was your age.'' He shook his head and chuckled. ''Who'd have thought it, eh? Me, made to back down by a kid! Well...just goes to show.'' He pressed his temples between his finger and thumb to relieve his throbbing head; then he loosened the braided leather lanyard that he had taken from the prison guard. ''Guess I'm getting old, Matthew. I got aches and pains where I didn't even know I had *places*. And talk about itches! I swear I have provided a meal for every flea in that hotel.'' He scratched his side, reaching up under his green-and-gold-brocade waistcoat with his thumb and chasing the itch back toward his spine, his teeth bared in a rictus of gratification. ''Yes, sir, I guess I'll just have to find me another town with a treasure of precious metal to pay for my militia of pure-blood Americans who will rid this nation of—''

The shotgun blast penetrated his stomach and blew away the pistol he was slipping from his belt behind his back. Blew it away, hand and all. His hips were driven back faster than his head and heels, so his chin snapped down to his chest and his boots left tracks in the mud. He ended sitting with his forehead on his knees against the steps to the Mercantile, which were splattered with soft bits. Whimpering in misery, Matthew clawed the hot shell out and pushed a fresh one in. He fired again, and the lifeless body jumped. He clawed out the hot waxy shell and put another in and fired, and the chest erupted into pulp. He clawed out the shell and pushed one in and fired, and the head swung loose. He clawed out the shell and thumbed in another, then turned and walked up the street.

Jeff Calder had been peeking around the door of the Traveller's Welcome to see what was happening down at the Mercantile, and now he staggered backward to make way for Matthew as he pushed in through the doors, shrugged off the old soldier's congratulatory pat on the shoulder.

"What can I serve ya?" Jeff Calder asked. "Anything you want. On the house. Man, I'd of give anything to be out there, standing shoulder to shoulder with you, facing down them no-accounts, and I would of been too, but this damned stump of mine's been acting up something fierce. I guess it's winter coming in and—"

"You just stay out of my line of fire," Matthew said in a dull monotone.

Pressing the stock firmly into his shoulder to prevent further damage to his wrists, he aimed at the nest of bottles on the shelf behind the bar. They exploded with a roar as the bottom of the back-bar mirror fragmented, allowing the top to slide down the frame and crack in half. Calmly he pulled out the spent shell and replaced it with one from his pocket, then he shifted his position to give himself an enfilade shot at the bottles kept beneath the bar. These disintegrated in a spray of liquid and glass that blew a panel off the front of the bar.

Frenchy burst in, followed by Kersti. "What the hell's going on? What are you doing, boy?"

"There won't be no more drinking in Twenty-Mile, ma'am. Not while I'm marshal."

"While you're... *what?*"

"It's booze that turns weak men into bad ones," Matthew quoted from a Ringo Kid book as he reloaded. He fired again, destroying the rest of the bottles.

"Now, I know you got more hooch stashed down under the trapdoor," he said. "And that's where it better stay, you hear what I'm telling you?" He slipped in the last of his handmade shells and snapped the gun shut. "Ma'am?" he said, politely pulling at the brim of his hat. And he left the hotel.

On his way up to the Reverend's depot he passed Professor Murphy who, after seeing Tiny and Bobby-My-Boy killed, had vomited against the wall of his barbershop until he was empty. Now, his lips slack and moist, he was looking down at Tiny's naked body... his pulpy, suppurating chest and stomach, his limp little penis. He dry-retched, and revulsion caused his eyes to flinch away, but morbid fascination dragged them back again.

Matthew stood in the street in front of the depot. "Come out here, preacher!" he called.

The front door was ajar, creaking slightly in the breeze that was beginning to dissipate the mist.

"You can't hide in there forever."

Nothing stirred within.

He waited a full minute, perfectly patient. Then: "All right. Here we go." He mounted the steps to the porch.

He knew the Reverend had given his gun to Lieder, but there were still kitchen knives and a poker and a kindling hatchet; and Hibbard could be behind any door, ready to spring out. So Matthew cocked the shotgun before opening the front door wide with his toe and looking obliquely in . . . then he shook his head, uncocked his gun, and pushed his hat back with his thumb.

The disorder within said it all. Hibbard was gone. He had returned to the depot, snatched up a few clothes and valuables, then run off. Either he was on his way up the tracks to the Surprise Lode, or he was making the tortuous descent to Destiny. Feeling suddenly empty and sour inside, Matthew sank into the chair by the table where the Reverend used to work up his hellfire sermons. Both his wrists had been wrenched by recoil, and the swollen right one throbbed with each beat of his pulse. He knew he could lose the pain by letting himself slip even deeper into the Other Place, by just letting go and sliding into the velvety warmth. . . . No! He stood up, tipping the chair over with the backs of his knees.

When he stepped out onto the porch of the depot, the mist had blown off, revealing the year's first snow out on the high reaches of the westward mountains. Torn shreds of cloud scuttled across a taut, wintry sky while, down in the street, the chill breeze ruffled the muddy puddles. He drew a long sigh and started back up toward the Mercantile.

He stopped at the Tonsorial Palace and kicked at the door. Murphy appeared, his eyes red from drink, his cheeks pale from another bout of vomiting.

"Come with me."

"Listen, boy, I'm feeling awful, and I—"

"Just come along."

So carefully did Murphy keep his eyes away from Tiny's gory chest and limp penis that he tripped over Bobby-My-Boy's headless corpse, and he recoiled, gagging and spitting. But he meekly followed Matthew to the porch of the Traveller's Welcome.

"Calder!"

The old veteran stumped up to the door and looked out.

"Come with me."

"Right now?"

"Just do it."

The three of them continued down toward the Mercantile, where a primitive carrion fascination had drawn the Bjorkvist men across the street to look at the remains of Lieder, which Oskar couldn't resist prodding with his toe. An act of bravado that made him tingle with frightened titillation.

"Here's what I want you to do," Matthew told the four of them. "Go fetch shovels and brooms and whatever you need, and clear away what's left of these men. Then I want you—"

"Hey!" Mr. Bjorkvist objected. "Why should we—"

Matthew shifted his shotgun and let his eyes lie heavily on Bjorkvist before saying, "I'm pretty disgusted over how none of you lifted a hand to save Coots. So it'd be a big mistake to give me any back-sass." The marshal's eyes narrowed, and he slowly inventoried their faces, one by one, causing each in turn to look down or aside. "Now like I said, I want you to clear these men away. Dump it all over the cliff. I don't want them in the same burying ground as Coots. Then I want you to sluice water around everywhere and scatter dirt until there's not a trace left. Not . . . one . . . trace. I'll be sitting up yonder on my porch, watching you. Now get to it."

He glanced up at the doorway of the Mercantile, where Ruth Lillian was standing next to Mr. Kane, who had a bandage over his eyebrow. He nodded to them, touched his hat brim, then turned and walked up to the marshal's office.

All morning, B. J. lay in bed, staring up at the ceiling, his eyes gritty and dry, as old eyes are when they have shed all the tears their ducts can produce. He had heard the shooting out in the street, but he didn't care. He had heard Frenchy and Kersti run out of the house on their

way over to the hotel, but he didn't care. And now he
heard the scrape, scrape of shovels out in the street, but
he didn't care. For the first time, he knew that he was
old. Really old. There was nothing for him to do. No one
needed him. There was no one to take care of, or be
irritated with, or tease. So he'd just . . . lie there.

By noon the street had been cleared of the last traces
of Lieder and his men, dirt had been scattered over the
bloody places, and the reluctant clean-up party had returned to their houses. But still Matthew sat on a chair
on his porch, the ball-pointed star on his breast, the shotgun containing his last shell heavy on his lap.

Although he had been aware of her approach out of
the corner of his eye, he didn't turn toward Ruth Lillian
when she said, "We're waiting dinner for you."

"That's real good of you, ma'am. But I'm not a bit
hungry. And anyway . . ." He held out his swollen wrist
and sausage fingers. "I doubt I'd be any great shakes
with a fork."

She reached out and gingerly touched the hot, tight
skin of his hand.

"I'll be all right," he said.

But she went into the office and soaked a cloth in the
chipped enamel wash-up basin he had carried with him
all the way from Nebraska. He didn't object when she
wrapped the sodden bandage around his wrist. "There,
that'll help bring down the swelling."

"Feels better already. Thank you."

"I could bring a bowl of stew for you to eat here, if
you want?"

"No thank you, ma'am. I'm just fine as I am."

"Yes, but . . ." She didn't know what to say. That
"ma'am" was worrying. "Pa's not hurt. Just a bad headache."

"I'm glad to hear that."

"You'll be up for supper, I hope?" She smiled. "You

won't have to help with the dishes. Not with that wrist of yours. You can just sit and talk to Pa.''

He blinked and turned to her. ''I'm sorry . . . what was that?''

''I asked if you'd be coming for supper.''

He looked at her with a slightly puzzled frown until she said, ''Well, I . . . I've got to get back. Dinner's getting cold.''

He nodded slowly.

She felt she ought to say something else, but she couldn't think of anything, so she left.

Matthew did not come to supper that evening, nor did he show up at the Traveller's Welcome the next morning to make breakfast for the girls. His time as the town's odd-job man was over. Later in the afternoon he came into the Mercantile, still wearing the badge and carrying his shotgun over his shoulder, the muzzle in his fist. In his new, softly diffident voice he gave Mr. Kane an order for flour, dried beans, bacon, corn syrup, tinned tomatoes, and tinned peaches, which Mr. Kane put into his canvas satchel for him because his wrist was still swollen. When Ruth Lillian came down from above to greet him, he said he hoped she was feeling all right after that little dustup the day before. Then he told them he wouldn't be burdening them with his company at meals anymore. He'd just fix up his own grub, if it was all the same to them. Ruth Lillian was saying, no, it *wasn't* all the same to her . . . when he tugged the brim of his hat at each of them and left.

From then until the miners returned the next Saturday for their weekly blow-out, Matthew spent most of his time sitting on his porch, his chair tipped back against the wall, keeping an eye on things. Marshal of Twenty-Mile. A highly respected man.

He no longer read his Ringo Kid books.

The town slowly returned to its habitual routines and concerns. Professor Murphy found a hogshead out behind the depot to replace the barrel he had lost, and he paid Oskar Bjorkvist two-bits to scrub it clean enough for miners. The boy occasionally looked up from this work and glared at Matthew, sitting across the street, watching through half-closed eyes.

Frenchy assumed Mr. Delanny's authority at the Traveller's Welcome. She even sat at his table, occasionally laying out solitaire. After a crisp no-holds-barred talk with Jeff Calder that left his ears sizzling with accusations of kiss-ass, lick-spittle kowtowing toward those outlaws, she gave the war hero a choice between doing all the cleaning, sweeping, bed-changing, and laundry, in addition to his work as bartender, or getting the hell out and stumping his way down to Destiny. He also had to make the breakfast every morning, which he did with angry assaults on the Dayton Imperial and (when he was sure Frenchy was out of earshot) with growling mutters about uppity niggers that you can't give an inch, or they'll take an ell. His efforts at baking biscuits were so total a disaster that Frenchy told him not to bother, just go back to beans, bacon, and coffee—if he had the brass to call this gritty sludge coffee!

It was over a cup of that gritty sludge that Frenchy gave Kersti clear, unembroidered technical advice about how to work fast, keep herself clean, and handle the men. She explained that it was just a job. "That's the only way to think of it, honey. Just a job. And if anything happens that you can't handle, just walk out of the room and come down to me. I'll take care of it. I know it seems scary. It was the same with me when I started out, and I was a helluva lot younger than you. Don't worry, you'll do just fine. No, no, that's all right. Go ahead and cry, if you want to. You've got a right." But Kersti sniffed and shook her head, and Frenchy told her she could have any of her fancy dresses that could be made to fit, so she'd better go look through her own wardrobe and choose the prettiest.

Later that afternoon, Frenchy was looking on as Jeff Calder arranged the bottles of the whiskey he had carried up from the dug cellar beneath the trap door. The squeak-flap of the bat-winged doors caused her to turn. Matthew stood there, his shotgun cradled in the crook of his arm. She looked at him with a defiant cock of one eyebrow, automatically turning her scarred side toward him. He scowled at the row of bottles; then, knowing that he only had one shell left, he shrugged and left.

It was three days before B. J. found the heart to drag himself out of bed, weak from muscle atrophy and not having eaten. He got the forge going out in the shoeing shed and toiled away, clumsily burning some words into one of the mining company's standard wooden grave markers, now and again looking up into the low-hanging sky from which descended that chill, flat, no-smell smell of snow. Winter was coming in, and soon. He ruined the first two markers because burning in the epitaphs had been Coots's job. And anyway, B. J. had always been inept with tools. Coots used to rag him about it. In the end, the words looked as though a child had painstakingly scrawled them.

AARON COOTS

DIED OCTOBER 4, 1898

A BELOVED COMPANION ON THE BRIEF

JOURNEY

He squinted at this last line critically, knowing that Coots would have scoffed at the sentimentalism. He considered doing another marker with just "Aaron Coots" on it, but in the end he justified his declaration of affection by reminding himself that burials and funerals had nothing to do with the dead. It was all for the consolation of the living. And if the message was sentimental . . . ?

Well, he was a sentimental man, and he wanted to say publicly that he had loved Aaron Coots.

Quis desiderio sit pudor aut modus tam cari captis?

The swelling in Matthew's wrist had almost gone by Saturday evening when the ore train pulled in, its kerosene headlamp picking out snow crystals that hung in the cold dry air. Its whistle screamed, and steam hissed against the trouser legs of the miners as they clambered down whooping and shouting. They knew nothing, of course, of what had happened in Twenty-Mile since their last visit.

Matthew sat on his porch, his chair tipped back against the wall, watching them tramp their boisterous way past him and up the street to grub down at the boardinghouse before making purchases at the Mercantile and beginning their funning. When the fastest eaters started back up toward the barbershop and the Traveller's Welcome, Matthew met them in the middle of the street.

"Here's what you better know, men," he said. He spoke without raising his voice, but the miners responded with impatient attention to the quiet authority of his tone—to say nothing of that huge granddaddy of a shotgun over his arm! He explained that they were free to laugh and josh around and cut up all they wanted. And they could have the girls over in the hotel, so long as the girls were willing. "But there will be no more drinking in Twenty-Mile, because whiskey causes too much of this world's pain and woe. And it's my job to protect people."

A man in the front grumbled that he'd be goddamned if any kid—

"Hold your mouth!" Matthew snapped. Then he retrieved his calm. "I'm sorry if some of you don't like it, but that's the way things are going to be from now on, and you'd best not cross me."

The grumbler faded back into the crowd because

the story of the shoot-out between Matthew and the three outlaws had been the principal topic of conversation during the chow-down—that and wondering what had become of the blonde waitress with the big udders.

But the crowd grew ill-tempered as it thickened with men who had poured out of the boardinghouse on their way up for their weekly ration of whiskey and poontang. Professor Murphy came down from where his boiler was puffing and hissing as steam from the barrels of hot water rose into the lightly falling snow. He asked what the hell was going on. Didn't anyone want a shave and a bath? Mrs. Bjorkvist arrived with her son and husband, who still bore yellowing bruises and crusted scabs from having had their faces clapped together. She addressed the miners, saying that Matthew didn't have no right to boss people around! She pushed her face close to Matthew's and said she wasn't going to stand by and let him ruin her business, because if the miners stopped coming down, then what would become of Twenty-Mile, she'd like to know!

Matthew was confused. But... these were the people he was protecting!

"Who does he think he is, anyway?" Jeff Calder asked from deep within the crowd. "Nobody ever elected him marshal!"

But... these people *respected* him. He'd faced down those outlaws to keep them safe.

Professor Murphy reminded the miners that they all had guns! "Hell, he's nothing but an uppity kid that's barely stopped shittin' yaller!"

A riffle of snorting laugher made Matthew's ears burn with humiliation.

Oskar Bjorkvist took this opportunity to throw a rock that hit Matthew, cutting his cheekbone.

The miners pressed forward.

Matthew's lips compressed as he thumbed back the

hammer, causing those closest to push back against the chests of those behind.

Doc elbowed his way through. "Come on now, Ringo. There's no call to—" Matthew repeated that the men could blow off steam as much as they wanted, but no drinking. "No drinking?" Doc said. "You gotta be joshing! Me, I intend to have myself a couple of stiff belts before dipping into the poontang. It's a man's right, Ringo, after a whole week up in that hellhole."

"If you try to walk past me, Doc," Ringo said in Anthony Bradford Chumms' words, "you'll be walking into history." A snowflake landed on his eyelash, but he didn't blink.

Keeping well back in the crowd, Sven Bjorkvist told the men that they didn't have to stand for that! "That kid ain't right upstairs! Are you men or not? You got guns!"

Doc forced a two-note laugh. "Now come on, Ringo! A joke's a joke, but things are getting pretty het up." When Matthew didn't react, Doc abandoned his laugh-it-off tone. "Now listen to me, kid. I'm going down to the hotel, and you can do whatever you've got the grit to do." He started to pass, but Matthew swung the barrel level with his middle.

"Don't do it, Doc." An anxious boyish note replaced the Ringo Kid's soft burr.

Doc squinted, trying to read Matthew's eyes through the gathering twilight and the snowfall.

"Don't do it, Doc," Matthew repeated. Then he whispered, "Please don't."

"Matthew?" Ruth Lillian was edging her way through the crowd. "Matthew?"

He tightened his jaw and shook his head.

Doc swallowed hard.

B. J. Stone stood on the edge, knowing he ought to do something, but not knowing what.

Ruth Lillian arrived at Matthew's side. "Give me the gun, Matthew."

"You'd best get out of the way, ma'am."

"No, I won't get out of the way. Now give me the gun."

Matthew shook his head, tears welling in his eyes.

"Here, Matthew, use my handkerchief. Your cheek's bleeding."

He slapped her hand away. "Get away from me, god-damn you! Just...get away!" His eyes searched hers desperately. "Leave me alone! Don't make me...Please ...please...*please!*" A long, thin moan of soul-pain escaped him, and he lowered the gun. B. J. stepped forward and took it from his slack grip as, with a whoop, the miners surged past them on their way to hot baths, tepid rotgut, and sizzling poontang! Boy-oh-boy! Look out, girls, here I come! They were momentarily surprised to hear the insistent tooting of the narrow-gauge train as it returned to town, backing up the line, pulling a cone of headlamp-lit snowfall behind it. What the hell...? But the miners weren't going to let anything stand in the way of their few hours of well-deserved fun. "That kid's nuttier'n a fruitcake! You remember ol' Mule? The fella who used to do odd jobs before he went around the bend? That kid's just like ol' Mule!"

Matthew stood at the edge of the cliff between Ruth Lillian and B. J., the outlines of the westward mountains just visible through the falling snow. Grunting with the effort, B. J. flung the shotgun out into the swirling void.

Matthew hung his head and let go, just...let go and slipped deep into the delicious calm of the Other Place, where he remained forever after.

Holding his hand, Ruth Lillian led him upstream against the flow of jostling, laughing miners, bringing him through the snow to the Mercantile, where her father awaited them.

February, 1998
St. Etienne de Baïgorry

WHEN I FINISHED READING Mr. Pedersen's manuscript of recollections of Twenty-Mile, I thanked him and, after another cup of coffee, I pushed on west, putting what I already called the "Twenty-Mile Tale" on the back burner, where it would simmer for much longer than I anticipated.

But I returned to Wyoming now and again to sip Mr. Pedersen's rye and listen to his stories, stories that I would amplify with research in the "living heritage" section of the archives of Cheyenne's Historical Society, where I found memoirs of train engineers, bank clerks, miners, prison guards, frontier journalists ... all sorts of people, many of them written by widows eager to give significance to the lives of departed husbands. I emptied filing boxes and pored over those shards and orts of the living past that can animate a writer's fancy: newspaper accounts, legal documents, municipal registers, memoirs, bills and records from stores, banks, railroad ticket offices.

I also went to see what is left of Tie Siding: a few foundation stones barely visible in the red earth, the roofless ruin of the old stone jail, a grave surrounded by a weathered, frequently vandalized fence. And several times I made the hard climb up to Twenty-Mile, where I would sit near the edge of the cliff, looking out toward the westward hills as I let the characters of my someday novel play out their encounters in my imagination.

During my last visit I was saddened to see how much Mr. Pedersen had faded and diminished. But then, he was nearly ninety. After we finished breakfast, he gave me his manuscript tied up in brown wrapping paper.

"Here, take this with you."

"You're sure?"

"I'm sure."

He died that winter.

Years passed as other work occupied my time and mind; then, not long ago, it occurred to me that the centenary of the incidents at Twenty-Mile was approaching, so I decided the time had come to write my only book in the Western genre, giving a new twist to the Western's conventional characters: the "kid," the tubercular gambler, the heart-o'-gold dance-hall gals, the philosophic shopkeeper, the frontier preacher, the "prairie rose" heroine, the embittered outsider, the outlaw who descends on the town like a biblical plague.

While the rudimentary narrative architecture and the psychological simplifications of the Western left ample room for those story/message shell games expected by Trevanian readers, I found the genre's insistence upon a quick wrap-up constricting because I yearned to answer such questions as: Why was the ore train backing up the track to Twenty-Mile while Ruth Lillian was leading Matthew home against the flow of the fun-seeking miners? And why did Twenty-Mile become a ghost town within two days of that event? And what became of Ruth Lillian, B. J. Stone, Kersti, Frenchy, Mr. Kane, Reverend Hibbard, and the rest?

Take the case of the ore train. You will recall how it came backing up the hill into town, the excited scream of its whistle ignored by the miners pressing down the street in pursuit of hot baths, rotgut, and poontang. The train had traveled about three miles down the line from Twenty-Mile when the driver's eyes suddenly widened in alarm. He snatched down the break lever that locked the wheels in a skidding, spark-spraying stop that left the cow-catcher hanging over an abyss created when a huge plate of rock fell into the ravine during the storm. (Remember that strange splitting sound from lower down on the mountain that interrupted Matthew's account of his pa's constant bad luck, and made Coots's neck muscles flinch as he pressed against the wall beneath the kitchen window of the Traveller's Welcome?) Through the swirling snowflakes, the train's feeble kerosene headlamp had picked out some twenty yards of twisted track suspended over the gap, its wooden ties no longer supporting the steel rails, but dangling from them. His trembling hand on the steam cock, the engineer backed off as slowly as he could, but the vibration caused the threads of steel to torque and fall into the ravine as the train backed up to Twenty-Mile, where it arrived with its whistle shrieking to alert everyone to the fact that the track was cut. Only a few miners delayed their pleasure long enough to find out what the hell all the ruckus was about, but the news spread quickly, and both miners and townsfolk assembled in the Traveller's Welcome to decide what to do, while outside the falling snow thickened to plump flakes that fluttered down so densely that Ruth Lillian, staring dully out her window, had the sensation that she was rising into the heavens.

The miners' first reaction to learning that they were cut off from the world was a raucous cheer at the prospect of an enforced holiday, but there were anxious mutterings from those townsfolk who feared an interruption in their profits, should the Surprise Lode be obliged to close down for any time. The meeting began in an unruly fashion with laughter and catcalls and hoots, but this ochlocratic chaos gave way to more-serious discussion after Doc was unanimously chosen to represent the interests of the miners and B. J. Stone was grudgingly selected to represent those of the townsfolk, leaving the rest of the assemblage to return to the business of consuming and providing fun.

B. J. and Doc decided that the train should go back up to the Lode to pick up the maintenance crew, and on its return it should bring back all remaining stocks of food. Doc suggested that everyone should then sit tight in Twenty-Mile while a couple of the hardiest miners tried to work their way down to Destiny, using the steep, dangerous old trail that had been opened during the blasting of the railroad cut. But B. J. couldn't see the logic in that. The people down in Destiny already knew something was wrong when the train didn't come in, but what could they do? The difference in gauge between the main line and their mountain spur prevented any engine from coming to their rescue. And anyway, how could it cross the gap caused by the infall of the rock face? No, the plain fact was that everyone, townsfolk and miners alike, would have to make it down the old trail, which was at this minute filling with snow. Doc asked how long B. J. thought it would take them to get down, and B. J. shrugged. If the trail hadn't suffered too much decay and erosion over the years, and if the snow wasn't too thick, the strongest of the miners could make it in . . . oh, maybe a day and a half? They'd have to bivouac at nightfall, because trying to work their way down in the dark would be suicidal. ''And what about those who ain't all that hardy?'' Doc asked. ''What about the women and the . . .''

''The old turds?'' B. J. asked, saving Doc the embarrassment. ''Well, the women are probably tougher than most of the men. And we old turds will just have to do the best we can.''

They decided that the next day, Sunday, should be spent organizing the descent, which would start with first light on Monday, the strongest men going first to break a path through the snow.

Some miners chose to return to the Surprise Lode to pick up their possessions, but most entrusted their bindles

to friends while they stayed down in town to continue
their hell-raising.

Up at the Lode, everything useful (and much that was
not) was crammed into gondolas or loaded onto flatbeds,
and the entire work force left, all believing they would
return as soon as the Boston owners arranged to have the
cut blasted out and the track relaid. In fact, save for some
bits and pieces that have been taken by trophy-hunters,
the tools and machinery remain there to this day, looking
as though work came mysteriously to a stop in mid–pick-
swing. Those treacherous, crumbling mine shafts are still
relatively rich in silver ore, and over the years dozens of
enterprises for getting it have been proposed, but no one
has found a way to bring the ore down without incurring
expenses greater than the value of the silver.

The gathering of so many hungry miners was a boon
to Bjorkvist's boardinghouse, which put them up two to
a bed. Meals were the usual "steaks," biscuits (until the
flour ran out), and tinned peaches (until they too ran out).
Because there was no other place where they could eat
and bed down, Mrs. Bjorkvist felt obliged to charge the
miners three dollars for half a bed and an additional dollar for each meal.

Surprisingly—perhaps not all that surprisingly, considering the aphrodisiac effect of death as manifest in
soaring birthrates during times of war and disaster—
Frenchy's girls did land-office business that first night
and all of Sunday, working right up to the morning, when
the miners had to start their descent. The clients chose
among Queeny, Chinky, and Goldy, this last being the
most popular. Perhaps it was the novelty.

Less surprisingly, the Mercantile quickly sold out of
blankets, warm clothes, tinned food, and anything else
that might be of use during the arduous descent.*

———————————————————————————

*Remarkably, during the two-day mass descent through drifting
snow and unstable footing, only one miner was lost; and he was

Throughout the day-and-night press of eager, sometimes belligerent buyers, Matthew helped out behind the counter, fetching goods, making change, tying up bundles, always smiling, his eyes gentle and distant.

It is characteristic of Mr. Kane that he gave credit to those who didn't have the cash to pay for what they needed, and it is characteristic of the now-vanished Yankee ethos that a fair percentage of the miners paid Ruth Lillian what they owed when they got to their savings down in Destiny.

Doc took upon himself the melancholy duty of shooting the pair of ailing donkeys that Coots had brought down for rest and attention, and by noon on Monday the last miners had passed through the donkey meadow and disappeared down the steep trail, the falling snow patiently filling their footprints. The girls, under Frenchy's direction, were the first of the townsfolk to undertake the descent, waddling across the meadow in bizarre accretions of blankets, cloaks, and makeshift hoods, beneath which they wore layers of fancy dresses, because Frenchy wouldn't let them carry anything but food. It turned out to be a blessing in disguise that Lieder had burned all their shoes in Murphy's boiler, for the hardy (and not a bit too roomy) boots that Queeny borrowed from a miner served her better on the trail than her own flimsy ones would have done. Frenchy wore the boots B. J. had given her, and Chinky, whose little feet would have been lost in miner's boots, had a stout pair of Ruth Lillian's shoes to see her through.

It was afternoon before the band consisting of the Bjorkvists, Jeff Calder, and Professor Murphy was ready to start down. The night before, they had gathered in the

---

literally *lost*. According to the account in the *Destiny Sentinel*, after taunting the men he was descending with for dawdling, one young miner pushed on ahead. But he never showed up in Destiny and was never heard of again.

kitchen of the boardinghouse, where Murphy proposed that they take as much as they could carry of the silver ore that the train had been unable to deliver to Destiny. This crushed and dressed ore was almost 20 percent silver. Five pounds of ore was a pound of silver! When you subtracted the cost of smelting and refining, it would be worth maybe half of that. That would work out to a pound of silver for every ten pounds of ore! They scrounged up every sack they could find and waited until the miners had gone (why let everybody in on it?) before filling them with double handfuls of ore. Painful choices had to be made between extra clothes and ore, between food and ore. In the end they brought only the absolute minimum to see them through the two-day descent.

The snow-laden sky was thickening ominously by the time the four men and the woman crossed the donkey meadow, their feet dragging furrows through the snow, their bodies bent beneath the weight of their ore.

Their greed was to make them endure famine, fatigue, falls, and frostbite,—and that's just the *F*'s, as Coots would have said. By the middle of the second day, Jeff Calder's wooden stump made him fall behind, and when he realized that the others had no intention of risking their lives and silver by slowing down for him, he abandoned his sacks of loot. When he caught up, Mrs. Bjorkvist could not believe that he had left his ore! Profligacy is a sin! She browbeat her son and husband into going back to get it. While she and Professor Murphy awaited their return, huddled together for warmth, Jeff Calder continued on ahead, unencumbered. And that's how it came to pass that, despite having only one leg, he was the first of them to get to Destiny, where he basked in the attention of a young reporter of the *Destiny Tribune*, as we shall see in a moment.

The others continued to stagger down, their legs wobbly beneath their burdens, frequently dropping to their knees and panting, drool melting holes in the snow be-

neath their chins. Eventually, they were forced to choose
between the ore and their lives. With tears of rage and
frustration, Mrs. Bjorkvist clenched her fist at the sky and
cursed the cruel God who was ripping her just reward
from her grasp, after all she had suffered! All right! All
right, she would leave the ore behind! But she insisted
that it be thrown over the cliff. If they couldn't have it,
no one would! When the four of them finally stumbled
into Destiny, they were in such bad condition that they
had to spend more than a week in bed in a boardinghouse
that cruelly overcharged them. It is said that Mrs. Bjorkvist was never the same, and that can only have been a
blessing for those who had to deal with her.

B. J. watched the party of five cross his donkey
meadow, each bent beneath a pair of sacks tied together
behind the neck. He shook his head and gathered up a
few possessions—just some clothes and his treasured Lucilius—then he went down to help the Kanes prepare for
their descent. As it turned out, they didn't leave until the
next morning.

Throughout the day and night that the Mercantile had
been besieged by panicked buyers, Mr. Kane had re-
peatedly brushed off his daughter's pleas not to exert
himself. ''Matthew and me can do everything, Pa!'' Now
they were the last people left in Twenty-Mile, and he was
bringing a small pasteboard box of memorabilia down
the stairs for B. J. to put into one of the slim blanket rolls
that were to be their only burdens on the descent. B. J.
reached up to receive the box, but Mr. Kane grasped both
his hands, letting the box drop. He sat heavily on the
bottom step and looked up, bewildered. ''I think...oh,
Mr. Stone, I think...'' And he died, holding the hands
of the man who, if things had worked out differently,
might have been a friend.

Later, when she was going through the box of memorabilia, Ruth Lillian discovered a lock of fine reddish
baby hair...hers..., the fine German scissors that her

grandfather had brought from the old country, and a yellowed photograph of her grandparents and their young son . . . her father . . . standing proudly before a sign announcing: *The American High-Class Finishing Materials Company (Reliable Service at Competitive Prices)*.

Although she had been preparing herself for her father's death for years, she still had difficulty swallowing back her silent tears.

Using the same barrow that had carried Coots, they brought Mr. Kane to the burying ground. Matthew could only manage a shallow grave in the stiffening earth, and the best B. J. could do for a marker was to drive in a fence post onto which he had nailed a board with the scratched-on words: "David Kane . . . A good man."

At the last minute, Matthew returned to the marshal's office to roll up his possessions. He took only his Hudson Bay blanket, his broken-backed dictionary, a scarf and pair of gloves Ruth Lillian had laid aside for him before the miners emptied the Mercantile of stock, and the canvas bag containing his treasures: the little blue glass bottle that had been buried so mysteriously, the marble with a real American flag suspended in the middle, and the rock with gold flakes that someone had said was only fool's gold, but who knows? His other treasure, the ball-pointed marshal's badge, he always wore pinned to his jacket.

The three of them paused for a moment by the fence to look through the sifting snow to where Coots and Mr. Kane lay side by side. Then they started across the donkey meadow.

———————

THIS IS THE PLACE to confess my debt to the *Destiny Tribune*, and particularly to its reporter-of-all-desks, C. R. Harriman. (I have no idea what the initials stood for.) Writing in the succulent, sesquipedalian journalese of the era, young Harriman chronicled the arrival of the refugees from Twenty-Mile; and it was he who, some thirty years later, wrote the account of his own last days in Destiny that I shall soon have cause to mention.

Combing through the yellow-edged, friable pages of the *Tribune* in the Historical Society's archives, I learned of Reverend Hibbard's arrival in Destiny three days after Coots's lynching, and five days before the first miners came stumbling in. He was found wandering in the street, muddy, bruised, completely worn-out. It was through C. R. Harriman's interview with Hibbard that Destiny found out what had become of those three insane escapees from the state prison who had dropped out of sight after killing that retired schoolteacher in Tie Siding and doing those terrible things to that poor woman who happened to come visiting. Hibbard described their reign of terror in Twenty-Mile, and he told of the death of Mr. Delanny, owner of the hotel, and the lynching of a mixed-blood named Coots. The Reverend explained that after doing everything in his power to prevent the lynching but—alas—failing, he had volunteered to make the dangerous descent to alert Destiny of the dreadful events in Twenty-Mile. The reporter congratulated Reverend Hibbard for his courage and suggested that the mayor might want to demonstrate the community's gratitude in some more-material way, but the next morning Hibbard was not to be found, having withdrawn his savings from the Destiny Bank and Trust and taken the morning train west.

I was going through the *Destiny Tribune*'s account of Hibbard's arrival, when it suddenly struck me: Why did it take *three days* for Hibbard to get down to Destiny? Descending the thirty or so miles of serpentine railroad line—even a very cautious descent—shouldn't have taken more than one full day. After all, the snow hadn't started yet; and two months earlier Matthew had climbed *up* in a little over twelve hours.

Then I realized that Hibbard couldn't have come down the tracks. The rock slide precipitated by the storm had already cut the line. What must have happened was this: after snatching up a few valuables from his depot, he must have started down the track in the storm, but when he came to the break in the line, he was obliged to return to Twenty-Mile, probably with the intention of slipping around the edge of town, crossing the donkey meadow, and working his way down the steep old access trail to Destiny, the same trail that was later used by the miners and townsfolk. If my calculations are roughly correct, he would have been hiding somewhere (perhaps in one of the abandoned buildings) when B. J., Matthew, and Frenchy were burying Coots.

I find it distasteful to think of Reverend Hibbard peering out from his hiding place, watching the burial of Coots.

It was from C. R. Harriman's interview with a "...redoubtable old soldier who, despite the loss of a leg in the service of his country, led the dangerous trek down to Destiny, guiding four others to safety," that I gleaned details of the ore-bearers' descent. But many particulars were vague because (as Harriman obliquely put it) "the fatigues of the colorful old soldier's journey did not prevent him from accepting bibulous congratulations proffered by gentlemen at the local oases."

In a column headed "Dramatic Incident at Twenty-Mile," this soldier, who gave his name as Sergeant-Major Jefferson M. Calder, described the shoot-out between Matthew and the escaped madmen from the state prison. He told how the young boy had faced down the desperados, using tactics he'd learned from the old soldier himself. But the strain of this confrontation had "...pretty much gutted the kid. Made him go sort of simple. Shoot, he even started thinking he was the town marshal!"

My debt to C. R. Harriman does not end with his interviews in the *Tribune*. A few years ago a colleague sent me a book he thought might interest me. When I unwrapped the package, the name C. R. Harriman on the cover immediately ignited my curiosity. It was a privately published account of his early years in Wyoming, concentrating on what the title called: *The End of Destiny*. Three hundred numbered exemplars of the book were printed in 1928, and I suppose that copy No. 132, which sits on my desk at this moment, is the only one extant, though I should be delighted to hear otherwise from a reader.

After a lively anecdotal description of the birth and growth of Destiny, Harriman's book focuses on the six weeks between the arrival of the frozen, bone-weary miners who had threaded their way down the snow-clogged trail from Twenty-Mile, and the economic panic that led to Destiny's collapse.

As soon as the miners had rested up, they were out roving the streets, creating a hectic holiday atmosphere. After drawing their wages from the mine's agent in town, they applied themselves diligently to joy-seeking, sure that their respite would be short, and that they would be back slaving in the mine as soon as the Boston owners repaired the collapsed rail line.

Information concerning the broken line was indeed telegraphed back to Boston, and days of silence ensued while the company weighed the considerable investment necessary to repair the track against the return they could expect from the mine. Then instructions came to the company office: After detaching the Surprise Lode from its mother company so as to avoid further liability, the Boston owners declared it bankrupt, leaving the miners without jobs, and leaving Destiny's dozen or so small service enterprises with unpaid accounts. The town was staggered by the news, for this was before the legalized scam of "chapter 11" bankruptcy, back when avoiding one's debts was considered dishonorable, and men driven to bankruptcy were expected to—and often did—commit suicide. Having assured the angry townsfolk that the Boston owners were entirely sensible of their responsibilities, the company agent quietly locked the door of his office and took the 2 A.M. eastbound to avoid the unpleasant distinction of being tarred and feathered.

Within weeks of the arrival of the miners and townsfolk from Twenty-Mile, the Destiny Bank and Trust had failed, and most of the merchants had sold out and departed, together with the doctor, the preacher, the lawyer, and the town's public girls; and what kind of a town is it where you can't get healed, saved, sued, or laid? Not long after, the undertaker left and the last bar nailed up its doors. And hey! If you can't even get drunk or buried . . . !

But this collapse was totally unthinkable when Frenchy and her girls first emerged, randomly shod, from the harrowing back trail into a town echoing with the miners' holiday zeal. While the girls were recuperating from their trek in the Destiny Regal Hotel's tin bathtubs, Frenchy made arrangements with the biggest saloon, and C. R. Harriman tells us that within two days her "ladies of the evening" were lightening the hours of miners and townsmen alike. I shall quote from this reference to give you a sample of Harriman's sumptuous, if occasionally tangle-footed, frontier journalese: "The trio of rough-hewn odalisques was managed by one 'Frenchy,' an enterprising woman of decidedly Nubian inclinations.* This 'Frenchy' did not offer herself for sale—or, more precisely, for *rent*—and considering a rather off-putting façade resulting from the application of a broken bottle to her left cheek, it is not likely that she would have found many customers among the refined townsfolk, although rough-and-ready miners would doubtless over-

---

*The reader is reminded that Mr. Harriman wrote long before political correctness became more important than Freedom of Speech.

look such superficial cosmetic nuances. But her troika of girls provided a variety calculated to tempt every appetite (save for the fastidious). There was 'Queeny,' a full-blown, full-blooded, full-voiced woman no longer burdened by the coy inhibitions of youth (or indeed those of middle age); and there was 'Chinky,' a shy, retiring visitor from the Celestial Kingdom; and finally there was the clear favorite, 'Goldy,' a brawny Viking girl of more-than-averagely plain features, but crowned with the luxuriant golden locks that inspired her sobriquet.''

In an appendix to his book, Harriman recounts how he crossed the trail of one of Twenty-Mile's denizens through what he called ''one of those 'wondrous' coincidences so common in our Nation of Drifters that the real wonder is that we continue to be amazed by them.'' A couple of years after he had left Destiny and found a post with a San Francisco daily, he was assigned to do a ''color piece'' on a community of outcasts living in a makeshift village across the bay, in the hills behind Oakland. There he found Reverend Hibbard, who had become the spiritual leader of a small band of fanatics who were convinced that the apocalyptic Second Coming would coincide with the arrival of the Twentieth Century. When that ominous date came and went without cataclysmic incident, Hibbard reexamined the texts of John and Daniel, and lo! he discovered an error of twenty-one years in their calculations—twenty-one being exactly the Trinity times the Seven Seals. So it now became obvious that the apocalypse would come on New Year's Eve, 1921, when Hibbard's followers would be wafted up to heaven, while the fornicators, the scoffers, the meat-eaters, the Darwinians, the blasphemers, and all the rest of us rubbish would be hurled, twisting and screaming, into eternal fires. While awaiting this gratifying spectacle, Reverend Hibbard commanded his followers to live in prayer, poverty, chastity, and grateful obedience to their leader. By the time a diminished handful of sect members stood in white gowns on their hilltop in the drenching rain, only to see the first dawn of 1922 appear with no greater catastrophe than half a dozen head-colds (and much ridicule and nose-thumbing from local flappers and cake-eaters), Reverend Hibbard had already preceded them to their reward, leaving behind a child he had begot upon the body of the thirteen-year-old daughter of a devoted follower. But Hibbard was not the first sin-merchant to cash in on America's penchant for wrathful, anti-intellectual fundamentalism and the addiction of its Lost and its Damaged for the narcotic of cultism, nor, sadly, would he be the last.

We learn little about Matthew, Ruth Lillian, and B. J. Stone from the *Destiny Tribune* beyond a mention of them as the last arrivals from Twenty-Mile, and two passing references to the shoot-out between Matthew and the prison escapees. I suppose it is only natural that the closure of the mine should occupy most of the newspaper's attention, considering the devastating effect it had on the town's prosperity. Records from the Destiny Bank and Trust show that Gerald (Doc) Kerry drew his savings out of the bank as soon as he got down to Destiny. He had always doubted the willingness of the Boston owners to provide additional investment, should something happen to the mine (as he told Matthew that night while they gobbled peaches and syrup on baking-powder biscuits). It can be inferred that Doc told B. J. Stone of his doubts, for the very next day B. J., Ruth Lillian, and all of Frenchy's girls withdrew their savings, and not a minute too soon, because two days later a rush on the bank forced it to shut down, never to open its doors again. ·

I confess to feeling wickedly pleased when I discovered from the records that among the many savings wiped out by the bank's collapse was a small account in the name of Professor Michael Francis Murphy and a very considerable one in the name of Mrs. Sven Bjorkvist.

Ruth Lillian must have been surprised to discover that

her father had kept all his savings in her name, and that they amounted to a very tidy sum. From records of bank transactions, we discover that during Destiny's financial panic she (or rather, B. J. Stone operating as her agent) purchased the entire stock of two clothing shops, a hardware store, a notions shop, and a harness maker's, all at dirt cheap panic prices; and from railroad shipping invoices, we learn that this stock came with them when they left for Seattle.

Evidently Frenchy read the writing on the wall too, for two days later she and her girls also bought tickets for Seattle, pursuing a clientele that was attracted to the Klondike Gold Rush, and my researches in Seattle turned up Frenchy's name (Marie-Thérèse Courbin) on a lease for a "resort-hotel" on Skid Road (soon to be corrupted to "skid *row*" and applied to any area of down-and-outs).

Because I've grown fond of them, it would be pleasant to confect happy futures for those four women. I can picture Frenchy returning rich to New Orleans and establishing herself in a fine old house from which she dominates local society through her generous support of the First American United Tabernacle of the Glorious Message of the Risen Christ, where none of the congregation even *dares* to comment on the succession of handsome, well-muscled young "nephews" she keeps in splendid clothes and expensive cigars. And Kersti? Well, I can envision Kersti using her professional nest egg to buy a fertile half-section where, with some full-blooded young man, she raises a clan of tow-headed rascals. Queeny? I can see Queeny winning the heart of some grizzled Klondike miner who, having struck it rich, opens a theater that features her performing her Famous Dance of the Seven Veils. Then, when finally her time comes, she dies of a sudden and painless heart attack while taking a seventh curtain call before a wildly appreciative audience. And Chinky? Poor Chinky, one of nature's victims, condemned to be used and discarded by a long parade of faceless, mean-hearted strangers. I'm afraid the best life I could reasonably project for Chinky would be a short one.

But all this is fantasy. The fact is that after Frenchy signed that lease, she and her girls disappeared into the eddies of time without a trace. But at least we know that Frenchy set up shop in Seattle, where her girls could harvest Johns fresh off the ships, rather than being dragged through the rigors of the Chilicoot Pass to the gold fields, where they would have had to compete with those hard-faced, sapphomorphic professionals of the Yukon who serviced queues of prospectors with a production-line efficiency that would have impressed young Henry Ford.

Following Ruth Lillian's trail in Seattle was not difficult, for she became a minor financial legend and, inevitably, the subject of an unpublished (indeed, unfinished) thesis.* I owe many details of Ruth Lillian's later life to this biography, where we learn that she, B. J. Stone, and Matthew Dubchek arrived in Seattle with three boxcar loads of tools, clothing, and other equipment just as thousands of men were amassing to try their luck in the Alaskan gold fields. It would appear that Ruth Lillian benefited from her father's story about the old Yankee peddler who said that the surest path to a fortune lay not in digging for gold, but in selling picks and shovels to the fools who did. Saved from the shriveling effects of grief and self-pity by having two young people to care for, B. J. Stone became the manager of Ruth Lillian's store, over which an ornately lettered sign proclaimed: *Kane's Mercantile Emporium.*

One can picture Matthew working happily in the Mercantile during its early, hectic, enormously profitable

---

R. Lillian Marx: The Woman and Her Times: Michele Goldman-Harris.

years. But later his activities seem to have been limited to gardening and doing odd chores around the house that Ruth Lillian had built only half a block from the store.

Until 1917 most of the Mercantile's orders and sales records bear B. J. Stone's signature (although all legal and banking documents are signed by Ruth Lillian, who had by then become R. Lillian Kane). Then suddenly, we find Ruth Lillian's signature on everything, because B. J. died the year American doughboys surged up the gangways of troop ships to the tune of "Over There," on their way to die in the "war to end war."

At the age of thirty-six, Ruth Lillian married David S. Marx, an earnest, hard-working rival whose mail-order business in outdoor supplies and work clothes ("Every Item Made in America by Americans!") had earned a reputation for quality throughout Alaska and the Northwest. It was both daring and canny of Mr. Marx to abandon his company's identity and unite their activities under the name of Ruth Lillian's store, recognizing that "Mercantile Emporium" lent their combined enterprise a nostalgic aura of reliability and honesty. He accented this image by using old-fashioned lettering on the cover of his catalogues, a practice continued by the multinational combine that owns the business today, although the target consumer has shifted from farmers and homesteaders to young urban dwellers eager to proclaim their concerns about ecology, and the American Past, and the Good Old Days, and . . . all that sort of thing. The clothing is now made by underpaid women in Asiatic sweatshops.

It would appear that Mr. Marx accepted Ruth Lillian's moral obligations, for Matthew went with them when they moved into what is now on show as the Marx-Kane House (appointment required). This ornate pile in the parvenu "Timber Baron" style is one of the few houses to survive the Great Fire that left Seattle an architectural wasteland. Matthew was described by a neighbor as a ". . . jack-of-all-work around the house. He went about his chores with placid good humor, always wearing a six-pointed marshal's badge pinned to his jacket. He was well known in the Queen Ann Hill neighborhood, where he used to take long rambling walks every evening. Occasionally a badly brought-up child would follow him chanting 'moron' or 'Simple-Simon,' but a short, stormy visit from Mrs. Marx always sufficed to put an end to that.''*

Mr. Marx died at his desk from overwork a year after the Wall Street Collapse threatened not only their company's profits but the jobs of their expanded enterprise's four hundred employees, for they had only three years earlier bought out two of their principal suppliers.

In 1931, American business's darkest moment, Ruth Lillian Marx became president of the Mercantile Emporium. By taking everyday management into her own hands and instigating more efficient practices, by declaring a moratorium on profits, by maintaining her company's reputation for high-quality goods even while prices plunged, and above all by tapping into the creativity of her work force, soliciting their suggestions and rewarding those accepted, she managed to navigate the treacherous waters of the Great Depression without having to fire a single person or reduce benefits.† Thus, when the nation's entry into the Second World War lifted American business from the doldrums into soaring profits, the Mercantile Emporium's eleven outlets, its mail-

---

*These details come from the Goldman-Harris biography where, in quoted interviews with an elderly Ruth Lillian, I also discovered her habit of describing persons and behaviors she disapproved of as *small!*

†It is difficult to avoid comparison of Ruth Lillian's treatment of her workers and colleagues with today's piratical practice of wringing every last cent of profit out of the work force, and "downsizing" to the point of hectic inefficiency, while denying workers the dignity that comes with civilized benefits and secure futures.

order division, and its manufacturing activities enjoyed the commercial advantages of a strong reputation for quality and fair dealing, a faithful clientele, and a fiercely loyal work force.

During the second year of that war, when radios across the country were echoing the soldier's metaphorical plea that the girl back home refrain from sitting under the apple tree with anyone else but me, anyone else but me, anyone else but me. No! No! No! . . . Matthew died in his sleep.

The war ended, and Ruth Lillian retired from active leadership of her now-robust and profitable company, to become a stern and feared force in liberal politics, and a generous, if slightly scornful, supporter of what passed for culture. She was recognized on the streets by the gray-shot russet hair she wore piled up and held in place by antique silver combs, and by her outdated, handmade dresses, which were in disapproving contrast to the post-war "New Look" with its graceless calf-bisecting skirts.

Full of years, Ruth Lillian Marx died in 1963. Seattle was surprised to learn that of the many millions of dollars she was reputed to be worth, all that remained was her rambling house on Queen Ann Hill, and even this was mortgaged down to the ashes in the fireplaces. It came out that all her money had gone to organizations seeking to combat what she held to be the greatest menace facing humankind: the worldwide population explosion. (It is sobering to realize that since Ruth Lillian's death world population has more than doubled, and will double again within the next twenty-seven years.)

Eleven years ago I found myself in Seattle, attending the funeral of an old friend (the one who sent me C. R. Harriman's book). I stayed on for a couple of weeks, doing research for this novel. Among other things, I discovered that Ruth Lillian and Mr. Marx were buried in the oldest of Seattle's cemeteries, one that now serves only as an out-of-the-way "green zone" where old people and lovers occasionally stroll. An examination of the cemetery's records revealed B. J. Stone's name . . . but no Matthew Dubchek. I need not say how disappointed I was, for I had imagined myself standing beside his grave, silently reviewing all that had happened in Twenty-Mile so long ago.

Having decided there was no point in visiting the burying ground since Matthew wasn't there, I was sitting in my hotel room with a couple of hours before my flight back to my home in France, when a sudden impulse caused me to go down and get a cab for the cemetery after all, hoping its gates would still be open, for it was almost evening.

I walked down the central path between trees dripping with the regular, gentle rain that is Seattle, and at length I came to the Marx–Kane plot, with a wrought-iron fence enclosing sufficient space for the children and grandchildren the Marxes never had. Ruth Lillian's stone stood beside her husband's, both weighty bourgeois statements in polished black marble. In one corner of the plot I found B. J.'s monument:

BENJAMIN JOSEPH STONE
DIED NOVEMBER 6, 1917
A BELOVED COMPANION ON THE BRIEF JOURNEY

So Ruth Lillian had remembered the words B. J. had painfully, clumsily inscribed on Coots's wooden marker. How like her. It was comforting to know that although he lay half a continent away from his Coots, B. J. was at least with family.

But it was in the opposite corner of the plot that I found what thrilled the sentimental man in me. No wonder I hadn't found "Matthew Dubchek" in the cemetery records!

The stone is rough-hewn Rocky Mountain granite.

The epitaph Ruth Lillian had inscribed must surely arouse the curiosity of passersby, but it would have pleased Matthew greatly:

1880–1943
THE RINGO KID

Characters in
INCIDENT AT TWENTY-MILE
(in order of appearance)

From the author's working biographies

Pedersen, Niels, *Carpenter, later Last Citizen of Destiny and Collector of Stories.* b: Destiny, Wyoming, 1888; d: Destiny, Wyoming, 1976.

Tillman, John Arthur "B B," *Prison Guard.* b: Cheyenne, Wyoming, 1875; d: Laramie, Wyoming, 1898.

Davidson, Lawrence ("The Acid-Thrower"), *Chastizer of Children.* b: Glens Falls, New York, 1838; d: State Penitentiary, Rawlings, Wyoming, 1909.

Childs, Elmer William ("The Politician"), b: Leeds, Yorkshire (date unknown); d: State Penitentiary, Rawlings, Wyoming, 1903.

Wheelwright, James ("The Spook"), *Punisher of Prostitutes, later Producer of Slapstick Film Comedies.* b: Evanston, Illinois, 1851; d: Hollywood, California, 1926.

Lieder, Hamilton Adams, *Patriot.* b: farm near Tie Siding, Wyoming, 1858; d: Twenty-Mile, Wyoming, 1898.

Quincy, Alphonse Xavier ("The Warrior"), *Writer of fantastic hate-propaganda, Spent most of his life in institutions.* b: Montreal, Canada, 1832; d: Poughkeepsie, New York, 1889.

Delanny, Henry Evans, *Gambler.* b: Macon, Georgia, 1856; d: Twenty-Mile, Wyoming, 1898.

Bjorkvist, Olga, *Owner of an eating house.* b: Töcksfors, Sweden, 1852; d: Fremont, California, 1928.

Kane, David, *Merchant.* b: Dortmund, Westphalia, 1841; d: Twenty-Mile, Wyoming, 1898.

Kane, Ruth Lillian (Marx), *Merchant. Daughter of David and Kathleen.* b: Blair, Nebraska, 1881; d: Seattle, Washington, 1963.

Stone, Benjamin Joseph, *Teacher, later Livery man, later Business Manager.* b: Boston, Massachusetts, 1839; d: Seattle, Washington, 1917.

Coots, Aaron, *Soldier, Gunfighter, Livery man.* b: Cateechee, South Carolina, 1841; d: Twenty-Mile, Wyoming, 1898.

Dubchek, Matthew, *Odd-Job Man, briefly Marshal.* b: Tarkio, Missouri, 1880; d: Seattle, Washington, 1943.

Chumms, Anthony Bradford, *Pseudonym of Lewis W. Milford, Social Critic and clandestine Writer of pulp Westerns.* b: Ramsden Heath, Essex, 1858; d: Dinder, Somerset, 1951.

Murphy, Francis ("Professor"), *Barber.* b: Worcester, Massachusetts, 1858; date and place of death unknown.

Calder, Jefferson M., *Soldier, Bartender, Odd-Job Man.* b: Cairo, Illinois, 1839; date and place of death unknown.

Bjorkvist, Sven, *Husband of Olga.* b: Töcksfors, Sweden, 1849; d: Fremont, California, 1922.

Bjorkvist, Kersti ("Goldy"), *Daughter of Olga and Sven, later Prostitute.* b: Töcksfors, Sweden, 1876; date and place of death unknown.

Bjorkvist, Oskar, *Son of Olga and Sven.* b: What Cheer, Iowa, 1882; date and place of death unknown.

Callahan, Bridget Mary ("Queeny"), *Entertainer, later Prostitute.* b: Trenton, New Jersey, 1837; date and place of death unknown.

Courbin, Marie-Thérèse ("Frenchy"), *Prostitute, later Entremetteuse.* b: Goudeau, Louisiana, 1859; date and place of death unknown.

Tchang, (first name unregistered) ("Chinky"), *Prostitute.* b: Zhejiang Province, 1878; date and place of death unknown.

Kane, Samuel, *Father of David, Tailor, later Small Entrepreneur.* b: Dortmund, Westphalia, 1810; d: New York, New York, 1854.

Kane, Sarah, *Wife of Samuel, Mother of David.* b: Dortmund, Westphalia, 1814; d: New York, New York, 1854.

Pike, Barnaby, *Yankee Drummer, early Mentor of David Kane.* Date and place of birth unknown; d: South Dayton, New York.

Hibbard, Leroy, *Preacher, later Apocalyptic Prophet.* b: Ellsworth, Maine, 1858; d: Richmond, California, 1919.

Tillman, Mary Elizabeth, *Widow of John, later Christian Missionary.* b: West Florence, Ohio, 1881; d: Gansu Province, China, 1939.

Milford, Stanley ("Tiny"), Date and place of birth unknown; d: Twenty-Mile, Wyoming, 1898.

Mabois, Robert ("Bobby-My-Boy"), Date and place of birth unknown; d: Twenty-Mile, Wyoming, 1898.

Kerry, Gerald ("Doc"), *Mining Technician.* b: Latham, Tennessee, 1849; d: Dawson, Yukon Territory, 1903.

White, Roger ("Razz"), *Miner; Clown of the mine crew.* Date and place of birth and death unknown.

Benson, Luke and Bradford, *School Bullies.* b: Bushnell, Nebraska. Dates and places of birth and death unknown.

Pickering, Mary Ellis (Montgomery), *Schoolmistress, later Wife of L. Montgomery.* Date and place of birth and death unknown.

Montgomery, Lawrence, *Examiner of Schools, adept at handling boys.* Date and place of birth and death unknown.

Bowles, T. W., *Farmer; neighbor who discovered Mr. and Mrs. Dubchek and gave vivid report to the* Nebraska Plainsman. Date and place of birth and death unknown.

Ballard, Edgar Mather, *Schoolmaster.* b: New Haven, Connecticut, 1831; d: Tie Siding, Wyoming, 1898.

Sklodowska, Angelica, *Casual Victim.* b: Tie Siding, Wyoming, 1859; d: Tie Siding, Wyoming, 1898.

Kane, Kathleen (née Evans), *Wife of David, Mother of Ruth Lillian.* b: Troy, New York, 1859; date and place of death unknown.

Bradford, Chester, *briefly Marshal of Twenty-Mile, briefly Lover of Kathleen Kane.* Date and place of birth and death unknown.

Utuburu, Beñat, *Basque immigrant; first Shepherd then, after a serious accident left him befuddled, Odd-Job Man.* (His hard-to-pronounce name was shortened to "Burro" and then changed to "Mule"). b: Ste. Engrace, Soule, France, 1853; d: Twenty-Mile, Wyoming, 1892.

Cooper, John ("Lucky Jack"), *Prospector.* b: Eureka Springs, Arkansas, 1841; d: Lodgepole Creek Gully, Wyoming, 1898.

Mitchell, Arthur, *Principal of Home for Wayward Boys; skilled disciplinarian.* Date and place of birth and death unknown.

Dubchek, Martha (née Taylor), *Mother of Matthew.* b: Tarkio, Missouri, 1856; d: Bushnell, Nebraska, 1898.

Dubchek, Karl Anton, *Father of Matthew.* b: near Odzaci, Serbia, 1854; d: Bushnell, Nebraska, 1898.

Taylor, John, *Farmer, Father of Martha Dubchek.* b: 1819, place unknown; d: Tarkio, Missouri, 1881.

Kilmer, Paul, *Miner; only person who didn't make the descent from Twenty-Mile.* Date and place of birth unknown; d: (presumed) Medicine Bow Range, 1898.

Harriman, C. R., *Journalist.* b: Richmond, Virginia, 1874; d: San Francisco, California, 1951.

Snopes, Chastity Ann, *"Spiritual wife" of Reverend Hibbard and Mother of his child. Died of pneumonia contracted while awaiting Ascension.* b: Niles, California, 1907; d: Richmond, California, 1922.

Marx, David S., *Businessman and Husband of Ruth Lillian Kane.* b: New York, New York, 1867; d: Seattle, Washington, 1930.

Goldman-Harris, Michele, *Doctoral Candidate, Writer of unfinished biography of Ruth Lillian Kane-Marx.* b: Redmond, Washington, 1961.